THE BURWASH EDITION OF THE COMPLETE
WORKS IN PROSE AND VERSE OF

RUDYARD KIPLING

VOLUME XV

THE LIGHT THAT FAILED
THE NAULAHKA

*The Collected Works Of*

# RUDYARD KIPLING

# The Light That Failed
# The Naulahka
### WRITTEN IN COLLABORATION WITH
### WOLCOTT BALESTIER

## AMS PRESS
### NEW YORK

This is a numbered set, of which this is number ...

Reprinted from a copy in the collection of the
Harvard University Libraries
From the edition of 1941, Garden City
First AMS EDITION published 1970
Manufactured in the United States of America

With permission of the estate of Rudyard Kipling,
Doubleday and Company, Inc., and Macmillan and Company, Ltd.

International Standard Book Number:
complete set: 0-404-03740-2
volume 15: 0-404-03755-0

Library of Congress Catalog Card Number: 75-120920

AMS PRESS, INC.
NEW YORK, N.Y. 10003

# CONTENTS

*ix*

# THE LIGHT THAT FAILED

*The Light that Failed* was first published in 1891

# DEDICATION

*If I were hanged on the highest hill,*
  Mother o' mine, O mother o' mine!
*I know whose love would follow me still,*
  Mother o' mine, O mother o' mine!

*If I were drowned in the deepest sea,*
  Mother o' mine, O mother o' mine!
*I know whose tears would come down to me,*
  Mother o' mine, O mother o' mine!

*If I were damned of body and soul,*
*I know whose prayers would make me whole,*
  Mother o' mine, O mother o' mine!

# PREFACE

THIS is the story of *The Light that Failed* as it was originally conceived by the Writer.—RUDYARD KIPLING

# CHAPTER I

*So we settled it all when the storm was done*
*As comfy as comfy could be;*
*And I was to wait in the barn, my dears,*
*Because I was only three,*
*And Teddy would run to the rainbow's foot,*
*Because he was five and a man—*
*And that's how it all began, my dears,*
*And that's how it all began!*

BIG BARN STORIES.

'WHAT DO YOU THINK she'd do if she caught us? We oughtn't to have it, you know,' said Maisie.

'Beat me, and lock you up in your bedroom,' Dick answered, without hesitation. 'Have you got the cartridges?'

'Yes; they're in my pocket, but they're joggling horribly. Do pin-fire cartridges go off of their own accord?'

'Don't know. Take the revolver, if you are afraid, and let me carry them.'

'I'm *not* afraid.' Maisie strode forward swiftly, a hand in her pocket and her chin in the air. Dick followed with a small pin-fire revolver.

The children had discovered that their lives would be unendurable without pistol-practice. After much forethought and self-denial, Dick had saved seven shillings and sixpence, the price of a badly constructed Belgian revolver. Maisie could only contribute half a crown to the syndicate for the purchase of a hundred cartridges. 'You can save better than I can, Dick,' she explained; 'I like nice things to eat, and it doesn't matter to you. Besides, boys ought to do these things.'

XV—2                    I

Dick grumbled a little at the arrangement, but went out and made the purchases, which the children were then on their way to test. Revolvers did not lie in the scheme of their daily life as decreed for them by the guardian who was incorrectly supposed to stand in the place of a mother to these two orphans. Dick had been under her care for six years, during which time she had made her profit of the allowances supposed to be expended on his clothes, and, partly through thoughtlessness, partly through a natural desire to pain,—she was a widow of some years anxious to marry again,—had made his days burdensome on his young shoulders. Where he had looked for love, she gave him first aversion and then hate. Where he growing older had sought a little sympathy, she gave him ridicule. The many hours that she could spare from the ordering of her small house she devoted to what she called the home-training of Dick Heldar. Her religion, manufactured in the main by her own intelligence and a keen study of the Scriptures, was an aid to her in this matter. At such times as she herself was not personally displeased with Dick, she left him to understand that he had a heavy account to settle with his Creator; wherefore Dick learned to loathe his God as intensely as he loathed Mrs. Jennett; and this is not a wholesome frame of mind for the young. Since she chose to regard him as a hopeless liar, when dread of pain drove him to his first untruth, he naturally developed into a liar, but an economical and self-contained one, never throwing away the least unnecessary fib, and never hesitating at the blackest, were it only plausible, that might make his life a little easier. The treatment taught him at least the power of living alone,—a power that was of service to him when he went to a public school and the boys laughed at his clothes, which were poor in quality and much mended. In the holidays he returned to the teachings of Mrs. Jennett, and, that the chain of discipline might not be weakened by association with the world, was generally beaten, on one count or another, before he had been twelve hours under her roof.

The autumn of one year brought him a companion in bond-age, a long-haired, grey-eyed little atom, as self-contained as himself, who moved about the house silently, and for the first few weeks spoke only to the goat that was her chiefest friend on earth and lived in the back-garden. Mrs. Jennett objected to the goat on the grounds that he was un-Christian,—which he certainly was. 'Then,' said the atom, choosing her words very deliberately, 'I shall write to my lawyer-peoples and tell them that you are a very bad woman. Amomma is mine, mine, mine!' Mrs. Jennett made a movement to the hall, where certain um-brellas and canes stood in a rack. The atom understood as clearly as Dick what this meant. 'I have been beaten before,' she said, still in the same passionless voice; 'I have been beaten worse than you can ever beat me. If you beat me I shall write to my lawyer-peoples and tell them that you do not give me enough to eat. I am not afraid of you.' Mrs. Jennett did not go into the hall, and the atom, after a pause to assure herself that all danger of war was past, went out, to weep bitterly on Amomma's neck.

Dick learned to know her as Maisie, and at first mistrusted her profoundly, for he feared that she might interfere with the small liberty of action left to him. She did not, however; and she volunteered no friendliness until Dick had taken the first steps. Long before the holidays were over, the stress of punishment shared in common drove the children together, if it were only to play into each other's hands as they prepared lies for Mrs. Jennett's use. When Dick returned to school, Maisie whispered, 'Now I shall be all alone to take care of myself; but,' and she nodded her head bravely, 'I can do it. You promised to send Amomma a grass collar. Send it soon.' A week later she asked for that collar by return of post, and was not pleased when she learned that it took time to make. When at last Dick forwarded the gift she forgot to thank him for it.

Many holidays had come and gone since that day, and Dick had grown into a lanky hobbledehoy more than ever conscious of his bad clothes. Not for a moment had Mrs. Jennett relaxed her tender care of him, but the average canings of a public school—Dick fell under punishment about three times a month—filled him with contempt for her powers. 'She doesn't hurt,' he explained to Maisie, who urged him to rebellion, 'and she is kinder to you after she has whacked me.' Dick shambled through the days unkept in body and savage in soul, as the smaller boys of the school learned to know, for when the spirit moved him he would hit them, cunningly and with science. The same spirit made him more than once try to tease Maisie, but the girl refused to be made unhappy. 'We are both miserable as it is,' said she. 'What is the use of trying to make things worse? Let's find things to do, and forget things.'

The pistol was the outcome of that search. It could only be used on the muddiest foreshore of the beach, far away from bathing-machines and pier-heads, below the grassy slopes of Fort Keeling. The tide ran out nearly two miles on that coast, and the many-coloured mud-banks, touched by the sun, sent up a lamentable smell of dead weed. It was late in the afternoon when Dick and Maisie arrived on their ground, Amomma trotting patiently behind them.

'Mf!' said Maisie, sniffing the air. 'I wonder what makes the sea so smelly. I don't like it.'

'You never like anything that isn't made just for you,' said Dick bluntly. 'Give me the cartridges, and I'll try first shot. How far does one of these little revolvers carry?'

'Oh, half a mile,' said Maisie promptly. 'At least it makes an awful noise. Be careful with the cartridges; I don't like those jagged stick-up things on the rim. Dick, do be careful.'

'All right. I know how to load. I'll fire at the breakwater out there.'

He fired, and Amomma ran away bleating. The bullet threw up a spurt of mud to the right of the weed-wreathed piles.

'Throws high and to the right. You try, Maisie. Mind, it's loaded all round.'

Maisie took the pistol and stepped delicately to the verge of the mud, her hand firmly closed on the butt, her mouth and left eye screwed up. Dick sat down on a tuft of bank and laughed. Amomma returned very cautiously. He was accustomed to strange experiences in his afternoon walks, and, finding the cartridge-box unguarded, made investigations with his nose. Maisie fired, but could not see where the bullet went.

'I think it hit the post,' she said, shading her eyes and looking out across the sailless sea.

'I know it has gone out to the Marazion bell-buoy,' said Dick, with a chuckle. 'Fire low and to the left; then perhaps you'll get it. Oh, look at Amomma!—He's eating the cartridges!'

Maisie turned, the revolver in her hand, just in time to see Amomma scampering away from the pebbles Dick threw after him. Nothing is sacred to a billy-goat. Being well fed and the adored of his mistress, Amomma had naturally swallowed two loaded pin-fire cartridges. Maisie hurried up to assure herself that Dick had not miscounted the tale.

'Yes, he's eaten two.'

5

'Horrid little beast! Then they'll joggle about inside him and blow up, and serve him right. . . . Oh, Dick! have I killed you?'

Revolvers are tricky things for young hands to deal with. Maisie could not explain how it had happened, but a veil of reeking smoke separated her from Dick, and she was quite certain that the pistol had gone off in his face. Then she heard him sputter, and dropped on her knees beside him, crying, 'Dick, you aren't hurt, are you? I didn't mean it.'

'Of course you didn't,' said Dick, coming out of the smoke and wiping his cheek. 'But you nearly blinded me. That powder stuff stings awfully.' A neat little splash of grey lead on a stone showed where the bullet had gone. Maisie began to whimper.

'Don't,' said Dick, jumping to his feet and shaking himself. 'I'm not a bit hurt.'

'No, but I might have killed you,' protested Maisie, the corners of her mouth drooping. 'What should I have done then?'

'Gone home and told Mrs. Jennett.' Dick grinned at the thought; then, softening, 'Please don't worry about it. Besides, we are wasting time. We've got to get back to tea. I'll take the revolver for a bit.'

Maisie would have wept on the least encouragement, but Dick's indifference, albeit his hand was shaking as he picked up the pistol, restrained her. She lay panting on the beach while Dick methodically bombarded the breakwater. 'Got it at last!' he exclaimed, as a lock of weed flew from the wood.

'Let me try,' said Maisie imperiously. 'I'm all right now.'

They fired in turns till the rickety little revolver nearly shook itself to pieces, and Amomma the outcast—because he might blow up at any moment—browsed in the background and wondered why stones were thrown at him. Then they found a balk of timber floating in a pool which was commanded by the seaward slope of Fort Keeling, and they sat down together before this new target.

'Next holidays,' said Dick, as the now thoroughly fouled revolver kicked wildly in his hand, 'we'll get another pistol,—central fire,—that will carry farther.'

'There won't be any next holidays for me,' said Maisie. 'I'm going away.'

'Where to?'

'I don't know. My lawyers have written to Mrs. Jennett, and I've got to be educated somewhere,—in France, perhaps,—I don't know where; but I shall be glad to go away.'

'I shan't like it a bit. I suppose I shall be left. Look here, Maisie, is it really true you're going? Then these holidays will be the last I shall see anything of you; and I go back to school next week. I wish——'

The young blood turned his cheeks scarlet. Maisie was picking grass-tufts and throwing them down the slope at a yellow sea-poppy nodding all by itself to the illimitable levels of the mud-flats and the milk-white sea beyond.

'I wish,' she said, after a pause, 'that I could see you again some time. You wish that too?'

'Yes, but it would have been better if—if—you had—shot straight over there—down by the breakwater.'

Maisie looked with large eyes for a moment. And this was the boy who only ten days before had decorated Amomma's horns with cut-paper ham-frills and turned him out, a bearded derision, among the public ways! Then she dropped her eyes: this was not the boy.

'Don't be stupid,' she said reprovingly, and with swift instinct attacked the side-issue. 'How selfish you are! Just think what I should have felt if that horrid thing had killed you! I'm quite miserable enough already.'

'Why? Because you're going way from Mrs. Jennett?'

'No.'

'From me, then?'

No answer for a long time. Dick dared not look at her. He felt, though he did not know, all that the past four years had been to him, and this the more acutely since he had no knowledge to put his feelings in words.

'I don't know,' she said. 'I suppose it is.'

'Maisie, you must know. *I*'m not supposing.'

'Let's go home,' said Maisie weakly.

But Dick was not minded to retreat.

'I can't say things,' he pleaded, 'and I'm awfully sorry for teasing you about Amomma the other day. It's all different now, Maisie, can't you see? And you might have told me that you were going, instead of leaving me to find out.'

'You didn't. I did tell. Oh, Dick, what's the use of worrying?'

'There isn't any; but we've been together years and years, and I didn't know how much I cared.'

'I don't believe you ever did care.'

'No, I didn't; but I do,—I care awfully now. Maisie,' he gulped,—'Maisie, darling, say you care too, please.'

'I do; indeed I do; but it won't be any use.'

'Why?'

'Because I am going away.'

'Yes, but if you promise before you go. Only say—will you?' A second 'darling' came to his lips more easily than the first. There were few endearments in Dick's home or school life; he had to find them by instinct. Dick caught the little hand blackened with the escaped gas of the revolver.

'I promise,' she said solemnly; 'but if I care, there is no need for promising?'

'And you do care?' For the first time in the past few minutes their eyes met and spoke for them who had no skill in speech. . . .

'Oh, Dick, don't! please don't! It was all right when we said good-morning; but now it's all different!' Amomma looked on from afar. He had seen his property quarrel frequently, but he had never seen kisses exchanged before. The yellow sea-poppy was wiser, and nodded its head approvingly. Considered as a kiss, that was a failure, but since it was the first, other than those demanded by duty, in all the world that either had ever given or taken, it opened to them new worlds, and every one of them glorious, so that they were lifted above the consideration of any worlds at all, especially those in which tea is necessary, and sat still, holding each other's hands and saying not a word.

'You can't forget now,' said Dick at last. There was that on his cheek that stung more than gunpowder.

'I shouldn't have forgotten anyhow,' said Maisie, and they looked at each other and saw that each was changed from the companion of an hour ago to a wonder and a mystery they could not understand. The sun began to set, and a night-wind thrashed along the bents of the foreshore.

'We shall be awfully late for tea,' said Maisie. 'Let's go home.'

'Let's use the rest of the cartridges first,' said Dick; and he helped Maisie down the slope of the fort to the sea,—a descent that she was quite capable of covering at full speed. Equally gravely Maisie took the grimy hand. Dick bent forward clumsily; Maise drew the hand away, and Dick blushed.

'It's very pretty,' he said.

'Pooh!' said Maisie, with a little laugh of gratified vanity. She stood close to Dick as he loaded the revolver for the last time and fired over the sea, with a vague notion at the back of his head that he was protecting Maisie from all the evils in the world. A puddle far across the mud caught the last rays of the sun and turned into a wrathful red disc. The light held Dick's attention for a moment, and as he raised his revolver there fell upon him a renewed sense of the miraculous, in that he was standing by Maisie who had promised to care for him for an indefinite length of time till such date as—— A gust of the growing wind drove the girl's long black hair across his face as she stood with her hand on his shoulder calling Amomma 'a little beast,' and for a moment he was in the dark, —a darkness that stung. The bullet went singing out to the empty sea.

'Spoilt my aim,' said he, shaking his head. 'There aren't any more cartridges; we shall have to run home.' But they did not run. They walked very slowly, arm in arm. And it was a matter of indifference to them whether the neglected Amomma with two pin-fire cartridges in his inside blew up or trotted beside them; for they had come into a golden heritage and were disposing of it with all the wisdom of all their years.

'And I shall be——' quoth Dick valiantly. Then he checked himself: 'I don't know what I shall be. I don't seem to be able to pass any exams., but I can make awful caricatures of the masters. Ho! ho!'

'Be an artist, then,' said Maisie. 'You're always laughing at my trying to draw; and it will do you good.'

'I'll never laugh at anything you do,' he answered. 'I'll be an artist, and I'll do things.'

'Artists always want money, don't they?'

'I've got a hundred and twenty pounds a year of my own. My guardians tell me I'm to have it when I come of age. That will be enough to begin with.'

'Ah, I'm rich,' said Maisie. 'I've got three hundred a year all my own when I'm twenty-one. That's why Mrs. Jennett is kinder to me than she is to you. I wish, though, that I had somebody that belonged to me,—just a father or a mother.'

'You belong to me,' said Dick, 'for ever and ever.'

'Yes, we belong—for ever. It's very nice.' She squeezed his arm. The kindly darkness hid them both, and, emboldened because he could only just see the profile of Maisie's cheek with the long lashes veiling the grey eyes, Dick at the front door delivered himself of the words he had been boggling over for the last two hours.

'And I—love you, Maisie,' he said, in a whisper that seemed to him to ring across the world,—the world that he would to-morrow or the next day set out to conquer.

There was a scene, not, for the sake of discipline, to be reported, when Mrs. Jennett would have fallen upon him, first for disgraceful unpunctuality, and secondly, for nearly killing himself with a forbidden weapon.

'I was playing with it, and it went off by itself,' said Dick, when the powder-pocked cheek could no longer be hidden, 'but if you think you're going to lick me you're wrong. You are never going to touch me again. Sit down and give me my tea. You can't cheat us out of that, anyhow.'

Mrs. Jennett gasped and became livid. Maisie said nothing, but encouraged Dick with her eyes, and he behaved abominably all that evening. Mrs. Jennett prophesied an immediate judgment of Providence and a descent into Tophet later, but Dick walked in Paradise and would not hear. Only when he was going to bed Mrs. Jennett recovered and asserted herself. He had bidden Maisie good-night with down-dropped eyes and from a distance.

'If you aren't a gentleman you might try to behave like

one,' said Mrs. Jennett spitefully. 'You've been quarrelling with Maisie àgain.'

This meant that the usual good-night kiss had been omitted. Maisie, white to the lips, thrust her cheek forward with a fine air of indifference, and was duly pecked by Dick, who tramped out of the room red as fire. That night he dreamed a wild dream. He had won all the world and brought it to Maisie in a cartridge-box, but she turned it over with her foot, and, instead of saying, 'Thank you,' cried:—

'Where is the grass collar you promised for Amomma? Oh, how selfish you are!'

# CHAPTER II

*Then we brought the lances down, then the bugles blew,*
*When we went to Kandahar, ridin' two an' two,*
*Ridin', ridin', ridin', two an' two,*
*Ta-ra-ra-ra-ra-ra-ra,*
*All the way to Kandahar, ridin' two an' two.*

BARRACK-ROOM BALLAD.

'I'M NOT ANGRY with the British public, but I wish we had a few thousand of them scattered among these rocks. They wouldn't be in such a hurry to get at their morning papers then. Can't you imagine the regulation householder—Lover of Justice, Constant Reader, Paterfamilias, and all that lot—frizzling on hot gravel?'

'With a blue veil over his head, and his clothes in strips. Has any man here a needle? I've got a bit of sugar-sack.'

'I'll lend you a packing-needle for six square inches of it then. Both my knees are worn through.'

'Why not six square acres, while you're about it? But lend me the needle, and I'll see what I can do with the selvage. I don't think there's enough to protect my royal body from the cold blast as it is. What are you doing with that everlasting sketch-book of yours, Dick?'

'Study of our Special Correspondent repairing his wardrobe,' said Dick gravely, as the other man kicked off a pair of sorely worn riding-breeches and began to fit a square of coarse canvas over the most obvious open space. He grunted disconsolately as the vastness of the void developed itself.

*13*

'Sugar-bags, indeed! Hi! you pilot-man there! Lend me all the sails of that whale-boat.'

A fez-crowned head bobbed up in the stern-sheets, divided itself into exact halves with one flashing grin, and bobbed down again. The man of the tattered breeches, clad only in a Norfolk jacket and a grey flannel shirt, went on with his clumsy sewing, while Dick chuckled over the sketch.

Some twenty whale-boats were nuzzling a sandbank which was dotted with English soldiery of half-a-dozen corps, bathing or washing their clothes. A heap of boat-rollers, commissariat-boxes, sugar-bags, and flour- and small-arm-ammunition-cases showed where one of the whale-boats had been compelled to unload hastily; and a regimental carpenter was swearing aloud as he tried, on a wholly insufficient allowance of white lead, to plaster up the sun-parched gaping seams of the boat herself.

'First the bloomin' rudder snaps,' said he to the world in general; 'then the mast goes; an' then, s' 'elp me, when she can't do nothin' else, she opens 'erself out like a cock-eyed Chinese lotus.'

'Exactly the case with my breeches, whoever you are,' said the tailor, without looking up. 'Dick, I wonder when I shall see a decent shop again.'

There was no answer, save the incessant angry murmur of the Nile as it raced round a basalt-walled bend and foamed across a rock-ridge half a mile up-stream. It was as though the brown weight of the river would drive the white men back to their own country. The indescribable scent of Nile mud in the air told that the stream was falling and that the next few miles would be no light thing for the whale-boats to overpass. The desert ran down almost to the banks, where, among grey, red, and black hillocks, a camel-corps was encamped. No man dared even for a day lose touch of the slow-moving boats; there had been no fighting for weeks past, and throughout all that time the Nile had never spared them. Rapid had followed rapid, rock rock, and island-group island-group, till the rank and file had long since lost all count of direction and very nearly of time. They were moving somewhere, they did not know why, to do something, they did not know what. Before them lay the Nile, and at the other end of it was one Gordon, fighting for the dear life, in a town called Khartoum. There were columns of British troops in the desert, or in one of the many deserts; there were columns on the river; there were yet more columns waiting to embark on the river; there were fresh drafts waiting at Assiut and Assuan; there were lies and rumours running over the face of the hopeless land from Suakin to the Sixth Cataract, and men supposed generally that there must be some one in authority to direct the general scheme of the many movements. The duty of that particular river-column was to keep the whale-boats afloat in the water, to avoid trampling on the villagers' crops when the gangs 'tracked' the boats with lines thrown from midstream, to get as much sleep and food as was possible, and, above all, to press on without delay in the teeth of the churning Nile.

With the soldiers sweated and toiled the correspondents of the newspapers, and they were almost as ignorant as their companions. But it was above all things necessary that England at breakfast should be amused and thrilled and interested, whether Gordon lived or died, or half the British army went to pieces in the sands. The Sudan campaign was a picturesque one, and lent itself to vivid word-painting. Now and again a 'Special' managed to get slain,—which was not altogether a disadvantage to the paper that employed him,—and more often the hand-to-hand nature of the fighting allowed of miraculous escapes which were worth telegraphing home at eighteenpence the word. There were many correspondents with many corps and columns,—from the veterans who had followed on the heels of the cavalry that occupied Cairo in '82, what time Arabi Pasha called himself king, who had seen the first miserable work round Suakin when the sentries were cut up nightly and the scrub swarmed with spears, to youngsters jerked into the business at the end of a telegraph-wire to take the place of their betters killed or invalided.

Among the seniors—those who knew every shift and change in the perplexing postal arrangements, the value of the seediest, weediest Egyptian garron offered for sale in Cairo or Alexandria, who could talk a telegraph-clerk into amiability and soothe the ruffled vanity of a newly appointed Staff-officer when Press regulations became burdensome—was the man in the flannel shirt, the black-browed Torpenhow. He represented the Central Southern Syndicate in the campaign, as he had represented it in the Egyptian war, and elsewhere. The syndicate did not concern itself greatly with criticisms of attack and the like. It supplied the masses, and all it demanded was picturesqueness and abundance of detail; for there is more joy in England over a soldier who insubordinately steps out of square to rescue a comrade than over twenty generals slaving even to baldness at the gross details of transport and commissariat.

He had met at Suakin a young man, sitting on the edge of a recently abandoned redoubt about the size of a hat-box, sketching a clump of shell-torn bodies on the gravel plain.

'What are you for?' said Torpenhow. The greeting of the correspondent is that of the commercial traveller on the road.

'My own hand,' said the young man, without looking up. 'Have you any tobacco?'

Torpenhow waited till the sketch was finished, and when he had looked at it said, 'What's your business here?'

'Nothing. There was a row, so I came. I'm supposed to be doing something down at the painting-slips among the boats, or else I'm in charge of the condenser on one of the water-ships. I've forgotten which.'

'You've cheek enough to build a redoubt with,' said Torpenhow, and took stock of the new acquaintance. 'Do you always draw like that?'

The young man produced more sketches. 'Row on a Chinese pig-boat,' said he sententiously, showing them one after another.—'Chief mate dirked by a comprador.—Junk ashore off Hakodate.—Somali muleteer being flogged.—Star-shell bursting over camp at Berbera.—Slave-dhow being chased round Tajurrah Bay.—Soldier lying dead in the moonlight outside Suakin,—throat cut by Fuzzies.'

'H'm!' said Torpenhow, 'can't say I care for Verestchagin-and-water myself, but there's no accounting for tastes. Doing anything now, are you?'

'No. I'm amusing myself here.'

Torpenhow looked at the aching desolation of the place. 'Faith, you've queer notions of amusement. Got any money?'

'Enough to go on with. Look here: do you want me to do war work?'

'*I* don't. My syndicate may, though. You can draw more than a little, and I don't suppose you care much what you get, do you?'

'Not this time. I want my chance first.'

Torpenhow looked at the sketches again, and nodded. 'Yes, you're right to take your first chance when you can get it.'

He rode away swiftly through the Gate of the Two War-Ships, rattled across the causeway into the town, and wired to his syndicate, 'Got man here, picture-work. Good and cheap. Shall I arrange? Can do letterpress with sketches.'

# THE LIGHT THAT FAILED

The man on the redoubt sat swinging his legs and murmuring, 'I knew the chance would come, sooner or later. By Gad, they'll have to sweat for it if I come through this business alive!'

In the evening Torpenhow was able to announce to his friend that the Central Southern Agency was willing to take him on trial, paying expenses for three months. 'And, by the way, what's your name?' said Torpenhow.

'Heldar. Do they give me a free hand?'

'They've taken you on chance. You must justify the choice. You'd better stick to me. I'm going up-country with a column, and I'll do what I can for you. Give me some of your sketches taken here, and I'll send 'em along.' To himself he said, 'That's the best bargain the Central Southern has ever made; and they got *me* cheaply enough.'

So it came to pass that, after some purchase of horse-flesh and arrangements financial and political, Dick was made free of the New and Honourable Fraternity of war-correspondents, who all possess the inalienable right of doing as much work as they can and getting as much for it as Providence and their owners shall please. To these things are added in time, if the brother be worthy, the power of glib speech that neither man nor woman can resist when a meal or a bed is in question, the eye of a horse-coper, the skill of a cook, the constitution of a bullock, the digestion of an ostrich, and an infinite adaptability to all circumstances. But many die before they attain to this degree, and the past-masters in the craft appear for the most part in dress-clothes when they are in England, and thus their glory is hidden from the multitude.

Dick followed Torpenhow wherever the latter's fancy chose to lead him, and between the two they managed to accomplish some work that almost satisfied themselves. It was not an easy life in any way, and under its influence the two were drawn very closely together, for they ate from the same dish, they shared the same water-bottle, and, most binding tie of all, their mails went off together. It was Dick who managed to make gloriously drunk a telegraph-clerk in a palm hut far beyond the Second Cataract, and, while the man lay in bliss on the floor, possessed himself of some laboriously acquired exclusive information, forwarded by a confiding correspondent of an opposition syndicate, made a careful duplicate of the matter, and brought the result to Torpenhow, who said that all was fair in love or war-correspondence, and built an excellent descriptive article from his rival's riotous waste of words. It was Torpenhow who—but the tale of their adventures, together and apart, from Philae to the waste wilderness of Herawi and Muella, would fill many books. They had been penned into a square side by side, in deadly fear of being shot by over-excited soldiers; they had fought with baggage-camels in the chill dawn; they had jogged along in silence under blinding sun on indefatigable little Egyptian horses; and they had floundered on the shallows of the Nile when the whale-boat in which they had found a berth chose to hit a hidden rock and rip out half her bottom-planks.

Now they were sitting on the sand-bank, and the whale-boats were bringing up the remainder of the column.

'Yes,' said Torpenhow, as he put the last rude stitches into his over-long-neglected gear, 'it has been a beautiful business.'

'The patch or the campaign?' said Dick. 'Don't think much of either, myself.'

'You want the *Eurylas* brought up above the Third Cataract, don't you? and eighty-one-ton guns at Jakdul? Now, *I'm* quite satisfied with my breeches.' He turned round gravely to exhibit himself, after the manner of a clown.

'It's very pretty. Specially the lettering on the sack. G. B. T. —Government Bullock Train. That's a sack from India.'

'It's my initials,—Gilbert Belling Torpenhow. I stole the cloth on purpose. What the mischief are the camel-corps doing yonder?' Torpenhow shaded his eyes and looked across the scrub-strewn gravel.

A bugle blew furiously, and the men on the bank hurried to their arms and accoutrements.

' "Pisan soldiery surprised while bathing," ' remarked Dick calmly. 'D'you remember the picture? It's by Michael Angelo. All beginners copy it. That scrub's alive with enemy.'

The camel-corps on the bank yelled to the infantry to come to them, and a hoarse shouting down the river showed that the remainder of the column had wind of the trouble and was hastening to take share in it. As swiftly as a reach of still water is crisped by the wind, the rock-strewn ridges and scrub-topped hills were troubled and alive with armed men. Mercifully, it occurred to these to stand far off for a time, to shout and gesticulate joyously. One man even delivered himself of a long story. The camel-corps did not fire. They were only too glad of a little breathing-space, until some sort of square could be formed. The men on the sand-bank ran to their side; and the whale-boats, as they toiled up within shouting distance, were thrust into the nearest bank and emptied of all save the sick and a few men to guard them. The Arab orator ceased his outcries, and his friends howled.

'They look like the Mahdi's men,' said Torpenhow, elbowing himself into the crush of the square. 'But what thousands of 'em there are! The tribes hereabout aren't against us, I know.'

'Then the Mahdi's taken another town,' said Dick, 'and set all these yelping devils free to chaw us up. Lend us your glass.'

'Our scouts should have told us of this. We've been trapped,' said a subaltern. 'Aren't the camel-guns ever going to begin? Hurry up, you men!'

There was no need for any order. The men flung themselves panting against the sides of the square, for they had good reason to know that whoso was left outside when the fighting began would very probably die in an extremely unpleasant fashion. The little hundred-and-fifty-pound camel-guns posted at one corner of the square opened the ball as the square moved forward by its right to get possession of a knoll of rising ground. All had fought in this manner many times before, and there was no novelty in the entertainment: always the same hot and stifling formation, the smell of dust and leather, the same boltlike rush of the enemy, the same pressure on the weakest side of the square, the few minutes of desperate hand-to-hand scuffle, and then the silence of the desert, broken only by the yells of those whom the handful of cavalry attempted to pursue. They had grown careless. The camel-guns spoke at intervals, and the square slouched forward amid the protests of the camels. Then came the attack of three thousand men who had not learned from books that it is impossible for troops in close order to attack against breech-loading fire. A few dropping shots heralded their approach, and a few horsemen led, but the bulk of the force was naked humanity, mad with rage, and armed with the spear and the sword. The instinct of the desert, where there is always much war, told them that the right flank of the square was the weakest, for they swung clear of the front. The camel-guns shelled them as they passed, and opened for an instant lanes through their midst, most like those quick-closing vistas in a Kentish hop-garden seen when the train races by at full speed; and the infantry fire, held till the opportune moment, dropped them in close-packed hundreds. No civilised troops in the world could have endured the hell through which they came, the living leaping high to avoid the dying who clutched at their heels, the wounded cursing and staggering forward, till they fell—a torrent black as the sliding water above a mill-dam—full on the right flank of the square. Then the line of the dusty troops and the faint blue desert sky overhead went out in rolling smoke, and the little stones on the heated ground and the tinder-dry clumps of scrub became matters of surpassing interest, for men measured their agonised retreat and recovery by these things, counting mechanically and hewing their way back to chosen pebble and branch. There was no semblance of any concerted fighting. For aught the men knew, the enemy might be attempting all four sides of the square at once. Their business was to destroy what lay in front of them, to bayonet in the back those who passed over them, and, dying, to drag down the slayer till he could be knocked on the head by some avenging gun-butt. Dick waited quietly with Torpenhow and a young doctor till the stress became unendurable. There was no hope of attending to the wounded till the attack was repulsed, so the three moved forward gingerly towards the weakest side. There was a rush from without, the short *hough-hough* of the stabbing spears, and a man on a horse, followed by thirty or forty others, dashed through, yelling and hacking. The right flank of the square sucked in after them, and the other sides sent help. The wounded, who knew that they had but a few hours more to live, caught at the enemy's feet and brought them down, or, staggering to a discarded rifle, fired blindly into the scuffle that raged in the centre of the square. Dick was conscious that somebody had cut him violently across his helmet, that he had fired his revolver into a black, foam-flecked face which forth-with ceased to bear any resemblance to a face, and that Torpenhow had gone down under an Arab whom he had tried to 'collar low,' and was turning over and over with his captive, feeling for the man's eyes. The doctor was jabbing at a venture with a bayonet, and a helmetless soldier was firing over Dick's shoulder. The flying grains of powder stung his cheek. It was to Torpenhow that Dick turned by instinct. The representative of the Central Southern Syndicate had shaken himself clear of his enemy, and rose, wiping his thumb on his trousers. The Arab, both hands to his forehead, screamed aloud, then snatched up his spear and rushed at Torpenhow, who was panting under shelter of Dick's revolver. Dick fired twice, and the man dropped limply. His upturned face lacked one eye. The musketry-fire redoubled, but cheers mingled with it. The rush had failed, and the enemy were flying. If the heart of the square were a shambles, the ground beyond was a butcher's shop. Dick thrust his way forward between the maddened men. The remnant of the enemy were retiring, as the few—the very few—English cavalry rode down the laggards.

Beyond the lines of the dead, a broad blood-stained Arab spear cast aside in the retreat lay across a stump of scrub, and beyond this again the illimitable dark levels of the desert. The sun caught the steel and turned it into a savage red disc. Some one behind him was saying, 'Ah, get away, you brute!' Dick raised his revolver and pointed towards the desert. His eye was held by the red splash in the distance, and the clamour about him seemed to die down to a very far-away whisper, like the whisper of a level sea. There was the revolver and the red light, . . . and the voice of some one scaring something away, exactly as had fallen somewhere before,—probably in a past life. Dick waited for what should happen afterwards. Something seemed to crack inside his head, and for an instant he stood in the dark,—a darkness that stung. He fired at random, and the bullet went out across the desert as he muttered, 'Spoilt my aim. There aren't any more cartridges. We shall have to run home.' He put his hand to his head and brought it away covered with blood.

'Old man, you're cut rather badly,' said Torpenhow. 'I owe you something for this business. Thanks. Stand up! I say, you can't be sick here!'

Dick had fallen stiffly on Torpenhow's shoulder, and was muttering something about aiming low and to the left. Then he sank to the ground and was silent. Torpenhow dragged him off to a doctor, and sat down to work out an account of what he was pleased to call 'a sanguinary battle, in which our arms had acquitted themselves,' etc.

All that night, when the troops were encamped by the whale-boats, a black figure danced in the strong moonlight on the sand-bar and shouted that Gordon the accursed one was dead, —was dead,—was dead,—that two steamers were rock-staked on the Nile outside the city, and that of all their crews there remained not one; and Gordon was dead,—was dead,—was dead!

But Torpenhow took no heed. He was watching Dick, who was calling aloud to the restless Nile for Maisie,—and again Maisie!

'Behold a phenomenon,' said Torpenhow, rearranging the blanket. 'Here is a man, presumably human, who mentions the name of one woman only. And I've seen a good deal of de-lirium, too.—Dick, here's some fizzy drink.'

'Thank you, Maisie,' said Dick.

# CHAPTER III

*So he thinks he shall take to the sea again*
*For one more cruise with his buccaneers,*
*To singe the beard of the King of Spain,*
*And capture another Dean of Jaen*
*And sell him in Algiers.*

LONGFELLOW.

THE SUDAN CAMPAIGN and Dick's broken head had been some months ended and mended, and the Central Southern Syndicate had paid Dick a certain sum on account for work done, which work they were careful to assure him was not altogether up to their standard. Dick heaved the letter into the Nile at Cairo, cashed the draft in the same town, and bade a warm farewell to Torpenhow at the station.

'I am going to lie up for a while and rest,' said Torpenhow. 'I don't know where I shall live in London, but if God brings us to meet, we shall meet. Are you staying here on the off-chance of another row? There will be none till the Southern Sudan is reoccupied by our troops. Mark that. Good-bye; bless you. Come back when your money's spent; and give me your address.'

Dick loitered in Cairo, Alexandria, Ismailia, and Port Said, —especially Port Said. There is iniquity in many parts of the world, and vice in all, but the concentrated essence of all the iniquities and all the vices in all the continents finds itself at Port Said. And through the heart of that sand-bordered hell, where the mirage flickers day long above the Bitter Lakes, move, if you will only wait, most of the men and women you have known in this life. Dick established himself in quarters more riotous than respectable. He spent his evenings on the quay, and boarded many ships, and saw very many friends, —gracious Englishwomen with whom he had talked not too wisely in the veranda of Shepheard's Hotel, hurrying war-correspondents, skippers of the contract troop-ships employed in the campaign, Army officers by the score, and others of less reputable trades. He had choice of all the races of the East and West for studies, and the advantage of seeing his subjects under the influence of strong excitement at the gaming-tables, saloons, dancing-hells and elsewhere. For recreation there was the straight vista of the Canal, the blazing sands, the procession of shipping, and the white hospitals where the English soldiers lay. He strove to set down in black and white and colour all that Providence sent him, and when that supply was ended sought about for fresh material. It was a fascinating employment, but it ran away with his money, and he had drawn in advance the hundred and twenty pounds to which he was entitled yearly. 'Now I shall have to work and starve!' thought he, and was addressing himself to this new fate when a mysterious telegram arrived from Torpenhow in England, which said, 'Come back quick. You have caught on. Come.'

A large smile overspread his face. 'So soon! that's good hearing,' said he to himself. 'There will be an orgy to-night. I'll stand or fall by my luck. Faith, it's time it came!' He deposited half of his funds in the hands of his well-known friends Monsieur and Madame Binat, and ordered himself a Zanzibar dance of the finest. Monsieur Binat was shaking with drink, but Madame smiled sympathetically:—

'Monsieur needs a chair, of course, and of course Monsieur will sketch: Monsieur amuses himself strangely.'

Binat raised a blue-white face from a cot in the inner room. 'I understand,' he quavered. 'We all know Monsieur. Monsieur is an artist, as I have been.' Dick nodded. 'In the end,' said Binat, with gravity, 'Monsieur will descend alive into Hell, as I have descended.' And he laughed.

'You must come to the dance, too,' said Dick; 'I shall want you.'

'For my face? I knew it would be so. For my face? My God! And for my degradation so tremendous! I will not. Take him away. He is a devil. Or at least do thou, Céleste, demand of him more.' The excellent Binat began to kick and scream.

'All things are for sale in Port Said,' said Madame. 'If my husband comes it will be so much more. Eh, 'ow you call— 'alf a sovereign.'

The money was paid, and the mad dance was held at night in a walled courtyard at the back of Madame Binat's house. The lady herself, in faded mauve silk always about to slide from her yellow shoulders, played the piano, and to the tin-pot music of a Western waltz the naked Zanzibari girls danced furiously by the light of kerosene lamps. Binat sat upon a chair and stared with eyes that saw nothing, till the whirl of the dance and the clang of the rattling piano stole into the drink that took the place of blood in his veins, and his face glistened. Dick took him by the chin brutally and turned that face to the light. Madame Binat looked over her shoulder and smiled with many teeth. Dick leaned against the wall and sketched for an hour, till the kerosene lamps began to smell, and the girls threw themselves panting on the hard-beaten ground. Then he shut his book with a snap and moved away, Binat plucking feebly at his elbow. 'Show me,' he whimpered. 'I too was once an artist, even I!' Dick showed him the rough sketch. 'Am I that?' he screamed. 'Will you take that away with you and show all the world that it is I,—Binat?' He moaned and wept.

'Monsieur has paid for all,' said Madame. 'To the pleasure of seeing Monsieur again.'

The courtyard gate shut, and Dick hurried up the sandy street to the nearest gambling-hell, where he was well known. 'If the luck holds, it's an omen; if I lose, I must stay here.' He placed his money picturesquely about the board, hardly daring to look at what he did. The luck held. Three turns of the wheel left him richer by twenty pounds, and he went down to the shipping to make friends with the captain of a decayed cargo-steamer, who landed him in London with fewer pounds in his pocket than he cared to think about.

A thin grey fog hung over the city, and the streets were very cold; for summer was in England.

'It's a cheerful wilderness, and it hasn't the knack of altering much,' Dick thought, as he tramped from the Docks westward. 'Now, what must I do?'

The packed houses gave no answer. Dick looked down the long lightless streets and at the appalling rush of traffic. 'Oh, you rabbit-hutches!' said he, addressing a row of highly respectable semi-detached residences. 'Do you know what you've got to do later on? You have to supply me with men-servants and maid-servants,'—here he smacked his lips,—'and the peculiar treasure of kings. Meantime I'll get clothes and boots, and presently I will return and trample on you.' He stepped forward energetically; he saw that one of his shoes was burst at the side. As he stooped to make investigations, a man jostled him into the gutter. 'All right,' he said. 'That's another nick in the score. I'll jostle you later on.'

# THE LIGHT THAT FAILED

Good clothes and boots are not cheap, and Dick left his last shop with the certainty that he would be respectably arrayed for a time, but with only fifty shillings in his pocket. He returned to streets by the Docks, and lodged himself in one room, where the sheets on the bed were almost audibly marked in case of theft, and where nobody seemed to go to bed at all. When his clothes arrived he sought the Central Southern Syndicate for Torpenhow's address, and got it, with the intimation that there was still some money owing to him.

'How much?' said Dick, as one who habitually dealt in millions.

'Between thirty and forty pounds. If it would be any convenience to you, of course we could let you have it at once; but we usually settle accounts monthly.'

'If I show that I want anything now, I'm lost,' he said to himself. 'All I need I'll take later on.' Then, aloud, 'It's hardly worth while; and I'm going into the country for a month, too. Wait till I come back, and I'll see about it.'

'But we trust, Mr. Heldar, that you do not intend to sever your connection with us?'

Dick's business in life was the study of faces, and he watched the speaker keenly. 'That man means something,' he said. 'I'll do no business till I've seen Torpenhow. There's a big deal coming.' So he departed, making no promises, to his one little room by the Docks. And that day was the seventh of the month, and that month, he reckoned with awful distinctness, had thirty-one days in it!

It is not easy for a man of catholic tastes and healthy appetites to exist for twenty-four days on fifty shillings. Nor is it cheering to begin the experiment alone in all the loneliness of London. Dick paid seven shillings a week for his lodging, which left him rather less than a shilling a day for food and

drink. Naturally, his first purchase was of the materials of
his craft; he had been without them too long. Half a day's
investigation and comparison brought him to the conclusion
that sausages and mashed potatoes, twopence a plate, were
the best food. Now sausages once or twice a week for breakfast are not unpleasant. As lunch, even, with mashed potatoes, they become monotonous. As dinner they are impertinent.
At the end of three days Dick loathed sausages, and, going
forth, pawned his watch to revel on sheep's head, which is
not as cheap as it looks, owing to the bones and the gravy.
Then he returned to sausages and mashed potatoes. Then he
confined himself entirely to mashed potatoes for a day, and
was unhappy because of pains in his inside. Then he pawned
his waistcoat and his tie, and thought regretfully of money
thrown away in times past. There are few things more edify-
ing unto Art than the actual belly-pinch of hunger, and Dick
in his rare walks abroad—he did not care for exercise, it raised
desires that could not be satisfied—found himself dividing
mankind into two classes,—those who looked as if they might
give him something to eat, and those who looked otherwise.
'I never knew what I had to learn about the human face before,' he thought; and, as a reward for his humility, Providence
caused a cab-driver at a sausage-shop where Dick fed that night
to leave half eaten a great chunk of bread. Dick took it,—
would have fought all the world for its possession,—and it
cheered him.

The month dragged through at last, and, nearly prancing
with impatience, he went to draw his money. Then he hastened to Torpenhow's address and smelt the smell of cooking
meats all along the corridors of the chambers. Torpenhow
was on the top floor, and Dick burst into his room, to be received with a hug which nearly cracked his ribs, as Torpen-

how dragged him to the light and spoke of twenty different things in the same breath.

'But you're looking tucked up,' he concluded.

'Got anything to eat?' said Dick, his eye roaming round the room.

'I shall be having breakfast in a minute. What do you say to sausages?'

'No, anything but sausages! Torp, I've been starving on that accursed horseflesh for thirty days and thirty nights.'

'Now what lunacy has been your latest?'

Dick spoke of the last few weeks with unbridled speech. Then he opened his coat; there was no waistcoat below. 'I ran it fine, awfully fine, but I've just scraped through.'

'You haven't much sense, but you've got a backbone, anyhow. Eat, and talk afterwards.' Dick fell upon eggs and bacon and gorged till he could gorge no more. Torpenhow handed him a filled pipe, and he smoked as men smoke who for three weeks have been deprived of good tobacco.

'Ouf!' said he. 'That's heavenly! Well?'

'Why in the world didn't you come to me?'

'Couldn't; I owe you too much already, old man. Besides, I had a sort of superstition that this temporary starvation— that's what it was, and it hurt—would bring me more luck later. It's over and done with now, and none of the syndicate know how hard up I was. Fire away. What's the exact state of affairs as regards myself?'

'You had my wire? You've caught on here. People like your work immensely. I don't know why, but they do. They say you have a fresh touch and a new way of drawing things. And, because they're chiefly home-bred English, they say you have insight. You're wanted by half-a-dozen papers. You're wanted to illustrate books.'

Dick grunted scornfully.

'You're wanted to work up your smaller sketches and sell them to the dealers. They seem to think the money sunk in you is a good investment. Good Lord! who can account for the fathomless folly of the public?'

'They're a remarkably sensible people.'

'They are subject to fits, if that's what you mean; and you happen to be the object of the latest fit among those who are interested in what they call Art. Just now you're a fashion, a phenomenon, or whatever you please. I appeared to be the only person who knew anything about you here, and I have been showing the most useful men a few of the sketches you gave me from time to time. Those coming after your work on the Central Southern Syndicate appear to have done your business. You're in luck.'

'Huh! call it luck! Do call it luck, when a man has been kicking about the world like a dog, waiting for it to come! I'll luck 'em later on. I want a place to work in first.'

'Come here,' said Torpenhow, crossing the landing. 'This place is a big box-room really, but it will do for you. There's your skylight, or your north light, or whatever window you call it, and plenty of room to thrash about in, and a bedroom beyond. What more do you need?'

'Good enough,' said Dick, looking round the large room that took up a third of a top storey in the rickety chambers overlooking the Thames. A pale yellow sun shone through the skylight and showed the much dirt of the place. Three steps led from the door to the landing, and three more to Torpenhow's room. The well of the staircase disappeared into darkness, pricked by tiny gas-jets, and there were sounds of men talking and doors slamming seven flights below, in the warm gloom.

'Do they give you a free hand here?' said Dick cautiously. He was Ishmael enough to know the value of liberty.

'Anything you like: latchkeys and licence unlimited. We are permanent tenants for the most part here. 'Tisn't a place I would recommend for a Young Men's Christian Association, but it will serve. I took these rooms for you when I wired.'

'You're a great deal too kind, old man.'

'You didn't suppose you were going away from me, did you?' Torpenhow put his hand on Dick's shoulder, and the two walked up and down the room, henceforward to be called the studio, in sweet and silent communion. They heard rapping at Torpenhow's door. 'That's some ruffian come up for a drink,' said Torpenhow; and he raised his voice cheerily. There entered no one more ruffianly than a portly middle-aged gentleman in a satin-faced frock-coat. His lips were parted and pale, and there were deep pouches under the eyes.

'Weak heart,' said Dick to himself, and, as he shook hands, 'very weak heart. His pulse is shaking his fingers.'

The man introduced himself as the head of the Central Southern Syndicate and 'one of the most ardent admirers of your work, Mr. Heldar. I assure you, in the name of the syndicate, that we are immensely indebted to you; and I trust, Mr. Heldar, you won't forget that we were largely instrumental in bringing you before the public.' He panted because of the seven flights of stairs.

Dick glanced at Torpenhow, whose left eyelid lay for a moment dead on his cheek.

'I shan't forget,' said Dick, every instinct of defence roused in him. 'You've paid me so well that I couldn't, you know. By the way, when I am settled in this place I should like to send and get my sketches. There must be nearly a hundred and fifty of them with you.'

'That is—er—is what I came to speak about. I fear we can't allow it exactly, Mr. Heldar. In the absence of any specified agreement the sketches are our property, of course.'

'Do you mean to say that you are going to keep them?'

'Yes; and we hope to have your help, on your own terms, Mr. Heldar, to assist us in arranging a little exhibition, which, backed by our name and the influence we naturally command among the Press, should be of material service to you. Sketches such as yours——'

'Belong to me. You engaged me by wire, you paid me the lowest rates you dared. You can't mean to keep them! Good God alive, man, they're all I've got in the world!'

Torpenhow watched Dick's face and whistled.

Dick walked up and down, thinking. He saw the whole of his little stock-in-trade, the first weapon of his equipment, annexed at the outset of his campaign by an elderly gentleman whose name Dick had not caught aright, who said that he represented a syndicate, which was a thing for which Dick had not the least reverence. The injustice of the proceedings did not much move him. He had seen the strong hand prevail too often in other places to be squeamish over the moral aspects of right and wrong. But he ardently desired the blood of the gentleman in the frock-coat, and when he spoke again it was with a strained sweetness that Torpenhow knew well for the beginning of strife.

'Forgive me, sir, but you have no—no younger man who can arrange this business with me?'

'I speak for the syndicate. I see no reason for a third party to——'

'You will in a minute. Be good enough to give back my sketches.'

The man stared blankly at Dick, and then at Torpenhow,

who was leaning against the wall. He was not used to ex-employees who ordered him to be good enough to do things.

'Yes, it is rather a cold-blooded steal,' said Torpenhow critically; 'but I'm afraid, I am very much afraid, you've struck the wrong man. Be careful, Dick. Remember, this isn't the Sudan.'

'Considering what services the syndicate have done you in putting your name before the world——'

This was not a fortunate remark; it reminded Dick of certain vagrant years lived out in loneliness and strife and unsatisfied desires. The memory did not contrast well with the prosperous gentleman who proposed to enjoy the fruit of those years.

'I don't know quite what to do with you,' began Dick meditatively. 'Of course you're a thief, and you ought to be half killed, but in your case you'd probably die. I don't want you dead on this floor, and, besides, it's unlucky just as one's moving in. Don't hit, sir; you'll only excite yourself.' He put one hand on the man's forearm and ran the other down the plump body beneath the coat. 'My goodness!' said he to Torpenhow, 'and this grey beast dares to be a thief! I have seen an Esneh camel-driver have the black hide taken off his body in strips for stealing half a pound of wet dates, and *he* was as tough as whipcord. This thing's soft all over—like a woman.' There are few things more poignantly humiliating than being handled by a man who does not intend to strike. The head of the syndicate began to breathe heavily. Dick walked round him, pawing him, as a cat paws a soft hearthrug. Then he traced with his forefinger the leaden pouches underneath the eyes, and shook his head. 'You were going to steal my things,—mine, mine, mine!—you, who don't know when you may die. Write a note to your office,—you say you're the head of it,—

and order them to give Torpenhow my sketches,—every one of them. Wait a minute: your hand's shaking. Now!' He thrust a pocket-book before him. The note was written. Torpenhow took it and departed without a word, while Dick walked round and round the spellbound captive, giving him such advice as he conceived best for the welfare of his soul. When Torpenhow returned with a gigantic portfolio, he heard Dick say, almost soothingly, 'Now, I hope this will be a lesson to you; and if you worry me when I have settled down to work with any nonsense about actions for assault, believe me, I'll catch you and man-handle you, and you'll die. You haven't very long to live, any-how. Go! *Imshi, Vootsak!*—Get out!' The man departed, stag-gering and dazed. Dick drew a long breath: 'Phew! what a law-less lot these people are! The first thing a poor orphan meets is gang robbery—organised burglary! Think of the hideous black-ness of that man's mind! Are my sketches all right, Torp?'

'Yes; one hundred and forty-seven of them. Well, I *must* say, Dick, you've begun well.'

'He was interfering with me. It only meant a few pounds to him, but it was everything to me. I don't think he'll bring an action. I gave him some medical advice gratis about the state of his body. It was cheap at the little flurry it cost him. Now let's look at my things.'

Two minutes later Dick had thrown himself down on the floor and was deep in the portfolio, chuckling lovingly as he turned the drawings over and thought of the price at which they had been bought.

The afternoon was well advanced when Torpenhow came to the door and saw Dick dancing a wild saraband under the skylight.

'I builded better than I knew, Torp,' he said, without stop-ping the dance. 'They're good! They're damned good! They'll go like smoke! I shall have an exhibition of them on my own brazen hook. And that man would have cheated me out of it! Do you know that I'm sorry now that I didn't actually hit him?'

'Go out,' said Torpenhow,—'go out and pray to be delivered from the sin of arrogance, which you never will be. Bring your things up from whatever place you're staying in, and we'll try to make this barn a little more shipshape.'

'And then—oh, then,' said Dick, still capering, 'we'll spoil the Egyptians!'

# CHAPTER IV

*The wolf-cub at even lay hid in the corn,*
  *When the smoke of the cooking hung grey:*
*He knew where the doe made a couch for her fawn,*
  *And he looked to his strength for his prey.*
*But the moon swept the smoke-wreaths away;*
*And he turned from his meal in the villager's close,*
*And he bayed to the moon as she rose.*

IN SEEONEE.

'WELL, AND HOW DOES SUCCESS TASTE?' said Torpenhow, some three months later. He had just returned to the chambers after a holiday in the country.

'Good,' said Dick, as he sat licking his lips before the easel in the studio. 'I want more,—heaps more. The lean years have passed, and I approve of these fat ones.'

'Be careful, old man. That way lies bad work.'

Torpenhow was sprawling in a long chair with a small fox-terrier asleep on his chest, while Dick was preparing a canvas. A dais, a background, and a lay-figure were the only fixed objects in the place. They rose from a wreck of oddments that began with felt-covered water-bottles, belts, and regimental badges, and ended with a small bale of second-hand uniforms and a stand of mixed arms. The mark of muddy feet on the dais showed that a military model had just gone away. The watery autumn sunlight was failing, and shadows sat in the corners of the studio.

'Yes,' said Dick deliberately, 'I like the power; I like the fun; I like the fuss; and above all I like the money. I almost like the people who make the fuss and pay the money. Almost. But they're a queer gang,—an amazingly queer gang!'

'They have been good enough to you, at any rate. That tin-pot exhibition of your sketches must have paid. Did you see that the papers called it the "Wild Work Show"?'

'Never mind. I sold every shred of canvas I wanted to; and, on my word, I believe it was because they believed I was a self-taught flagstone artist. I should have got better prices if I had worked my things on wool or scratched them on camel-bone instead of using mere black and white and colour. But they are a queer gang, these people. Limited isn't the word to describe 'em. I met a fellow the other day who told me that it was impossible that shadows on white sand should be blue,—ultramarine,—as they are. I found out, later, that that man had been as far as Brighton beach; but he knew all about Art, confound him. He gave me a lecture on it, and recommended me to go to school to learn technique. I wonder what old Kami would have said to that.'

'When were you under Kami, man of extraordinary beginnings?'

'I studied with him for two years in Paris. He taught by personal magnetism. All he ever said was, "*Continuez, mes enfants*," and you had to make the best you could of that. He had a divine touch, and he knew something about colour. Kami used to dream colour. I swear he could never have seen the genuine article; but he evolved it, and it was good.'

'Recollect some of those views in the Sudan?' said Torpenhow, with a provoking drawl.

Dick squirmed in his place. 'Don't! It makes me want to get out there again. What colour that was! Opal and umber and amber and claret and brick-red and sulphur—cockatoo-crest sulphur—against brown, with a nigger-black rock sticking up in the middle of it all, and a decorative frieze of camels festooning in front of a pure pale turquoise sky.' He began to walk up and down. 'And yet, you know, if you try to give these people the thing as God gave it keyed down to their comprehension and according to the powers He has given you——'

'Modest man! Go on.'

'Half-a-dozen epicene young pagans who haven't even been to Algiers will tell you, first, that your notion is borrowed, and, secondly, that it isn't Art.'

'This comes of my leaving Town for a month. Dickie, you've been promenading among the toy-shops and hearing people talk.'

'I couldn't help it,' said Dick penitently. 'You weren't here, and it was lonely these long evenings. A man can't work for ever.'

'A man might have gone to a pub, and got decently drunk.'

'I wish I had; but I foregathered with some men of sorts. They said they were artists, and I knew some of them could draw,—but they wouldn't draw. They gave me tea,—tea at five in the afternoon!—and talked about Art and the state of their souls. As if their souls mattered! I've heard more about Art and seen less of her in the last six months than in the whole of my life. Do you remember Cassavetti, who worked for some continental syndicate, out with the desert column? He was a regular Christmas-tree of contraptions when he took the field in full fig, with his water-bottle, lanyard, revolver, writing-case, housewife, gig-lamps, and the Lord knows what all. He used to fiddle about with 'em and show us how they worked; but he never seemed to do much except fudge his reports from the Nilghai. See?'

'Dear old Nilghai! He's in Town, fatter than ever. He

ought to be up here this evening. I see the comparison perfectly. You should have kept clear of all that man-millinery. Serves you right, and I hope it will unsettle your mind.'

'It won't. It has taught me what Art—holy sacred Art—means.'

'You've learnt something while I've been away. What is Art?'

'Give 'em what they know, and when you've done it once do it again.' Dick dragged forward a canvas laid face to the wall. 'Here's a sample of real Art. It's going to be a facsimile reproduction for a weekly. I called it "His Last Shot." It's worked up from the little water-colour I made outside El Maghrib. Well, I lured my model, a beautiful rifleman, up here with drink; I drored him, and I redrored him, and I tredrored him, and I made him a flushed, dishevelled, bedevilled scallawag, with his helmet at the back of his head, and the living fear of death in his eye, and the blood oozing out of a cut over his ankle-bone. He wasn't pretty, but he was all soldier and very much man.'

'Once more, modest child!'

Dick laughed. 'Well, it's only to you I'm talking. I did him just as well as I knew how, making allowance for the slickness of oils. Then the art-manager of that abandoned paper said that his subscribers wouldn't like it. It was brutal and coarse and violent,—man being naturally gentle when he's fighting for his life. They wanted something more restful, with a little more colour. I could have said a good deal, but you might as well talk to a sheep as an art-manager. I took my "Last Shot" back. Behold the result! I put him into a lovely red coat without a speck on it. That is Art. I polished his boots, —observe the high light on the toe. That is Art. I cleaned his rifle,—rifles are always clean on service,—because that is Art.

I pipeclayed his helmet,—pipeclay is always used on active service, and is indispensable to Art. I shaved his chin, I washed his hands, and gave him an air of fatted peace. Result, military tailor's pattern-plate. Price, thank Heaven, twice as much as for the first sketch, which was moderately decent.'

'And do you suppose you're going to give that thing out as your work?'

'Why not? I did it. Alone I did it, in the interests of sacred, home-bred Art and *Dickenson's Weekly.*'

Torpenhow smoked in silence for a while. Then came the verdict, delivered from rolling clouds: 'If you were only a mass of blathering vanity, Dick, I wouldn't mind,—I'd let you go to the deuce on your own mahl-stick; but when I consider what you are to me, and when I find that to vanity you add the two-penny-halfpenny pique of a twelve-year-old girl, then I bestir myself in your behalf. Thus!'

The canvas ripped as Torpenhow's booted foot shot through it, and the terrier jumped down, thinking rats were about.

'If you have any bad language to use, use it. You have not. I continue. You are an idiot, because no man born of woman is strong enough to take liberties with his public, even though they be—which they ain't—all you say they are.'

'But they don't know any better. What can you expect from creatures born and bred in this light? Dick pointed to the yellow fog. 'If they want furniture-polish, let them have furniture-polish, so long as they pay for it. They are only men and women. You talk as though they were gods.'

'That sounds very fine, but it has nothing to do with the case. They are the people you have to work for, whether you like it or not. They are your masters. Don't be deceived, Dickie, you aren't strong enough to trifle with them,—or with yourself, which is more important. Moreover,—Come back, Binkie: that red daub isn't going anywhere,—unless you take precious good care you will fall under the damnation of the cheque-book, and that's worse than death. You will get drunk —you're half drunk already—on easily-acquired money. For that money and your own infernal vanity you are willing to deliberately turn out bad work. You'll do quite enough bad work without knowing it. And, Dickie, as I love you and as I know you love me, I am not going to let you cut off your nose to spite your face for all the gold in England. That's settled. Now swear.'

'Don't know,' said Dick. 'I've been trying to make myself angry, but I can't; you're so abominably reasonable. There will be a row on *Dickenson's Weekly*, I fancy.'

'Why the Dickenson do you want to work on a weekly paper? It's slow bleeding of power.'

'It brings in the very desirable dollars,' said Dick, his hands in his pockets.

Torpenhow watched him with large contempt. 'Why, I thought it was a man!' said he. 'It's a child.'

'No, it isn't,' said Dick, wheeling quickly. 'You've no notion what the certainty of cash means to a man who has always wanted it badly. Nothing will pay me for some of my life's joys. On that Chinese pig-boat, for instance, when we ate bread and jam for every meal, because Ho-Wang wouldn't allow us anything better, and it all tasted of pig,—Chinee pig. I've worked for this, I've sweated for and I've starved for this, line on line and month after month. And now I've got it I am going to make the most of it while it lasts. Let them pay— they've no knowledge.'

'What does Your Majesty please to want? You can't smoke more than you do; you won't drink; you're a gross feeder;

and you dress in the dark, by the look of you. You wouldn't keep a horse, the other day when I suggested, because, you said, it might fall lame, and whenever you cross the street you take a hansom. Even you are not foolish enough to suppose that theatres and all the live things you can buy thereabouts mean Life. What earthly need have you for money?'

'It's there, bless its golden heart,' said Dick. 'It's there all the time. Providence has sent me nuts while I have teeth to crack 'em with. I haven't yet found the nut I wish to crack, but I'm keeping my teeth filed. Perhaps some day you and I will go for a walk round the wide earth.'

'With no work to do, nobody to worry us, and nobody to compete with? You would be unfit to speak to in a week. Besides, I shouldn't go. I don't care to profit by the price of a man's soul,—for that's what it would mean. Dick, it's no use arguing. You're a fool.'

'Don't see it. When I was on that Chinese pig-boat our captain got enormous credit for saving about twenty-five thousand very seasick little pigs, when our old tramp of a steamer fell foul of a timber-junk. Now, taking those pigs as a parallel——'

'Oh, confound your parallels! Whenever I try to improve your soul you always drag in some irrelevant anecdote from your very shady past. Pigs aren't the British public; credit on the high seas isn't credit here; and self-respect is self-respect all the world over. Go out for a walk and try to catch some self-respect. And, I say, if the Nilghai comes up this evening can I show him your diggings?'

'Surely. You'll be asking whether you must knock at my door, next.' And Dick departed, to take counsel with himself in the rapidly-gathering London fog.

Half an hour after he had left, the Nilghai laboured up the staircase. He was the chiefest, as he was the hugest, of the war-correspondents, and his experiences dated from the birth of the needle-gun. Saving only his ally, Keneu the Great War Eagle, there was no man mightier in the craft than he, and he always opened his conversation with the news that there would be trouble in the Balkans in the spring. Torpenhow laughed as he entered.

'Never mind the trouble in the Balkans. Those little states are always screeching. You've heard about Dick's luck?'

'Yes; he has been called up to notoriety, hasn't he? I hope you keep him properly humble. He wants suppressing from time to time.'

'He does. He's beginning to take liberties with what he thinks is his reputation.'

'Already! By Jove, he has cheek! I don't know about his reputation, but he'll come a cropper if he tries that sort of thing.'

'So I told him. I don't think he believes it.'

'They never do when they first start off. What's that wreck on the ground there?'

'Specimen of his latest impertinence.' Torpenhow thrust the torn edges of the canvas together and showed the well-groomed picture to the Nilghai, who looked at it for a moment and whistled.

'It's a chromo,' said he,—'a chromo-litholeo-margarine fake! What possessed him to do it? And yet how thoroughly he has caught the note that catches a public who think with their boots and read with their elbows! The cold-blooded insolence of the work almost saves it; but he mustn't go on with this. Hasn't he been praised and cockered up too much? You know these people here have no sense of proportion. They'll call him a second Detaille and a third-hand Meissonier while his fashion lasts. It's windy diet for a colt.'

'I don't think it affects Dick much. You might as well call

a young wolf a lion and expect him to take the compliment in exchange for a shin-bone. Dick's soul is in the bank. He's working for cash.'

'Now he has thrown up war work, I suppose he doesn't see that the obligations of the service are just the same, only the proprietors are changed.'

'How should he know? He thinks he is his own master.'

'Does he? I could undeceive him for his good if there's any virtue in print. He wants the whip-lash.'

'Lay it on with science, then. I'd flay him myself, but I like him too much.'

'I've no scruples. He had the audacity to try to cut me out with a woman at Cairo once. I forgot that, but I remember now.'

'Did he cut you out?'

'You'll see when I have dealt with him. But, after all, what's the good? Leave him alone and he'll come home, if he has any stuff in him, dragging or wagging his tail behind him. There's more in a week of life than in a lively weekly. None the less I'll slate him. I'll slate him ponderously in the *Cataclysm*.'

'Good luck to you; but I fancy nothing short of a crowbar would make Dick wince. His soul seems to have been fired before we came across him. He's intensely suspicious and utterly lawless.'

'Matter of temper,' said the Nilghai. 'It's the same with horses. Some you wallop and they work, some you wallop and they jib, and some you wallop and they go out for a walk with their hands in their pockets.'

'That's exactly what Dick has done,' said Torpenhow. 'Wait till he comes back. In the meantime you can begin your slating here. I'll show you some of his last and worst work in his studio.'

Dick had instinctively sought running water for a comfort to his mood of mind. He was leaning over the Embankment wall, watching the rush of the Thames through the arches of Westminster Bridge. He began by thinking of Torpenhow's advice, but, as of custom, lost himself in the study of the faces flocking past. Some had death written on their features, and Dick marvelled that they could laugh. Others, clumsy and coarse-built for the most part, were alight with love; others were merely drawn and lined with work; but there was something, Dick knew, to be made out of them all. The poor at least should suffer that he might learn, and the rich should pay for the output of his learning. Thus his credit in the world and his cash balance at the bank would be increased. So much the better for him. He had suffered. Now he would take toll of the ills of others.

The fog was driven apart for a moment, and the sun shone, a blood-red wafer, on the water. Dick watched the spot till he heard the voice of the tide between the piers die down like the wash of the sea at low tide. A girl hard pressed by her lover shouted shamelessly, 'Ah, get away, you beast!' and a shift of the same wind that had opened the fog drove across Dick's face the black smoke of a river-steamer at her berth below the wall. He was blinded for the moment, then spun round and found himself face to face with—Maisie.

There was no mistaking. The years had turned the child to a woman, but they had not altered the dark-grey eyes, the thin scarlet lips, or the firmly-modelled mouth and chin; and, that all should be as it was of old, she wore a closely-fitting grey dress.

Since the human soul is finite and not in the least under its own command, Dick, advancing, said, 'Hullo!' after the manner of schoolboys, and Maisie answered, 'Oh, Dick, is that

you?' Then, against his will, and before the brain, newly released from considerations of the cash balance, had time to
dictate to the nerves, every pulse of Dick's body throbbed furiously and his palate dried in his mouth. The fog shut down
again, and Maisie's face was pearl-white through it. No word
was spoken, but Dick fell into step at her side, and the two
paced the Embankment together, keeping the step as perfectly as in their afternoon excursions to the mud-flats. Then
Dick, a little hoarsely:

'What has happened to Amomma?'

'He died, Dick. Not cartridges. Over-eating. He was always
greedy. Isn't it funny?'

'Yes. No. Do you mean Amomma?'

'Ye—es. No. This. Where have you come from?'

'Over there.' He pointed eastward through the fog. 'And
you?'

'Oh, I'm in the North,—the black North, across all the
Park. I am very busy.'

'What do you do?'

'I paint a great deal. That's all I have to do.'

'Why, what's happened? You had three hundred a year.'

'I have that still. I'm painting; that's all.'

'Are you alone, then?'

'There's a girl living with me. Don't walk so fast, Dick.
You're out of step.'

'Then you noticed it too?'

'Of course I did. You're always out of step.'

'So I am. I'm sorry. You went on with the painting?'

'Of course. I said I should. I was at the Slade, then at Mer-
ton's in St. John's Wood, the big studio, then I pepper-potted,
—I mean I went to the National,—and now I'm working
under Kami.'

'But Kami is in Paris surely?'

'No; he has his teaching-studio at Vitry-sur-Marne. I work with him in the summer, and I live in London in the winter. I'm a householder.'

'Do you sell much?'

'Now and again, but not often. There is my 'bus, I must take it or lose half an hour. Good-bye, Dick.'

'Good-bye, Maisie. Won't you tell me where you live? I must see you again; and perhaps I could help you. I—I paint a little myself.'

'I may be in the Park to-morrow if there is no working light. I walk from the Marble Arch down and back again; that is my little excursion. But of course I shall see you again.' She stepped into the omnibus and was swallowed up by the fog.

'Well,—I—am—damned!' exclaimed Dick, and returned to the chambers.

Torpenhow and the Nilghai found him sitting on the steps to the studio door, repeating the phrase with an awful gravity.

'You'll be more damned when I've done with you,' said the Nilghai, upheaving his bulk from behind Torpenhow's shoulder and waving a sheaf of half-dry manuscript. 'Dick, it is of common report that you are suffering from swelled head.'

'Hullo, Nilghai. Back again? How are the Balkans and all the little Balkans? One side of your face is out of drawing, as usual.'

'Never mind that. I am commissioned to smite you in print. Torpenhow refuses from false delicacy. I've been overhauling the pot-boilers in your studio. They are simply disgraceful.'

'Oho! that's it, is it? If you think you can slate me, you're wrong. You can only describe, and you need as much room to turn in, on paper, as a cargo-boat. But continue, and be swift. I'm going to bed.'

'H'm! h'm! h'm! The first part only deals with your pictures. Here's the peroration: "For work done without conviction, for power wasted on trivialities, for labour expended with levity for the deliberate purpose of winning the easy applause of a fashion-driven public——" '

'That's "His Last Shot," second edition. Go on.'

'——"public, there remains but one end,—the oblivion that is preceded by toleration and cenotaphed with contempt. From that fate Mr. Heldar has yet to prove himself out of danger." '

'*Wow—wow—wow—wow—wow!*' said Dick profanely. 'It's a clumsy ending and vile journalese, but it's quite true. And yet,'—he sprang to his feet and snatched at the manuscript,— 'you scarred, deboshed, battered old gladiator! You're sent out when a war begins, to minister to the blind, brutal, British public's bestial thirst for blood. They have no arenas now, but they must have special correspondents. You're a fat gladiator who comes up through a trap-door and talks of what he's seen. You stand on precisely the same level as an energetic bishop, an affable actress, a devastating cyclone, or—my own sweet self. And you presume to lecture me about my work! Nilghai, if it were worth while I'd caricature you in four papers!'

The Nilghai winced. He had not thought of this.

'As it is, I shall take this stuff and tear it small—so!' The manuscript fluttered in slips down the dark well of the staircase. 'Go home, Nilghai,' said Dick. 'Go home to your lonely little bed, and leave me in peace. I am about to turn in till to-morrow.'

'Why, it isn't seven yet!' said Torpenhow, with amazement.

'It shall be two in the morning, if I choose,' said Dick,

backing to the studio door. 'I go to grapple with a serious crisis, and I shan't want any dinner.'

The door shut and was locked.

'What can you do with a man like that?' said the Nilghai.

'Leave him alone. He's as mad as a hatter.'

At eleven there was kicking on the studio door. 'Is the Nilghai with you still?' said a voice from within. 'Then tell him he might have condensed the whole of his lumbering nonsense into an epigram: "Only the free are bond, and only the bond are free." Tell him he's an idiot, Torp, and tell him I'm another.'

'All right. Come out and have supper. You're smoking on an empty stomach.'

There was no answer.

## CHAPTER V

*'I have a thousand men,' said he,*
*'To wait upon my will,*
*And towers nine upon the Tyne,*
*And three upon the Till.'*

*'And what care I for your men,' said she,*
*'Or towers from Tyne to Till,*
*Sith you must go with me,' she said,*
*'To wait upon my will?'*
SIR HOGGIE AND THE FAIRIES.

NEXT MORNING Torpenhow found Dick sunk in deepest repose of tobacco.

'Well, madman, how d'you feel?'

'I don't know. I'm trying to find out.'

'You had much better do some work.'

'Maybe; but I'm in no hurry. I've made a discovery, Torp. There's too much Ego in my Cosmos.'

'Not really! Is this revelation due to my lectures, or the Nilghai's?'

'It came to me suddenly, all on my own account. Much too much Ego; and now I'm going to work.'

He turned over a few half-finished sketches, drummed on a new canvas, cleaned three brushes, set Binkie to bite the toes of the lay-figure, rattled through his collection of arms and accoutrements, and then went out abruptly, declaring that he had done enough for the day.

'This is positively indecent,' said Torpenhow, 'and the first time that Dick has ever broken up a light morning. Perhaps he has found out that he has a soul, or an artistic temperament, or something equally valuable. That comes of leaving him alone for a month. Perhaps he has been going out of evenings. I must look to this.' He rang for the bald-headed old housekeeper, whom nothing could astonish or annoy.

'Beeton, did Mr. Heldar dine out at all while I was out of town?'

'Never laid 'is dress-clothes out once, sir, all the time. Mostly 'e dined in; but 'e brought some most remarkable fancy young gentlemen up 'ere after theatres once or twice. Remarkable fancy they was. You gentlemen on the top floor does very much as you likes, but it do seem to me, sir, droppin' a walkin'-stick down five flights o' stairs an' then goin' down four abreast to pick it up again at half-past two in the mornin' singin', "Bring back the whisky, Willie darlin',"—not once or twice, but scores o' times,—ain't charity to the other tenants. What I say is, "Do as you would be done by." That's my motto.'

'Of course! of course! I'm afraid the top floor isn't the quietest in the house.'

'I make no complaints, sir. I have spoke to Mr. Heldar friendly, an' he laughed, an' did me a picture of the missis that is as good as a coloured print. It 'asn't the 'igh shine of a photograph, but what I say is, "Never look a gift-horse in the mouth." Mr. Heldar's dress-clothes 'aven't been on him for weeks.'

'Then it's all right,' said Torpenhow to himself. 'Orgies are healthy, and Dick has a head of his own, but when it comes to women making eyes I'm not so certain.—Binkie, never you be a man, little dorglums. They're contrary brutes, and they do things without any reason.'

Dick had turned northward across the Park, but he was

walking in the spirit on the mud-flats with Maisie. He laughed aloud as he remembered the day when he had decked Amomma's horns with the ham-frills, and Maisie, white with rage, had cuffed him. How long those four years seemed in review, and how closely Maisie was connected with every hour of them! Storm across the sea, and Maisie in a grey dress on the beach, sweeping her drenched hair out of her eyes and laughing at the homeward race of the fishing-smacks; hot sunshine on the mud-flats, and Maisie sniffing scornfully, with her chin in the air; Maisie flying before the wind that threshed the foreshore and drove the sand like small shot about her ears; Maisie, very composed and independent, telling lies to Mrs. Jennett while Dick supported her with coarser perjuries; Maisie picking her way delicately from stone to stone, a pistol in her hand and her teeth firm-set; and Maisie in a grey dress sitting on the grass between the mouth of a cannon and a nodding yellow sea-poppy. The pictures passed before him one by one, and the last stayed the longest. Dick was perfectly happy with a quiet peace that was as new to his mind as it was foreign to his experience. It never occurred to him that there might be other calls upon his time than loafing across the Park in the forenoon.

'There's a good working light now,' he said, watching his shadow placidly. 'Some poor devil ought to be grateful for this. And there's Maisie!'

She was walking towards him from the Marble Arch, and he saw that no mannerism of her gait had been changed. It was good to find her still Maisie, and, so to speak, his next-door neighbour. No greeting passed between them, because there had been none in the old days.

'What are you doing out of your studio at this hour?' said Dick, as one who was entitled to ask.

'Idling. Just idling. I got angry with a chin and scraped it out. Then I left it in a little heap of paint-chips and came away.'

'I know what palette-knifing means. What was the piccy?'

'A fancy head that wouldn't come right,—horrid thing!'

'I don't like working over scraped paint when I'm doing flesh. The grain comes up woolly as the paint dries.'

'Not if you scrape properly.' Maisie waved her hand to illustrate her methods. There was a dab of paint on the white cuff. Dick laughed.

'You're as untidy as ever.'

'That comes well from you. Look at your own cuff!'

'By Jove, yes! It's worse than yours. I don't think we've much altered in anything. Let's see, though.' He looked at Maisie critically. The pale blue haze of an autumn day crept between the tree-trunks of the Park and made a background for the grey dress, the black velvet toque above the black hair, and the resolute profile.

'No, there's nothing changed. How good it is! D'you remember when I fastened your hair into the snap of a handbag?'

Maisie nodded, with a twinkle in her eyes, and turned her full face to Dick.

'Wait a minute,' said he. 'That mouth is down at the corners a little. Who's been worrying you, Maisie?'

'No one but myself. I never seem to get on with my work, and yet I try hard enough, and Kami says——'

' "Continuez, mesdemoiselles. Continuez toujours, mes enfants." Kami is depressing. I beg your pardon.'

'Yes, that's what he says. He told me last summer that I was doing better and he'd let me exhibit this year.'

'Not in this place, surely?'

'Of course not. The Salon.'

'You fly high.'

'I've been beating my wings long enough. Where do you exhibit, Dick?'

'I don't exhibit. I sell.'

'What is your line, then?'

'Haven't you heard?' Dick's eyes opened. Was this thing possible? He cast about for some means of conviction. They were not far from the Marble Arch. 'Come up Oxford Street a little and I'll show you.'

A small knot of people stood round a print-shop that Dick knew well. 'Some reproduction of my work inside,' he said, with suppressed triumph. Never before had success tasted so sweet upon the tongue. 'You see the sort of things I paint. D'you like it?'

Maisie looked at the wild whirling rush of a field-battery going into action under fire. Two artillerymen stood behind her in the crowd.

'They've chucked the off lead-'orse,' said one to the other. ' 'E's tore up awful, but they're makin' good time with the others. That lead-driver drives better nor you, Tom. See 'ow cunnin' 'e's nursin' 'is 'orse.'

'Number Three'll be off the limber, next jolt,' was the answer.

'No, 'e won't. See 'ow 'is foot's braced against the iron? 'E's all right.'

Dick watched Maisie's face and swelled with joy—fine, rank, vulgar triumph. She was more interested in the little crowd than in the picture. That was something that she could understand.

'And I wanted it so! Oh, I did want it so!' she said at last, under her breath.

'Me,—all me!' said Dick placidly. 'Look at their faces. It

56

hits 'em. They don't know what makes their eyes and mouths open; but I know. And I know my work's right.'

'Yes. I see. Oh, what a thing to have come to one!'

'Come to one, indeed! I had to go out and look for it. What do you think?'

'I call it success. Tell me how you got it.'

They returned to the Park, and Dick delivered himself of the saga of his own doings, with all the arrogance of a young man speaking to a woman. From the beginning he told the tale, the I—I—I's flashing through the records as telegraph-poles fly past the traveller. Maisie listened and nodded her head. The histories of strife and privation did not move her a hair's-breadth. At the end of each canto he would conclude, 'And *that* gave me some notion of handling colour,' or light, or whatever it might be that he had set out to pursue and understand. He led her breathless across half the world, speaking as he had never spoken in his life before. And in the flood-tide of his exaltation there came upon him a great desire to pick up this maiden who nodded her head and said, 'I understand. Go on,'—to pick her up and to carry her away with him, because she was Maisie, and because she understood, and because she was his right, and a woman to be desired above all women.

Then he checked himself abruptly. 'And so I took all I wanted,' he said, 'and I had to fight for it. Now you tell.'

Maisie's tale was almost as grey as her dress. It covered years of patient toil backed by savage pride that would not be broken though dealers laughed, and fogs delayed work, and Kami was unkind and even sarcastic, and girls in other studios were painfully polite. It had a few bright spots, in pictures accepted at provincial exhibitions, but it wound up with the oft-repeated wail, 'And so you see, Dick, I had no success, though I worked so hard.'

Then pity filled Dick. Even thus had Maisie spoken when she could not hit the breakwater, half an hour before she had kissed him. And that had happened yesterday.

'Never mind,' he said. 'I'll tell you something if you'll believe it.' The words were shaping themselves of their own accord. 'The whole thing, lock, stock, and barrel, isn't worth one big yellow sea-poppy below Fort Keeling.'

Maisie flushed a little. 'It's all very well for you to talk, but you've had the success and I haven't.'

'Let me talk, then. I know you'll understand. Maisie, dear, it sounds a bit absurd, but those ten years never existed, and I've come back again. It really is just the same. Can't you see? You're alone now and I'm alone. What's the use of worrying? Come to me instead, darling!'

Maisie poked the gravel with her parasol. They were sitting on a bench. 'I understand,' she said slowly. 'But I've got my work to do, and I must do it.'

'Do it with me, then, dear. I won't interrupt.'

'No, I couldn't. It's my work,—mine,—mine,—mine! I've been alone all my life in myself, and I'm not going to belong to anybody except myself. I remember things as well as you do, but that doesn't count. We were babies then, and we didn't know what was before us. Dick, don't be selfish. I think I see my way to a little success next year. Don't take it away from me.'

'I beg your pardon, darling. It's my fault for speaking stupidly. I can't expect you to throw up all your life just because I'm back. I'll go to my own place and wait a little.'

'But, Dick, I don't want you to—go—out of—my life, now you've just come back.'

'I'm at your orders; forgive me.' Dick devoured the troubled little face with his eyes. There was triumph in them, because he could not conceive that Maisie should refuse sooner or later to love him, since he loved her.

'It's wrong of me,' said Maisie, more slowly than before; 'it's wrong and selfish. But, oh, I've been so lonely! No, you misunderstand. Now I've seen you again,—it's absurd, but I want to keep you in my life.'

'Naturally. We belong.'

'We don't; but you always understood me, and there is so much in my work that you could help me in. You know things and the ways of doing things. You must.'

'I do, I fancy, or else I don't know myself. Then I suppose you won't care to lose sight of me altogether, and you want me to help you in your work?'

'Yes; but remember, Dick, nothing will ever come of it. That's why I feel so selfish. Let things stay as they are. I *do* want your help.'

'You shall have it. But let's consider. I must see your piccys first, and overhaul your sketches, and find out about your tendencies. You should see what the papers say about *my* tendencies! Then I'll give you good advice, and you shall paint according. Isn't that it, Maisie?'

Again there was unholy triumph in Dick's eye.

'It's too good of you,—much too good. Because you are consoling yourself with what will never happen, and I know that, and yet I wish to keep you. Don't blame me later, please.'

'I'm going into the matter with my eyes open. Moreover, the Queen can do no wrong. It isn't your selfishness that impresses me. It's your audacity in proposing to make use of *me*.'

'Pooh! You're only Dick,—and a print-shop.'

'Very good: that's all I am. But, Maisie, you believe, don't you, that I love you? I don't want you to have any false notions about brothers and sisters.'

Maisie looked up for a moment and dropped her eyes.

'It's absurd, but—I believe. I wish I could send you away before you get angry with me. But—but the girl that lives with me is red-haired, and an impressionist, and all our notions clash.'

'So do ours, I think. Never mind. Three months from to-day we shall be laughing at this together.'

Maisie shook her head mournfully. 'I knew you wouldn't understand, and it will only hurt you more when you find out. Look at my face, Dick, and tell me what you see.'

They stood up and faced each other for a moment. The fog was gathering, and it stifled the roar of the traffic of London beyond the railings. Dick brought all his painfully-acquired knowledge of faces to bear on the eyes, mouth, and chin underneath the black velvet toque.

'It's the same Maisie, and it's the same me,' he said. 'We've both nice little wills of our own, and one or other of us has to be broken. Now about the future. I must come and see your pictures some day,—I suppose when the red-haired girl is on the premises.'

'Sundays are my best times. You must come on Sundays. There are such heaps of things I want to talk about and ask your advice about. Now I must get back to work.'

'Try to find out before next Sunday what I am,' said Dick. 'Don't take my word for anything I've told you. Good-bye, darling, and bless you.'

Maisie stole away like a little grey mouse. Dick watched her till she was out of sight, but he did not hear her say to herself, very soberly, 'I'm a wretch,—a horrid, selfish wretch. But it's Dick, and Dick will understand.'

No one has yet explained what actually happens when an irresistible force meets the immovable post, though many have thought deeply, even as Dick thought. He tried to assure himself that Maisie would be led in a few weeks by his mere presence and discourse to a better way of thinking. Then he remembered much too distinctly her face and all that was written on it.

'If I know anything of heads,' he said, 'there's everything in that face but love. I shall have to put that in myself; and that chin and mouth won't be got for nothing. But she's right. She knows what she wants, and she's going to get it. What insolence! Me! Of all the people in the wide world, to use me! But then she's Maisie. There's no getting over that fact; and it's good to see her again. This business must have been simmering at the back of my head for years. . . . She'll use me as I used Binat at Port Said. She's quite right. It will hurt a little. I shall have to see her every Sunday,—like a young man courting a housemaid. She's sure to come round; and yet—that mouth isn't a yielding one. I shall be wanting to kiss her all the time, and I shall have to look at her pictures,—I don't even know what sort of work she does yet,— and I shall have to talk about Art,—Woman's Art! Therefore, particularly and perpetually, damn all varieties of Art. It did me a good turn once, and now it's in my way. I'll go home and do some Art.'

Half-way to the studio Dick was smitten with a terrible thought. The figure of a solitary woman in the fog suggested it.

'She's all alone in London, with a red-haired impressionist girl, who probably has the digestion of an ostrich. Most red-haired people have. Maisie's a bilious little body. They'll eat like lone women,—meals at all hours, and tea with all meals. I remember how the students in Paris used to pig along. She may fall ill at any minute, and I shan't be able to help. Whew! this is ten times worse than owning a wife.'

Torpenhow came into the studio at dusk, and looked at

Dick with his eyes full of the austere love that springs up between men who have tugged at the same oar together and are yoked by custom and use and the intimacies of toil. This is a good love, and, since it allows, and even encourages strife, recrimination, and the most brutal sincerity, does not die, but increases, and is proof against any absence and evil conduct.

Dick was silent after he handed Torpenhow the filled pipe of council. He thought of Maisie and her possible needs. It was a new thing to think of anybody but Torpenhow, who could think for himself. Here at last was an outlet for that cash balance. He could adorn Maisie barbarically with jewelry,—a thick gold necklace round that little neck, bracelets upon the rounded arms, and rings of price upon her hands,— the cool, temperate, ringless hands that he had taken between his own. It was an absurd thought, for Maisie would not even allow him to put one ring on one finger, and she would laugh at golden trappings. It would be better to sit with her quietly in the dusk, his arm round her neck and her face on his shoulder, as befitted husband and wife. Torpenhow's boots creaked that night, and his strong voice jarred. Dick's brows contracted and he murmured an evil word because he had taken all his success as a right and part payment for past dis-comfort, and now he was checked in his stride by a woman who admitted all the success and did not instantly care for him.

'I say, old man,' said Torpenhow, who had made one or two vain attempts at conversation, 'I haven't put your back up by anything I've said lately, have I?'

'You! No. How could you?'

'Liver out of order?'

'The truly healthy man doesn't know he has a liver. I'm only a bit worried about things in general. I suppose it's my soul.'

'The truly healthy man doesn't know he has a soul. What business have you with luxuries of that kind?'

'It came of itself. Who's the man that says that we're all islands shouting lies to each other across seas of misunderstanding?'

'He's right, whoever he is,—except about the misunderstanding. I don't think we could misunderstand each other.'

The blue smoke curled back from the ceiling in clouds. Then Torpenhow, insinuatingly:—

'Dick, is it a woman?'

'Be hanged if it's anything remotely resembling a woman; and if you begin to talk like that, I'll hire a red-brick studio with white paint trimmings, and begonias and petunias and blue Hungarians to play among three-and-sixpenny pot-palms, and I'll mount all my piccys in aniline-dye plush plasters, and I'll invite every woman who yelps and maunders and moans over what her guide-books tell her is Art, and you shall receive 'em, Torp,—in a snuff-brown velvet coat with yellow trousers and an orange tie. You'll like that.'

'Too thin, Dick. A better man than you denied with cursing and swearing on a memorable occasion. You've overdone it, just as he did. It's no business of mine, of course, but it's comforting to think that somewhere under the stars there's saving up for you a tremendous thrashing. Whether it'll come from Heaven or Earth I don't know, but it's bound to come and break you up a little. You want hammering.'

Dick shivered. 'All right,' said he. 'When this island is disintegrated it will call for you.'

'I shall come round the corner and help to disintegrate it some more. We're talking nonsense. Come along to a theatre.'

# CHAPTER VI

*'And you may lead a thousand men,*
*Nor ever draw the rein,*
*But ere ye lead the Faery Queen*
*'Twill burst your heart in twain.'*

*He has slipped his foot from the stirrup-bar,*
*The bridle from his hand,*
*And he is bound by hand and foot*
*To the Queen o' Faery-land.*
SIR HOGGIE AND THE FAIRIES.

SOME WEEKS LATER, on a very foggy Sunday, Dick was returning across the Park to his studio. 'This,' he said, 'is evidently
the thrashing that Torp meant. It hurts more than I expected;
but the Queen can do no wrong; and she certainly has some
notion of drawing.'

He had just finished a Sunday visit to Maisie,—always under
the green eyes of the red-haired impressionist girl, whom he
learned to hate at sight,—and was tingling with a keen sense
of shame. Sunday after Sunday, putting on his best clothes, he
had walked over to the untidy house north of the Park, first
to see Maisie's pictures, and then to criticise and advise upon
them as he realised that they were productions on which advice would not be wasted. Sunday after Sunday, and his love
grew with each visit, he had been compelled to cram his heart
back from between his lips when it prompted him to kiss
Maisie several times and very much indeed. Sunday after Sunday, the head above the heart had warned him that Maisie was
not yet attainable, and that it would be better to talk as con-

64

nectedly as possible upon the mysteries of the craft that was all in all to her. Therefore it was his fate to endure weekly torture in the studio built out over the clammy back garden of a frail, stuffy little villa where nothing was ever in its right place and nobody ever called,—to endure and to watch Maisie moving to and fro with the teacups. He abhorred tea, but, since it gave him a little longer time in her presence, he drank it devoutly, and the red-haired girl sat in an untidy heap and eyed him without speaking. She was always watching him. Once, and only once, when she had left the studio Maisie showed him an album that held a few poor cuttings from provincial papers,—the briefest of hurried notes on some of her pictures sent to outlying exhibitions. Dick stooped and kissed the paint-smudged thumb on the open page. 'Oh, my love, my love,' he muttered, 'do you value these things? Chuck 'em into the waste-paper basket!'

'Not till I get something better,' said Maisie, shutting the book.

Then Dick, moved by no respect for his public and a very deep regard for the maiden, did deliberately propose, in order to secure more of these coveted cuttings, that he should paint a picture which Maisie should sign.

'That's childish,' said Maisie, 'and I didn't think it of you. It must be my work. Mine,—mine,—mine!'

'Go and design decorative medallions for rich brewers' houses. You are thoroughly good at that.' Dick was sick and savage.

'Better things than medallions, Dick,' was the answer, in tones that recalled a grey-eyed atom's fearless speech to Mrs. Jennett. Dick would have abased himself utterly, but that the other girl trailed in.

Next Sunday he laid at Maisie's feet small gifts of pencils that could almost draw of themselves and colours in whose permanence he believed, and he was ostentatiously attentive to the work in hand. It demanded, among other things, an exposition of the faith that was in him. Torpenhow's hair would have stood on end had he heard the fluency with which Dick preached his own gospel of Art.

A month before, Dick would have been equally astonished; but it was Maisie's will and pleasure, and he dragged his words together to make plain to her comprehension all that had been hidden to himself of the whys and wherefores of work. There is not the least difficulty in doing a thing if you only know how to do it; the trouble is to explain your method.

'I could put this right if I had a brush in my hand,' said Dick despairingly, over the modelling of a chin that Maisie complained would not 'look flesh,'—it was the same chin that she had scraped out with the palette-knife,—'but I find it almost impossible to teach you. There's a queer grim Dutch touch about your painting that I like; but I've a notion that you're weak in drawing. You foreshorten as though you never used the model, and you've caught Kami's pasty way of dealing with flesh in shadow. Then, again, though you don't know it yourself, you shirk hard work. Suppose you spend some of your time on line alone. Line doesn't allow of shirking. Oils do, and three square inches of flashy, tricky stuff in the corner of a pic sometimes carry a bad thing off,—as I know. That's immoral. Do line-work for a little while, and then I can tell more about your powers, as old Kami used to say.'

Maisie protested. She did not care for the pure line.

'I know,' said Dick. 'You want to do your fancy heads with a bunch of flowers at the base of the neck to hide bad modelling.' The red-haired girl laughed a little. 'You want to do landscapes with cattle knee-deep in grass to hide bad drawing. You want to do a great deal more than you can do. You *have* sense of colour, but you want form. Colour's a gift,—put it aside and think no more about it,—but form you can be drilled into. Now, all your fancy heads—and some of them are very good—will keep you exactly where you are. With line you must go forward or backward, and it will show up all your weaknesses.'

'But other people——' began Maisie.

'You mustn't mind what other people do. If their souls were your soul it would be different. You stand and fall by your own work, remember, and it's waste of time to think of any one else in this battle.'

Dick paused, and the longing that had been so resolutely put away came back into his eyes. He looked at Maisie, and the look asked as plainly as words, Was it not time to leave all this barren wilderness of canvas and counsel and join hands with Life and Love?

Maisie assented to the new programme of schooling so adorably that Dick could hardly restrain himself from picking her up then and there and carrying her off to the nearest registrar's office. It was the implicit obedience to the spoken word and the blank indifference to the unspoken desire that baffled and buffeted his soul. He held authority in that house,—authority limited, indeed, to one-half of one afternoon in seven, but very real while it lasted. Maisie had learned to appeal to him on many subjects, from the proper packing of pictures to the condition of a smoky chimney. The red-haired girl never consulted him about anything. On the other hand, she accepted his appearances without protest, and watched him always. He discovered that the meals of the establishment were irregular and fragmentary. They depended chiefly on tea, pickles, and biscuit, as he had suspected from the beginning. The girls were supposed to market week and week about, but they lived, with the help of a charwoman, as casually as the young ravens. Maisie spent most of her income on models, and the other girl revelled in apparatus as refined as her work was rough. Armed with knowledge dear-bought from the Docks, Dick warned Maisie that the end of semi-starvation meant the crippling of power to work, which was considerably worse than death. Maisie took the warning, and gave more thought to what she ate and drank. When his trouble returned upon him, as it generally did in the long winter twilights, the remembrance of that little act of domestic authority and his coercion with a hearth-brush of the smoky drawing-room chimney stung Dick like a whip-lash.

He conceived that this memory would be the extreme of his sufferings, till, one Sunday, the red-haired girl announced that she would make a study of Dick's head, and that he would be good enough to sit still, and—quite as an afterthought—look at Maisie. He sat, because he could not well refuse, and for the space of half an hour he reflected on all the people in the past whom he had laid open for the purposes of his own craft. He remembered Binat most distinctly,—that Binat who had once been an artist and talked about degradation.

It was the merest monochrome roughing in of a head, but it presented the dumb waiting, the longing, and, above all, the hopeless enslavement of the man, in a spirit of bitter mockery.

'I'll buy it,' said Dick promptly, 'at your own price.'

'My price is too high, but I daresay you'll be as grateful if——' The wet sketch fluttered from the girl's hand and fell into the ashes of the studio stove. When she picked it up it was hopelessly smudged.

'Oh, it's all spoiled!' said Maisie. 'And I never saw it. Was it like?'

'Thank you,' said Dick under his breath to the red-haired girl, and he removed himself swiftly.

'How that man hates me!' said the girl. 'And how he loves you, Maisie!'

'What nonsense! I know Dick's very fond of me, but he has his work to do, and I have mine.'

'Yes, he is fond of you, and I think he knows there is something in impressionism, after all. Maisie, can't you *see*?'

'See? See what?'

'Nothing; only I know that if I could get any man to look at me as that man looks at you, I'd—I don't know what I'd do. But he hates me. Oh, how he hates me!'

She was not altogether correct. Dick's hatred was tempered with gratitude for a few moments, and then he forgot the girl entirely. Only the sense of shame remained, and he was nursing it across the Park in the fog. 'There'll be an explosion one of these days,' he said wrathfully. 'But it isn't Maisie's fault; she's right, quite right, as far as she knows, and I can't blame her. This business has been going on for three months nearly. Three months!—and it cost me ten years' knocking about to get at the notion, the merest raw notion, of my work. That's true; but then I didn't have pins, drawing-pins and palette-knives, stuck into me every Sunday. Oh, my little darling, if ever I break you, somebody will have a very bad time of it. No, she won't. I'd be as big a fool about her as I am now. I'll poison that red-haired girl on my wedding-day,—she's unwholesome,—and now I'll pass on these present bad times to Torp.'

Torpenhow had been moved to lecture Dick more than once lately on the sin of levity, and Dick had listened and replied not a word. In the weeks between the first few Sundays of his discipline he had flung himself savagely into his work, resolved that Maisie should at least know the full stretch of his powers. Then he had taught Maisie that she must not pay the least attention to any work outside her own, and Maisie had obeyed him all too well. She took his counsels, but was not interested in his pictures.

'Your things smell of tobacco and blood,' she said once. 'Can't you do anything except soldiers?'

'I could do a head of you that would startle you,' thought Dick,—this was before the red-haired girl had brought him under the guillotine,—but he only said, 'I am very sorry,' and harrowed Torpenhow's soul that evening with blasphemies against Art. Later, insensibly and to a large extent against his own will, he ceased to interest himself in his own work. For Maisie's sake, and to soothe the self-respect that it seemed to him he lost each Sunday, he would not consciously turn out bad stuff, but, since Maisie did not care even for his best, it were better not to do anything at all save wait and mark time between Sunday and Sunday. Torpenhow was disgusted as the weeks went by fruitless, and then attacked him one Sunday evening when Dick felt utterly exhausted after three hours' biting self-restraint in Maisie's presence. There was Language, and Torpenhow withdrew to consult the Nilghai, who had come in to talk continental politics.

'Bone-idle, is he? Careless, and touched in the temper?' said the Nilghai. 'It isn't worth worrying over. Dick is probably playing the fool with a woman.'

'Isn't that bad enough?'

'No. She may throw him out of gear and knock his work to pieces for a while. She may turn up here some day and make a scene on the staircase. One never knows. But until Dick speaks of his own accord you had better not touch him. He is no easy-tempered man to handle.'

'No; I wish he were. He is such an aggressive, cocksure, you-be-damned fellow.'

'He'll get that knocked out of him in time. He must learn that he can't storm up and down the world with a box of moist tubes and a slick brush. You're fond of him?'

'I'd take any punishment that's in store for him if I could; but the worst of it is, no man can save his brother.'

'No, and the worser of it is, there is no discharge in this war. Dick must learn his lesson like the rest of us. Talking of war, there'll be trouble in the Balkans in the spring.'

'That trouble is long coming. I wonder if we could drag Dick out there when it comes off?'

Dick entered the room soon afterwards, and the question was put to him. 'Not good enough,' he said shortly. 'I'm too comfy where I am.'

'Surely you aren't taking all the stuff in the papers seriously?' said the Nilghai. 'Your vogue will be ended in less than six months,—the public will know your touch and go on to something new,—and where will you be then?'

'Here, in England.'

'When you might be doing decent work among us out there? Nonsense! I shall go, the Keneu will be there, Torp will be there, Cassavetti will be there, and the whole lot of us will be there, and we shall have as much as ever we can do, with unlimited fighting and the chance for you of seeing things that would make the reputation of three Verestchagins.'

'Um!' said Dick, pulling at his pipe.

'You prefer to stay here and imagine that all the world is gaping at your pictures? Just think how full an average man's life is of his own pursuits and pleasures. When twenty thousand of him find time to look up between mouthfuls and grunt something about something they aren't the least interested in, the net result is called fame, reputation, or notoriety, according to the taste and fancy of the speller, me lord.'

'I know that as well as you do. Give me credit for a little gumption.'

'Be hanged if I do!'

71

'*Be* hanged, then; you probably will be,—for a spy, by excited Turks. Heigh-ho! I'm weary, dead weary, and virtue has
gone out of me.' Dick dropped into a chair, and was fast
asleep in a minute.

'That's a bad sign,' said the Nilghai, in an undertone.

Torpenhow picked the pipe from the waistcoat where it was
beginning to burn, and put a pillow behind the head. 'We
can't help; we can't help,' he said. 'It's a good ugly sort of old
coconut, and I'm fond of it. There's the scar of the wipe he
got when he was cut over in the square.'

'Shouldn't wonder if that has made him a trifle mad.'

'*I* should. He's a most businesslike madman.'

Then Dick began to snore furiously.

'Oh, here, no affection can stand this sort of thing. Wake up,
Dick, and go and sleep somewhere else, if you intend to make
a noise about it.'

'When a cat has been out on the tiles all night,' said the
Nilghai in his beard, 'I notice that she usually sleeps all day.
This is natural history.'

Dick staggered away rubbing his eyes and yawning. In the
night-watches he was overtaken with an idea, so simple and
so luminous that he wondered he had never conceived it before. It was full of craft. He would seek Maisie on a week-day,
—would suggest an excursion, and would take her by train to
Fort Keeling, over the very ground that they two had trodden
together ten years ago.

'As a general rule,' he explained to his chin-lathered reflection in the morning, 'it isn't safe to cross an old trail twice.
Things remind one of things, and a cold wind gets up, and
you feel sad. But this is an exception to every rule that ever
was. I'll go to Maisie at once.'

Fortunately, the red-haired girl was out shopping when he

arrived, and Maisie in a paint-spattered blouse was warring with her canvas. She was not pleased to see him; for week-day visits were a stretch of the bond; and it needed all his courage to explain his errand.

'I know you've been working too hard,' he concluded, with an air of authority. 'If you do that you'll break down. You had much better come.'

'Where?' said Maisie wearily. She had been standing before her easel too long, and was very tired.

'Anywhere you please. We'll take a train to-morrow and see where it stops. We'll have lunch somewhere, and I'll bring you back in the evening.'

'If there's a good working light to-morrow I lose a day.' Maisie balanced the heavy white chestnut palette irresolutely.

Dick held back an oath that was hurrying to his lips. He had not yet learned patience with the maiden to whom her work was all in all.

'You'll lose ever so many more, dear, if you use every hour of working light. Overwork's only murderous idleness. Don't be unreasonable. I'll call for you to-morrow after breakfast early.'

'But surely you are going to ask——'

'No, I am not. I want you and nobody else. Besides, she hates me as much as I hate her. She won't care to come. To-morrow, then; and pray that we get sunshine.'

Dick went away delighted, and by consequence did no work whatever. He strangled a wild desire to order a special train, but bought a great grey kangaroo cloak lined with glossy black marten, and then retired into himself to consider things.

'I'm going out for the day to-morrow with Dick,' said Maisie to the red-haired girl when the latter returned, tired, from marketing in the Edgware Road.

'He deserves it. I shall have the studio floor thoroughly scrubbed while you're away. It's very dirty.'

Maisie had enjoyed no sort of holiday for months, and looked forward to the little excitement, but not without misgivings.

'There's nobody nicer than Dick when he talks sensibly,' she thought, 'but I'm sure he'll be silly and worry me, and I'm sure I can't tell him anything he'd like to hear. If he'd only be sensible I should like him so much better.'

Dick's eyes were full of joy when he made his appearance next morning and saw Maisie, grey-ulstered and black-velvet-hatted, standing in the hall-way. Palaces of marble, and not sordid imitations of grained wood, were surely the fittest background for such a divinity. The red-haired girl drew her into the studio for a moment and kissed her hurriedly. Maisie's eyebrows climbed to the top of her forehead. She was altogether unused to these demonstrations. 'Mind my hat,' she said, hurrying away, and ran down the steps to Dick waiting by the hansom.

'Are you quite warm enough? Are you sure you wouldn't like some more breakfast? Put this cloak over your knees.'

'I'm quite comfy, thanks. Where are we going, Dick? Oh, do stop singing like that. People will think we're mad.'

'Let 'em think,—if the exertion doesn't kill them. They don't know who we are, and I'm sure I don't care who they are. My faith, Maisie, you're looking lovely!'

Maisie stared directly in front of her and did not reply. The wind of a keen, clear winter morning had put colour into her cheeks. Overhead, the creamy-yellow smoke-clouds were thinning away one by one against a pale-blue sky, and the improvident sparrows broke off from water-spout committees and cab-rank cabals to clamour of the coming of spring.

'It will be perfect weather in the country,' said Dick.

'But where are we going?'

'Wait and see.'

They stopped at Victoria, and Dick sought tickets. For less than half the fraction of an instant it occurred to Maisie, comfortably settled by the waiting-room fire, that it was much more pleasant to send a man to the booking-office than to elbow one's own way through the crowd. Dick put her into a Pullman,—solely on account of the warmth there; and she regarded the extravagance with grave scandalised eyes as the train moved out into the country.

'I wish I knew where we are going,' she repeated for the twentieth time. The name of a well-remembered station flashed by, towards the end of the run, and Maisie was enlightened.

'Oh, Dick, you villain!'

'Well, I thought you might like to see the place again. You haven't been here since old times, have you?'

'No. I never cared to see Mrs. Jennett again; and she was all that was ever there.'

'Not quite. Look out a minute. There's the windmill above the potato-fields; they haven't built villas there yet. D'you remember when I shut you up in it?'

'Yes. How she beat you for it! *I* never told it was you.'

'She guessed. I jammed a stick under the door and told you that I was burying Amomma alive in the potatoes, and you believed me. You had a trusting nature in those days.'

They laughed and leaned to look out, identifying ancient landmarks with many reminiscences. Dick fixed his weather eye on the curve of Maisie's cheek, very near his own, and watched the blood rise under the clear skin. He congratulated himself upon his cunning, and looked that the evening would bring him a great reward.

When the train stopped they went out to look at an old town with new eyes. First, but from a distance, they regarded the house of Mrs. Jennett.

'Suppose she should come out now, what would you do?' said Dick, with mock terror.

'I should make a face.'

'Show, then,' said Dick, dropping into the speech of childhood.

Maisie made that face in the direction of the mean little villa, and Dick laughed aloud.

' "This is disgraceful," ' said Maisie, mimicking Mrs. Jennett's tone. ' "Maisie, you run in at once, and learn the collect, gospel, and epistle for the next three Sundays. After all I've taught you, too, and three helps every Sunday at dinner! Dick's always leading you into mischief. If you aren't a gentleman, Dick, you might at least——" '

The sentence ended abruptly. Maisie remembered when it had last been used.

' "Try to behave like one," ' said Dick promptly. 'Quite right. Now we'll get some lunch and go on to Fort Keeling,—unless you'd rather drive there?'

'We must walk, out of respect to the place. How little changed it all is!'

They turned in the direction of the sea through unaltered streets, and the influence of old things lay upon them. Presently they passed a confectioner's shop much considered in the days when their joint pocket-money amounted to a shilling a week.

'Dick, have you any pennies?' said Maisie, half to herself.

'Only three; and if you think you're going to have two of 'em to buy peppermints with, you're wrong. She says peppermints aren't ladylike.'

76

Again they laughed, and again the colour came into Maisie's cheeks as the blood boiled through Dick's heart. After a large lunch they went down to the beach and to Fort Keeling across the waste, wind-bitten land that no builder had thought it worth his while to defile. The winter breeze came in from the sea and sang about their ears.

'Maisie,' said Dick, 'your nose is getting a crude Prussian blue at the tip. I'll race you as far as you please for as much as you please.'

She looked round cautiously, and with a laugh set off, swiftly as the ulster allowed, till she was out of breath.

'We used to run miles,' she panted. 'It's absurd that we can't run now.'

'Old age, dear. This it is to get fat and sleek in Town. When I wished to pull your hair you generally ran for three miles, shrieking at the top of your voice. I ought to know, because those shrieks were meant to call up Mrs. Jennett with a cane and——'

'Dick, I never got you a beating on purpose in my life.'

'No, of course you never did. Good heavens, look at the sea.'

'Why, it's the same as ever!' said Maisie.

Torpenhow had gathered from Mr. Beeton that Dick, properly dressed and shaved, had left the house at half-past eight in the morning with a travelling-rug over his arm. The Nilghai rolled in at mid-day for chess and polite conversation.

'It's worse than anything I imagined,' said Torpenhow.

'Oh, the everlasting Dick, I suppose! You fuss over him like a hen with one chick. Let him run riot if he thinks it'll amuse him. You can whip a young pup off feather, but you can't whip a young man.'

'It isn't a woman. It's one woman; and it's a girl.'

'Where's your proof?'

'He got up and went out at eight this morning,—got up in the middle of the night, by Jove! a thing he never does except when he's on service. Even then, remember, we had to kick him out of his blankets before the fight at El-Maghrib. It's disgusting.'

'It looks odd; but maybe he's decided to buy a horse at last. He might get up for that, mightn't he?'

'Buy a blazing wheelbarrow! He'd have told us if there was a horse in the wind. It's a girl.'

'Don't be certain. Perhaps it's only a married woman.'

'Dick has some sense of humour, if you haven't. Who gets up in the grey dawn to call on another man's wife? It's a girl.'

'Let it be a girl, then. She may teach him that there's somebody else in the world besides himself.'

'She'll spoil his hand. She'll waste his time, and she'll marry him, and ruin his work for ever. He'll be a respectable married man before we can stop him, and—he'll never go on the long trail again.'

'All quite possible, but the earth won't spin the other way when it happens. . . . Ho! ho! I'd give something to see Dick "go wooing with the boys." Don't worry about it. These things be with Allah, and we can only look on. Get the chessmen.'

The red-haired girl was lying down in her own room, staring at the ceiling. The footsteps of people on the pavement sounded, as they grew indistinct in the distance, like a many-times-repeated kiss that was all one long kiss. Her hands were by her side, and they opened and shut savagely from time to time.

The charwoman in charge of the scrubbing of the studio knocked at her door: 'Beg y' pardon, miss, but in cleanin' of a floor there's two, not to say three, kind of soap, which is yaller, an' mottled, an' disinfectink. Now, jist before I took my pail into the passage I thought it would be pre'aps jest as well if I was to come up 'ere an' ask you what sort of soap you was wishful that I should use on them boards. The yaller soap, miss——'

There was nothing in the speech to have caused the paroxysm of fury that drove the red-haired girl into the middle of the room, almost shouting:—

'Do you suppose *I* care what you use? Any kind will do!— *any* kind!'

The woman fled, and the red-haired girl looked at her own reflection in the glass for an instant and covered her face with her hands. It was as though she had shouted some shameful secret aloud.

# CHAPTER VII

*Roses red and roses white*
*Plucked I for my love's delight.*
*She would none of all my posies,—*
*Bade me gather her blue roses.*

*Half the world I wandered through,*
*Seeking where such flowers grew;*
*Half the world unto my quest*
*Answered but with laugh and jest.*

*It may be beyond the grave*
*She shall find what she would have.*
*Mine was but an idle quest,—*
*Roses white and red are best!*

BLUE ROSES.

INDEED THE SEA had not changed. Its waters were low on the mud-banks, and the Marazion bell-buoy clanked and swung in the tideway. On the white beach-sand dried stumps of sea-poppy shivered and chattered together.

'I don't see the old breakwater,' said Maisie under her breath.

'Let's be thankful that we have as much as we have. I don't believe they've mounted a single new gun on the fort since we were here. Come and look.'

They came to the glacis of Fort Keeling, and sat down in a nook sheltered from the wind under the tarred throat of a forty-pounder cannon.

'Now, if Amomma were only here!' said Maisie.

For a long time both were silent. Then Dick took Maisie's hand and called her by her name.

She shook her head and looked out to sea.

'Maisie, darling, doesn't it make any difference?'

'No!' between clenched teeth. 'I'd—I'd tell you if it did; but it doesn't. Oh, Dick, please be sensible.'

'Don't you think that it ever will?'

'No, I'm sure it won't.'

'Why?'

Maisie rested her chin on her hand, and, still regarding the sea, spoke hurriedly:

'I know what you want perfectly well, but I can't give it you, Dick. It isn't my fault; indeed it isn't. If I felt that I could care for any one—— But I don't feel that I care. I simply don't understand what the feeling means.'

'Is that true, dear?'

'You've been very good to me, Dickie; and the only way I can pay you back is by speaking the truth. I daren't tell a fib. I despise myself quite enough as it is.'

'What in the world for?'

'Because—because I take everything that you give me and I give you nothing in return. It's mean and selfish of me, and whenever I think of it, it worries me.'

'Understand once for all, then, that I can manage my own affairs, and if I choose to do anything you aren't to blame. You haven't a single thing to reproach yourself with, darling.'

'Yes, I have, and talking only makes it worse.'

'Then don't talk about it.'

'How can I help myself? If you find me alone for a minute you are always talking about it; and when you aren't you look it. You don't know how I despise myself sometimes.'

'Great goodness!' said Dick, nearly jumping to his feet. 'Speak the truth now, Maisie, if you never speak it again! Do I—does this worrying bore you?'

'No. It does not.'

'You'd tell me if it did?'

'I should let you know, I think.'

'Thank you. The other thing is fatal. But you must learn to forgive a man when he's in love. He's always a nuisance. You must have known that?'

Maisie did not consider the last question worth answering, and Dick was forced to repeat it.

'There were other men, of course. They always worried just when I was in the middle of my work, and wanted me to listen to them.'

'Did you listen?'

'At first; and they couldn't understand why I didn't care. And they used to praise my pictures; and I thought they meant it. I used to be proud of the praise, and tell Kami, and—I shall never forget—once Kami laughed at me.'

'You don't like being laughed at, Maisie, do you?'

'I hate it. I never laugh at other people unless—unless they do bad work. Dick, tell me honestly what you think of my pictures generally,—of everything of mine that you've seen.'

' "Honest, honest, and honest over!" ' quoted Dick from a catchword of long ago. 'Tell me what Kami always says.'

Maisie hesitated. 'He—he says that there is feeling in them.'

'How dare you tell me a fib like that? Remember, I was under Kami for two years. I know exactly what he says.'

'It isn't a fib.'

'It's worse; it's a half-truth. Kami says, when he puts his head on one side,—so,—"Il y a du sentiment, mais il n'y a pas de parti pris." ' He rolled the r threateningly, as Kami used to do.

'Yes, that is what he says; and I'm beginning to think that he is right.'

'Certainly he is.' Dick admitted that two people in the world could do and say no wrong. Kami was the man.

'And now you say the same thing. It's so disheartening.'

'I'm sorry, but you asked me to speak the truth. Besides, I love you too much to pretend about your work. It's strong, it's patient sometimes,—not always,—and sometimes there's power in it, but there's no special reason why it should be done at all. At least, that's how it strikes me.'

'There's no special reason why anything in the world should ever be done. You know that as well as I do. I only want success.'

'You're going the wrong way to get it, then. Hasn't Kami ever told you so?'

'Don't quote Kami to me. I want to know what you think. My work's bad, to begin with.'

'I didn't say that, and I don't think it.'

'It's amateurish, then.'

'That it most certainly is not. You're a work-woman, darling, to your boot-heels, and I respect you for that.'

'You don't laugh at me behind my back?'

'No, dear. You see, you are more to me than any one else. Put this cloak thing round you, or you'll get chilled.'

Maisie wrapped herself in the soft marten skins, turning the grey kangaroo fur to the outside.

'This is delicious,' she said, rubbing her chin thoughtfully along the fur. 'Well? Why am I wrong in trying to get a little success?'

'Just because you try. Don't you understand, darling? Good work has nothing to do with—doesn't belong to—the person who does it. It's put into him or her from outside.'

'But how does that affect——'

83

'Wait a minute. All we can do is to learn how to do our work, to be masters of our materials instead of servants, and never to be afraid of anything.'

'I understand that.'

'Everything else comes from outside ourselves. Very good. If we sit down quietly to work out notions that are sent to us, we may or we may not do something that isn't bad. A great deal depends on being master of the bricks and mortar of the trade. But the instant we begin to think about success and the effect of our work—to play with one eye on the gallery—we lose power and touch and everything else. At least that's how I have found it. Instead of being quiet and giving every power you possess to your work, you're fretting over something which you can neither help nor hinder by a minute. See?'

'It's so easy for you to talk in that way. People like what you do. Don't you ever think about the gallery?'

'Much too often; but I'm always punished for it by loss of power. It's as simple as the Rule of Three. If we make light of our work by using it for our own ends, our work will make light of us, and, as we're the weaker, we shall suffer.'

'*I* don't treat my work lightly. You know that it's everything to me.'

'Of course; but, whether you realise it or not, you give two strokes for yourself to one for your work. It isn't your fault, darling. I do exactly the same thing, and know that I'm doing it. Most of the French schools, and all the schools here, drive the students to work for their own credit, and for the sake of their pride. I was told that all the world was interested in my work, and everybody at Kami's talked turpentine, and I honestly believed that the world needed elevating and influencing, and all manner of impertinences, by my brushes. By Jove, I actually believed that! When my little head was bursting with a notion that I couldn't handle because I hadn't sufficient knowledge of my craft, I used to run about wondering at my own magnificence and getting ready to astonish the world.'

'But surely one can do that sometimes?'

'Very seldom with malice aforethought, darling. And when it's done it's such a tiny thing, and the world's so big, and all but a millionth part of it doesn't care. Maisie, come with me and I'll show you something of the size of the world. One can no more avoid working than eating,—that goes on by itself,—but try to see what you are working for. I know such little heavens that I could take you to,—islands tucked away under the Line. You sight them after weeks of crashing through water as black as black marble because it's so deep, and you sit in the fore-chains day after day and see the sun rise almost afraid because the sea's so lonely.'

'Who is afraid?—you, or the sun?'

'The sun, of course. And there are noises under the sea, and sounds overhead in a clear sky. Then you find your island alive with hot moist orchids that make mouths at you, and can do everything except talk. There's a waterfall in it three hundred feet high, just like a sliver of green jade laced with silver; and millions of wild bees live up in the rocks; and you can hear the fat coconuts falling from the palms; and you order an ivory-white servant to sling you a long yellow hammock with tassels on it like ripe maize, and you put up your feet and hear the bees hum and the water fall till you go to sleep.'

'Can one work there?'

'Certainly. One must do something always. You hang your canvas up in a palm-tree and let the parrots criticise. When they scuffle you heave a ripe custard-apple at them, and it bursts in a lather of cream. There are hundreds of places. Come and see them.'

'I don't quite like that place. It sounds lazy. Tell me another.'

'What do you think of a big, red, dead city built of red sandstone, with raw green aloes growing between the stones, lying out neglected on honey-coloured sands? There are forty dead kings there, Maisie, each in a gorgeous tomb finer than all the others. You look at the palaces and streets and shops and tanks, and think that men must live there, till you find a wee grey squirrel rubbing its nose all alone in the market-place, and a jewelled peacock struts out of a carved doorway and spreads its tail against a marble screen as fine-pierced as point-lace. Then a monkey—a little black money—walks through the main square to get a drink from a tank forty feet deep. He slides down the creepers to the water's edge, and a friend holds him by the tail in case he should fall in.'

'Is all that true?'

'I have been there and seen. Then evening comes, and the lights change till it's just as though you stood in the heart of a king-opal. A little before sundown, as punctually as clock-work, a big bristly wild boar, with all his family following, trots through the city gate, churning the foam on his tusks. You climb on the shoulder of a blind black stone god and watch that pig choose himself a palace for the night and stump in wagging his tail. Then the night-wind gets up, and the sands move, and you hear the desert outside the city singing, "Now I lay me down to sleep," and everything is dark till the moon rises. Maisie, darling, come with me and see what the world is really like. It's very lovely, and it's very horrible,— but I won't let you see anything horrid,—and it doesn't care your life or mine for pictures or anything else except doing its own work and making love. Come, and I'll show you how to brew sangaree, and sling a hammock, and—oh, thousands of things, and you'll see for yourself what colour means, and we'll find out together what love means, and then, maybe, we shall be allowed to do some good work. Come away!'

'Why?' said Maisie.

'How can you do anything until you have seen everything, or as much as you can? And besides, darling, I love you. Come along with me. You have no business here. You don't belong to this place; you're half a gipsy,—your face tells that; and I— even the smell of open water makes me restless. Come across the sea and be happy!'

He had risen to his feet, and stood in the shadow of the gun, looking down at the girl. The very short winter afternoon had worn away, and, before they knew, the winter moon was walking the untroubled sea. Long ruled lines of silver showed where a ripple of the rising tide was turning over the mud-banks. The wind had dropped, and in the intense stillness they could hear a donkey cropping the frosty grass many yards away. A faint beating like that of a muffled drum came out of the moon-haze.

'What's that?' said Maisie quickly. 'It sounds like a heart beating. Where is it?'

Dick was so angry at this sudden wrench to his pleadings that he could not trust himself to speak, and in this silence caught the sound. Maisie from her seat under the gun watched him with a certain amount of fear. She wished so much that he would be sensible and cease to worry her with over-sea emotion that she both could and could not understand. She was not prepared, however, for the change in his face as he listened.

'It's a steamer,' he said,—'a twin-screw steamer, by the beat.

*87*

I can't make her out, but she must be standing very close inshore. Ah!' as the red of a rocket streaked the haze, 'she's standing in to signal before she clears the Channel.'

'Is it a wreck?' said Maisie, to whom these words were as Greek.

Dick's eyes were turned to the sea. 'Wreck! What nonsense! She's only reporting herself. Red rocket forward—there's a green light aft now, and two red rockets from the bridge.'

'What does that mean?'

'It's the signal of the Cross Keys Line running to Australia. I wonder which boat it is.' The note of his voice had changed. He seemed to be talking to himself, and Maisie did not approve of it. The moonlight broke the haze for a moment, touching the black sides of a long steamer working down Channel. 'Four masts and three funnels—she's in deep draught, too. That must be the *Barralong*, or the *Bhutia*. No, the *Bhutia* has a clipper bow. It's the *Barralong*, to Australia. She'll lift the Southern Cross in a week,—lucky old tub!—oh, lucky old tub!'

He stared intently, and moved up the slope of the fort to get a better view, but the mist on the sea thickened again, and the beating of the screws grew fainter. Maisie called to him a little angrily, and he returned, still keeping his eyes to seaward. 'Have you ever seen the Southern Cross blazing right over your head?' he asked. 'It's superb!'

'No,' she said shortly, 'and I don't want to. If you think it's so lovely why don't you go and see it yourself?'

She raised her face from the soft blackness of the marten skins about her throat, and her eyes shone like diamonds. The moonlight on the grey kangaroo fur turned it to frosted silver of the coldest.

'By Jove, Maisie, you look like a little heathen idol tucked up there.' The eyes showed that they did not appreciate the compliment. 'I'm sorry,' he continued. 'The Southern Cross isn't worth looking at unless some one helps you to see. That steamer's out of hearing.'

'Dick,' she said quietly, 'suppose I were to come to you now, —be quiet a minute,—just as I am, and caring for you just as much as I do.'

'Not as a brother, though? You said you didn't—in the Park.'

'I never had a brother. Suppose I said, "Take me to those places, and in time, perhaps, I might really care for you," what would you do?'

'Send you straight back to where you came from, in a cab. No, I wouldn't; I'd let you walk. But you couldn't do it, dear. And I wouldn't run the risk. You're worth waiting for till you can come without reservation.'

'Do you honestly believe that?'

'I have a hazy sort of idea that I do. Has it never struck you in that light?'

'Ye—es. I feel so wicked about it.'

'Wickeder than usual?'

'You don't know all I think. It's almost too awful to tell.'

'Never mind. You promised to tell me the truth—at least.'

'It's so ungrateful of me, but—but, though I know you care for me, and I like to have you with me, I'd—I'd even sacrifice you, if that would bring me what I want.'

'My poor little darling! I know that state of mind. It doesn't lead to good work.'

'You aren't angry? Remember, I do despise myself.'

'I'm not exactly flattered,—I had guessed as much before,— but I'm not angry. I'm sorry for you. Surely you ought to have left a littleness like that behind you, years ago.'

'You've no right to patronise me! I only want what I have worked for so long. It came to *you* without any trouble, and—and I don't think it's fair.'

'What can I do? I'd give ten years of my life to get you what you want. But I can't help you; even I can't help.'

A murmur of dissent from Maisie. He went on:—

'And I know by what you have just said that you're on the wrong road to success. It isn't got at by sacrificing other people,—I've had that much knocked into me; you must sacrifice yourself, and live under orders, and never think for yourself, and never have real satisfaction in your work except just at the beginning, when you're reaching out after a notion.'

'How can you believe all that?'

'There's no question of belief or disbelief. That's the law, and you take it or refuse it as you please. I try to obey, but I can't, and then my work turns bad on my hands. Under any circumstances, remember, four-fifths of everybody's work must be bad. But the remnant is worth the trouble for its own sake.'

'Isn't it nice to get credit even for bad work?'

'It's much too nice. But—— May I tell you something? It isn't a pretty tale, but you're so like a man that I forget when I'm talking to you.'

'Tell me.'

'Once when I was out in the Sudan I went over some ground that we had been fighting on for three days. There were twelve hundred dead; and we hadn't had time to bury them.'

'How ghastly!'

'I had been at work on a big double-sheet sketch, and I was wondering what people would think of it at home. The sight of that field taught me a good deal. It looked just like a bed of horrible toadstools in all colours, and—I'd never seen men in bulk go back to their beginnings before. So I began to understand that men and women were only material to work with, and that what they said or did was of no consequence. See? Strictly speaking, you might just as well put your ear down to the palette to catch what your colours are saying.'

'Dick, that's disgraceful!'

'Wait a minute. I said, strictly speaking. Unfortunately, everybody must be either a man or a woman.'

'I'm glad you allow that much.'

'In your case I don't. You aren't a woman. But ordinary people, Maisie, must behave and work as such. That's what makes me so savage.' He hurled a pebble towards the sea as he spoke. 'I know that it is outside my business to care what people say; I can see that it spoils my output if I listen to 'em; and yet, confound it all,'—another pebble flew seaward,—'I can't help purring when I'm rubbed the right way. Even when I can see on a man's forehead that he is lying his way through a clump of pretty speeches, those lies make me happy and play the mischief with my hand.'

'And when he doesn't say pretty things?'

'Then, belovedest,'—Dick grinned,—'I forget that I am the steward of these gifts, and I want to make that man love and appreciate my work with a thick stick. It's too humiliating altogether; but I suppose even if one were an angel and painted humans altogether from outside, one would lose in touch what one gained in grip.'

Maisie laughed at the idea of Dick as an angel.

'But you seem to think,' she said, 'that everything nice spoils your hand.'

'I don't think. It's the law,—just the same as it was at Mrs. Jennett's. Everything that is nice *does* spoil your hand. I'm glad you see so clearly.'

'I don't like the view.'

'Nor I. But—have got orders. What can do? Are you strong enough to face it alone?'

'I suppose I must.'

'Let me help, darling. We can hold each other very tight and try to walk straight. We shall blunder horribly, but it will be better than stumbling apart. Maisie, can't you see reason?'

'I don't think we should get on together. We should be two of a trade, so we should never agree.'

'How I should like to meet the man who made that proverb! He lived in a cave and ate raw bear, I fancy. I'd make him chew his own arrow-heads. Well?'

'I should be only half married to you. I should worry and fuss about my work, as I do now. Four days out of the seven I'm not fit to speak to.'

'You talk as if no one else in the world had ever used a brush. D'you suppose that I don't know the feeling of worry and bother and can't-get-at-ness? You're lucky if you only have it four days out of the seven. What difference would that make?'

'A great deal—if you had it too.'

'Yes, but I could respect it. Another man might not. He might laugh at you. But there's no use talking about it. If you can think in that way you can't care for me—yet.'

The tide had nearly covered the mud-banks, and twenty little ripples broke on the beach before Maisie chose to speak.

'Dick,' she said slowly, 'I believe very much that you are better than I am.'

'This doesn't seem to bear on the argument—but in what way?'

'I don't quite know, but in what you said about work and things; and then you're so patient. Yes, you're better than I am.'

Dick considered rapidly the murkiness of an average man's life. There was nothing in the review to fill him with a sense of virtue. He lifted the hem of the cloak to his lips.

'Why,' said Maisie, making as though she had not noticed, 'can you see things that I can't? I don't believe what you believe; but you're right, I believe.'

'If I've seen anything, God knows I couldn't have seen it but for you, and I know that I couldn't have said it except to you. You seemed to make everything clear for a minute; but I don't practise what I preach. You would help me. . . . There are only us two in the world for all purposes, and—and you like to have me with you?'

'Of course I do. I wonder if you can realise how utterly lonely I am!'

'Darling, I think I can.'

'Two years ago, when I first took the little house, I used to walk up and down the back-garden trying to cry. I never can cry. Can you?'

'It's some time since I tried. What was the trouble? Overwork?'

'I don't know; but I used to dream that I had broken down, and had no money, and was starving in London. I thought about it all day, and it frightened me—oh, how it frightened me!'

'I know that fear. It's the most terrible of all. It wakes me up in the night sometimes. You oughtn't to know anything about it.'

'How do *you* know?'

'Never mind. Is your three hundred a year safe?'

'It's in Consols.'

'Very well. If any one comes to you and recommends a better investment,—even if I should come to you,—don't you listen. Never shift the money for a minute, and never lend a penny of it,—even to the red-haired girl.'

'Don't scold me so! I'm not likely to be foolish.'

'The earth is full of men who'd sell their souls for three hundred a year; and women come and talk, and borrow a five-pound note here and a ten-pound note there; and a woman has no conscience in a money debt. Stick to your money, Maisie. There's nothing more ghastly in the world than poverty in London. It's scared me. By Jove, it put the fear into *me*! And one oughtn't to be afraid of anything.'

To each man is appointed his particular dread,—the terror that, if he does not fight against it, must cow him even to the loss of his manhood. Dick's experience of the sordid misery of want had entered into the deeps of him, and, lest he might find virtue too easy, that memory stood behind him, tempting to shame, when dealers came to buy his wares. As the Nilghai quaked against his will at the still green water of a lake or a mill-dam, as Torpenhow flinched before any white arm that could cut or stab and loathed himself for flinching, Dick feared the poverty he had once tasted half in jest. His burden was heavier than the burdens of his companions.

Maisie watched the face working in the moonlight.

'You've plenty of pennies now,' she said soothingly.

'I shall never get enough,' he began, with vicious emphasis. Then, laughing, 'I shall always be threepence short in my accounts.'

'Why threepence?'

'I carried a man's bag once from Liverpool Street Station to Blackfriars Bridge. It was a sixpenny job,—you needn't laugh; indeed it was,—and I wanted the money desperately. He only gave me threepence; and he hadn't even the decency to pay in silver. Whatever money I make I shall never get that odd threepence out of the world.'

This was not language befitting the man who had preached of the sanctity of work. It jarred on Maisie, who preferred her payment in applause, which, since all men desire it, must be of the right. She hunted for her little purse and gravely took out a threepenny bit.

'There it is,' she said. 'I'll pay you, Dickie; and don't worry any more; it isn't worth while. Are you paid?'

'I am,' said the very human apostle of fair craft, taking the coin. 'I'm paid a thousand times, and we'll close that account. It shall live on my watch-chain; and you're an angel, Maisie.'

'I'm very cramped, and I'm feeling a little cold. Good gracious! the cloak is all white, and so is your moustache! I never knew it was so chilly.'

A light frost lay white on the shoulder of Dick's ulster. He, too, had forgotten the state of the weather. They laughed together, and with that laugh ended all serious discourse.

They ran inland across the waste to warm themselves, then turned to look at the glory of the full tide under the moonlight and the intense black shadows of the furze-bushes. It was an additional joy to Dick that Maisie could see colour even as he saw it,—could see the blue in the white of the mist, the violet that is in grey palings, and all things else as they are,— not of one hue, but a thousand. And the moonlight came into Maisie's soul, so that she, usually reserved, chattered of herself and of the things she took interest in,—of Kami, wisest of teachers, and of the girls in the studio,—of the Poles, who will kill themselves with overwork if they are not checked; of the French, who talk at great length of much more than they will ever accomplish; of the slovenly English, who toil hopelessly and cannot understand that inclination does not imply power; of the Americans, whose rasping voices in the hush of a hot afternoon strain tense-drawn nerves to breaking-point, and whose suppers lead to indigestion; of tempestuous Russians, neither to hold nor to bind, who tell the girls ghost-stories till the girls shriek; of stolid Germans, who come to learn one thing, and, having mastered that much, stolidly go away and copy pictures for evermore. Dick listened enraptured because it was Maisie who spoke. He knew the old life.

'It hasn't changed much,' he said. 'Do they still steal colours at lunch-time?'

'Not steal. "Attract" is the word. Of course they do. I'm good—I only attract ultramarine; but there are students who'd attract flake-white.'

'I've done it myself. You can't help it when the palettes are hung up. Every colour is common property once it runs down, —even though you start it with a drop of oil. It teaches people not to waste their tubes.'

'I should like to "attract" some of your colours, Dick. Perhaps I might catch your success with them.'

'I mustn't say a bad word, but I should like to. What in the world, which you've just missed a lovely chance of seeing, does success or want of success, or a three-storeyed success, matter compared with—— No, I won't open that question again. It's time to go back to Town.'

'I'm sorry, Dick, but——'

'You're much more interested in that than you are in me.'

'I don't know. I don't think I am.'

'What will you give me if I tell you a sure short-cut to everything you want,—the trouble and the fuss and the tangle and all the rest? Will you promise to obey me?'

'Of course.'

'In the first place, you must never forget a meal because you happen to be at work. You forgot your lunch twice last week,' said Dick, at a venture, for he knew with whom he was dealing.

'No, no,—only once, really.'

'That's bad enough. And you mustn't take a cup of tea and a biscuit in place of a regular dinner, because dinner happens to be a trouble.'

'You're making fun of me!'

'I never was more in earnest in my life. Oh, my love, my love, hasn't it dawned on you yet what you are to me? Here's the whole earth in a conspiracy to give you a chill, or run over you, or drench you to the skin, or cheat you out of your money, or let you die of overwork and underfeeding, and I haven't the mere right to look after you. Why, I don't even know if you have sense enough to put on warm things when the weather's cold.'

'Dick, you're the most awful boy to talk to—really! How do you suppose I managed when you were away?'

'I wasn't here, and I didn't know. But now I'm back I'd give everything I have for the right of telling you to come in out of the rain.'

'Your success too?'

This time it cost Dick a severe struggle to refrain from bad words.

'As Mrs. Jennett used to say, you're a trial, Maisie! You've been cooped up in the schools too long, and you think every one is looking at you. There aren't twelve hundred people in the world who understand pictures. The others pretend and don't care. Remember, I've seen twelve hundred men dead in toadstool-beds. It's only the voice of the tiniest little fraction of people that makes success. The real world doesn't care a tinker's—doesn't care a bit. For aught you or I know, every man in the world may be arguing with a Maisie of his own.'

'Poor Maisie!'

'Poor Dick, I think. Do you believe while he's fighting for

what's dearer than his life he wants to look at a picture? And even if he did, and if all the world did, and a thousand million people rose up and shouted hymns to my honour and glory, would that make up to me for the knowledge that you were out shopping in the Edgware Road on a rainy day without an umbrella? Now we'll go to the station.'

'But you said on the beach——' persisted Maisie with a certain fear.

Dick groaned aloud: 'Yes, I know what I said. My work is everything I have, or am, or hope to be, to me, and I believe I've learnt the law that governs it; but I've some lingering sense of fun left,—though you've nearly knocked it out of me. I can just see that it isn't everything to all the world. "Do what I say, and not what I do." '

Maisie was careful not to reopen debatable matters, and they returned to London joyously. The terminus stopped Dick in the midst of an eloquent harangue on the beauties of exercise. He would buy Maisie a horse,—such a horse as never yet bowed head to bit,—would stable it, with a companion, some twenty miles from London, and Maisie, solely for her health's sake, should ride with him twice or thrice a week.

'That's absurd,' said she. 'It wouldn't be proper.'

'Now who in all London to-night would have sufficient interest or audacity to call us two to account for anything we chose to do?'

Maisie looked at the lamps, the fog, and the hideous turmoil. Dick was right; but horseflesh did not make for Art as she understood it.

'You're very nice sometimes, but you're very foolish more times. I'm not going to let you give me horses, or take you out of your way to-night. I'll go home by myself. Only I want you to promise me something. You won't think any more about that extra threepence, will you? Remember, you've been paid; and I won't allow you to be spiteful and do bad work for a little thing like that. You can be so big that you mustn't be tiny.'

This was turning the tables with a vengeance. There remained only to put Maisie into her hansom.

'Good-bye,' she said simply. 'You'll come on Sunday. It has been a beautiful day, Dick. Why can't it be like this always?'

'Because love's like line-work: you must go forward or backward; you can't stand still. By the way, go on with your line-work. Good-night, and, for my—for any sake, take care of yourself.'

He turned to walk home, meditating. The day had brought him nothing that he hoped for, but—surely this was worth many days—it had brought him nearer to Maisie. The end was only a question of time now, and the prize well worth the waiting. By instinct, once more, he turned to the river.

'And she understood at once,' he said, looking at the water. 'She found out my pet besetting sin on the spot, and paid it off. My God, how she understood! And she said I was better than she was! Better than she was!' He laughed at the absurdity of the notion. 'I wonder if girls guess at one-half a man's life. They can't, or—they wouldn't marry us.' He took her gift out of his pocket, and considered it in the light of a miracle and a pledge of the comprehension that, one day, would lead to perfect happiness. Meantime Maisie was alone in London, with none to save her from danger. And the packed wilderness was very full of danger.

Dick made his prayer to Fate disjointedly after the manner of the heathen as he threw the piece of silver into the river. If any evil were to befall, let him bear the burden and let Maisie go unscathed, since the threepenny piece was dearest to him of all his possessions. It was a small coin in itself, but Maisie had given it, and the Thames held it, and surely the Fates would be bribed for this once.

The drowning of the coin seemed to cut him free from thought of Maisie for the moment. He took himself off the bridge and went whistling to his chambers with a strong yearning for some man-talk and tobacco after his first experience of an entire day spent in the society of a woman. There was a stronger desire at his heart when there rose before him an unsolicited vision of the *Barralong* dipping deep and sailing free for the Southern Cross.

# CHAPTER VIII

*And these two, as I have told you,*
*Were the friends of Hiawatha,*
*Chibiabos, the musician,*
*And the very strong man, Kwasind.*

HIAWATHA.

TORPENHOW WAS PAGING the last sheets of some manuscript, while the Nilghai, who had come for chess and remained to talk tactics, was reading through the first part, commenting scornfully the while.

'It's picturesque enough and it's sketchy,' said he; 'but as a serious consideration of affairs in Eastern Europe, it's not worth much.'

'It's off my hands at any rate. . . . Thirty-seven, thirty-eight, thirty-nine slips altogether, aren't there? That should make between eleven and twelve pages of valuable misinformation. Heigho!' Torpenhow shuffled the writing together and hummed:—

> *'Young lambs to sell, young lambs to sell,*
> *If I'd as much money as I could tell,*
> *I never would cry, Young lambs to sell!'*

Dick entered, self-conscious and a little defiant, but in the best of tempers with all the world.

'Back at last?' said Torpenhow.

'More or less. What have you been doing?'

'Work. Dickie, you behave as though the Bank of England

were behind you. Here's Sunday, Monday, and Tuesday gone and you haven't done a line. It's scandalous.'

'The notions come and go, my children—they come and go like our 'baccy,' he answered, filling his pipe. 'Moreover,'— he stooped to thrust a spill into the grate—'Apollo does not always stretch his—— Oh, confound your clumsy jests, Nilghai!'

'This is not the place to preach the theory of direct inspiration,' said the Nilghai, returning Torpenhow's large and workmanlike bellows to their nail on the wall. 'We believe in cobblers' wax. *Là!*—where you sit down.'

'If you weren't so big and fat,' said Dick, looking round for a weapon, 'I'd——'

'No skylarking in my rooms. You two smashed half my furniture last time you threw the cushions about. You might have the decency to say How d'you do? to Binkie. Look at him.'

Binkie had jumped down from the sofa and was fawning round Dick's knee, and scratching at his boots.

'Dear man!' said Dickie, snatching him up, and kissing him on the black patch above his right eye. 'Did ums was, Binks? Did that ugly Nilghai turn you off the sofa? Bite him, Mr. Binkle.' He pitched him on the Nilghai's stomach, as the big man lay at ease, and Binkie pretended to destroy the Nilghai inch by inch, till a sofa-cushion extinguished him, and panting he stuck out his tongue at the company.

'The Binkie-boy went for a walk this morning before you were up, Torp. I saw him making love to the butcher at the corner when the shutters were being taken down—just as if he hadn't enough to eat in his own proper house,' said Dick.

'Binks, is that a true bill?' said Torpenhow severely. The little dog retreated under the sofa-cushion, and showed by the fat white back of him that he really had no further interest in the discussion.

'Strikes me that another disreputable dog went for a walk, too,' said the Nilghai. 'What made you get up so early? Torp said you might be buying a horse?'

'He knows it would need three of us for a serious business like that. No, I felt lonesome and unhappy, so I went out to look at the sea, and watch the pretty ships go by.'

'Where did you go?'

'Somewhere on the Channel. Progly or Snigly, or some one-horse watering-place was its name; I've forgotten; but it was only two hours' run from London and the ships went by.'

'Did you see anything you knew?'

'Only the *Barralong* outwards to Australia, and an Odessa grain-boat loaded down by the head. It was a thick day, but the sea smelt good.'

'Wherefore put on one's best trousers to see the *Barralong*?' said Torpenhow, pointing.

'Because I've nothing except these things and my painting duds. Besides, I wanted to do honour to the sea.'

'Did she make you feel restless?' asked the Nilghai keenly.

'Crazy. Don't speak of it. I'm sorry I went.'

Torpenhow and the Nilghai exchanged a look as Dick, stooping, busied himself among the former's boots and trees.

'These will do,' he said at last; 'I can't say I think much of your taste in slippers, but the fit's the thing.' He slipped his feet into a pair of sock-like sambhur-skin foot-coverings, found a long chair, and lay at length.

'They're my own pet pair,' Torpenhow said. 'I was just going to put them on myself.'

'All your reprehensible selfishness. Just because you see me happy for a minute, you want to worry me and stir me up. Find another pair.'

'Good for you that Dick can't wear your clothes, Torp. You two live communistically,' said the Nilghai.

'Dick never has anything that I can wear. He's only useful to sponge upon.'

'Confound you, have you been rummaging round among my caches, then?' said Dick. 'I put a sovereign in the tobacco-jar yesterday. How do you expect a man to keep his accounts properly if you——'

Here the Nilghai began to laugh, and Torpenhow joined him.

'Hid a sovereign yesterday! You're no sort of a financier. You lent me a fiver about a month back. Do you remember?' Torpenhow said.

'Yes, of course.'

'Do you remember that I paid it you ten days later, and you put it at the bottom of the tobacco?'

'By Jove, did I? I thought it was in one of my colour-boxes.'

'You thought! About a week ago I went into your studio to get some 'baccy and found it.'

'What did you do with it?'

'Took the Nilghai to a theatre and fed him.'

'You couldn't feed the Nilghai under twice the money—not though you gave him Army beef. Well, I suppose I should have found it out sooner or later. What is there to laugh at?'

'You're a most amazing cuckoo in many directions,' said the Nilghai, still chuckling over the thought of the dinner. 'Never mind. We had both been working very hard, and it was your unearned increment we spent, and as you're only a loafer it didn't matter.'

'That's pleasant—from the man who is bursting with my meat, too. I'll get that dinner back one of these days. Suppose we go to a theatre now.'

'Put our boots on,—and dress,—*and* wash?' The Nilghai spoke very lazily.

'I withdraw the motion.'

'Suppose, just for a change—as a startling variety, you know —we, that is to say *we*, get our charcoal and our canvas and go on with our work.' Torpenhow spoke pointedly, but Dick only wriggled his toes inside the soft leather moccasins.

'What a one-idea'd clucker it is! If I had any unfinished figures on hand, I haven't any model; if I had my model, I haven't any spray, and I never leave charcoal unfixed overnight; and if I had my spray and twenty photographs of backgrounds, I couldn't do anything to-night. I don't feel that way.'

'Binkie-dog, he's a lazy hog, isn't he?' said the Nilghai.

'Very good, I *will* do some work,' said Dick, rising swiftly. 'I'll fetch the Nungapunga Book, and we'll add another picture to the Nilghai Saga.'

'Aren't you worrying him a little too much?' asked the Nilghai, when Dick had left the room.

'Perhaps, but I know what he can turn out if he likes. It makes me savage to hear him praised for past work when I know what he ought to do. You and I are arranged for—'

'By Kismet and our own powers, more's the pity. I have dreamed of a good deal.'

'So have I, but we know our limitations now. I'm dashed if I know what Dick's may be when he gives himself to his work. That's what makes me so keen about him.'

'And when all's said and done, you will be put aside—quite rightly—for a female girl.'

'I wonder. . . . Where do you think he has been to-day?'

'To the sea. Didn't you see the look in his eyes when he talked about her? He's as restless as a swallow in autumn.'

'Yes; but did he go alone?'

'I don't know, and I don't care, but he has the beginnings of the go-fever upon him. He wants to up-stakes and move out.

There's no mistaking the signs. Whatever he may have said before, he has the call upon him now.'

'It might be his salvation,' Torpenhow said.

'Perhaps—if you care to take the responsibility of being a saviour: I'm averse to tampering with souls myself.'

Dick returned with a great clasped sketch-book that the Nilghai knew well and did not love too much. In it Dick had drawn in his playtime all manner of moving incidents, experienced by himself or related to him by the others, of all the four corners of the earth. But the wider range of the Nilghai's body and life attracted him most. When truth failed here he fell back on fiction of the wildest, and represented incidents in the Nilghai's career that were unseemly,—his marriages with many African princesses, his shameless betrayal, for Arab wives, of army corps to the Mahdi, his tattooment by skilled operators in Burma, his interview (and his fears) with the yellow headsman in the blood-stained execution-ground of Canton, and finally, the passings of his spirit into the bodies of whales, elephants, and toucans. Torpenhow from time to time had added rhymed descriptions, and the whole was a curious piece of art, because Dick decided, having regard to the name of the book, which being interpreted means 'naked,' that it would be wrong to draw the Nilghai with any clothes on, under any circumstances. Consequently the last sketch, representing that much-enduring man calling on the War Office to press his claims to the Egyptian medal, was hardly delicate. He settled himself comfortably at Torpenhow's table and turned over the pages.

'What a fortune you would have been to Blake, Nilghai!' he said. 'There's a succulent pinkness about some of these sketches that's more than life-like. "The Nilghai surrounded while bathing by the Mahdieh"—that was founded on fact, eh?'

'It was very nearly my last bath, you irreverent dauber. Has Binkie come into the Saga yet?'

'No; the Binkie-boy hasn't done anything except eat and kill cats. Let's see. Here you are as a stained-glass saint in a church. Deuced decorative lines about your anatomy; you ought to be grateful for being handed down to posterity in this way. Fifty years hence you'll exist in rare and curious facsimiles at ten guineas each. What shall I try this time? The domestic life of the Nilghai?'

'Hasn't got any.'

'The undomestic life of the Nilghai, then. Of course. Mass-meeting of his wives in Trafalgar Square. That's it. They came from the ends of the earth to attend the Nilghai's wedding to an English bride. This shall be in sepia. It's a sweet material to work with.'

'It's a scandalous waste of time,' said Torpenhow.

'Don't worry; it keeps one's hand in—specially when you begin without the pencil.' He set to work rapidly. 'That's Nelson's Column. Presently the Nilghai will appear shinning up it.'

'Give him some clothes this time.'

'Certainly—a veil and an orange-wreath, because he's been married.'

'Gad, that's clever enough!' said Torpenhow over his shoulder, as Dick brought out of the paper with three twirls of the brush a very fat back and labouring shoulder pressed against the stone.

'Just imagine,' Dick continued, 'if we could publish a few of these dear little things every time the Nilghai subsidises a man who can write, to give the public an honest opinion of my pictures.'

'Well, you'll admit I always tell you when I have done any-

thing of that kind. I know I can't hammer you as you ought
to be hammered, so I give the job to another. Young Maclagan,
for instance——'

'No-o—one half-minute, old man; stick your hand out
against the dark of the wall-paper—you only burble and call
me names. That left shoulder's out of drawing. I must literally
throw a veil over that. Where's my penknife? Well, what about
Maclagan?'

'I only gave him his riding-orders to—to lambaste you on
general principles for not producing work that will last.'

'Whereupon that young fool,'—Dick threw back his head
and shut one eye as he shifted the page under his hand,—
'being left alone with an ink-pot and what he conceived were
his own notions, went and spilt them both over me in the
papers. You might have engaged a grown man for the business,
Nilghai. How do you think the bridal veil looks now, Torp?'

'How the deuce do three dabs and two scratches make the
stuff stand away from the body as it does?' said Torpenhow,
to whom Dick's methods were always new.

'It just depends on where you put 'em. If Maclagan had
known that much about his business he might have done
better.'

'Why don't you put the damned dabs into something that
will stay, then?' insisted the Nilghai, who had really taken
considerable trouble in hiring for Dick's benefit the pen of a
young gentleman who devoted most of his waking hours to an
anxious consideration of the aims and ends of Art, which, he
wrote, was one and indivisible.

'Wait a minute till I see how I am going to manage my pro-
cession of wives. You seem to have married extensively, and
I must rough 'em in with the pencil—Medes, Parthians,
Edomites. . . . Now, setting aside the weakness and the

wickedness and—and the fat-headedness of deliberately trying to do work that will live, as they call it, I'm content with the knowledge that I've done my best up to date, and I shan't do anything like it again for some hours at least—probably years. Most probably never.'

'What! any stuff you have in stock your best work?' said Torpenhow.

'Anything you've sold?' said the Nilghai.

'Oh no. It isn't here and it isn't sold. Better than that, it can't be sold, and I don't think any one knows where it is. I'm sure I don't. . . . And yet more and more wives, on the north side of the Square. Observe the virtuous horror of the lions!'

'You may as well explain,' said Torpenhow, and Dick lifted his head from the paper.

'The sea reminded me of it,' he said slowly. 'I wish it hadn't. It weighs some few thousand tons—unless you cut it out with a cold chisel.'

'Don't be an idiot. You can't pose with us here,' said the Nilghai.

'There's no pose in the matter at all. It's a fact. I was loafing from Lima to Auckland in a big, old, condemned passenger-ship turned into a cargo-boat and owned by a second-hand Italian firm. She was a crazy basket. We were cut down to fifteen ton of coal a day, and we thought ourselves lucky when we kicked seven knots out of her. Then we used to stop and let the bearings cool down, and wonder whether the crack in the shaft was spreading.'

'Were you a steward or a stoker in those days?'

'I was flush for the time being, so I was a passenger, or else I should have been a steward, I think,' said Dick with perfect gravity, returning to the procession of angry wives. 'I was the only other passenger from Lima, and the ship was half empty, and full of rats and cockroaches and scorpions.'

'But what has this to do with the picture?'

'Wait a minute. She had been in the China passenger trade and her lower deck had bunks for two thousand pigtails. Those were all taken down, and she was empty up to her nose, and the lights came through the port-holes—most annoying lights to work in till you got used to them. I hadn't anything to do for weeks. The ship's charts were in pieces and our skipper daren't run south for fear of catching a storm. So he did his best to knock all the Society Islands out of the water one by one, and I went into the lower deck, and did my picture on the port side as far forward in her as I could go. There was some brown paint and some green paint that they used for the boats, and some black paint for ironwork, and that was all I had.'

'The passengers must have thought you mad.'

'There was only one, and it was a woman; but it gave me the notion of my picture.'

'What was the she like?' said Torpenhow.

'She was a sort of Negroid-Jewess-Cuban; with morals to match. She couldn't read or write, and she didn't want to, but she used to come down and watch me paint, and the skipper didn't like it, because he was paying her passage and had to be on the bridge occasionally.'

'I see. That must have been cheerful.'

'It was the best time I ever had. To begin with, we didn't know whether we should go up or go down any minute when there was a sea on; and when it was calm it was Paradise; and the woman used to mix the paints and talk broken English, and the skipper used to steal down every few minutes to the lower deck, because he said he was afraid of fire. So, you see, we could never tell when we might be caught, and I had a splendid notion to work out in only three keys of colour.'

'What was the notion?'

'Two lines in Poe—

*"Neither the angels in Heaven above nor the demons down
   under the sea,*
*Can ever dissever my soul from the soul of the beautiful
   Annabel Lee."*

It came out of the sea—all by itself. I drew that fight, fought out in green water over the naked, choking soul, and the woman served as the model for the devils and the angels both —sea-devils and sea-angels, and the soul half drowned between them. It doesn't sound much, but when there was a good light on the lower deck it looked very fine and creepy. It was seven by fourteen feet, all done in shifting light for shifting light.'

'Did the woman inspire you much?' said Torpenhow.

'She and the sea between them—immensely. There was a heap of bad drawing in that picture. I remember I went out of my way to foreshorten for sheer delight of doing it, and I foreshortened damnably, but for all that it's the best thing I've ever done; and now I suppose the ship's broken up or gone down. Whew! What a time that was!'

'What happened after all?'

'It all ended. They were loading her with wool when I left the ship, but even the stevedores kept the picture clear to the last. The eyes of the demons scared them, I honestly believe.'

'And the woman?'

'She was scared too when it was finished. She used to cross herself before she went down to look at it. Just three colours and no chance of getting any more, and the sea outside and unlimited love-making inside, and the fear of death atop of everything else, O Lord!' He had ceased to look at the sketch, but was staring straight in front of him across the room.

'Why don't you try something of the same kind now?' said the Nilghai.

'Because those things come not by fasting and prayer. When I find a cargo-boat and a Jewess-Cuban and another notion and the same old life, I may.'

'You won't find them here,' said the Nilghai.

'No, I shall not.' Dick shut the sketch-book with a bang. 'This room's as hot as an oven. Open the window, some one.'

He leaned into the darkness, watching the greater darkness of London below him. The chambers stood much higher than the other houses, commanding a hundred chimneys—crooked cowls that looked like sitting cats as they swung round, and other uncouth brick and zinc mysteries supported by iron stanchions and clamped by S-pieces. Northward the lights of Piccadilly Circus and Leicester Square threw a copper-coloured glare above the black roofs, and southward lay all the orderly lights of the Thames. A train rolled out across one of the railway bridges, and its thunder drowned for a minute the dull roar of the streets. The Nilghai looked at his watch and said shortly, 'That's the Paris night-mail. You can book from here to St. Petersburg if you choose.'

Dick crammed head and shoulders out of the window and looked across the river. Torpenhow came to his side, while the Nilghai passed over quietly to the piano and opened it. Binkie, making himself as large as possible, spread out upon the sofa with the air of one who is not to be lightly disturbed.

'Well,' said the Nilghai to the two pairs of shoulders, 'have you never seen this place before?'

A steam-tug on the river hooted as she towed her barges to wharf. Then the boom of the traffic came into the room.

Torpenhow nudged Dick. 'Good place to bank in—bad place to bunk in, Dickie, isn't it?'

Dick's chin was in his hand as he answered, in the words of a general not without fame, still looking out on the darkness: ' "My God, what a city to loot!" '

Binkie found the night air tickling his whiskers and sneezed plaintively.

'We shall give the Binkie-dog a cold,' said Torpenhow. 'Come in,' and they withdrew their heads. 'You'll be buried in Kensal Green, Dick, one of these days, if it isn't closed by the time you want to go there—buried within two feet of some one else, his wife and his family.'

'Allah forbid! I shall get away before that time comes. Give a man room to stretch his legs, Mr. Binkle.' Dick flung himself down on the sofa and tweaked Binkie's velvet ears, yawning heavily the while.

'You'll find that wardrobe-case very much out of tune,' Torpenhow said to the Nilghai. 'It's never touched except by you.'

'A piece of gross extravagance,' Dick grunted. 'The Nilghai only comes when I'm out.'

'That's because you're always out. Howl, Nilghai, and let him hear.'

*'The life of the Nilghai is fraud and slaughter,*
*His writings are watered Dickens and water;*
*But the voice of the Nilghai raised on high*
*Makes even the Mahdieh glad to die!'*

Dick quoted from Torpenhow's letterpress in the Nungapunga Book. 'How do they call moose in Canada, Nilghai?'

The man laughed. Singing was his one polite accomplishment, as many Press-tents in far-off lands had known.

'What shall I sing?' said he, turning in the chair.

' "Moll Roe in the Morning," ' said Torpenhow at a venture. 'No,' said Dick sharply, and the Nilghai opened his eyes. The old chanty whereof he, among a very few, possessed all the words was not a pretty one, but Dick had heard it many times before without wincing. Without prelude he launched into that stately tune that calls together and troubles the hearts of the gipsies of the sea:—

> 'Farewell and adieu to you, fair Spanish ladies,
> Farewell and adieu to you, ladies of Spain.'

Dick turned uneasily on the sofa, for he could hear the bows of the *Barralong* crashing into the green seas on her way to the Southern Cross. Then came the chorus:—

> 'We'll rant and we'll roar like true British sailors,
> We'll rant and we'll roar across the salt seas,
> Until we take soundings in the Channel of Old England,
> From Ushant to Scilly 'tis forty-five leagues.'

'Thirty-five—thirty-five,' said Dick petulantly. 'Don't tamper with Holy Writ. Go on, Nilghai.'

> 'The first land we made it was called the Deadman,'

and they sang to the end very vigorously.

'That would be a better song if her head were turned the other way—to the Ushant light, for instance,' said the Nilghai.

'Flinging its arms about like a mad windmill,' said Torpenhow. 'Give us something else, Nilghai. You're in fine fog-horn form to-night.'

'Give us "The Ganges Pilot": you sang that in the square

the night before El-Maghrib. By the way, I wonder how many of the chorus are alive to-night,' said Dick.

Torpenhow considered for a minute. 'By Jove! I believe only you and I. Raynor, Vickery, and Deenes—all dead; Vincent caught smallpox in Cairo, carried it here and died of it. Yes, only you and I and the Nilghai.'

'Umph! And yet the men here who've done their work in a well-warmed studio all their lives, with a policeman at each corner, say that I charge too much for my pictures.'

'They are buying your work, not your insurance policies, dear child,' said the Nilghai.

'I gambled with one to get at the other. Don't preach. Go on with the "Pilot." Where in the world did you get that song?'

'On a tombstone,' said the Nilghai. 'On a tombstone in a distant land. I made it an accompaniment with heaps of bass chords.'

'Oh, Vanity! Begin.' And the Nilghai began:—

'*I have slipped my cable, messmates, I'm drifting down with the tide,*
*I have my sailing orders, while ye at anchor ride.*
*And never on fair June morning have I put out to sea*
*With clearer conscience or better hope, or a heart more light and free.*

'*Shoulder to shoulder, Joe, my boy, into the crowd like a wedge.*
*Strike with the hangers, messmates, but do not cut with the edge.*
*Cries Charnock, "Scatter the faggots, double that Brahmin in two.*
*The tall pale widow for me, Joe, the little brown girl for you!"*

# THE LIGHT THAT FAILED

*'Young Joe (you're nearing sixty), why is your hide so dark?*
*Katie has soft fair blue eyes, who blackened yours?—Why,*
*hark!'*

They were all singing now, Dick with the roar of the wind
of the open sea about his ears as the deep bass voice let
itself go.

*'The morning gun—Ho, steady!—the arquebuses to me!*
*I ha' sounded the Dutch High Admiral's heart as my lead doth*
*sound the sea.*

*'Sounding, sounding the Ganges, floating down with the tide,*
*Moor me close to Charnock, next to my nut-brown bride.*
*My blessing to Kate at Fairlight—Holwell, my thanks to you;*
*Steady! We steer for Heaven, through sand-drifts cold and*
*blue.'*

'Now what is there in that nonsense to make a man restless?'
said Dick, hauling Binkie from his feet to his chest.

'It depends on the man,' said Torpenhow.

'The man who has been down to look at the sea,' said the
Nilghai.

'I didn't know she was going to upset me in this fashion.'

'That's what men say when they go to say good-bye to a
woman. It's more easy, though, to get rid of three women than
a piece of one's life and surroundings.'

'But a woman can be——' began Dick unguardedly.

'A piece of one's life,' continued Torpenhow. 'No, she can't.'
His face darkened for a moment. 'She says she wants to sympathise with you and help you in your work, and everything else

that clearly a man must do for himself. Then she sends round five notes a day to ask why the dickens you haven't been wasting your time with her.'

'Don't generalise,' said the Nilghai. 'By the time you arrive at five notes a day you must have gone through a good deal and behaved accordingly. Shouldn't begin these things, my son.'

'I shouldn't have gone down to the sea,' said Dick, just a little anxious to change the conversation. 'And you shouldn't have sung.'

'The sea isn't sending you five notes a day,' said the Nilghai.

'No, but I'm fatally compromised. She's an enduring old hag, and I'm sorry I ever met her. Why wasn't I born and bred and dead in a three-pair back?'

'Hear him blaspheming his first love! Why in the world shouldn't you listen to her?' said Torpenhow.

Before Dick could reply the Nilghai lifted up his voice with a shout that shook the windows, in 'The Men of the Sea,' that begins, as all know, 'The sea is a wicked old woman,' and after racing through eight lines whose imagery is truthful, ends in a refrain, slow as the clacking of a capstan when the boat comes unwillingly up to the bars where the men sweat and tramp in the shingle.

> ' "Ye that bore us, oh, restore us!
> She is kinder than ye;
> For the call is on our heart-strings!"
> Said The Men of the Sea.'

The Nilghai sang that verse twice, with simple craft, intending that Dick should hear. But Dick was waiting for the farewell of the men to their wives.

# THE LIGHT THAT FAILED

*' "Ye that love us, can ye move us?*
*She is dearer than ye;*
*And your sleep will be the sweeter,"*
*Said The Men of the Sea.'*

The rough words beat like the blows of the waves on the
bows of the rickety boat from Lima in the days when Dick was
mixing paints, making love, drawing devils and angels in the
half-dark, and wondering whether the next minute would
place the Italian captain's knife between his shoulder-blades.
And the go-fever, which is more real than many doctor's
diseases, waked and raged, urging him who loved Maisie beyond anything in the world to go away and taste the old hot,
unregenerate life again,—to scuffle, swear, gamble, and love
light loves with his fellows; to take ship and know the sea
once more, and by her beget pictures; to talk to Binat among
the sands of Port Said while Yellow 'Tina mixed the drinks;
to hear the crackle of musketry, and see the smoke roll outward, thin and thicken again till the shining black faces came
through, and in that hell every man was strictly responsible
for his own head, and his own alone, and struck with an unfettered arm. It was impossible, utterly impossible, but—

*' "Oh, our fathers, in the churchyard,*
*She is older than ye,*
*And our graves will be the greener,"*
*Said The Men of the Sea.'*

'What *is* there to hinder?' said Torpenhow, in the long hush
that followed the song.

'You said a little time since that you wouldn't come for a
walk round the world, Torp.'

'That was months ago, and I only objected to your making

money for travelling expenses. You've shot your bolt here and it has gone home. Go away and do some work, and see some things.'

'Get some of the fat off you; you're disgracefully out of condition,' said the Nilghai, making a plunge from the chair and grasping a handful of Dick generally over the right ribs. 'Soft as putty—pure tallow born of over-feeding. Train it off, Dickie.'

'We're all equally gross, Nilghai. Next time you have to take the field you'll sit down, wink your eyes, gasp, and die in a fit.'

'Never mind. You go away on a ship. Go to Lima again, or to Brazil. There's always trouble in South America.'

'Do you suppose I want to be told where to go? Great Heavens, the only difficulty is to know where I'm to stop. But I shall stay here, as I told you before.

'Then you'll be buried in Kensal Green and turn into adipocere with the others,' said Torpenhow. 'Are you thinking of commissions in hand? Pay forfeit and go. You've money enough to travel as a king if you please.'

'You've the grisliest notions of amusement, Torp. I think I see myself shipping first class on a six-thousand-ton hotel, and asking the third engineer what makes the engines go round, and whether it isn't very warm in the stokehold. Ho! ho! I should ship as a loafer if ever I shipped at all, which I'm not going to do. I shall compromise, and go for a small trip to begin with.'

'That's something at any rate. Where will you go?' said Torpenhow. 'It would do you all the good in the world, old man.'

The Nilghai saw the twinkle in Dick's eye and refrained from speech.

'I shall go in the first place to Rathray's stable, where I shall hire one horse, and take him very carefully as far as Richmond Hill. Then I shall walk him back again, in case he should accidentally burst into a lather and make Rathray angry. I shall do that to-morrow for the sake of air and exercise.'

'Bah!' Dick had barely time to throw up his arm and ward off the cushion that the disgusted Torpenhow heaved at his head.

'Air and exercise indeed,' said the Nilghai, sitting down heavily on Dick. 'Let's give him a little of both. Get the bellows, Torp.'

At this point the conference broke up in disorder, because Dick would not open his mouth till the Nilghai held his nose fast, and there was some trouble in forcing the nozzle of the bellows between his teeth; and even when it was there he weakly tried to puff against the force of the blast, and his cheeks blew up with a great explosion; and the enemy becoming helpless with laughter he so beat them over the head with a soft sofa-cushion that that became unsewn and distributed its feathers, and Binkie, interfering in Torpenhow's interests, was bundled into the half-empty bag and advised to scratch his way out, which he did after a while, travelling rapidly up and down the floor in the shape of an agitated green haggis, and when he came out looking for satisfaction, the three pillars of his world were picking feathers out of their hair.

'A prophet has no honour in his own country,' said Dick ruefully, dusting his knees. 'This filthy fluff will never brush off my bags.'

'It was all for your good,' said the Nilghai. 'Nothing like air and exercise.'

'All for your good,' said Torpenhow, not in the least with reference to past clowning. 'It would let you focus things at their proper worth and prevent your becoming slack in this hothouse of a town. Indeed it would, old man. I shouldn't have spoken if I hadn't thought so. Only, you make a joke of everything.'

'Before God, I do no such thing,' said Dick quickly and earnestly. 'You don't know me if you think that.'

'*I* don't think it,' said the Nilghai.

'How can fellows like ourselves, who know what life and death really mean, dare to make a joke of anything? I know we pretend it, to save ourselves from breaking down or going to the other extreme. Can't I see, old man, how you're always anxious about me, and try to advise me to make my work better? Do you suppose I don't think about that myself? But you can't help me—you can't help me—not even you. I must play my own hand alone in my own way.'

'Hear, hear,' from the Nilghai.

'What's the one thing in the Nilghai Saga that I've never drawn in the Nungapunga Book?' Dick continued to Torpenhow, who was a little astonished at the outburst.

Now there was one blank page in the book given over to the sketch that Dick had not drawn of the crowning exploit in the Nilghai's life; when that man, being young and forgetting that his body and bones belonged to the paper that employed him, had ridden over sunburned slippery grass in the rear of Bredow's brigade on the day that the troopers flung themselves at Canrobert's artillery, and for aught they knew twenty battalions in front, to save the battered 24th German Infantry, to give time to decide the fate of Vionville, and to learn ere their remnant came back to Flavigny that cavalry can attack and crumple and break unshaken infantry. Whenever he was inclined to think over a life that might have been better, an income that might have been larger, and a soul that might have been considerably cleaner, the Nilghai would comfort himself with the thought, 'I rode with Bredow's brigade at Vionville,' and take heart for any lesser battle the next day might bring.

'I know,' he said very gravely. 'I was always glad that you left it out.'

'I left it out because Nilghai taught me what the German Army learned then, and what Schmidt taught their cavalry. I don't know German. What is it? "Take care of the time and the dressing will take care of itself." I must ride my own line to my own beat, old man.'

'*Tempo ist Richtung.* You've learned your lesson well,' said the Nilghai. 'He must go alone. He speaks truth, Torp.'

'Maybe I'm as wrong as I can be—hideously wrong. I must find that out for myself, as I have to think things out for myself, but I daren't turn my head to dress by the next man. It hurts me a great deal more than you know not to be able to go, but I cannot, that's all. I must do my own work and live my own life in my own way, because I'm responsible for both. Only don't think I frivol about it, Torp. I have my own matches and sulphur, and I'll make my own Hell, thanks.'

There was an uncomfortable pause. Then Torpenhow said blandly, 'What did the Governor of North Carolina say to the Governor of South Carolina?'

'Excellent notion. It *is* a long time between drinks. There are the makings of a very fine prig in you, Dick,' said the Nilghai.

'I've liberated my mind, estimable Binkie, with the feathers in his mouth.' Dick picked up the still indignant one and shook him tenderly. 'You're tied up in a sack and made to run about blind, Binkie-wee, without any reason, and it has hurt your little feelings. Never mind. *Sic volo, sic jubeo, stet pro ratione voluntas,* and don't sneeze in my eye because I talk Latin. Good-night.'

# THE LIGHT THAT FAILED

He went out of the room.

'That's distinctly one for you,' said the Nilghai. 'I told you it was hopeless to meddle with him. He's not pleased.'

'He'd swear at me if he weren't. I can't make it out. He has the go-fever upon him and he won't go. I only hope that he mayn't have to go some day when he doesn't want to,' said Torpenhow.

In his own room Dick was settling a question with himself— and the question was whether all the world, and all that was therein, and a burning desire to exploit both, was worth one threepenny piece thrown into the Thames.

'It came of seeing the sea, and I'm a cur to think about it,' he decided. 'After all, the honeymoon will be that tour—with reservations; only . . . only I didn't realise that the sea was so strong. I didn't feel it so much when I was with Maisie. Those damnable songs did it. He's beginning again.'

But it was only Herrick's Nightpiece to Julia that the Nilghai sang, and before it was ended Dick re-appeared on the threshold, not altogether clothed indeed, but in his right mind, thirsty and at peace.

The mood had come and gone with the rising and the falling of the tide by Fort Keeling.

# CHAPTER IX

*'If I have taken the common clay*
*And wrought it cunningly*
*In the shape of a God that was digged a clod,*
*The greater honour to me.'*

*'If thou hast taken the common clay,*
*And thy hands be not free*
*From the taint of the soil, thou hast made thy spoil*
*The greater shame to thee.'*
                    THE TWO POTTERS.

HE DID NO WORK of any kind for the rest of the week. Then
came another Sunday. He dreaded and longed for the day
always, but since the red-haired girl had sketched him there
was rather more dread than desire in his mind.

He found that Maisie had entirely neglected his suggestions
about line-work. She had gone off at score filled with some
absurd notion for a 'fancy head.' It cost Dick something to
command his temper.

'What's the good of suggesting anything?' he said pointedly.

'Ah, but this will be a picture,—a real picture; and I know
that Kami will let me send it to the Salon. You don't mind,
do you?'

'I suppose not. But you won't have time for the Salon.'

Maisie hesitated a little. She even felt uncomfortable.

'We're going over to France a month sooner because of it.
I shall get the idea sketched out here and work it up at Kami's.'

Dick's heart stood still, and he came very near to being disgusted with his Queen who could do no wrong. 'Just when I thought I had made some headway, she goes off chasing butterflies. It's maddening!'

There was no possibility of arguing, for the red-haired girl was in the studio. Dick could only look unutterable reproach.

'I'm sorry,' he said, 'and I think you make a mistake. But what's the idea of your new picture?'

'I took it from a book.'

'That's bad, to begin with. Books aren't the places for pictures. And——'

'It's this,' said the red-haired girl behind him. 'I was reading it to Maisie the other day from *The City of Dreadful Night.* D'you know the book?'

'A little. I'm sorry I spoke. There are pictures in it. What has taken her fancy?'

'The description of the Melancolia:——

*"Her folded wings as of a mighty eagle,*
*But all too impotent to lift the regal*
*Robustness of her earth-born strength and pride."*

And here again. (Maisie, get the tea, dear.)

*"The forehead charged with baleful thoughts and dreams,*
*The household bunch of keys, the housewife's gown,*
*Voluminous indented, and yet rigid*
*As though a shell of burnished metal frigid,*
*Her feet thick-shod to tread all weakness down."'*

There was no attempt to conceal the scorn of the lazy voice. Dick winced.

'But that has been done already by an obscure artist of the name of Dürer,' said he. 'How does the thing run?—

> *"Three centuries and threescore years ago,*
> *With phantasies of his peculiar thought."*

You might as well try to rewrite *Hamlet*. It will be waste of time.'

'No, it won't,' said Maisie, putting down the teacups with clatter to reassure herself. 'And I mean to do it. Can't you see what a beautiful thing it would make?'

'How in perdition can one do work when one hasn't had the proper training? Any fool can get a notion. It needs training to drive the thing through,—training and conviction; not rushing after the first fancy.' Dick spoke between his teeth.

'You don't understand,' said Maisie. 'I think I can do it.'

Again the voice of the girl behind him:—

> ' *"Baffled and beaten back, she works on still;*
> *Weary and sick of soul, she works the more.*
> *Sustained by her indomitable will,*
> *The hands shall fashion, and the brain shall pore,*
> *And all her sorrow shall be turned to labour——"*

I fancy Maisie means to embody herself in the picture.'

'Sitting on a throne of rejected pictures? No, I shan't, dear. The notion in itself has fascinated me.—Of course you don't care for fancy heads, Dick. I don't think you could do them. You like blood and bones.'

'That's a direct challenge. If you can do a Melancolia that isn't merely a sorrowful female head, I can do a better one. And I will, too. What d'you know about Melancolias?' Dick firmly believed that he was even then tasting three-quarters of all the sorrow in the world.

'She was a woman,' said Maisie, 'and she suffered a great deal,—till she could suffer no more. Then she began to laugh at it all, and then I painted her and sent her to the Salon.'

The red-haired girl rose up and left the room, laughing.

Dick looked at Maisie humbly and hopelessly.

'Never mind about the picture,' he said. 'Are you really going back to Kami's a month before your time?'

'I must, if I want to get the picture done.'

'And that's all you want?'

'Of course. Don't be stupid, Dick.'

'You haven't the power. You have only the ideas—the ideas and the little cheap impulses. How you could have kept at your work for ten years steadily is a mystery to me. So you are really going,—a month before you need?'

'I must do my work.'

'Your work—bah! . . . No, I didn't mean that. It's all right, dear. Of course you must do your work, and—I think I'll say good-bye for this week.'

'Won't you even stay for tea?'

'No, thank you. Have I your leave to go, dear? There's nothing more you particularly want me to do, and the line-work doesn't matter.'

'I wish you could stay, and then we could talk over my picture. If only one single picture's a success it draws attention to all the others. I *know* some of my work is good, if only people could see. And you needn't have been so rude about it.'

'I'm sorry. We'll talk the Melancolia over some one of the other Sundays. There are four more—yes, one, two, three, four—before you go. Good-bye, Maisie.'

Maisie stood by the studio window, thinking, till the red-haired girl returned, a little white at the corners of her lips.

'Dick's gone off,' said Maisie. 'Just when I wanted to talk about the picture. Isn't it selfish of him?'

Her companion opened her lips as if to speak, shut them again, and went on reading *The City of Dreadful Night*.

Dick was in the Park, walking round and round a tree that he had chosen as his confidante for many Sundays past. He was swearing audibly, and when he found that the infirmities of the English tongue hemmed in his rage, he sought consolation in Arabic, which is expressly designed for the use of the afflicted. He was not pleased with the reward of his patient service; nor was he pleased with himself; and it was long before he arrived at the proposition that the Queen could do no wrong.

'It's a losing game,' he said. 'I'm worth nothing when a whim of hers is in question. But in a losing game at Port Said we used to double the stakes and go on. She do a Melancolia! She hasn't the power, or the insight, or the training. Only the desire. She's cursed with the curse of Reuben. She won't do line-work, because it means real work; and yet she's stronger than I am. I'll make her understand that I can beat her on her own Melancolia. Even then she wouldn't care. She says I can only do blood and bones. I don't believe she has blood in her veins. All the same I love her; and I must go on loving her; and if I can humble her vanity I will. I'll do a Melancolia that shall be something like a Melancolia,—"the Melancolia that transcends all wit." I'll do it at once, con—bless her.'

He discovered that the notion would not come to order, and that he could not free his mind for an hour from the thought of Maisie's departure. He took very small interest in her rough studies for the Melancolia when she showed them next week. The Sundays were racing past, and the time was at hand when all the church bells in London could not ring Maisie back to him. Once or twice he said something to Binkie about 'hermaphroditic futilities,' but the little dog received so many confidences both from Torpenhow and Dick that he did not trouble his tulip-ears to listen.

Dick was permitted to see the girls off. They were going by the Dover night-boat, and they hoped to return in August. It was then February, and Dick felt that he was being hardly used. Maisie was so busy stripping the small house across the Park, and packing her canvases, that she had no time for thought. Dick went down to Dover and wasted a day there fretting over a wonderful possibility. Would Maisie at the very last allow him one small kiss? He reflected that he might capture her by the strong arm, as he had seen women captured in the Southern Sudan, and lead her away; but Maisie would never be led. She would turn her grey eyes upon him and say, 'Dick, how selfish you are!' Then his courage would fail him. It would be better, after all, to beg for that kiss.

Maisie looked more than usually kissable as she stepped from the night-mail on to the windy pier, in a grey waterproof and a little grey cloth travelling-cap. The red-haired girl was not so lovely. Her green eyes were hollow and her lips were dry. Dick saw the trunks aboard, and went to Maisie's side in the darkness under the bridge. The mail-bags were thundering into the forehold, and the red-haired girl was watching them.

'You'll have a rough passage to-night,' said Dick. 'It's blowing outside. I suppose I may come over and see you if I'm good?'

'You mustn't. I shall be busy. At least, if I want you I'll send for you. But I shall write from Vitry-sur-Marne. I shall have heaps of things to consult you about. Oh, Dick, you have been so good to me!—So good to me!'

'Thank you for that, dear. It hasn't made any difference, has it?'

'I can't tell a fib. It hasn't—in that way. But don't think I'm not grateful.'

'Damn the gratitude!' said Dick huskily to the paddle-box.

'What's the use of worrying? You know I should ruin your life, and you'd ruin mine, as things are now. You remember what you said when you were so angry that day in the Park? One of us has to be broken. Can't you wait till that day comes?'

'No, love. I want you unbroke—all to myself.'

Maisie shook her head. 'My poor Dick, what can I say?'

'Don't say anything. Give me a kiss? Only one kiss, Maisie. I'll swear I won't take any more. You might as well, and then I can be sure you're grateful.'

Maisie put her cheek forward, and Dick took his reward in the darkness. It was only one kiss, but, since there was no time-limit specified, it was a long one. Maisie wrenched herself free angrily, and Dick stood abashed and tingling from head to heel.

'Good-bye, darling. I didn't mean to scare you. I'm sorry. Only—keep well and do good work,—specially the Melancolia. I'm going to do one, too. Remember me to Kami, and be careful what you drink. Country drinking-water is bad everywhere, but it's worst in France. Write to me if you want anything, and good-bye. Say good-bye to the what-you-call-um girl, and—can't I have another kiss? No. You're quite right. Good-bye.'

A shout told him that it was not seemly to charge up the mail-bag incline. He reached the pier as the steamer began to move off, and he followed her with his heart.

'And there's nothing—nothing in the wide world—to keep

us apart except her obstinacy. These Calais night-boats are much too small. I'll get Torp to write to the papers about it. She's beginning to pitch already.'

Maisie stood where Dick had left her till she heard a little gasping cough at her elbow. The red-haired girl's eyes were alight with cold flame.

'He kissed you!' she said. 'How could you let him, when he wasn't anything to you? How dared you take a kiss from him? Oh, Maisie, let's go to the ladies' cabin. I'm sick,—deadly sick.'

'We aren't into open water yet. Go down, dear, and I'll stay here. I don't like the smell of the engines. . . . Poor Dick! He deserved one,—only one. But I didn't think he'd frighten me so.'

Dick returned to Town next day just in time for lunch, for which he had telegraphed. To his disgust, there were only empty plates in the studio. He lifted up his voice like all the bears in the fairy-tale, and Torpenhow entered, looking very guilty.

'H'sh!' said he. 'Don't make such a noise. I took it. Come into my rooms, and I'll show you why.'

Dick paused amazed at the threshold, for on Torpenhow's sofa lay a girl asleep and breathing heavily. The little cheap sailor hat, the blue-and-white dress, fitter for June than for February, dabbled with mud at the skirts, the jacket trimmed with imitation astrakhan and ripped at the shoulder-seams, the one-and-elevenpenny umbrella, and, above all, the disgraceful condition of the kid-topped boots, declared all things.

'Oh, I say, old man, this is too bad! You mustn't bring this sort up here. They steal things from the rooms.'

'It looks bad, I admit, but I was coming in after lunch, and she staggered into the hall. I thought she was drunk at first, but it was collapse. I couldn't leave her as she was, so I brought her up here and gave her your lunch. She was fainting from want of food. She went fast asleep the minute she had finished.'

'I know something of that complaint. She's been living on sausages, I suppose. Torp, you should have handed her over to a policeman for presuming to faint in a respectable house. Poor little wretch! Look at that face! There isn't an ounce of immorality in it. Only folly,—slack, fatuous, feeble, futile folly. It's a typical head. D'you notice how the skull begins to show through the flesh-padding on the face and cheek-bone?'

'What a cold-blooded barbarian it is! Don't hit a woman when she's down. Can't we do anything? She was simply dropping with starvation. She almost fell into my arms, and when she got to the food she ate like a wild beast. It was horrible.'

'I can give her money, which she would probably spend in drinks. Is she going to sleep for ever?'

The girl opened her eyes and glared at the men between terror and effrontery.

'Feeling better?' said Torpenhow.

'Yes. Thank you. There aren't many gentlemen that are as kind as you are. Thank you.'

'When did you leave service?' said Dick, who had been watching the scarred and chapped hands.

'How did you know I was in service? I was. General servant. I didn't like it.'

'And how do you like being your own mistress?'

'Do I look as if I liked it?'

'I suppose not. One moment. Would you be good enough to turn your face to the window?'

The girl obeyed, and Dick watched her face keenly,—so keenly that she made as if to hide behind Torpenhow.

'The eyes have it,' said Dick, walking up and down. 'They

are superb eyes for my business. And, after all, every head depends on the eyes. This has been sent from Heaven to make up for—what was taken away. Now the weekly strain's off my shoulders, I can get to work in earnest. Evidently sent from Heaven. Yes. Raise your chin a little, please.'

'Gently, old man, gently. You're scaring somebody out of her wits,' said Torpenhow, who could see the girl trembling.

'Don't let him hit me! Oh, please don't let him hit me! I've been hit cruel to-day because I spoke to a man. Don't let him look at me like that! He's reg'lar wicked, that one. Don't let him look at me like that, neither! Oh, I feel as if I hadn't nothing on when he looks at me like that!'

The overstrained nerves in the frail body gave way, and the girl wept like a little child and began to scream. Dick threw open the window, and Torpenhow flung the door back.

'There you are,' said Dick soothingly. 'My friend here can call for a policeman, and you can run through that door. Nobody is going to hurt you.'

The girl sobbed convulsively for a few minutes, and then tried to laugh.

'Nothing in the world to hurt you. Now listen to me for a minute. I'm what they call an artist by profession. You know what artists do?'

'They draw the things in red and black ink on the pop-shop labels.'

'I daresay. I haven't risen to pop-shop labels yet. Those are done by the Academicians. I want to draw your head.'

'What for?'

'Because it's pretty. That is why you will come to the room across the landing three times a week at eleven in the morning, and I'll give you three quid a week just for sitting still and being drawn. And there's a quid on account.'

'For nothing? Oh, my!' The girl turned the sovereign in her hand, and with more foolish tears: 'Ain't neither o' you two gentlemen afraid of my bilking you?'

'No. Only ugly girls do that. Try and remember this place. And, by the way, what's your name?'

'I'm Bessie,—Bessie—— It's no use giving the rest. Bessie Broke,—Stone-broke if you like. What's your names? But there,—no one ever gives the real ones.'

Dick consulted Torpenhow with his eyes.

'My name's Heldar, and my friend's called Torpenhow; and you must be sure to come here. Where do you live?'

'South-the-water,—one room,—five and sixpence a week. Aren't you making fun of me about that three quid?'

'You'll see later on. And, Bessie, next time you come, re-member, you needn't wear that paint. It's bad for the skin, and I have all the colours you'll be likely to need.'

Bessie withdrew, scrubbing her cheek with a ragged pocket-handkerchief. The two men looked at each other.

'You're a man,' said Torpenhow.

'I'm afraid I've been a fool. It isn't our business to run about the earth reforming Bessie Brokes. And a woman of any kind has no right on this landing.'

'Perhaps she won't come back.'

'She will if she thinks she can get food and warmth here. I know she will, worse luck. But remember, old man, she isn't a woman. She's my model; and be careful.'

'The idea! She's a dissolute little scarecrow,—a gutter-snip-pet and nothing more.'

'So you think. Wait till she has been fed a little and freed from fear. That fair type recovers itself very quickly. You won't know her in a week or two, when that abject funk has died out of her eyes. She'll be too happy and smiling for my purposes.'

'But surely you're taking her out of charity?—to please me?'

'I am not in the habit of playing with hot coals to please anybody. She has been sent from Heaven, as I may have remarked before, to help me with my Melancolia.'

'Never heard a word about the lady before.'

'What's the use of having a friend if you must sling your notions at him in words? *You* ought to know what I'm thinking about. You've heard me grunt lately?'

'Even so; but grunts mean anything in your language, from bad 'baccy to wicked dealers. And I don't think I've been much in your confidence for some time.'

'It was a high and soulful grunt. You ought to have understood that it meant the Melancolia.' Dick walked Torpenhow up and down the room, keeping silence. Then he smote him in the ribs. '*Now* don't you see it? Bessie's abject futility, and the terror in her eyes, welded on to one or two details in the way of sorrow that have come under my experience lately. Likewise some orange and black,—two keys of each. But I can't explain on an empty stomach.'

'It sounds mad enough. You'd better stick to your soldiers, Dick, instead of maundering about heads and eyes and experiences.'

'Think so?' Dick began to dance on his heels, singing:—

*'They're as proud as a turkey when they hold the ready cash,*
　*You ought to 'ear the way they laugh an' joke!*
*They are tricky an' they're funny when they've got the ready*
　　*money,—*
　*Ow! but see 'em when they're all stone-broke!'*

Then he sat down to pour out his heart to Maisie in a four-sheet letter of counsel and encouragement, and registered an oath that he would get to work with an undivided heart as soon as Bessie should reappear.

The girl kept her appointment unpainted and unadorned, afraid and overbold by turns. When she found that she was merely expected to sit still, she grew calmer, and criticised the appointments of the studio with freedom and some point. She liked the warmth and the comfort and the release from fear of physical pain. Dick made two or three studies of her head in monochrome, but the actual notion of the Melancolia would not arrive.

'What a mess you keep your things in!' said Bessie, some days later, when she felt herself thoroughly at home. 'I s'pose your clothes are just as bad. Gentlemen never think what buttons and tape are made for.'

'I buy things to wear, and wear 'em till they go to pieces. I don't know what Torpenhow does.'

Bessie made diligent inquiry in the latter's room, and unearthed a bale of disreputable socks. 'Some of these I'll mend now,' she said, 'and some I'll take home. D'you know, I sit all day long at home doing nothing, just like a lady, and no more noticing them other girls in the house than if they was so many flies? I don't have any unnecessary words, but I put 'em down quick, I can tell you, when they talk to me. No; it's quite nice these days. I lock my door, and they can only call me names through the keyhole, and I sit inside, just like a lady, mending socks. Mr. Torpenhow wears his socks out both ends at once.'

'Three quid a week from me, and the delights of my society. No socks mended. Nothing from Torp except a nod on the landing now and again, and all his socks mended. Bessie is very much a woman,' thought Dick; and he looked at her between half-shut eyes. Food and rest had transformed the girl, as Dick knew they would.

'What are you looking at me like that for?' she said quickly. 'Don't. You look reg'lar bad when you look that way. You don't think much o' me, do you?'

'That depends on how you behave.'

Bessie behaved beautifully. Only it was difficult at the end of a sitting to bid her go out into the grey streets. She very much preferred the studio and a big chair by the stove, with some socks in her lap as an excuse for delay. Then Torpenhow would come in, and Bessie would be moved to tell strange and wonderful stories of her past, and still stranger ones of her present improved circumstances. She would make them tea as though she had a right to make it; and once or twice on these occasions Dick caught Torpenhow's eyes fixed on the trim little figure, and because Bessie's flittings about the room made Dick ardently long for Maisie, he realised whither Torpenhow's thoughts were tending. And Bessie was exceedingly careful of the condition of Torpenhow's linen. She spoke very little to him, but sometimes they talked together on the landing.

'I was a great fool,' Dick said to himself. 'I know what red firelight looks like when a man's trampling through a strange town; and ours is a lonely, selfish sort of life at the best. I wonder Maisie doesn't feel that sometimes. But I can't order Bessie away. That's the worst of beginning things. One never knows where they'll stop.'

One evening after a sitting prolonged to the last limit of the light, Dick was roused from a nap by a broken voice in Torpenhow's room. He jumped to his feet. 'Now what ought I to do? It looks foolish to go in.—Oh, bless you, Binkie!' The little terrier thrust Torpenhow's door open with his nose and came out to take possession of Dick's chair. The door swung wide unheeded, and Dick across the landing could see Bessie in the half-light making her little supplication to Torpenhow.

She was kneeling by his side, and her hands were clasped across his knees.

'I know,—I know,' she said thickly. ' 'Tisn't right o' me to do this, but I can't help it; and you were so kind,—so kind; and you never took any notice o' me. And I've mended all your things so carefully,—I did. Oh, please, 'tisn't as if I was asking you to marry me. I wouldn't think of it. But cou—couldn't you take and live with me till Miss Right comes along? I'm only Miss Wrong, I know, but I'd work my hands to the bare bones for you. And I'm not ugly to look at. Say you will?'

Dick hardly recognised Torpenhow's voice in reply:—

'But look here. It's no use. I'm liable to be ordered off anywhere at a minute's notice if a war breaks out. At a minute's notice—dear.'

'What does that matter? Until you go, then. Until you go. 'Tisn't much I'm asking, and—you don't know how good I can cook.' She had put an arm round his neck and was drawing his head down.

'Until—I—go, then.'

'Torp,' said Dick across the landing. He could hardly steady his voice. 'Come here a minute, old man. I'm in trouble.— Heaven send he'll listen to me!' There was something very like an oath from Bessie's lips. She was afraid of Dick, and disappeared down the staircase in panic, but it seemed an age before Torpenhow entered the studio. He went to the mantelpiece, buried his head on his arms, and groaned like a wounded bull.

'What the devil right have you to interfere?' he said, at last.

'Who's interfering with which? Your own sense told you long ago you couldn't be such a fool. It was a tough rack, St. Anthony, but you're all right now.'

'I oughtn't to have seen her moving about these rooms as

if they belonged to her. That's what upset me. It gives a lonely man a sort of hankering, doesn't it?' said Torpenhow piteously.

'Now you talk sense. It does. But, since you aren't in a condition to discuss the disadvantages of double housekeeping, do you know what you're going to do?'

'I don't. I wish I did.'

'You're going away for a season on a brilliant tour to regain tone. You're going to Brighton, or Scarborough, or Prawle Point, to see the ships go by. And you're going at once. Isn't it odd? I'll take care of Binkie, but out you go immediately. Never resist the Devil. He holds the bank. Fly from him. Pack your things and go.'

'I believe you're right. Where shall I go?'

'And you call yourself a special correspondent! Pack first and inquire afterwards.'

An hour later Torpenhow was despatched into the night in a hansom. 'You'll probably think of some place to go to while you're moving,' said Dick. 'Go to Euston, to begin with, and— oh yes—get drunk to-night.'

He returned to the studio, and lighted more candles, for he found the room very dark.

'Oh, you Jezebel! you futile little Jezebel! Won't you hate me to-morrow?—Binkie, come here.'

Binkie turned over on his back on the hearthrug, and Dick stirred him with a meditative foot.

'I said she was not immoral. I was wrong. She said she could cook. That showed premeditated sin. Oh, Binkie, if you are a man you will go to perdition; but if you are a woman, and say that you can cook, you will go to a much worse place.'

# CHAPTER X

*What's yon that follows at my side?—*
*The foe that ye must fight, my lord.—*
*That hirples swift as I can ride?—*
*The shadow of your might, my lord.—*
*Then wheel my horse against the foe!—*
*He's down and overpast, my lord.*
*Ye war against the sunset glow:*
*The darkness gathers fast, my lord.*
THE FIGHT OF HERIOT'S FORD.

'THIS IS A CHEERFUL LIFE,' said Dick, some days later. 'Torp's away; Bessie hates me; I can't get at the notion of the Melancolia; Maisie's letters are scrappy; and I believe I have indigestion. What gives a man pains across his head and spots before his eyes, Binkie? Shall us take some liver pills?'

Dick had just gone through a lively scene with Bessie. She had for the fiftieth time reproached him for sending Torpenhow away. She explained her enduring hatred for Dick, and made it clear to him that she only sat for the sake of his money. 'And Mr. Torpenhow's ten times a better man than you,' she concluded.

'He is. That's why he went away. *I* should have stayed and made love to you.'

The girl sat with her chin on her hand, scowling. 'To me! I'd like to catch you! If I wasn't afraid o' being hung I'd kill you. That's what I'd do. D'you believe me?'

Dick smiled wearily. It is not pleasant to live in the company of a notion that will not work out, a fox-terrier that cannot talk, and a woman who talks too much. He would have answered, but at that moment there unrolled itself from one corner of the studio a veil, as it were, of the filmiest gauze. He rubbed his eyes, but the grey haze would not go.

'This is disgraceful indigestion. Binkie, we will go to a medicine-man. We can't have our eyes interfered with, for by these we get our bread; also mutton-chop bones for little dogs.'

The doctor was an affable local practitioner with white hair, and he said nothing till Dick began to describe the grey film in the studio.

'We all want a little patching and repairing from time to time,' he chirped. 'Like a ship, my dear sir,—exactly like a ship. Sometimes the hull is out of order, and we consult the surgeon; sometimes the rigging, and then I advise; sometimes the engines, and we go to the brain-specialist; sometimes the look-out on the bridge is tired, and then we see an oculist. I should recommend you to see an oculist. A little patching and repairing from time to time is all we want. An oculist, by all means.'

Dick sought an oculist,—the best in London. He was certain that the local practitioner did not know anything about his trade, and more certain that Maisie would laugh at him if he were forced to wear spectacles.

'I've neglected the warnings of my lord the stomach too long. Hence these spots before the eyes, Binkie. I can see as well as I ever could.'

As he entered the dark hall that led to the consulting-room a man cannoned against him. Dick saw the face as it hurried out into the street.

'That's the writer-type. He has the same modelling of the forehead as Torp. He looks very sick. Probably heard something he didn't like.'

Even as he thought, a great fear came upon Dick, a fear that made him hold his breath as he walked into the oculist's waiting-room, with the heavy carved furniture, the dark-green paper, and the sober-hued prints on the wall. He recognised a reproduction of one of his own sketches.

Many people were waiting their turn before him. His eye was caught by a flaming red-and-gold Christmas-carol book. Little children came to that eye-doctor, and they needed large-type amusement.

'That's idolatrous bad Art,' he said, drawing the book towards himself. 'From the anatomy of the angels, it has been made in Germany.' He opened it mechanically, and there leaped to his eyes a verse printed in red ink:—

> *The next good joy that Mary had,*
> *It was the joy of three,*
> *To see her good Son Jesus Christ*
> *Making the blind to see;*
> *Making the blind to see, good Lord,*
> *And happy may we be.*
> *Praise Father, Son, and Holy Ghost*
> *To all eternity!*

Dick read and re-read the verse till his turn came, and the doctor was bending above him seated in an arm-chair. The blaze of a gas-microscope in his eyes made him wince. The doctor's hand touched the scar of the sword-cut on Dick's head, and Dick explained briefly how he had come by it. When the flame was removed, Dick saw the doctor's face, and the fear came upon him again. The doctor wrapped himself in a mist of words. Dick caught allusions to 'scar,' 'frontal bone,' 'optic nerve,' 'extreme caution,' and the 'avoidance of mental anxiety.'

'Verdict?' he said faintly. 'My business is painting, and I daren't waste time. What do you make of it?'

Again the whirl of words, but this time they conveyed a meaning.

'Can you give me anything to drink?'

Many sentences were pronounced in that darkened room, and the prisoners often needed cheering. Dick found a glass of liqueur brandy in his hand.

'As far as I can gather,' he said, coughing above the spirit, 'you call it decay of the optic nerve, or something, and therefore hopeless. What is my time-limit, avoiding all strain and worry?'

'Perhaps one year.'

'My God! And if I don't take care of myself?'

'I really could not say. One cannot ascertain the exact amount of injury inflicted by the sword-cut. The scar is an old one, and—exposure to the strong light of the desert, did you say?—with excessive application to fine work? I really could not say.'

'I beg your pardon, but it has come without any warning. If you will let me, I'll sit here for a minute, and then I'll go. You have been very good in telling me the truth. . . . Without any warning . . . without any warning. Thanks.'

Dick went into the street, and was rapturously received by Binkie. 'We've got it very badly, little dog! Just as badly as we can get it. We'll go to the Park to think it out.'

They headed for a certain tree that Dick knew well, and they sat down to think, because his legs were trembling under him and there was cold fear at the pit of his stomach.

'How could it have come without any warning? It's as sudden as being shot. It's the living death, Binkie. We're to be shut up in the dark in one year if we're careful, and we shan't see anybody, and we shall never have anything we want, not though we live to be a hundred.' Binkie wagged his tail joy-ously. 'Binkie, we must think. Let's see how it feels to be blind.' Dick shut his eyes, and flaming commas and Catherine-wheels floated inside the lids. Yet when he looked across the Park the scope of his vision was not contracted. He could see perfectly, until a procession of slow-wheeling fireworks defiled across his eyeballs.

'Little dorglums, we aren't at all well. Let's go home. If only Torp were back, now!'

But Torpenhow was in the South of England, inspecting dockyards in the company of the Nilghai. His letters were brief and full of mystery.

Dick had never asked anybody to help him in his joys or his sorrows. He argued, in the loneliness of the studio, henceforward to be decorated with a film of grey gauze in one corner, that, if his fate were blindness, all the Torpenhows in the world could not save him. 'I can't call him off his trip to sit down and sympathise with me. I must pull through the business alone,' he said. He was lying on the sofa, eating his moustache and wondering what the darkness of the night would be like. Then came to his mind the memory of a quaint scene in the Sudan. A soldier had been nearly hacked in two by a broad-bladed Arab spear. For one instant the man felt no pain. Looking down, he saw that his life-blood was going from him. The stupid bewilderment on his face was so intensely comic that both Dick and Torpenhow, still panting and unstrung from a fight for life, had roared with laughter, in which the man seemed as if he would join, but, as his lips parted in a sheepish grin, the agony of death came upon him, and he pitched grunting at their feet. Dick laughed again, remembering the horror. It seemed so exactly like his own case. 'But I have a little more time allowed me,' he said. He paced up and down the room, quietly at first, but afterwards with the hurried feet of fear. It was as though a black shadow stood at his elbow and urged him to go forward; and there were only weaving circles and floating pin-dots before his eyes.

'We must be calm, Binkie. We must be calm.' He talked aloud for the sake of distraction. 'This isn't nice at all. What shall we do? We must do something. Our time is short. I shouldn't have believed that this morning; but now things are different. Binkie, where was Moses when the light went out?'

Binkie smiled from ear to ear, as a well-bred terrier should, but made no suggestion.

' "Were there but world enough and time, This coyness, Binkie, were no crime. . . . But at my back I always hear——" ' He wiped his forehead, which was unpleasantly damp. 'What can I do? What can I do? I haven't any notions left, and I can't think connectedly, but I must do something, or I shall go off my head.'

The hurried walk recommenced, Dick stopping every now and again to drag forth long-neglected canvases and old note-books; for he turned to his work by instinct, as a thing that could not fail. 'You won't do, and you won't do,' he said, at each inspection. 'No more soldiers. I couldn't paint 'em. Sudden death comes home too nearly, and this is battle and murder both for me.'

The day was failing, and Dick thought for a moment that the twilight of the blind had come upon him unawares. 'Allah Almighty!' he cried despairingly, 'help me through the time of waiting, and I won't whine when my punishment comes. What can I do now, before the light goes?'

There was no answer. Dick waited till he could regain some sort of control over himself. His hands were shaking, and he prided himself on their steadiness; he could feel that his lips were quivering, and the sweat was running down his face. He was lashed by fear, driven forward by the desire to get to work at once and accomplish something, and maddened by the refusal of his brain to do more than repeat the news that he was about to go blind. 'It's a humiliating exhibition,' he thought, 'and I'm glad Torp isn't here to see. The doctor said I was to avoid mental worry. Come here and let me pet you, Binkie.'

The little dog yelped because Dick nearly squeezed the bark out of him. Then he heard the man speaking in the twilight, and, doglike, understood that his trouble stood off from him:—

'Allah is good, Binkie. Not quite so gentle as we could wish, but we'll discuss that later. I think I see my way to it now. All those studies of Bessie's head were nonsense, and they nearly brought your master into a scrape. I have the notion now as clear as crystal,—"the Melancolia that transcends all wit." There shall be Maisie in that head, because I shall never get Maisie; and Bess, of course, because she knows all about Melancolia, though she doesn't know she knows; and there shall be some drawing in it, and it shall all end up with a laugh. That's for myself. Shall she giggle or grin? No, she shall laugh right out of the canvas, and every man and woman that ever had a sorrow of their own shall—what is it the poem says?—

> "Understand the speech and feel a stir
> Of fellowship in all disastrous fight."

"In all disastrous fight"? That's better than painting the thing merely to pique Maisie. I can do it now because I have it inside me. Binkie, I'm going to hold you up by your tail. You're an omen. Come here.'

Binkie swung head downward for a moment without speaking.

' 'Rather like holding a guinea-pig; but you're a brave little dog, and you don't yelp when you're hung up. It *is* an omen.'

Binkie went to his own chair, and as often as he looked saw Dick walking up and down, rubbing his hands and chuckling. That night Dick wrote a letter to Maisie full of the tenderest concern for her health, but saying very little about his own, and dreamed of the Melancolia to be born. Not till morning did he remember that something might happen to him in the future.

He fell to work, whistling softly, and was swallowed up in the clean, clear joy of creation, which does not come to man too often, lest he should consider himself the equal of his God, and so refuse to die at the appointed time. He forgot Maisie, Torpenhow, and Binkie at his feet, but remembered to stir Bessie, who needed very little stirring, into a tremendous rage, that he might watch the smouldering lights in her eyes. He threw himself without reservation into his work, and did not think of the doom that was to overtake him, for he was possessed with his notion, and the things of this world had no power upon him.

'You're pleased to-day?' said Bessie.

Dick waved his mahl-stick in mystic circles and went to the sideboard for a drink. In the evening, when the exaltation of the day had died down, he went to the sideboard again, and after some visits became convinced that the eye-doctor was a liar, since he still could see everything very clearly. He was of opinion that he would even make a home for Maisie, and that whether she liked it or not she should be his wife. The mood passed next morning, but the sideboard and all upon it remained for his comfort. Again he set to work, and his eyes troubled him with spots and dashes and blurs till he had taken counsel with the sideboard, and the Melancolia both on the canvas and in his own mind appeared lovelier than ever. There was a delightful sense of irresponsibility upon him, such as they feel who walking among their fellow-men know that the death-sentence of disease is upon them, and, since fear is but waste of the little time left, are riotously happy. The days passed without event. Bessie arrived punctually always, and, though her voice seemed to Dick to come from a distance, her face was always very near, and the Melancolia began to flame on the canvas, in the likeness of a woman who had known all the sorrow in the world and was laughing at it. It was true that the corners of the studio draped themselves in grey film and retired into the darkness, that the spots in his eyes and the pains across his head were very troublesome, and that Maisie's letters were hard to read and harder still to answer. He could not tell her of his trouble, and he could not laugh at her accounts of her own Melancolia which was always going to be finished. But the furious days of toil and the nights of wild dreams made amends for all, and the sideboard was his best friend on earth. Bessie was singularly dull. She used to shriek with rage when Dick stared at her between half-closed eyes. Now she sulked, or watched him with disgust, saying very little.

Torpenhow had been absent for six weeks. An incoherent note heralded his return. 'News! great news!' he wrote. 'The Nilghai knows, and so does the Keneu. We're all back on Thursday. Get lunch and clean your accoutrements.'

Dick showed Bessie the letter, and she abused him for that he had ever sent Torpenhow away and ruined her life.

'Well,' said Dick brutally, 'you're better as you are, instead of making love to some drunken beast in the street.' He felt that he had rescued Torpenhow from great temptation.

'I don't know if that's any worse than sitting to a drunken beast in a studio. *You* haven't been sober for three weeks.

You've been soaking the whole time; and yet you pretend you're better than me!'

'What do you mean?' said Dick.

'Mean! You'll see when Mr. Torpenhow comes back.'

It was not long to wait. Torpenhow met Bessie on the staircase without a sign of feeling. He had news that was more to him than many Bessies, and the Keneu and the Nilghai were trampling behind him, calling for Dick.

'Drinking like a fish,' Bessie whispered. 'He's been at it for nearly a month.' She followed the men stealthily to hear judgment done.

They came into the studio, rejoicing, to be welcomed over-effusively by a drawn, lined, shrunken, haggard wreck,—unshaven, blue-white about the nostrils, stooping in the shoulders, and peering under his eyebrows nervously. The drink had been at work as steadily as Dick.

'Is this you?' said Torpenhow.

'All that's left of me. Sit down. Binkie's quite well, and I've been doing some good work.' He reeled where he stood.

'You've done some of the worst work you've ever done in your life. Man alive, you're——'

Torpenhow turned to his companions appealingly, and they left the room to find lunch elsewhere. Then he spoke; but, since the reproof of a friend is much too sacred and intimate a thing to be printed, and since Torpenhow used figures and metaphors which were unseemly, and contempt untranslatable, it will never be known what was actually said to Dick, who blinked and winked and picked at his hands. After a time the culprit began to feel the need of a little self-respect. He was quite sure that he had not in any way departed from virtue, and there were reasons, too, of which Torpenhow knew nothing. He would explain.

He rose, tried to straighten his shoulders, and spoke to the face he could hardly see.

'You are right,' he said. 'But I am right, too. After you went away I had some trouble with my eyes. So I went to an oculist, and he turned a gasogene—I mean a gas-engine—into my eye. That was very long ago. He said, "Scar on the head,—sword-cut and optic nerve." Make a note of that. So I am going blind. I have some work to do before I go blind, and I suppose that I must do it. I cannot see much now, but I can see best when I am drunk. I did not know I was drunk till I was told, but I must go on with my work. If you want to see it, there it is.' He pointed to the all but finished Melancolia and looked for applause.

Torpenhow said nothing, and Dick began to whimper feebly, for joy at seeing Torpenhow again, for grief at misdeeds—if indeed they were misdeeds—that made Torpenhow remote and unsympathetic, and for childish vanity hurt, since Torpenhow had not given a word of praise to his wonderful picture.

Bessie looked through the keyhole after a long pause, and saw the two walking up and down as usual, Torpenhow's hand on Dick's shoulder. Hereat she said something so improper that it shocked even Binkie, who was dribbling patiently on the landing in the hope of seeing his master again.

# CHAPTER XI

*The lark will make her hymn to God,*
*The partridge call her brood,*
*While I forget the heath I trod,*
*The fields wherein I stood.*
*'Tis dule to know not night from morn,*
*But deeper dule to know*
*I can but hear the hunter's horn*
*That once I used to blow.*

BALLAD.

IT WAS THE THIRD DAY after Torpenhow's return, and his heart was heavy.

'Do you mean to tell me that you can't see to work without whisky? It's generally the other way about.'

'Can a drunkard swear on his honour?' said Dick.

'Yes, if he has been as good a man as you.'

'Then I give you my word of honour,' said Dick, speaking hurriedly through parched lips. 'Old man, I can hardly see your face now. You've kept me sober for two days,—if I ever was drunk,—and I've done no work. Don't keep me back any more. I don't know when my eyes may give out. The spots and dots and the pains and things are crowding worse than ever. I swear I can see all right when I'm—when I'm moderately screwed, as you say. Give me three more sittings from Bessie and all the—stuff I want, and the picture will be done. I can't kill myself in three days. It only means a touch of D.T. at the worst.'

'If I give you three days more will you promise me to stop work and—the other thing, whether the picture's finished or not?'

151

'I can't. You don't know what that picture means to me. But surely you could get the Nilghai to help you, and knock me down and tie me up. I shouldn't fight for the whisky, but I should for the work.'

'Go on, then. I give you three days; but you're breaking my heart.'

Dick returned to his work, toiling as one possessed; and the yellow devil of whisky stood by him and chased away the spots in his eyes. The Melancolia was nearly finished, and was all or nearly all that he had hoped she would be. Dick jested with Bessie, who reminded him that he was 'a drunken beast'; but the reproof did not move him.

'You can't understand, Bess. We are in sight of land now, and soon we shall lie back and think about what we've done. I'll give you three months' pay when the picture's finished, and next time I have any more work in hand—but that doesn't matter. Won't three months' pay make you hate me less?'

'No, it won't! I hate you, and I'll go on hating you. Mr. Torpenhow won't speak to me any more. He's always looking at map-things and red-backed books.'

Bessie did not say that she had again laid siege to Torpenhow, or that he had at the end of her passionate pleading picked her up, given her a kiss, and put her outside the door with a recommendation not to be a little fool. He spent most of his time in the company of the Nilghai, and their talk was of war in the near future, the hiring of transports, and secret preparations among the dockyards. He did not care to see Dick till the picture was finished.

'He's doing first-class work,' he said to the Nilghai, 'and it's quite out of his regular line. But, for the matter of that, so's his infernal soaking.'

'Never mind. Leave him alone. When he has come to his

senses again we'll carry him off from this place and let him breathe clean air. Poor Dick! I don't envy you, Torp, when his eyes fail.'

'Yes, it will be a case of "God help the man who's chained to our Davie." The worst is that we don't know when it will happen; and I believe the uncertainty and the waiting have sent Dick to the whisky more than anything else.'

'How the Arab who cut his head open would grin if he knew!'

'He's at perfect liberty to grin if he can. He's dead. That's poor consolation now.'

In the afternoon of the third day Torpenhow heard Dick calling for him. 'All finished!' he shouted. 'I've done it! Come in! Isn't she a beauty? Isn't she a darling? I've been down to Hell to get her; but isn't she worth it?'

Torpenhow looked at the head of a woman who laughed,— a full-lipped, hollow-eyed woman who laughed from out of the canvas as Dick had intended she should.

'Who taught you how to do it?' said Torpenhow. 'The touch and notion have nothing to do with your regular work. What a face it is! What eyes, and what insolence!' Unconsciously he threw back his head and laughed with her. 'She's seen the game played out,—I don't think she had a good time of it,—and now she doesn't care. Isn't that the idea?'

'Exactly.'

'Where did you get the mouth and chin from? They don't belong to Bess.'

'They're—some one else's. But isn't it good? Isn't it thundering good? Wasn't it worth the whisky? I did it. Alone I did it, and it's the best I can do.' He drew his breath sharply, and whispered, 'Just God! what could I not do ten years hence, if I can do this now!—By the way, what do you think of it, Bess?'

The girl was biting her lips. She loathed Torpenhow because he had taken no notice of her.

'I think it's just the horridest, beastliest thing I ever saw,' she answered, and turned away.

'More than you will be of that way of thinking, young woman.—Dick, there's a sort of murderous, viperine suggestion in the poise of the head that I don't understand,' said Torpenhow.

'That's trick-work,' said Dick, chuckling with delight of being completely understood. 'I couldn't resist one little bit of sheer swagger. It's a French trick, and you wouldn't understand; but it's got at by slewing round the head a trifle, and a tiny, tiny foreshortening of one side of the face from the angle of the chin to the top of the left ear. That, and deepening the shadow under the lobe of the ear. It was flagrant trick-work; but, having the notion fixed, I felt entitled to play with it.—Oh, you beauty!'

'Amen! She is a beauty. I can feel it.'

'So will every man who has any sorrow of his own,' said Dick, slapping his thigh. 'He shall see his trouble there, and, by the Lord Harry, just when he's feeling properly sorry for himself he shall throw back his head and laugh,—as she is laughing. I've put the life of my heart and the light of my eyes into her, and I don't care what comes. . . . I'm tired,—awfully tired. I think I'll get to sleep. Take away the whisky, it has served its turn, and give Bessie thirty-six quid, and three over for luck. Cover the picture.'

He dropped asleep in the long chair, his face white and haggard, almost before he had finished the sentence. Bessie tried to take Torpenhow's hand. 'Aren't you never going to speak to me no more?' she said; but Torpenhow was looking at Dick.

'What a stock of vanity the man has! I'll take him in hand

to-morrow and make much of him. He deserves it.—Eh! what was that, Bess?'

'Nothing. I'll put things tidy here a little, and then I'll go. You couldn't give me that three months' pay now, could you? He said you were to.'

Torpenhow gave her a cheque and went to his own rooms. Bessie faithfully tidied up the studio, set the door ajar for flight, emptied half a bottle of turpentine on a duster, and began to scrub the face of the Melancolia viciously. The paint did not smudge quickly enough. She took a palette-knife and scraped, following each stroke with the wet duster. In five minutes the picture was a formless, scarred muddle of colours. She threw the paint-stained duster into the studio stove, stuck out her tongue at the sleeper, and whispered, 'Bilked!' as she turned to run down the staircase. She would never see Torpenhow any more, but she had at least done harm to the man who had come between her and her desire and who used to make fun of her. Cashing the cheque was the very cream of the jest to Bessie. Then the little privateer sailed across the Thames, to be swallowed up in the grey wilderness of South-the-water.

Dick slept till late into the evening, when Torpenhow dragged him off to bed. His eyes were as bright as his voice was hoarse. 'Let's have another look at the picture,' he said, insistently as a child.

'You—go—to—bed,' said Torpenhow. 'You aren't at all well, though you mayn't know it. You're as jumpy as a cat.'

'I reform to-morrow. Good-night.'

As he repassed through the studio, Torpenhow lifted the cloth above the picture, and almost betrayed himself by outcries: 'Wiped out!—scraped out and turped out! If Dick knows this to-night he'll go raving mad. He's on the verge of jumps as it is. That's Bess,—the little devil! Only a woman could have done that!—with the ink not dry on the cheque, too! Dick will be off his head to-morrow. It was all my fault for trying to help gutter-devils. Oh, my poor Dick, the Lord is hitting you very hard!'

Dick could not sleep that night, partly for pure joy, and partly because the well-known Catherine-wheels inside his eyes had given place to crackling volcanoes of many-coloured fire. 'Spout away,' he said aloud. 'I've done my work, and now you can do what you please.' He lay still, staring at the ceiling, the long-pent-up delirium of drink in his veins, his brain on fire with racing thoughts that would not stay to be considered, and his hands crisped and dry. He had just discovered that he was painting the face of the Melancolia on a revolving dome ribbed with millions of lights, and that all his wondrous thoughts stood embodied hundreds of feet below his tiny swinging plank, shouting together in his honour, when something cracked inside his temples like an overstrained bowstring, the glittering dome broke inward, and he was alone in the thick night.

'I'll go to sleep. The room's very dark. Let's light a lamp and see how the Melancolia looks. There ought to have been a moon.'

It was then that Torpenhow heard his name called by a voice that he did not know,—in the rattling accents of deadly fear.

'He's looked at the picture,' was his first thought, as he hurried into the bedroom and found Dick sitting up and beating the air with his hands.

'Torp! Torp! Where are you? For pity's sake, come to me!'

'What's the matter?'

Dick clutched at his shoulder. 'Matter! I've been lying here for hours in the dark, and you never heard me. Torp, old man, don't go away. I'm all in the dark. In the dark, I tell you!'

Torpenhow held the candle within a foot of Dick's eyes, but there was no answer in those eyes. He lit the gas, and Dick heard the flame catch. The grip of his fingers on Torpenhow's shoulder made Torpenhow wince.

'Don't leave me. You wouldn't leave me alone now, would you? I can't see. D'you understand? It's black,—quite black,— and I feel as if I was falling through it all.'

'Steady does it.' Torpenhow put his arm round Dick and began to rock him gently to and fro.

'That's good. Now don't talk. If I keep very quiet for a while this darkness will lift. It seems just on the point of breaking. H'sh!' Dick knit his brows, and stared desperately in front of him. The night air was chilling Torpenhow's toes.

'Can you stay like that a minute?' he said. 'I'll get my dressing-gown and some slippers.'

Dick clutched the bed-head with both hands and waited for the darkness to clear away. 'What a time you've been!' he cried, when Torpenhow returned. 'It's as black as ever. What are you banging about in the doorway?'

'Long chair,—horse-blanket,—pillow. Going to sleep by you. Lie down now; you'll be better in the morning.'

'I shan't!' The voice rose to a wail. 'My God! I'm blind! I'm blind, and the darkness will never go away.' He made as if to leap from the bed, but Torpenhow's arms were round him, and Torpenhow's chin was on his shoulder, and his breath was squeezed out of him. He could only gasp, 'Blind!' and wriggle feebly.

'Steady, Dickie, steady!' said the deep voice in his ear, and the grip tightened. 'Bite on the bullet, old man, and don't let them think you're afraid.' The grip could draw no closer. Both men were breathing heavily. Dick threw his head from side to side and groaned.

'Let me go,' he panted. 'You're cracking my ribs. We—we mustn't let them think we're afraid, must we,—all the Powers of Darkness and that lot?'

'Lie down. It's all over now.'

'Yes,' said Dick obediently. 'But would you mind letting me hold your hand? I feel as if I wanted something to hold on to. One drops through the dark so.'

Torpenhow thrust out a large and hairy paw from the long chair. Dick clutched it tightly, and in half an hour had fallen asleep. Torpenhow withdrew his hand, and, stooping over Dick, kissed him lightly on the forehead, as men do sometimes kiss a wounded comrade in the hour of death, to ease his departure.

In the grey dawn Torpenhow heard Dick talking to himself. He was adrift on the shoreless tides of delirium, speaking very quickly:—

'It's a pity,—a great pity; but it's helped, and it must be eaten, Master George. . . . Sufficient unto the day is the blindness thereof, and, further, putting aside all Melancolias and false humours, it is of obvious notoriety—such as mine was—that the Queen can do no wrong. Torp doesn't know that. I'll tell him when we're a little farther into the desert. What a bungle those boatmen are making of the steamer-ropes! They'll have that four-inch hawser chafed through in a minute. I told you so—there she goes! . . . White foam on green water, and the steamer slewing round. How good that looks! I'll sketch it. No, I can't. I'm afflicted with ophthalmia. That was one of the ten plagues of Egypt, and it extends up the Nile in the shape of cataract. Ha! that's a joke, Torp.

Laugh, you graven image, and stand clear of the hawser. . . .
It'll knock you into the water and make your dress all dirty,
Maisie dear.'

'Oh!' said Torpenhow. 'This happened before. That night
on the river.'

'She'll be sure to say it's my fault if you get muddy, and
you're quite near enough to the breakwater. . . . Maisie,
that's not fair. Ah! I knew you'd miss. Low and to the left,
dear. But you've no conviction. Everything in the world except conviction. Don't be angry, darling. I'd cut my hand off
if it would give you anything more than obstinacy. My right
hand, if it would serve.'

'Now we mustn't listen. Here's an island shouting across
seas of misunderstanding with a vengeance. But it's shouting
truth, I fancy,' said Torpenhow.

The babble continued. It all bore upon Maisie. Sometimes
Dick lectured at length on his craft, then he cursed himself for
his folly in being enslaved. He pleaded to Maisie for a kiss—
only one kiss—before she went away, and called to her to come
back from Vitry-sur-Marne, if she would; but through all his
ravings he bade Heaven and Earth witness that the Queen
could do no wrong.

Torpenhow listened attentively, and learned every detail
of Dick's life that had been hidden from him. For three days
Dick raved through his past, and then slept a natural sleep.
'What a strain he has been running under, poor chap!' said
Torpenhow. 'Dick, of all men, handing himself over like a
dog! And I was lecturing him on arrogance! I ought to have
known that it is no use to judge a man. But I did it. What a
demon that girl must be! Dick's given her his life,—confound
him!—and she's given him one kiss apparently.'

'Torp,' said Dick from the bed, 'go out for a walk. You've

been here too long. I'll get up. Hi! This is annoying. I can't dress myself. Oh, it's too absurd!'

Torpenhow helped him into his clothes and led him to the big chair in the studio. He sat quietly waiting under strained nerves for the darkness to lift. It did not lift that day, nor the next. Dick adventured on a voyage round the walls. He hit his shins against the stove, and this suggested to him that it would be better to crawl on all-fours, one hand in front of him. Torpenhow found him on the floor.

'I'm trying to get the geography of my new possessions,' said he. 'D'you remember that nigger you gouged in the square? Pity you didn't keep the odd eye. It would have been useful. Any letters for me? Give me all the ones in fat grey envelopes with a sort of crown thing outside. They're of no importance.'

Torpenhow gave him a letter with a black M. on the envelope flap. Dick put it into his pocket. There was nothing in it that Torpenhow might not have read, but it belonged to himself and to Maisie, who would never belong to him.

'When she finds that I don't write she'll stop writing. It's better so. I couldn't be any use to her now,' Dick argued, and the tempter suggested that he should make known his condition. Every nerve in him revolted. 'I have fallen low enough already. I'm not going to beg for pity. Besides, it would be cruel to her.' He strove to put Maisie out of his thoughts; but the blind have many opportunities for thinking, and as the tides of his strength came back to him in the long employless days of dead darkness, Dick's soul was troubled to the core. Another letter, and another, came from Maisie. Then there was silence, and Dick sat by the window, the pulse of summer in the air, and pictured her being won by another man, stronger than himself. His imagination, the keener for the dark background it worked against, spared him no single detail that might send him raging up and down the studio, to stumble over the stove that seemed to be in four places at once. Worst of all, tobacco would not taste in the darkness. The arrogance of the man had disappeared, and in its place were settled despair that Torpenhow knew, and blind passion that Dick confided to his pillow at night. The intervals between the paroxysms were filled with intolerable waiting and the weight of intolerable darkness.

'Come out into the Park,' said Torpenhow. 'You haven't stirred out since the beginning of things.'

'What's the use? There's no movement in the dark; and, besides,'—he paused irresolutely at the head of the stairs,— 'something will run over me.'

'Not if I'm with you. Proceed gingerly.'

The roar of the streets filled Dick with nervous terror, and he clung to Torpenhow's arm. 'Fancy having to feel for a gutter with your foot!' he said petulantly, as he turned into the Park. 'Let's curse God and die.'

'Sentries are forbidden to pay unauthorised compliments. By Jove, there are the Guards!'

Dick's figure straightened. 'Let's get near 'em. Let's go in and look. Let's get on the grass and run. I can smell the trees.'

'Mind the low railing. That's all right!' Torpenhow kicked out a tuft of grass with his heel. 'Smell that,' he said. 'Isn't it good?' Dick snuffed luxuriously. 'Now pick up your feet and run.' They approached as near to the regiment as was possible. The clank of bayonets being unfixed made Dick's nostrils quiver.

'Let's get nearer. They're in column, aren't they?'

'Yes. How did you know?'

'Felt it. Oh, my men!—my beautiful men!' He edged forward as though he could see. 'I could draw those chaps once. Who'll draw 'em now?'

'They'll move off in a minute. Don't jump when the band begins.'

'Huh! I'm not a new charger. It's the silences that hurt. Nearer, Torp!—nearer! Oh, my God, what wouldn't I give to see 'em for a minute!—one half-minute!'

He could hear the armed life almost within reach of him, could hear the slings tighten across the bandsman's chest as he heaved the big drum from the ground.

'Sticks crossed above his head,' whispered Torpenhow.

'I know. *I* know! Who should know if I don't? H'sh!'

The drumsticks fell with a boom, and the men swung forward to the crash of the band. Dick felt the wind of the massed movement in his face, heard the maddening tramp of feet and the friction of the pouches on the belts. The big drum pounded out the tune. It was a music-hall refrain that made a perfect quickstep:—

> *He must be a man of decent height,*
> *He must be a man of weight,*
> *He must come home on a Saturday night*
> *In a thoroughly sober state;*
>
> *He must know how to love me,*
> *And he must know how to kiss;*
> *And if he's enough to keep us both*
> *I can't refuse him bliss.*

'What's the matter?' said Torpenhow, as he saw Dick's head fall when the last of the regiment had departed.

'Nothing. I feel a little bit out of the running,—that's all. Torp, take me back. Why did you bring me out?'

## CHAPTER XII

*There were three friends that buried the fourth,*
*The mould in his mouth and the dust in his eyes;*
*And they went south, and east, and north,—*
*The strong man fights, but the sick man dies.*

*There were three friends that spoke of the dead,—*
*The strong man fights, but the sick man dies.—*
*'And would he were here with us now,' they said,*
*'The sun in our face and the wind in our eyes.'*

BALLAD.

THE NILGHAI WAS ANGRY with Torpenhow. Dick had been sent to bed,—blind men are ever under the orders of those who can see,—and since he had returned from the Park had fluently sworn at Torpenhow because he was alive, and all the world because it was alive and could see, while he, Dick, was dead in the death of the blind, who, at the best, are only burdens upon their associates. Torpenhow had said something about a Mrs. Gummidge, and Dick had retired in a black fury to handle and rehandle three unopened letters from Maisie.

The Nilghai, fat, burly, and aggressive, was in Torpenhow's rooms. Behind him sat the Keneu, the Great War Eagle, and between them lay a large map embellished with black- and white-headed pins.

'I was wrong about the Balkans,' said the Nilghai. 'But I'm not wrong about this business. The whole of our work in the Southern Sudan must be done over again. The public doesn't care, of course, but the Government does, and they are making their arrangements quietly. You know that as well as I do.'

'I remember how the people cursed us when our troops withdrew from Omdurman. It was bound to crop up sooner or later. But I can't go,' said Torpenhow. He pointed through the open door; it was a hot night. 'Can you blame me?'

The Keneu purred above his pipe like a large and very happy cat:—

'Don't blame you in the least. It's uncommonly good of you, and all the rest of it, but every man—even you, Torp—must consider his work. I know it sounds brutal, but Dick's out of the race,—down,—*gastado*, expended, finished, done for. He has a little money of his own. He won't starve, and you can't pull out of your stride for his sake. Think of your own reputation.'

'Dick's was five times bigger than mine and yours put together.'

'That was because he signed his name to everything he did. It's all ended now. You must hold yourself in readiness to move out. You can command your own prices, and you do better work than any three of us.'

'Don't tell me how tempting it is. I'll stay here to look after Dick for a while. He's as cheerful as a bear with a sore head, but I think he likes to have me near him.'

The Nilghai said something uncomplimentary about soft-headed fools who throw away their careers for other fools. Torpenhow flushed angrily. The constant strain of attendance on Dick had worn his nerves thin.

'There remains a third fate,' said the Keneu thoughtfully. 'Consider this, and be not larger fools than is necessary. Dick is—or rather was—an able-bodied man of moderate attractions and a certain amount of audacity.'

'Oho!' said the Nilghai, who remembered an affair at Cairo. 'I begin to see.—Torp, I'm sorry.'

Torpenhow nodded forgiveness: 'You were more sorry when he cut you out, though.—Go on, Keneu.'

'I've often thought, when I've seen men die out in the desert, that if the news could be sent through the world, and the means of transport were quick enough, there would be one woman at least at each man's bedside.'

'There would be some mighty quaint revelations. Let us be grateful things are as they are,' said the Nilghai.

'Let us rather reverently consider whether Torp's three-cornered ministrations are exactly what Dick needs just now. —What do you think yourself, Torp?'

'I know they aren't. But what can I do?'

'Lay the matter before the Board. We are all Dick's friends here. You've been most in his life.'

'But I picked it up when he was off his head.'

'The greater chance of its being true. I thought we should arrive. Who is she?'

Then Torpenhow told a tale in plain words, as a special correspondent who knows how to make a verbal *précis* should tell it. The men listened without interruption.

'Is it possible that a man can come back across the years to his calf-love?' said the Keneu. 'Is it possible?'

'I give the facts. He says nothing about it now, but he sits fumbling three letters from her when he thinks I'm not looking. What am I to do?'

'Speak to him,' said the Nilghai.

'Oh yes! Write to her,—I don't know her full name, remember,—and ask her to accept him out of pity. I believe you once told Dick you were sorry for him, Nilghai. You remember what happened, eh? Go into the bedroom and suggest full confession and an appeal to this Maisie girl, whoever she is. I honestly believe he'd try to kill you; and the blindness has made him rather muscular.'

'Torpenhow's course is perfectly clear,' said the Keneu. 'He will go to Vitry-sur-Marne, which is on the Bézières-Landes Railway,—single track from Tourgas. The Prussians shelled it out in '70 because there was a poplar on the top of a hill eighteen hundred yards from the church spire. There's a squadron of cavalry quartered there,—or ought to be. Where this studio Torp spoke about may be I cannot tell. That is Torp's business. I have given him his route. He will dispassionately explain the situation to the girl, and she will come back to Dick,—the more especially because, to use Dick's words, "there is nothing but her damned obstinacy to keep them apart." '

'And they have four hundred and twenty pounds a year between 'em. Dick never lost his head for figures, even in his delirium. You haven't the shadow of an excuse for not going,' said the Nilghai.

Torpenhow looked very uncomfortable. 'But it's absurd and impossible. I can't drag her back by the hair.'

'Our business—the business for which we draw our money—is to do absurd and impossible things,—generally with no reason whatever except to amuse the public. Here we have a reason. The rest doesn't matter. I shall share these rooms with the Nilghai till Torpenhow returns. There will be a batch of unbridled "specials" coming to Town in a little while, and these will serve as their headquarters. Another reason for sending Torpenhow away. Thus Providence helps those who help others, and'—here the Keneu dropped his measured speech—'we can't have you tied by the leg to Dick when the trouble begins. It's your only chance of getting away; and Dick will be grateful.'

'He will,—worse luck! I can but go and try. I can't conceive a woman in her senses refusing Dick.'

'Talk that out with the girl. I have seen you wheedle an angry Mahdieh woman into giving you dates. This won't be a tithe as difficult. You had better not be here to-morrow after-noon, because the Nilghai and I will be in possession. It is an order. Obey.'

'Dick,' said Torpenhow next morning, 'can I do anything for you?'

'No! Leave me alone. How often must I remind you that I'm blind?'

'Nothing I could go for to fetch for to carry for to bring?'

'No. Take those infernal creaking boots of yours away.'

'Poor chap!' said Torpenhow to himself. 'I must have been sitting on his nerves lately. He wants a lighter step.' Then, aloud, 'Very well. Since you're so independent I'm going off for four or five days. Say good-bye at least. The housekeeper will look after you, and Keneu has my rooms.'

Dick's face fell. 'You won't be longer than a week at the outside? I know I'm touched in the temper, but I can't get on without you.'

'Can't you? You'll have to do without me in a little time, and you'll be glad I'm gone.'

Dick felt his way back to the big chair, and wondered what these things might mean. He did not wish to be tended by the housekeeper, and yet Torpenhow's constant tenderness jarred on him. He did not exactly know what he wanted. The dark-ness would not lift, and Maisie's unopened letters felt worn and old from much handling. He could never read them for himself as long as life endured; but Maisie might have sent him some fresh ones to play with. The Nilghai entered with a gift,—a piece of red modelling-wax. He fancied that Dick might find interest in using his hands. Dick poked and patted the stuff for a few minutes, and, 'Is it like anything in the world?' he said drearily. 'Take it away. I may get the touch of the blind in fifty years. Do you know where Torpenhow has gone?'

The Nilghai knew nothing. 'We're staying in his rooms till he comes back. Can we do anything for you?'

'I'd like to be left alone, please. Don't think I'm ungrateful, but I'm best alone.'

The Nilghai chuckled, and Dick resumed his drowsy brooding and sullen rebellion against fate. He had long since ceased to think about the work he had done in the old days, and the desire to do more work had departed from him. He was exceedingly sorry for himself, and the completeness of his tender grief soothed him. But his soul and his body cried for Maisie, —Maisie who would understand. His mind pointed out that Maisie, having her own work to do, would not care. His experience had taught him that when money was exhausted women went away, and that when a man was knocked out of the race the others trampled on him. 'Then at the least,' said Dick, in reply, 'she could use me as I used Binat,—for some sort of a study. I wouldn't ask more than to be near her again, even though I knew that another man was making love to her. Ugh! what a dog I am!'

A voice on the staircase began to sing joyfully:—

'When we go—go—go away from here,
　Our creditors will weep and they will wail,
Our absence much regretting when they find that we've been
　　getting
　Out of England by next Tuesday's Indian mail.'

Following the trampling of feet, slamming of Torpenhow's door, and the sound of voices in strenuous debate, some one squeaked, 'And see, you good fellows, I have found a new water-bottle,—firs'-class patent—eh, how you say? Open himself inside out.'

Dick sprang to his feet. He knew the voice well. 'That's Cassavetti, back from the Continent. Now I know why Torp went away. There's a row somewhere, and—I'm out of it!'

The Nilghai commanded silence in vain. 'That's for my sake,' Dick said bitterly. 'The birds are getting ready to fly, and they wouldn't tell me. I can hear Morten-Sutherland and Mackaye. Half the war-correspondents in London are there;—and I'm out of it.'

He stumbled across the landing and plunged into Torpenhow's room. He could feel that it was full of men. 'Where's the trouble?' said he. 'In the Balkans at last? Why didn't some one tell me?'

'We thought you wouldn't be interested,' said the Nilghai shamefacedly. 'It's the Sudan, as usual.'

'You lucky dogs! Let me sit here while you talk. I shan't be a skeleton at the feast.—Cassavetti, where are you? Your English is as bad as ever.'

Dick was led into a chair. He heard the rustle of the maps, and the talk swept forward, carrying him with it. Everybody spoke at once, discussing Press censorships, railway-routes, transport, water-supply, the capacities of generals,—these in language that would have horrified a trusting public,—ranting, asserting, denouncing, and laughing at the top of their voices. There was the glorious certainty of war in the Sudan at any moment. The Nilghai said so, and it was well to be in readiness. The Keneu had telegraphed to Cairo for horses; Cassavetti had stolen a perfectly inaccurate list of troops that would be ordered forward, and was reading it out amid profane interruptions, and the Keneu introduced to Dick some man unknown who would be employed as war artist by the Central Southern Syndicate. 'It's his first outing,' said the Keneu. 'Give him some tips—about riding camels.'

'Oh, those camels!' groaned Cassavetti. 'I shall learn to ride him again, and now I am so much all soft! Listen, you good fellows. I know your military arrangement very well. There will go the Royal Argalshire Sutherlanders. So it was read to me upon best authority.'

A roar of laughter interrupted him.

'Sit down,' said the Nilghai. 'The lists aren't even made out in the War Office.'

'Will there be any force at Suakin?' said a voice.

Then the outcries redoubled, and grew mixed, thus: 'How many Egyptian troops will they use?——God help the Fellaheen!——There's a railway in Plumstead marshes doing duty as a fives-court.——We shall have the Suakin-Berber line built at last.——Canadian voyageurs are too careful. Give me a half-drunk Krooman in a whale-boat.——Who commands the Desert column?——No, they never blew up the big rock at the Ghizeh bend. We shall have to be hauled up, as usual.—— Somebody tell me if there's an Indian contingent, or I'll break everybody's head.——Don't tear the map in two.—It's a war of occupation, I tell you, to connect with the African Companies in the South.——There's guinea-worm in most of the wells on that route.' Then the Nilghai, despairing of peace, bellowed like a fog-horn and beat upon the table with both hands.

'But what becomes of Torp?' said Dick, in the silence that followed.

'Torp's in abeyance just now. He's off love-making somewhere, I suppose,' said the Nilghai.

'He said he was going to stay at home,' said the Keneu.

'Is he?' said Dick with an oath. 'He won't. I'm not much good now, but if you and the Nilghai hold him down I'll engage to trample on him till he sees reason. He stay behind, indeed! He's the best of you all. There'll be some tough work by Omdurman. We shall come there to stay, this time. But I forgot. . . . I wish I were going with you.'

'So do we all, Dickie,' said the Keneu.

'And I most of all,' said the new artist of the Central Southern Syndicate. 'Could you tell me——'

'I'll give you one piece of advice,' Dick answered, moving towards the door. 'If you happen to be cut over the head in a scrimmage, don't guard. Tell the man to go on cutting. You'll find it cheapest in the end. Thanks for letting me look in.'

'There's grit in Dick,' said the Nilghai, an hour later, when the room was emptied of all save the Keneu.

'It was the sacred call of the war-trumpet. Did you notice how he answered to it? Poor fellow! Let's look at him,' said the Keneu.

The excitement of the talk had died away. Dick was sitting by the studio table, with his head on his arms, when the men came in. He did not change his position.

'It hurts,' he moaned. 'God forgive me, but it hurts cruelly; and yet, y'know, the world has a knack of spinning round all by itself. Shall I see Torp before he goes?'

'Oh yes. You'll see him,' said the Nilghai.

# CHAPTER XIII

*The sun went down an hour ago,*
*I wonder if I face towards home,*
*If I lost my way in the light of day*
*How shall I find it now night is come?*
OLD SONG.

'MAISIE, come to bed.'

'It's so hot I can't sleep. Don't worry.'

Maisie put her elbows on the window-sill and looked at the moonlight on the straight, poplar-flanked road. Summer had come upon Vitry-sur-Marne and parched it to the bone. The grass was dry-burnt in the meadows, the clay by the bank of the river was caked to brick, the roadside flowers were long since dead, and the roses in the garden hung withered on their stalks. The heat in the little low bedroom under the eaves was almost intolerable. The very moonlight on the wall of Kami's studio across the road seemed to make the night hotter, and the shadow of the big bell-handle by the closed gate cast a bar of inky black that caught Maisie's eye and annoyed her.

'Horrid thing! It should be all white,' she murmured. 'And the gate isn't in the middle of the wall, either. I never noticed that before.'

Maisie was hard to please at that hour. First, the heat of the past few weeks had worn her down; secondly, her work, and particularly the study of a female head intended to represent the Melancolia and not finished in time for the Salon, was unsatisfactory; thirdly, Kami had said as much two days before; fourthly,—but so completely fourthly that it was hardly worth thinking about,—Dick, her property, had not written to her for more than six weeks. She was angry with the heat, with Kami, and with her work, but she was exceedingly angry with Dick.

She had written to him three times,—each time proposing a fresh treatment of her Melancolia. Dick had taken no notice of these communications. She had resolved to write no more. When she returned to England in the autumn—for her pride's sake she could not return earlier—she would speak to him. She missed the Sunday afternoon conferences more than she cared to admit. All that Kami said was, *'Continuez, mademoiselle, continuez toujours,'* and he had been repeating his wearisome counsel through the hot summer, exactly like a cicala,—an old grey cicala in a black alpaca coat, white trousers, and a huge felt hat. But Dick had tramped masterfully up and down her little studio north of the cool green London park, and had said things ten times worse than *Continuez*, before he snatched the brush out of her hand and showed her where her error lay. His last letter, Maisie remembered, contained some trivial advice about not sketching in the sun or drinking water at wayside farm-houses; and he had said that not once, but three times,—as if he did not know that Maisie could take care of herself.

But what was he doing, that he could not trouble to write? A murmur of voices in the road made her lean from the window. A cavalryman of the little garrison in the town was talking to Kami's cook. The moonlight glittered on the scabbard of his sabre, which he was holding in his hand lest it should clank inopportunely. The cook's cap cast deep shadows on her face, which was close to the conscript's. He slid his arm round her waist, and there followed the sound of a kiss.

'Faugh!' said Maisie, stepping back.

'What's that?' said the red-haired girl, who was tossing uneasily outside her bed.

'Only a conscript kissing the cook,' said Maisie. 'They've gone away now.' She leaned out of the window again, and put a shawl over her nightgown to guard against chills. There was a very small night-breeze abroad, and a sun-baked rose below nodded its head as one who knew unutterable secrets. Was it possible that Dick should turn his thoughts from her work and his own and descend to the degradation of Suzanne and the conscript? He could not! The rose nodded its head and one leaf therewith. It looked like a naughty little devil scratching its ear. Dick could not, 'because,' thought Maisie, 'he is mine,—mine,—mine. He said he was. I'm sure I don't care what he does. It will only spoil his work if he does; and it will spoil mine too.'

The rose continued to nod in the futile way peculiar to flowers. There was no earthly reason why Dick should not disport himself as he chose, except that he was called by Providence, which was Maisie, to assist Maisie in her work. And her work was the preparation of pictures that went sometimes to English provincial exhibitions, as the notices in the scrap-book proved, and that were invariably rejected by the Salon when Kami was plagued into allowing her to send them up. Her work in the future, it seemed, would be the preparation of pictures on exactly similar lines which would be rejected in exactly the same way——

(The red-haired girl threshed distressfully across the sheets. 'It's too hot to sleep,' she moaned; and the interruption jarred.)

Exactly the same way. Then she would divide her years between the little studio in England and Kami's big studio at

Vitry-sur-Marne. No, she would go to another master, who should force her into the success that was her right, if patient toil and desperate endeavour gave one a right to anything. Dick had told her that he had worked ten years to understand his craft. She had worked ten years, and ten years were nothing. Dick had said that ten years were nothing,—but that was in regard to herself only. He had said—this very man who could not find time to write—that he would wait ten years for her, and that she was bound to come back to him sooner or later. He had said this in the absurd letter about sunstroke and diphtheria; and then he had stopped writing. He was wandering up and down moonlit streets, kissing cooks. She would like to lecture him now,—not in her nightgown, of course, but properly dressed, severely and from a height. Yet if he was kissing other girls he certainly would not care whether she lectured him or not. He would laugh at her. Very good. She would go back to her studio and prepare pictures that went, etc. etc. The mill-wheel of thought swung round slowly, that no section of it might be slurred over, and the red-haired girl tossed and turned behind her.

Maisie put her chin in her hands and decided that there could be no doubt whatever of the villainy of Dick. To justify herself, she began, unwomanly, to weigh the evidence. There was a boy, and he had said he loved her. And he kissed her— kissed her on the cheek—by a yellow sea-poppy that nodded its head exactly like the maddening dry rose in the garden. Then there was an interval, and men had told her that they loved her—just when she was busiest with her work. Then the boy came back, and at their very second meeting had told her that he loved her. Then he had—— But there was no end to the things he had done. He had given her his time and his powers. He had spoken to her of Art, housekeeping, technique, teacups, the abuse of pickles as a stimulant,—that was rude,—sable-hair brushes,—he had given her the best in her stock,—she used them daily; he had given her advice that she had profited by, and now and again—a look. Such a look! The look of a beaten hound waiting for the word to crawl to his mistress's feet. In return she had given him nothing whatever, except—here she brushed her mouth against the openwork sleeve of her nightgown—the privilege of kissing her once. And on the mouth, too. Disgraceful! Was that not enough, and more than enough? and if it was not, had he not cancelled the debt by not writing and—probably kissing other girls?

'Maisie, you'll catch a chill. Do go and lie down,' said the wearied voice of her companion. 'I can't sleep a wink with you at the window.'

Maisie shrugged her shoulders and did not answer. She was reflecting on the meannesses of Dick, and on other meannesses with which he had nothing to do. The remorseless moonlight would not let her sleep. It lay on the skylight of the studio across the road in cold silver; she stared at it intently, and her thoughts began to slide one into the other. The shadow of the big bell-handle in the wall grew short, lengthened again, and faded out as the moon went down behind the pasture and a hare came limping home across the road. Then the dawn-wind washed through the upland grasses, and brought coolness with it, and the cattle lowed by the drought-shrunk river. Maisie's head fell forward on the window-sill, and the tangle of black hair covered her arms.

'Maisie, wake up. You'll catch a chill.'

'Yes, dear; yes, dear.' She staggered to her bed like a wearied child, and as she buried her face in the pillows she muttered, 'I think—I think. . . . But he ought to have written.'

Day brought the routine of the studio, the smell of paint and turpentine, and the monotonous wisdom of Kami, who was a leaden artist, but a golden teacher if the pupil were only in sympathy with him. Maisie was not in sympathy that day, and she waited impatiently for the end of the work. She knew when it was coming; for Kami would gather his black alpaca coat into a bunch behind him, and, with faded blue eyes that saw neither pupils nor canvas, look back into the past to recall the history of one Binat. 'You have all done not so badly,' he would say. 'But you shall remember that it is not enough to have the method, and the art, and the power, nor even that which is touch, but you shall have also the conviction that nails the work to the wall. Of the so many I have taught,'—here the students would begin to unfix drawing-pins or get their tubes together,—'the very so many that I have taught, the best was Binat. All that comes of the study and the work and the knowledge was to him even when he came. After he left me he should have done all that could be done with the colour, the form, and the knowledge. Only, he had not the conviction. So to-day I hear no more of Binat,—the best of my pupils,—and that is long ago. So to-day, too, you will be glad to hear no more of me. *Continuez, mesdemoiselles,* and, above all, with conviction.'

He went into the garden to smoke and mourn over the lost Binat as the pupils dispersed to their several cottages or loitered in the studio to make plans for the cool of the afternoon.

Maisie looked at her very unhappy Melancolia, restrained a desire to grimace before it, and was hurrying across the road to write a letter to Dick, when she was aware of a large man on a white troop-horse. How Torpenhow had managed in the course of twenty hours to find his way to the hearts of the cavalry officers in quarters at Vitry-sur-Marne, to discuss with them the certainty of a glorious revenge for France, to reduce the Colonel to tears of pure affability, and to borrow the best horse in the squadron for the journey to Kami's studio, is a mystery that only special correspondents can unravel.

'I beg your pardon,' said he. 'It seems an absurd question to ask, but the fact is that I don't know her by any other name: Is there any young lady here that is called Maisie?'

'I am Maisie,' was the answer from the depths of a great sun-hat.

'I ought to introduce myself,' he said, as the horse capered in the blinding white dust. 'My name is Torpenhow. Dick Heldar is my best friend, and—and—the fact is that he has gone blind.'

'Blind!' said Maisie stupidly. 'He can't be blind.'

'He has been stone-blind for nearly two months.'

Maisie lifted up her face, and it was pearly white. 'No! No! Not blind! I won't have him blind!'

'Would you care to see for yourself?' said Torpenhow.

'Now—at once?'

'Oh no! The Paris train doesn't go through this place till eight to-night. There will be ample time.'

'Did Mr. Heldar send you to me?'

'Certainly not. Dick wouldn't do that sort of thing. He's sitting in his studio, turning over some letters that he can't read because he's blind.'

There was a sound of choking from the sun-hat. Maisie bowed her head and went into the cottage, where the red-haired girl was on a sofa, complaining of a headache.

'Dick's blind!' said Maisie, taking her breath quickly as she steadied herself against a chair-back. 'My Dick's blind!'

'What?' The girl was on the sofa no longer.

'A man has come from England to tell me. He hasn't written to me for six weeks.'

'Are you going to him?'

'I must think.'

'Think! *I* should go back to London and see him, and I should kiss his eyes, and kiss them and kiss them until they got well again! If you don't go I shall. Oh, what am I talking about? You wicked little idiot! Go to him at once. Go!'

Torpenhow's neck was blistering, but he preserved a smile of infinite patience as Maisie appeared bare-headed in the sunshine.

'I am coming,' said she, her eyes on the ground.

'You will be at Vitry Station, then, at seven this evening.' This was an order delivered by one who was used to being obeyed. Maisie said nothing, but she felt grateful that there was no chance of disputing with this big man who took everything for granted and managed a squealing horse with one hand. She returned to the red-haired girl, who was weeping bitterly, and between tears, kisses,—very few of those,—menthol, packing, and an interview with Kami, the sultry afternoon wore away. Thought might come afterwards. Her present duty was to go to Dick,—Dick who owned the wondrous friend and sat in the dark playing with her unopened letters.

'But what will you do?' she said to her companion.

'I? Oh, I shall stay here and—finish your Melancolia,' she said, smiling pitifully. 'Write to me afterwards.'

That night there ran a legend through Vitry-sur-Marne of a mad Englishman, doubtless suffering from sunstroke, who had drunk all the officers of the garrison under the table, had borrowed a horse from the lines, and had then and there eloped, after the English custom, with one of those more than mad English girls who drew pictures down there under the care of that good Monsieur Kami.

'They are very droll,' said Suzanne to the conscript in the moonlight by the studio wall. 'She walked always with those

*179*

big eyes that saw nothing, and yet she kisses me on both cheeks as though she were my sister, and gives me—see—ten francs!'

The conscript levied a contribution on both gifts; for he prided himself on being a good soldier.

Torpenhow spoke very little to Maisie during the journey to Calais; but he was careful to attend to all her wants, to get her a compartment entirely to herself, and to leave her alone. He was amazed at the ease with which the matter had been accomplished.

'The safest thing would be to let her think things out. By Dick's showing,—when he was off his head,—she must have ordered him about very thoroughly. Wonder how she likes being under orders.'

Maisie never told. She sat in the empty compartment often with her eyes shut, that she might realise the sensation of blindness. It was an order that she should return to London swiftly, and she found herself at last almost beginning to enjoy the situation. This was better than looking after luggage and a red-haired friend who never took any interest in her sur-roundings. But there appeared to be a feeling in the air that she, Maisie,—of all people,—was in disgrace. Therefore she justified her conduct to herself with great success, till Tor-penhow came up to her on the steamer, and without preface began to tell the story of Dick's blindness, suppressing a few details, but dwelling at length on the miseries of delirium. He stopped before he reached the end, as though he had lost interest in the subject, and went forward to smoke. Maisie was furious with him and with herself.

She was hurried on from Dover to London almost before she could ask for breakfast, and—she was past any feeling of indignation now—was bidden curtly to wait in a hall at the foot of some lead-covered stairs while Torpenhow went up to make inquiries. Again the knowledge that she was being treated like a naughty little girl made her pale cheeks flame. It was all Dick's fault for being so stupid as to go blind.

Torpenhow led her up to a shut door, which he opened very softly. Dick was sitting by the window, with his chin on his chest. There were three envelopes in his hand, and he turned them over and over. The big man who gave orders was no longer by her side, and the studio door snapped behind her.

Dick thrust the letters into his pocket as he heard the sound. 'Hullo, Torp! Is that you? I've been so lonely.'

His voice had taken the peculiar flatness of the blind. Maisie pressed herself up into a corner of the room. Her heart was beating furiously, and she put one hand on her breast to keep it quiet. Dick was staring directly at her, and she realised for the first time that he was blind. Shutting her eyes in a railway-carriage to open them when she pleased was child's play. This man was blind though his eyes were wide open.

'Torp, is that you? They said you were coming.' Dick looked puzzled and a little irritated at the silence.

'No: it's only me,' was the answer, in a strained little whisper. Maisie could hardly move her lips.

'H'm!' said Dick composedly, without moving. 'This is a new phenomenon. Darkness I'm getting used to; but I object to hearing voices.'

Was he mad, then, as well as blind, that he talked to himself? Maisie's heart beat more wildly, and she breathed in gasps. Dick rose and began to feel his way across the room, touching each table and chair as he passed. Once he caught his foot on a rug, and swore, dropping on his knees to feel what the obstruction might be. Maisie remembered him walking in the Park as though all the earth belonged to him, tramping up and down her studio two months ago, and flying up the gangway of the Channel steamer. The beating of her heart was making her sick, and Dick was coming nearer, guided by the sound of her breathing. She put out a hand mechanically to ward him off or to draw him to herself, she did not know which. It touched his chest, and he stepped back as though he had been shot.

'It's Maisie!' said he, with a dry sob. 'What are you doing here?'

'I came—I came—to see you, please.'

Dick's lips closed firmly.

'Won't you sit down, then? You see, I've had some bother with my eyes, and——'

'I know. I know. Why didn't you tell me?'

'I couldn't write.'

'You might have told Mr. Torpenhow.'

'What has he to do with my affairs?'

'He—he brought me from Vitry-sur-Marne. He thought I ought to see you.'

'Why, what has happened? Can I do anything for you? No, I can't. I forgot.'

'Oh, Dick, I'm so sorry! I've come to tell you, and—— Let me take you back to your chair.'

'Don't! I'm not a child. You only do that out of pity. I never meant to tell you anything about it. I'm no good now. I'm down and done for. Let me alone!'

He groped back to his chair, his chest labouring as he sat down.

Maisie watched him, and the fear went out of her heart, to be followed by a very bitter shame. He had spoken a truth that had been hidden from the girl through every step of the impetuous flight to London; for he was, indeed, down and done for—masterful no longer, but rather a little abject;

neither an artist stronger than she, nor a man to be looked up to—only some blind one that sat in a chair and seemed on the point of crying. She was immensely and unfeignedly sorry for him—more sorry than she had ever been for any one in her life, but not sorry enough to deny his words. So she stood still and felt ashamed and a little hurt, because she had honestly intended that her journey should end triumphantly; and now she was only filled with pity most startlingly distinct from love.

'Well?' said Dick, his face steadily turned away. 'I never meant to worry you any more. What's the matter?'

He was conscious that Maisie was catching her breath, but was as unprepared as herself for the torrent of emotion that followed. People who cannot cry easily weep unrestrainedly when the fountains of the great deep are broken up. She had dropped into a chair and was sobbing with her face hidden in her hands.

'I can't—I can't!' she cried desperately. 'Indeed, I can't. It isn't my fault. I'm so sorry. Oh, Dickie, I'm so sorry.'

Dick's shoulders straightened again, for the words lashed like a whip. Still the sobbing continued. It is not good to realise that you have failed in the hour of trial or flinched before the mere possibility of making sacrifices.

'I do despise myself—indeed I do. But I can't. Oh, Dickie, you wouldn't ask me—would you?' wailed Maisie.

She looked up for a minute, and by chance it happened that Dick's eyes fell on hers. The unshaven face was very white and set, and the lips were trying to force themselves into a smile. But it was the worn-out eyes that Maisie feared. Her Dick had gone blind and left in his place some one that she could hardly recognise till he spoke.

'Who is asking you to do anything, Maisie? I told you how

it would be. What's the use of worrying? For pity's sake don't cry like that. It isn't worth it.'

'You don't know how I hate myself. Oh, Dick, help me—help me!' The passion of tears had grown beyond her control and was beginning to alarm the man. He stumbled forward and put his arm round her, and her head fell on his shoulder.

'Hush, dear, hush! Don't cry. You're quite right, and you've nothing to reproach yourself with—you never had. You're only a little upset by the journey, and I don't suppose you've had any breakfast. What a brute Torp was to bring you over.'

'I wanted to come. I did indeed!' she protested.

'Very well. And now you've come and seen, and I'm—immensely grateful. When you're better you shall go away and get something to eat. What sort of a passage did you have coming over?'

Maisie was crying more subduedly, for the first time in her life glad that she had something to lean against. Dick patted her on the shoulder tenderly but clumsily, for he was not quite sure where her shoulder might be.

She drew herself out of his arms at last and waited, trembling and most unhappy. He had felt his way to the window to put the width of the room between them, and to quiet a little the tumult in his heart.

'Are you better now?' he said.

'Yes, but—don't you hate me?'

'I hate you? My God! I?'

'Isn't—isn't there anything I could do for you, then? I'll stay here in England to do it, if you like. Perhaps I could come and see you sometimes.'

'I think not, dear. It would be kindest not to see me any more, please. I don't want to seem rude, but—don't you think —perhaps you had almost better go now.'

He was conscious that he could not bear himself as a man if the strain continued much longer.

'I don't deserve anything else. I'll go, Dick. Oh, I'm so miserable.'

'Nonsense. You've nothing to worry about; I'd tell you if you had. Wait a moment, dear. I've got something to give you first. I meant it for you ever since this little trouble began. It's my Melancolia; she was a beauty when I last saw her. You can keep her for me, and if ever you're poor you can sell her. She's worth a few hundred in any state of the market.' He groped among his canvases. 'She's framed in black. Is this a black frame that I have my hand on? There she is. What do you think of her?'

He turned a scarred, formless muddle of paint towards Maisie, and the eyes strained as though they would catch her wonder and surprise. One thing and one thing only could she do for him.

'Well?'

The voice was fuller and more rounded, because the man knew he was speaking of his best work. Maisie looked at the blur, and a lunatic desire to laugh caught her by the throat. But for Dick's sake—whatever this mad blankness might mean —she must make no sign. Her voice choked with hard-held tears as she answered, still gazing on the wreck:

'Oh, Dick, it *is* good!'

He heard the little hysterical gulp and took it for tribute. 'Won't you have it, then? I'll send it over to your house if you will.'

'I? Oh yes—thank you. Ha! ha!' if she did not fly at once the laughter that was worse than tears would kill her. She turned and ran, choking and blinded, down the staircases that were empty of life, to take refuge in a cab and go to her house across the Park. There she sat down in the almost dismantled drawing-room and thought of Dick in his blindness, useless till the end of life, and of herself in her own eyes. Behind the sorrow, the shame, and the humiliation, lay fear of the cold wrath of the red-haired girl when Maisie should return. Maisie had never feared her companion before. Not until she found herself saying, 'Well, he never asked me,' did she realise her scorn of herself.

And that is the end of Maisie.

For Dick was reserved more searching torment. He could not realise at first that Maisie, whom he had ordered to go, had left him without a word of farewell. He was savagely angry against Torpenhow, who had brought upon him this humiliation and troubled his miserable peace. Then his dark hour came, and he was alone with himself and his desires to get what help he could from the darkness. The Queen could do no wrong, but in following her right, so far as it served her work, she had wounded her one subject more than his own brain would let him know.

'It's all I had and I've lost it,' he said, as soon as the misery permitted clear thinking. 'And Torp will think that he has been so infernally clever that I shan't have the heart to tell him. I must think this out quietly.'

'Hullo!' said Torpenhow, entering the studio after Dick had enjoyed two hours of thought. 'I'm back. Are you feeling any better?'

'Torp, I don't know what to say. Come here.' Dick coughed huskily, wondering, indeed, what he should say, and how to say it temperately.

'What's the need for saying anything? Get up and tramp.' Torpenhow was perfectly satisfied.

They walked up and down as of custom, Torpenhow's hand on Dick's shoulder, and Dick buried in his own thoughts.

'How in the world did you find it all out?' said Dick at last.

'You shouldn't go off your head if you want to keep secrets, Dickie. It was absolutely impertinent on my part; but if you'd seen me rocketing about on a half-trained French troop-horse under a blazing sun you'd have laughed. There will be a charivari in my rooms to-night. Seven other devils——'

'I know—the row in the Southern Sudan. I surprised their councils the other day, and it made me unhappy. Have you fixed your flint to go? Who d'you work for?'

'Haven't signed any contracts yet. I wanted to see how your business would turn out.'

'Would you have stayed with me, then, if—things had gone wrong?' He put his question cautiously.

'Don't ask me too much. I'm only a man.'

'You've tried to be an angel very successfully.'

'Oh ye—es! . . . Well, do you attend the function to-night? We shall be half screwed before the morning. All the men believe the war's a certainty.'

'I don't think I will, old man, if it's all the same to you. I'll stay quiet here.'

'And meditate? I don't blame you. You deserve a good time if ever a man did.'

That night there was tumult on the stairs. The correspondents poured in from theatre, dinner, and music-hall to Torpenhow's room that they might discuss their plan of campaign in the event of military operations being a certainty. Torpenhow, the Keneu, and the Nilghai had bidden all the men they had worked with to the orgy; and Mr. Beeton, the housekeeper, declared that never before in his checkered experience had he seen quite such a fancy lot of gentlemen. They waked the chambers with shoutings and song; and the elder men were quite as bad as the younger. For the chances of war were in front of them, and all knew what those meant.

Sitting in his own room a little perplexed by the noise across the landing, Dick suddenly began to laugh to himself.

'When one comes to think of it the situation is intensely comic. Maisie's quite right—poor little thing. I didn't know she could cry like that before; but now I know what Torp thinks, I'm sure he'd be quite fool enough to stay at home and try to console me—if he knew. Besides, it isn't nice to own that you've been thrown over like a broken chair. I must carry this business through alone—as usual. If there isn't a war, and Torp finds out, I shall look foolish, that's all. If there is a war I mustn't interfere with another man's chances. Business is business, and I want to be alone—I want to be alone. What a row they're making!'

Somebody hammered at the studio door.

'Come out and frolic, Dickie,' said the Nilghai.

'I should like to, but I can't. I'm not feeling frolicsome.'

'Then I'll tell the boys and they'll draw you like a badger.'

'Please not, old man. On my word, I'd sooner be left alone just now.'

'Very good. Can we send anything in to you? Fizz, for instance. Cassavetti is beginning to sing songs of the Sunny South already.'

For one minute Dick considered the proposition seriously.

'No, thanks. I've a headache already.'

'Virtuous child. That's the effect of emotion on the young. All my congratulations, Dick. I also was concerned in the conspiracy for your welfare.'

'Go to the devil and—oh, send Binkie in here.'

The little dog entered on elastic feet, riotous from having been made much of all the evening. He had helped to sing the choruses; but scarcely inside the studio he realised that this was no place for tail-wagging, and settled himself on Dick's

*188*

lap till it was bedtime. Then he went to bed with Dick, who counted every hour as it struck, and rose in the morning with a painfully clear head to receive Torpenhow's more formal congratulations and a particular account of the last night's revels.

'You aren't looking very happy for a newly-accepted man,' said Torpenhow.

'Never mind that—it's my own affair, and I'm all right. Do you really go?'

'Yes. With the old Central Southern as usual. They wired and I accepted on better terms than before.'

'When do you start?'

'The day after to-morrow—for Brindisi.'

'Thank God.' Dick spoke from the bottom of his heart.

'Well, that's not a pretty way of saying you're glad to get rid of me. But men in your condition are allowed to be selfish.'

'I didn't mean that. Will you get a hundred pounds cashed for me before you leave?'

'That's a slender amount for housekeeping, isn't it?'

'Oh, it's only for—marriage expenses.'

Torpenhow brought him the money, counted it out in fives and tens, and carefully put it away in the writing-table.

'Now I suppose I shall have to listen to his ravings about his girl until I go. Heaven send us patience with a man in love!' said he to himself.

But never a word did Dick say of Maisie or marriage. He hung in the doorway of Torpenhow's room when the latter was packing, and asked innumerable questions about the coming campaign, till Torpenhow began to feel annoyed.

'You're a secretive animal, Dickie, and you consume your own smoke, don't you?' he said on the last evening.

'I—I suppose so. By the way, how long do you think this war will last?'

'Days, weeks, or months. One can never tell. It may go on for years.'

'I wish I were going.'

'Good heavens! You're the most unaccountable creature! Hasn't it occurred to you that you're going to be married— thanks to me?'

'Of course, yes. I'm going to be married—so I am. Going to be married. I'm awfully grateful to you. Haven't I told you that?'

'You might be going to be hanged by the look of you,' said Torpenhow.

And the next day Torpenhow bade him good-bye and left him to the loneliness he had so much desired.

# CHAPTER XIV

*Yet at the last, ere our spearmen had found him,*
*Yet at the last, ere a sword-thrust could save,*
*Yet at the last, with his masters around him,*
*He of the Faith spoke as master to slave;*
*Yet at the last, tho' the Kafirs had maimed him,*
*Broken by bondage and wrecked by the reiver,—*
*Yet at the last, tho' the darkness had claimed him,*
*He called upon Allah, and died a believer.*

KIZILBASHI.

'BEG YOUR PARDON, Mr. Heldar, but—but isn't nothin' going to happen?' said Mr. Beeton.

'No!' Dick had just waked to another morning of blank despair and his temper was of the shortest.

' 'Taint my regular business, o' course, sir; and what I say is, "Mind your own business and let other people mind theirs"; but just before Mr. Torpenhow went away he give me to understand, like, that you might be moving into a house of your own, so to speak—a sort of house with rooms upstairs and downstairs where you'd be better attended to, though I try to act just by all our tenants. Don't I?'

'Ah! That must have been a mad-house. I shan't trouble you to take me there yet. Get me my breakfast, please, and leave me alone.'

'I hope I haven't done anything wrong, sir, but you know, I hope, that as far as a man can I tries to do the proper thing by all the gentlemen in chambers—and more particular those whose lot is hard—such as you, for instance, Mr. Heldar. You likes soft-roe bloater, don't you? Soft-roe bloaters is scarcer than hard-roe, but what I says is, "never mind a little extra trouble so long as you gives satisfaction to the tenants." '

Mr. Beeton withdrew and left Dick to himself. Torpenhow had been long away; there was no more rioting in the chambers, and Dick had settled down to his new life, which he was weak enough to consider nothing better than death.

It is hard to live alone in the dark, confusing the day and night; dropping to sleep through sheer weariness at mid-day, and rising restless in the chill of the dawn. At first Dick, on his awakenings, would grope along the corridors of the chambers till he heard some one snore. Then he would know that the day had not yet come, and return wearily to his bedroom. Later he learned not to stir till there was a noise and movement in the house and Mr. Beeton advised him to get up. Once dressed—and dressing, now that Torpenhow was away, was a lengthy business, because collars, ties, and the like, hid themselves in far corners of the room, and search meant head-beating against chairs and trunks—once dressed, there was nothing whatever to do except to sit still and brood till the three daily meals came. Centuries separated breakfast from lunch, and lunch from dinner, and though a man prayed for hundreds of years that his mind might be taken from him, God would never hear. Rather the mind was quickened and the revolting thoughts ground against each other as millstones grind when there is no corn between; and yet the brain would not wear out and give him rest. It continued to think, at length, with imagery and all manner of reminiscences. It recalled Maisie and past success, reckless travels by land and sea, the glory of doing work and feeling that it was good, and suggested all that might have happened had his eyes only been faithful to their duty. When thinking ceased through sheer weariness, there poured into Dick's soul tide on tide of over-whelming, purposeless fear—dread of starvation always, terror lest the unseen ceiling should crash down upon him, fear of fire in the chambers and a louse's death in red flame, and agonies of fiercer horror that had nothing to do with any fear of death. Then Dick bowed his head, and clutching the arms of his chair fought with his sweating self till the tinkle of plates told him that something to eat was being set before him.

Mr. Beeton would bring the meal when he had time to spare, and Dick learned to hang upon his speech, which dealt with badly-fitted gas-plugs, waste-pipes out of repair, little tricks for driving picture-nails into walls, and the sins of the charwoman or the housemaids. In the lack of better things the small gossip of a servants' hall becomes immensely interesting, and the screwing of a washer on a tap an event to be talked over for days.

Once or twice a week, too, Mr. Beeton would take Dick out with him when he went marketing in the morning to haggle with tradesmen over fish, lamp-wicks, mustard, tapioca, and so forth, while Dick rested his weight first on one foot and then on the other, and played aimlessly with the tins and string-ball on the counter. Then they would, perhaps, meet one of Mr. Beeton's friends, and Dick, standing aside a little, would hold his peace till Mr. Beeton was willing to go on again.

The life did not increase his self-respect. He abandoned shaving as a dangerous exercise, and being shaved in a barber's shop meant exposure of his infirmity. He could not see that his clothes were properly brushed, and since he had never taken any care of his personal appearance he became every known variety of sloven. A blind man cannot eat with

cleanliness till he has been some months used to the darkness.
If he demand attendance and grow angry at the want of it, he
must assert himself and stand upright. Then the meanest
menial can see that he is blind and, therefore, of no consequence. A wise man will keep his eyes on the floor and sit
still. For amusement he may pick coal lump by lump out of
the scuttle with the tongs, and pile it in a little heap in the
fender, keeping count of the lumps, which must all be put
back again, one by one and very carefully. He may set himself sums if he cares to work them out; he may talk to himself or to the cat if she chooses to visit him; and if his trade has
been that of an artist, he may sketch in the air with his forefinger; but that is too much like drawing a pig with the eyes
shut. He may go to his bookshelves and count his books, ranging them in order of their size; or to his wardrobe and count
his shirts, laying them in piles of two or three on the bed, as
they suffer from frayed cuffs or lost buttons. Even this entertainment wearies after a time; and all the times are very, very
long.

Dick was allowed to sort a tool-chest where Mr. Beeton kept
hammers, taps and nuts, lengths of gas-pipes, oil-bottles, and
string.

'If I don't have everything just where I know where to look
for it, why, then, I can't find anything when I do want it.
You've no idea, sir, the amount of little things that these
chambers uses up,' said Mr. Beeton. Fumbling at the handle
of the door as he went out: 'It's hard on you, sir. I *do* think
it's hard on you. Ain't you going to do anything, sir?'

'I'll pay my rent and messing. Isn't that enough?'

'I wasn't doubting for a moment that you couldn't pay your
way, sir; but I 'ave often said to my wife, "It's 'ard on 'im
because it isn't as if he was an old man, nor yet a middle-aged

one, but quite a young gentleman. *That*'s where it comes so
'ard." '

'I suppose so,' said Dick absently. This particular nerve
through long battering had ceased to feel—much.

'I was thinking,' continued Mr. Beeton, still making as if
to go, 'that you might like to hear my boy Alf read you the
papers sometimes of an evening. He do read beautiful, seeing
he's only nine.'

'I should be very grateful,' said Dick. 'Only let me make it
worth his while.'

'We wasn't thinking of *that,* sir, but of course it's in your
own 'ands; but only to 'ear Alf sing "A Boy's best Friend is 'is
Mother!" Ah!'

'I'll hear him sing that too. Let him come in this evening
with the newspapers.'

Alf was not a nice child, being puffed up with many school-
board certificates for good conduct, and inordinately proud of
his singing. Mr. Beeton remained, beaming, while the child
wailed his way through a song of some eight eight-line verses
in the usual whine of the young Cockney, and, after compliments, left him to read Dick the foreign telegrams. Ten minutes later Alf returned to his parents rather pale and scared.

' 'E said 'e couldn't stand it no more,' he explained.

'He never said you read badly, Alf?' Mrs. Beeton spoke.

'No. 'E said I read beautiful. Said 'e never 'eard any one
read like that, but 'e said 'e couldn't abide the stuff in the
papers.'

'P'raps he's lost some money in the Stocks. Were you readin'
him about Stocks, Alf?'

'No. It was all about fightin' out there where the soldiers is
gone—a great long piece with all the lines close together and
very hard words in it. 'E give me 'arf a crown because I read

so well. And 'e says the next time there's anything 'e wants read 'e'll send for me.'

'That's good hearing, but I do think for all the half-crown —put it into the kicking-donkey money-box, Alf, and let me see you do it—he might have kept you longer. Why, he couldn't have begun to understand how beautiful you read.'

'He's best left to hisself—gentlemen always are when they're downhearted,' said Mr. Beeton.

Alf's rigorously limited powers of comprehending Torpenhow's special correspondence had waked the devil of unrest in Dick. He could hear, through the boy's nasal chant, the camels grunting in the squares behind the soldiers outside Suakin; could hear the men swearing and chaffing across the cooking-pots, and could smell the acrid wood-smoke as it drifted over the camp before the wind of the desert.

That night he prayed to God that his mind might be taken from him, offering for proof that he was worthy of this favour the fact that he had not shot himself long ago. That prayer was not answered, and indeed Dick knew in his heart of hearts that only a lingering sense of humour and no special virtue had kept him alive. Suicide, he had persuaded himself, would be a ludicrous insult to the gravity of the situation as well as a weak-kneed confession of fear.

'Just for the fun of the thing,' he said to the cat, who had taken Binkie's place in his establishment, 'I should like to know how long this is going to last. I can live for a year on the hundred pounds Torp cashed for me. I must have two or three thousand at least at the Bank—twenty or thirty years more provided for, that is to say. Then I fall back on my hundred and twenty a year, which will be more by that time. Let's consider. Twenty-five—thirty-five—a man's in his prime then, they say—forty-five—a middle-aged man just entering politics —fifty-five—"died at the comparatively early age of fifty-five," according to the newspapers. Bah! How these Christians funk death! Sixty-five—we're only getting on in years. Seventy-five is just possible though. Great Hell, cat O! fifty years more of solitary confinement in the dark! You'll die, and Beeton will die, and Torp will die, and Mai—everybody else will die, but I shall be alive and kicking with nothing to do. I'm very sorry for myself. I should like some one else to be sorry for me. Evidently I'm not going mad before I die, but the pain's just as bad as ever. Some day when you're vivisected, cat O! they'll tie you down on a little table and cut you open—but don't be afraid; they'll take precious good care that you don't die. You'll live, and you'll be very sorry then that you weren't sorry for me. Perhaps Torp will come back or . . . I wish I could go to Torp and the Nilghai, even though I were in their way.'

Pussy left the room before the speech was ended, and Alf, as he entered, found Dick addressing the empty hearth-rug.

'There's a letter for you, sir,' he said. 'Perhaps you'd like me to read it.'

'Lend it to me for a minute and I'll tell you.'

The outstretched hand shook just a little and the voice was not over-steady. It was within the limits of human possibility that—that was no letter from Maisie. He knew the heft of three closed envelopes only too well. It was a foolish hope that the girl should write to him, for he did not realise that there is a wrong which admits of no reparation though the evildoer may with tears and the heart's best love strive to mend all. It is best to forget that wrong whether it be caused or endured, since it is as remediless as bad work once put forward.

'Read it, then,' said Dick, and Alf began intoning according to the rules of the Board School:—

"I could have given you love, I could have given you loyalty, such as you never dreamed of. Do you suppose I cared *what* you were? But you chose to whistle everything down the wind for nothing. My only excuse for you is that you are so young."

'That's all,' he said, returning the paper to be dropped into the fire.

'What was in the letter?' asked Mrs. Beeton when Alf returned.

'I don't know. I think it was a circular or a tract about not whistlin' at everything when you're young.'

'I must have stepped on something when I was alive and walking about, and it has bounced up and hit me. God help it, whatever it is—unless it was all a joke. But I don't know any one who'd take the trouble to play a joke on me. . . . Love and loyalty for nothing. It sounds tempting enough. I wonder whether I have lost anything really?'

Dick considered for a long time, but could not remember when or how he had put himself in the way of winning these trifles at a woman's hands.

Still, the letter as touching on matters that he preferred not to think about stung him into a fit of frenzy that lasted for a day and night. When his heart was so full of despair that it would hold no more, body and soul together seemed to be dropping without check through the darkness. Then came fear of darkness and desperate attempts to reach the light again. But there was no light to be reached. When that agony had left him sweating and breathless, the downward flight would recommence till the gathering torture of it spurred him into another fight as hopeless as the first. Followed some few minutes of sleep in which he dreamed that he saw. Then the procession of events would repeat itself till he was utterly worn out, and the brain took up its everlasting consideration of Maisie and might-have-beens.

At the end of everything Mr. Beeton came to his room and volunteered to take him out. 'Not marketing this time, but we'll go into the Parks if you like.'

'Be damned if I do,' quoth Dick. 'Keep to the streets and walk up and down. I like to hear the people round me.'

This was not altogether true. The blind in the first stages of their infirmity dislike those who can move with a free stride and unlifted arms—but Dick had no earthly desire to go to the Parks. Once and only once since Maisie had shut the door he had gone there under Alf's charge. Alf forgot him and fished for minnows in the Serpentine with some companions. After half an hour's waiting Dick, almost weeping with rage and wrath, caught a passer-by who introduced him to a friendly policeman, who led him to a four-wheeler opposite the Albert Hall. He never told Mr. Beeton of Alf's forgetfulness, but . . . this was not the manner in which he was used to walk the Parks aforetime.

'What streets would you like to walk down, then?' said Mr. Beeton sympathetically. His own ideas of a riotous holiday meant picnicking on the grass of the Green Park with his family, and half-a-dozen paper bags full of food.

'Keep to the river,' said Dick, and they kept to the river, and the rush of it was in his ears till they came to Blackfriars Bridge and struck thence on to the Waterloo Road, Mr. Beeton explaining the beauties of the scenery as he went on.

'And walking on the other side of the pavement,' said he, 'unless I'm much mistaken, is the young woman that used to come to your rooms to be drawed. I never forgets a face and I never remembers a name, except paying tenants, o' course!'

'Stop her,' said Dick. 'It's Bessie Broke. Tell her I'd like to speak to her again. Quick, man!'

Mr. Beeton crossed the road under the noses of the omnibuses and arrested Bessie then on her way northward. She recognised him as the man in authority who used to glare at her when she passed up Dick's staircase, and her first impulse was to run.

'Wasn't you Mr. Heldar's model?' said Mr. Beeton, planting himself in front of her. 'You was. He's on the other side of the road and he'd like to see you.'

'Why?' said Bessie faintly. She remembered—indeed had never for long forgotten—an affair connected with a newly-finished picture.

'Because he has asked me to do so, and because he's most particular blind.'

'Drunk?'

'No. 'Orspital blind. He can't see. That's him over there.'

Dick was leaning against the parapet of the bridge as Mr. Beeton pointed him out—a stub-bearded bowed creature wearing a dirty magenta-coloured neckcloth outside an unbrushed coat. There was nothing to fear from such an one. Even if he chased her, Bessie thought, he could not follow far. She crossed over and Dick's face lighted up. It was long since a woman of any kind had taken the trouble to speak to him.

'I hope you're well, Mr. Heldar,' said Bessie, a little puzzled. Mr. Beeton stood by with the air of an ambassador and breathed responsibly.

'I'm very well indeed, and, by Jove! I'm glad to see—hear you, I mean, Bess. You never thought it worth while to turn up and see us again after you got your money. I don't know why you should. Are you going anywhere in particular just now?'

'I was going for a walk,' said Bessie.

'Not the old business?' Dick spoke under his breath.

'Lor', no! I've paid my premium'—Bessie was very proud of that word—'for a barmaid, sleeping in, and I'm at the bar now quite respectable. Indeed I am.'

Mr. Beeton had no special reason to believe in the loftiness of human nature. Therefore he dissolved himself like a mist and returned to his gas-plugs without a word of apology. Bessie watched the flight with a certain uneasiness; but so long as Dick appeared to be ignorant of the harm that had been done to him. . . .

'It's hard work pulling the beer-handles,' she went on, 'and they've got one of them penny-in-the-slot cash-machines, so if you get wrong by a penny at the end of the day—but then I don't believe the machinery is right. Do you?'

'I've only seen it work. Mr. Beeton?'

'He's gone.'

'I'm afraid I must ask you to help me home, then. I'll make it worth your while. You see?' The sightless eyes turned towards her and Bessie saw.

'It isn't taking you out of your way?' he said hesitatingly. 'I can ask a policeman if it is.'

'Not at all. I come on at seven and I'm off at four. That's easy hours.'

'Good God!—but I'm on all the time. I wish I had some work to do too. Let's go home, Bess.'

He turned and cannoned into a man on the sidewalk, recoiling with an oath. Bessie took his arm and said nothing— as she had said nothing when he had ordered her to turn her face a little more to the light. They walked for some time in silence, the girl steering him deftly through the crowd.

'And where's—where's Mr. Torpenhow?' she inquired at last.

'He has gone away to the desert.'

'Where's that?'

Dick pointed to the right. 'East—out of the mouth of the river,' said he. 'Then west, then south, and then east again, all along the underside of Europe. Then south again, God

knows how far.' The explanation did not enlighten Bessie in
the least, but she held her tongue and looked to Dick's path
till they came to the chambers.

'We'll have tea and muffins,' he said joyously. 'I can't tell
you, Bessie, how glad I am to find you again. What made you
go away so suddenly?'

'I didn't think you'd want me any more,' she said, emboldened by his ignorance.

'I didn't as a matter of fact—but afterwards— At any rate
I'm glad you've come. You know the stairs.'

So Bessie led him home to his own place—there was no one
to hinder—and shut the door of the studio.

'What a mess!' was her first word. 'All these things haven't
been looked after for months and months.'

'No, only weeks, Bess. You can't expect them to care.'

'I don't know what you expect them to do. They ought to
know what you've paid them for. The dust's just awful. It's
all over the easel.'

'I don't use it much now.'

'All over the pictures and the floor, and all over your coat.
I'd like to speak to them housemaids.'

'Ring for tea, then.' Dick felt his way to the one chair he
used by custom.

Bessie saw the action and, as far as in her lay, was touched.
But there remained always a keen sense of new-found superior-
ity, and it was in her voice when she spoke.

'How long have you been like this?' she said wrathfully, as
though the blindness were some fault of the housemaids.

'How?'

'As you are.'

'The day after you went away with the cheque, almost as
soon as my picture was finished; I hardly saw her alive.'

'Then they've been cheating you ever since; that's all. I know their nice little ways.'

A woman may love one man and despise another, but on general feminine principles she will do her best to save the man she despises from being defrauded. Her loved one can look to himself, but the other man, being obviously an idiot, needs protection.

'I don't think Mr. Beeton cheats much,' said Dick. Bessie was flouncing up and down the room, and he was conscious of a keen sense of enjoyment as he heard the swish of her skirts and the light step between.

'Tea *and* muffins,' she said shortly, when the ring at the bell was answered; 'two teaspoonfuls and one over for the pot. I don't want the old teapot that was here when I used to come. It don't draw. Get another.'

The housemaid went away scandalised, and Dick chuckled. Then he began to cough as Bessie banged up and down the studio disturbing the dust.

'What are you trying to do?'

'Put things straight. This is like unfurnished lodgings. How could you let it go so?'

'How could I help it? Dust away.'

She dusted furiously, and in the midst of all the pother entered Mrs. Beeton. Her husband on his return had explained the situation, winding up with the peculiarly felicitous proverb, 'Do unto others as you would be done by.' She had ascended to put into her place the person who demanded muffins and an uncracked teapot as though she had a right to both.

'Muffins ready yet?' said Bess, still dusting. She was no longer a drab of the streets, but a young lady who, thanks to Dick's cheque, had paid her premium and was entitled to pull beer-handles with the best. Being neatly dressed in black she did not hesitate to face Mrs. Beeton, and there passed between the two women certain regards that Dick would have appreciated. The situation adjusted itself by eye. Bessie had won, and Mrs. Beeton returned to cook muffins and make scathing remarks about models, hussies, trollops, and the like, to her husband.

'There's nothing to be got of interfering with him, Liza,' he said. 'Alf, you go along into the street to play. When he isn't crossed he's as kindly as kind, but when he's crossed he's the devil and all. We took too many little things out of his rooms since he was blind to be that particular about what he does. They ain't no objects to a blind man, of course, but if it was to come into court we'd get the sack. Yes, I did introduce him to that girl because I'm a feelin' man myself.'

'Much too feelin'!' Mrs. Beeton slapped the muffins into the dish, and thought of comely housemaids long since dismissed on suspicion.

'I ain't ashamed of it, and it isn't for us to judge him hard so long as he pays quiet and regular as he do. I know how to manage young gentlemen; you know how to cook for them; and what I says is, let each stick to his own business and then there won't be any trouble. Take them muffins, Liza, and be sure you have no words with that young woman. His lot is cruel hard, and if he's crossed he do swear worse than any one I've ever served.'

'That's a little better,' said Bessie, sitting down to the tea. 'You needn't wait, thank you, Mrs. Beeton.'

'I had no intention of doing such, I do assure you.'

Bessie made no answer whatever. This, she knew, was the way in which real ladies routed their foes, and when one is a barmaid at a first-class public-house one may become a real lady at ten minutes' notice.

Her eyes fell on Dick opposite her and she was both shocked and displeased. There were droppings of food all down the front of his coat; the mouth, under the ragged ill-grown beard, drooped sullenly; the forehead was lined and contracted; and on the lean temples the hair was a dusty, indeterminate colour that might or might not have been called grey. The utter misery and self-abandonment of the man appealed to her, and at the bottom of her heart lay the wicked feeling that he was humbled and brought low who had once humbled her.

'Oh! it *is* good to hear you moving about,' said Dick, rubbing his hands. 'Tell us all about your bar successes, Bessie, and the way you live now.'

'Never mind that. I'm quite respectable, as you'd see by looking at me. *You* don't seem to live too well. What made you go blind that sudden? Why isn't there any one to look after you?'

Dick was too thankful for the sound of her voice to resent the tone of it.

'I was cut across the head a long time ago, and that ruined my eyes. I don't suppose anybody thinks it worth while to look after me any more. Why should they?—and Mr. Beeton really does everything I want.'

'Didn't you know any gentlemen and ladies, then, while you was—well?'

'A few, but I don't care to have them looking at me.'

'I suppose that's why you've growed a beard. Take it off, it don't become you.'

'Good gracious, child, do you imagine that I think of what becomes me these days?'

'You ought. Get that taken off before I come here again. I suppose I can come, can't I?'

'I'd be only too grateful if you did. I don't think I treated you very well in the old days. I used to make you angry.'

'Very angry, you did.'

'I'm sorry for it, then. Come and see me when you can and as often as you can. God knows, there isn't a soul in the world to take that trouble except you and Mr. Beeton.'

'A lot of trouble *he's* taking and *she* too.' This with a toss of the head. 'They've let you do anyhow, and they haven't done anything for you. I've only to look to see that much. I'll come, and I'll be glad to come, but you must go and be shaved, and you must get some other clothes—those ones aren't fit to be seen.'

'I have heaps somewhere,' he said helplessly.

'I know you have. Tell Mr. Beeton to give you a new suit and I'll brush it and keep it clean. You may be as blind as a barn-door, Mr. Heldar, but it doesn't excuse you looking like a sweep.'

'Do I look like a sweep then?'

'Oh, I'm sorry for you. I'm that sorry for you!' she cried impulsively, and took Dick's hands. Mechanically, he lowered his head as if to kiss—she was the only woman who had taken pity on him, and he was not too proud for a little pity now. She stood up to go.

'Nothing o' that kind till you look more like a gentleman. It's quite easy when you get shaved, and some clothes.'

He could hear her drawing on her gloves and rose to say good-bye. She passed behind him, kissed him audaciously on the back of the neck, and ran away as swiftly as on the day when she had destroyed the Melancolia.

'To think of me kissing Mr. Heldar,' she said to herself, 'after all he's done to me and all! Well, I'm sorry for him, and if he was shaved he wouldn't be so bad to look at, but . . . Oh, them Beetons, how shameful they've treated him! I know Beeton's wearing his shirt on his back to-day just as well as if I'd aired it. To-morrow, I'll see . . . I wonder if he has much of his own. It might be worth more than the bar—I wouldn't have to do any work—and just as respectable if no one knew.'

Dick was not grateful to Bessie for her parting gift. He was acutely conscious of it in the nape of his neck throughout the night, but it seemed, among very many other things, to enforce the wisdom of getting shaved. He was shaved accordingly in the morning, and felt the better for it. A fresh suit of clothes, white linen, and the knowledge that some one in the world said that she took an interest in his personal appearance, made him carry himself almost upright; for the brain was relieved for a while from thinking of Maisie, who, under other circumstances, might have given that kiss and a million others.

'Let us consider,' said he after lunch. 'The girl can't care, and it's a toss-up whether she comes again or not, but if money can buy her to look after me she shall be bought. Nobody else in the world would take the trouble, and I can make it worth her while. She's a child of the gutter holding brevet rank as a barmaid; so she shall have everything she wants if she'll only come and talk and look after me.' He rubbed his newly-shorn chin and began to perplex himself with the thought of her not coming. 'I suppose I did look rather a sweep,' he went on. 'I had no reason to look otherwise. I knew things dropped on my clothes, but it didn't matter. It would be cruel if she didn't come. She must. Maisie came once, and that was enough for her. She was quite right. She had something to work for. This creature has only beer-handles to pull, unless she has deluded some young man into keeping company with her. Fancy being cheated for the sake of a counter-jumper! We're falling pretty low.'

Something cried aloud within him: This will hurt more than anything that has gone before. It will recall and remind and suggest and tantalise, and in the end drive you mad.

'I know it, I know it!' Dick cried, clenching his hands despairingly; 'but, good heavens, is a poor blind beggar never to get anything out of his life except three meals a day and a greasy waistcoat? I wish she'd come.'

Early in the afternoon time she came, because there was no young man in her life just then, and she thought of material advantages which would allow her to be idle for the rest of her days.

'I shouldn't have known you,' she said approvingly. 'You look as you used to look—a gentleman that was proud of himself.'

'Don't you think I deserve another kiss then?' said Dick, flushing a little.

'Maybe—but you won't get it yet. Sit down and let's see what I can do for you. I'm certain sure Mr. Beeton cheats you, now that you can't go through the housekeeping books every month. Isn't that true?'

'You'd better come and housekeep for me, then, Bessie.'

'Couldn't do it in these chambers—you know that as well as I do.'

'I know, but we might go somewhere else, if you thought it worth your while.'

'I'd try to look after you, anyhow; but I shouldn't care to have to work for both of us.' This was tentative.

Dick laughed.

'Do you remember where I used to keep my bankbook?' said he. 'Torp took it to be balanced just before he went away. Look and see.'

'It was generally under the tobacco-jar. Ah!'

'Well?'

'Oh! Four thousand two hundred and ten pounds nine shillings and a penny! Oh my!'

'You can have the penny. That's not bad for one year's work. Is that and a hundred and twenty pounds a year good enough?'

The idleness and the pretty clothes were almost within her reach now, but she must, by being housewifely, show that she deserved them.

'Yes; but you'd have to move, and if we took an inventory, I think we'd find that Mr. Beeton has been prigging little things out of the rooms here and there. They don't look as full as they used.'

'Never mind, we'll let him have them. The only thing I'm particularly anxious to take away is that picture I used you for—when you used to swear at me. We'll pull out of this place, Bess, and get away as far as ever we can.'

'Oh yes,' she said uneasily.

'I don't know where I can go to get away from myself, but I'll try, and you shall have all the pretty frocks that you care for. You'll like that. Give me that kiss now, Bess. Ye Gods! it's good to put one's arm round a woman's waist again.'

Then came the fulfilment of the prophecy within the brain. If his arm were thus round Maisie's waist and a kiss had just been given and taken between them,—why, then. . . . He pressed the girl more closely to himself because the pain whipped him. She was wondering how to explain a little accident to the Melancolia. At any rate, if this man really desired the solace of her company—and certainly he would relapse into his original slough if she withdrew it—he would not be more than just a little vexed. It would be delightful at least to see what would happen, and by her teachings it was good for a man to stand in a certain awe of his companion.

She laughed nervously, and slipped out of his reach.

'I shouldn't worrit about that picture if I was you,' she began, in the hope of turning his attention.

'It's at the back of all my canvases somewhere. Find it, Bess; you know it as well as I do.'

'I know—but——'

'But what? You've wit enough to manage the sale of it to a dealer. Women haggle much better than men. It might be a matter of eight or nine hundred pounds to—to us. I simply didn't like to think about it for a long time. It was mixed up with my life so.—But we'll cover up our tracks and get rid of everything, eh? Make a fresh start from the beginning, Bess.'

Then she began to repent very much indeed, because she knew the value of money. Still, it was probable that the blind man was overestimating the value of his work. Gentlemen, she knew, were absurdly particular about their things. She giggled as a nervous housemaid giggles when she tries to explain the breakage of a pipe.

'I'm very sorry, but you remember I was—I was angry with you before Mr. Torpenhow went away?'

'You were very angry, child; and on my word I think you had some right to be.'

'Then I—but aren't you sure Mr. Torpenhow didn't tell you?'

'Tell me what? Good gracious, what are you making such a fuss about when you might just as well be giving me another kiss?'

He was beginning to learn, not for the first time in his experience, that kissing is a cumulative poison. The more you get of it, the more you want. Bessie gave the kiss promptly, whispering, as she did so, 'I was that angry I rubbed out that picture with the turpentine. You aren't angry, are you?'

'What? Say that again.' The man's hand had closed on her wrist.

'I rubbed it out with turps and the knife,' faltered Bessie. 'I thought you'd only have to do it over again. You did do it over again, didn't you? Oh, let go of my wrist; you're hurting me.'

'Isn't there anything left of the thing?'

'N'nothing that looks like anything. I'm sorry—I didn't know you'd take on about it; I only meant to do it in fun. You aren't going to hit me?'

'Hit you! No! Let's think.'

He did not relax his hold upon her wrist but stood staring toward the carpet. Then he shook his head as a young steer shakes it when the lash of the stock-whip across his nose warns him back to the path to the shambles that he would escape. For weeks he had forced himself not to think of the Melancolia, because she was a part of his dead life. With Bessie's return and certain new prospects that had developed themselves the Melancolia—lovelier in his imagination than she had ever been on canvas—reappeared. By her aid he might have procured more money wherewith to amuse Bess and to forget Maisie, as well as another taste of an almost forgotten success. Now, thanks to a vicious little wench's folly, there was nothing to look for—not even the hope that he might some day take an abiding interest in the wench. Worst of all, he had been made to appear ridiculous in Maisie's eyes. A woman will forgive the man who has ruined her life's work so long as he gives her love: a man may forgive those who ruin the love of his life, but he will never forgive the destruction of his work.

'Tck—tck—tck,' said Dick between his teeth, and then laughed softly. 'It's an omen, Bessie, and—a good many things considered, it serves me right for doing what I have done. By Jove! that accounts for Maisie's running away. She must have thought me perfectly mad—small blame to her! The whole picture ruined, isn't it so? What made you do it?'

'Because I was that angry. I'm not angry now—I'm awful sorry.'

'I wonder.—It doesn't matter, anyhow. I'm to blame for making the mistake.'

'What mistake?'

'Something you wouldn't understand, dear. Great heavens! to think that a little piece of dirt like you could throw me out of my stride!' Dick was talking to himself as Bessie tried to shake off his grip on her wrist.

'I ain't a piece of dirt, and you shouldn't call me so! I did it 'cause I hated you, and I'm only sorry now 'cause you're— 'cause you're——'

'Exactly—because I'm blind. There's nothing like tact in little things.'

Bessie began to sob. She did not like being shackled against her will; she was afraid of the blind face and the look upon it, and was sorry too that her great revenge had only made Dick laugh.

'Don't cry,' he said, and took her into his arms. 'You only did what you thought right.'

'I—I ain't a little piece of dirt, and if you say that I'll never come to you again.'

'You don't know what you've done to me. I'm not angry—indeed, I'm not. Be quiet for a minute.'

Bessie remained in his arms shrinking. Dick's first thought was connected with Maisie, and it hurt him as white-hot iron hurts an open sore.

Not for nothing is a man permitted to ally himself to the

wrong woman. The first pang—the first sense of things lost is but the prelude to the play, for the very just Providence who delights in causing pain has decreed that the agony shall return, and that in the midst of keenest pleasure. They know this pain equally who have forsaken or been forsaken by the love of their life, and in their new wives' arms are compelled to realise it. It is better to remain alone and suffer only the misery of being alone, so long as it is possible to find distraction in daily work. When that resource goes the man is to be pitied and left alone.

These things and some others Dick considered while he was holding Bessie to his heart.

'Though you mayn't know it,' he said, raising his head, 'the Lord is a just and a terrible God, Bess; with a very strong sense of humour. It serves me right—how it serves me right! Torp could understand it if he were here; he must have suffered something at your hands, child, but only for a minute or so. I saved him. Set that to my credit, some one.'

'Let me go,' said Bess, her face darkening. 'Let me go.'

'All in good time. Did you ever attend Sunday school?'

'Never. Let me go, I tell you; you're making fun of me.'

'Indeed, I'm not. I'm making fun of myself. . . . Thus. "He saved others, himself he cannot save." It isn't exactly a Board-School text.' He released her wrist, but since he was between her and the door she could not escape. 'What an enormous amount of mischief one little woman can do!'

'I'm sorry; I'm awfully sorry about the picture.'

'I'm not. I'm grateful to you for spoiling it. . . . What were we talking about before you mentioned the thing?'

'About getting away—and money. Me and you going away.'

'Of course. We will get away—that is to say, I will.'

'And me?'

'You shall have fifty whole pounds for spoiling a picture.'

'Then you won't——?'

'I'm afraid not, dear. Think of fifty pounds for pretty things all to yourself.'

'You said you couldn't do anything without me.'

'That was true a little while ago. I'm better now, thank you. Get me my hat.'

'S'pose I don't?'

'Beeton will, and you'll lose fifty pounds. That's all. Get it.'

Bessie cursed under her breath. She had pitied the man sincerely, had kissed him with almost equal sincerity, for he was not unhandsome. It pleased her to be in a way and for a time his protector, and above all there were four thousand pounds to be handled by some one. Now through a slip of the tongue and a little feminine desire to give a little, not too much, pain she had lost the money, the blessed idleness and the pretty things, the companionship, and the chance of looking outwardly as respectable as a real lady.

'Now fill me a pipe. Tobacco doesn't taste, but it doesn't matter, and I'll think things out. What's the day of the week, Bess?'

'Tuesday.'

'Then Thursday's mail-day. What a fool—what a blind fool I have been! Twenty-two pounds covers my passage home again. Allow ten for additional expenses. We must put up at Madame Binat's for old sake's sake. Thirty-two pounds altogether. Add a hundred for the cost of the last trip—Gad, won't Torp stare to see me!—a hundred and thirty-two leaves seventy-eight for *baksheesh*—I shall need it—and to play with. What are you crying for, Bess? It wasn't your fault, child; it was mine altogether. Oh, you funny little opossum, mop your eyes and take me out! I want the pass-book and the cheque-book. Stop a minute. Four thousand pounds at four per cent —that's safe interest—means a hundred and sixty pounds a year; one hundred and twenty pounds a year—also safe—is two eighty, and two hundred and eighty pounds added to three hundred a year means gilded luxury for a single woman. Bess, we'll go to the bank.'

Richer by two hundred and ten pounds stored in his money-belt, Dick caused Bessie, now thoroughly bewildered, to hurry from the bank to the P. & O. offices, where he explained things tersely.

'Port Said, single first; cabin as close to the baggage-hatch as possible. What ship's going?'

'The *Colgong*,' said the clerk.

'She's a wet little hooker. Is it Tilbury and a tender, or Gallions and the docks?'

'Gallions. Twelve-forty, Thursday.'

'Thanks. Change, please. I can't see very well—will you count it into my hand?'

'If they all took their passages like that instead of talking about their trunks, life would be worth something,' said the clerk to his neighbour, who was trying to explain to a harassed mother of many that condensed milk is just as good for babes at sea as daily dairy. Being nineteen and unmarried, he spoke with conviction.

'We are now,' quoth Dick, as they returned to the studio, patting the place where his money-belt covered ticket and money, 'beyond the reach of man, or devil, or woman—which is much more important. I've three little affairs to carry through before Thursday, but I needn't ask you to help, Bess. Come here on Thursday morning at nine. We'll breakfast, and you shall take me down to Gallions Station.'

'What are you going to do?'

'Going away, of course. What should I stay for?'

'But you can't look after yourself!'

'I can do anything. I didn't realise it before, but I can. I've done a great deal already. Resolution shall be treated to one kiss if Bessie doesn't object.' Strangely enough, Bessie objected and Dick laughed. 'I suppose you're right. Well, come at nine the day after to-morrow and you'll get your money.'

'Shall I sure?'

'I don't bilk, and you won't know whether I do or not unless you come. Oh, but it's long and long to wait! Good-bye, Bessie, —send Beeton here as you go out.'

The housekeeper came.

'What are all the fittings of my rooms worth?' said Dick imperiously.

'' 'Tisn't for me to say, sir. Some things is very pretty and some is wore out dreadful.'

'I'm insured for two hundred and seventy.'

'Insurance policies is no criterion, though I don't say——'

'Oh, damn your longwindedness! You've made your pickings out of me and the other tenants. Why, you talked of retiring and buying a public-house the other day. Give a straight answer to a straight question.'

'Fifty,' said Mr. Beeton, without a moment's hesitation.

'Double it; or I'll break up half my sticks and burn the rest.'

He felt his way to a bookstand that supported a pile of sketch-books, and wrenched out one of the mahogany pillars. 'That's sinful, sir,' said the housekeeper, alarmed.

'It's my own. One hundred or——'

'One hundred it is. It'll cost me three and six to get that there pilaster mended.'

'I thought so. What an out-and-out swindler you must have been to spring that price at once!'

'I hope I've done nothing to dissatisfy any of the tenants, least of all you, sir.'

'Never mind that. Get me the money to-morrow, and see that all my clothes are packed in the little brown bullock-trunk. I'm going.'

'But the quarter's notice?'

'I'll pay forfeit. Look after the packing and leave me alone.'

Mr. Beeton discussed this new departure with his wife, who decided that Bessie was at the bottom of it all. Her husband took a more charitable view.

'It's very sudden—but then he was always sudden in his ways. Listen to him now!'

There was a sound of chanting from Dick's room.

> *We'll never come back any more, boys,*
> *We'll never come back no more;*
> *We'll go to the deuce on any excuse,*
> *And never come back no more!*

> *Oh, say we're afloat or ashore, boys,*
> *Oh, say we're afloat or ashore;*
> *But we'll never come back any more, boys,*
> *We'll never come back no more!*

'Mr. Beeton! Mr. Beeton! Where the deuce is my pistol?'

'Quick, he's going to shoot himself—'avin' gone mad!' said Mrs. Beeton.

Mr. Beeton addressed Dick soothingly, but it was some time before the latter, threshing up and down his bedroom, could realise the intention of the promises to 'find everything to-morrow, sir.'

'Oh, you copper-nosed old fool—you impotent Academician!'

he shouted at last. 'Do you suppose I want to shoot myself?
Take the pistol in your silly shaking hand then. If *you* touch
it, it will go off, because it's loaded. It's among my campaign-
kit somewhere—in the parcel at the bottom of the trunk.'

Long ago Dick had carefully possessed himself of a forty-
pound-weight field-equipment constructed by the knowledge
of his own experience. It was this put-away treasure that he
was trying to find and rehandle. Mr. Beeton whipped the revolver out of its place on the top of the package, and Dick
drove his hand among the khaki coat and breeches, the blue
cloth leg-bands, and the heavy flannel shirts doubled over a
pair of swan-neck spurs. Under these and the water-bottle lay
a sketch-book and a pigskin case of stationery.

'These we don't want; you can have them, Mr. Beeton.
Everything else I'll keep. Pack 'em on the top right-hand side
of my trunk. When you've done that come into the studio
with your wife. I want you both. Wait a minute; get me a pen
and a sheet of note-paper.'

It is not an easy thing to write when you cannot see, and
Dick had particular reasons for wishing that his work should
be clear. So he began, following his right hand with his left:
' "The badness of this writing is because I am blind and cannot see my pen." H'mph!—Even a lawyer can't mistake that.
It must be signed, I suppose, but it needn't be witnessed. Now
an inch lower—why did I never learn to use a typewriter?—
"This is the last will and testament of me, Richard Heldar.
I am in sound bodily and mental health, and there is no
previous will to revoke."—That's all right. Damn the pen!
Whereabouts on the paper was I?—"I leave everything that I
possess in the world, including four thousand pounds, and
two thousand seven hundred and twenty-eight pounds held
for me"—Oh, I can't get this straight.' He tore off half the

sheet and began again with the caution about the handwriting. Then: 'I leave all the money I possess in the world to'—here followed Maisie's name, and the names of the two banks that held his money.

'It mayn't be quite regular, but no one has a shadow of a right to dispute it, and I've given Maisie's address. Come in, Mr. Beeton. This is my signature; you've seen it often enough to know it. I want you and your wife to witness it. Thanks. To-morrow you must take me to the landlord and I'll pay forfeit for leaving without notice, and I'll lodge this paper with him in case anything happens when I'm away. Now we're going to light up the studio stove. Stay with me, and give me my papers as I want 'em.'

No one knows until he has tried how fine a blaze a year's accumulation of bills, letters, and dockets can make. Dick stuffed into the stove every document in the studio—saving only three unopened letters: destroyed sketch-books, rough note-books, new and half-finished canvases alike.

'What a lot of rubbish a tenant gets about him if he stays long enough in one place, to be sure,' said Mr. Beeton at last.

'He does. Is there anything more left?' Dick felt round the walls.

'Not a thing, and the stove's nigh red-hot.'

'Excellent, and you've lost about a thousand pounds' worth of sketches. Ho! ho! Quite a thousand pounds' worth, if I can remember what I used to be.'

'Yes, sir,' politely. Mr. Beeton was quite sure that Dick had gone mad, otherwise he would have never parted with his excellent furniture for a song. The canvas things took up storage room and were much better out of the way.

There remained only to leave the little will in safe hands: that could not be accomplished till to-morrow. Dick groped about the floor picking up the last pieces of paper, assured himself again and again that there remained no written word or sign of his past life in drawer or desk, and sat down before the stove till the fire died out and the contracting iron cracked in the silence of the night.

# CHAPTER XV

*With a heart of furious fancies,*
*Whereof I am commander;*
*With a burning spear and a horse of air,*
*To the wilderness I wander.*
*With a knight of ghosts and shadows*
*I summoned am to tourney—*
*Ten leagues beyond the wide world's end,*
*Methinks it is no journey.*
                                    TOM A' BEDLAM'S SONG.

'GOOD-BYE, BESS. I promised you fifty. Here's a hundred—all that I got for my furniture from Beeton. That will keep you in pretty frocks for some time. You've been a good little girl, all things considered, but you've given me and Torpenhow a fair amount of trouble.'

'Give Mr. Torpenhow my love if you see him, won't you?'

'Of course I 'will, dear. Now take me up the gang-plank and into the cabin. Once aboard the lugger and the maid is—and I am free, I mean.'

'Who'll look after you on the ship?'

'The head-steward, if there's any use in money. The doctor when we come to Port Said, if I know anything of P. & O. doctors. After that, the Lord will provide, as He used to do.'

Bess found Dick his cabin in the wild turmoil of a ship full of leavetakers and weeping relatives. Then he kissed her, and laid himself down in his bunk until the decks should be clear. He who had taken so long to move about his own darkened rooms well understood the geography of a ship, and the neces-

sity of seeing to his own comforts was as wine to him. Before
the screw began to thrash the ship along the Docks he had been
introduced to the head-steward, had royally tipped him, secured a good place at table, opened out his baggage, and settled himself down with joy in the cabin. It was scarcely necessary to feel his way as he moved about, for he knew everything
so well. Then God was very kind. A deep sleep of weariness
came upon him just as he would have thought of Maisie, and
he slept till the steamer had cleared the mouth of the Thames
and was lifting to the pulse of the Channel.

The rattle of the engines, the reek of oil and paint, and a
very familiar sound in the next cabin roused him to his new
inheritance.

'Oh, it's good to be alive again!' He yawned, stretched himself vigorously, and went on deck to be told that they were
almost abreast of the lights of Brighton. This is no more open
water than Trafalgar Square is a common; the free levels
begin at Ushant; but none the less Dick could feel the healing of the sea at work upon him already. A boisterous little
cross-swell swung the steamer disrespectfully by the nose; and
one wave breaking far aft spattered the quarter-deck and the
pile of new deck-chairs. He heard the foam fall with the clash
of broken glass, was stung in the face by a cupful, and sniffing
luxuriously, felt his way to the smoking-room by the wheel.
There a strong breeze found him, blew his cap off and left him
bareheaded in the doorway, and the smoking-room steward,
understanding that he was a voyager of experience, said that
the weather would be stiff in the chops of the Channel and
more than half a gale in the Bay. These things fell as they
were foretold, and Dick enjoyed himself to the utmost. It is
allowable and even necessary at sea to lay firm hold upon
tables, stanchions, and ropes in moving from place to place.

# THE LIGHT THAT FAILED

On land the man who feels with his hands is patently blind.
At sea even a blind man who is not sea-sick can jest with the
doctor over the weakness of his fellows. Dick told the doctor
many tales—and these are coin of more value than silver if
properly handled—, smoked with him till unholy hours of the
night, and so won his shortlived regard that he promised Dick
a few hours of his time when they came to Port Said.

And the sea roared or was still as the winds blew, and the
engines sang their song day and night, and the sun grew
stronger day by day, and Tom the Lascar barber shaved Dick
of a morning under the opened hatch-grating where the cool
winds blew, and the awnings were spread and the passengers
made merry, and at last they came to Port Said.

'Take me,' said Dick to the doctor, 'to Madame Binat's—if
you know where that is.'

'Whew!' said the doctor, 'I do. There's not much to choose
between 'em; but I suppose you're aware that that's one of
the worst houses in the place. They'll rob you to begin with,
and knife you later.'

'Not they. Take me there, and I can look after myself.'

So he was brought to Madame Binat's and filled his nostrils
with the well-remembered smell of the East, that runs without a change from the Canal head to Hong-Kong, and his
mouth with the villainous Lingua Franca of the Levant. The
heat smote him between the shoulder-blades with the buffet
of an old friend, his feet slipped on the sand, and his coat-
sleeve was warm as new-baked bread when he lifted it to his
nose.

Madame Binat smiled with the smile that knows no aston-
ishment when Dick entered the drinking-shop which was one
source of her gains. But for a little accident of complete darkness he could hardly realise that he had ever quitted the old

life that hummed in his ears. Somebody opened a bottle of peculiarly strong Schiedam. The smell reminded Dick of Monsieur Binat, who, by the way, had spoken of Art and degradation. Binat was dead. Madame said as much when the doctor departed, scandalised, so far as a ship's doctor can be, at the warmth of Dick's reception. Dick was delighted at it. 'They remember me here after a year. They have forgotten me across the water by this time. Madame, I want a long talk with you when you're at liberty. It is good to be back again.'

In the evening she set an iron-topped café-table out on the sands, and Dick and she sat by it, while the house behind them filled with riot, merriment, oaths, and threats. The stars came out and the lights of the shipping in the harbour twinkled by the head of the Canal.

'Yes. The war is good for trade, my friend; but what dost thou do here? We have not forgotten thee.'

'I was over there in England and I went blind.'

'But there was the glory first. We heard of it here, even here—I and Binat; and thou hast used the head of Yellow 'Tina—she is still alive—so often and so well that 'Tina laughed when the papers arrived by the mail-boats. It was always something that we here could recognise in the paintings. And then there was always the glory and the money for thee.'

'I am not poor—I shall pay you well.'

'Not to me. Thou hast paid for everything.' Under her breath, 'Mon Dieu, to be blind and so young! What horror!'

Dick could not see her face with the pity on it, or his own with the discoloured hair at the temples. He did not feel the need of pity; he was too anxious to get to the Front once more, and explained his desire.

'And where? The Canal is full of the English ships. Sometimes they fire as they used to do when the war was here—ten years ago. Beyond Cairo there is fighting, but how canst thou go there without a correspondent's passport? And in the desert there is always fighting, but that is impossible also,' said she.

'I must go to Suakin.' He knew, thanks to Alf's readings, that Torpenhow was at work with the column that was protecting the construction of the Suakin-Berber line. P. & O. steamers do not touch at that port, and, besides, Madame Binat knew everybody whose help or advice was worth anything. They were not respectable folk, but they could cause things to be accomplished, which is much more important when there is work toward.

'But at Suakin they are always fighting. That desert breeds men always—and always more men. And they are so bold! Why to Suakin?'

'My friend is there.'

'Thy friend! Chtt! Thy friend is death, then.'

Madame Binat dropped a fat arm on the table-top, filled Dick's glass anew, and looked at him closely under the stars. There was no need that he should bow his head in assent and say:

'No. He is a man, but—if it should arrive . . . blamest thou?'

'I blame?' she laughed shrilly. 'Who am I that I should blame any one—except those who try to cheat me over their *consommations*. But it is very terrible.'

'I must go to Suakin. Think for me. A great deal has changed within the year, and the men I knew are not here. The Egyptian Lighthouse steamer goes down the Canal to Suakin—and the post-boats—but even then——'

'Do not think any longer. *I* know, and it is for me to think. Thou shalt go—thou shalt go and see thy friend. Be wise. Sit here until the house is a little quiet—I must attend to my guests—and afterwards go to bed. Thou shalt go, in truth, thou shalt go.'

'To-morrow?'

'As soon as may be.' She was talking as though he were a child.

He sat at the table listening to the voices in the harbour and the streets, and wondering how soon the end would come, till Madame Binat carried him off to bed and ordered him to sleep. The house shouted and sang and danced and revelled, Madame Binat moving through it with one eye on the liquor payments and the girls and the other on Dick's interests. To this latter end she smiled upon scowling and furtive Turkish officers of Fellaheen regiments, was gracious to Cypriote commissariat underlings, and more than kind to camel-agents of no nationality whatever.

In the early morning, being then appropriately dressed in a flaming red silk ball-dress, with a front of tarnished gold embroidery and a necklace of plate-glass diamonds, she made chocolate and carried it in to Dick.

'It is only I, and I am of discreet age, eh? Drink and eat the roll too. Thus in France mothers bring their sons, when those behave wisely, the morning chocolate.' She sat down on the side of the bed whispering:

'It is all arranged. Thou wilt go by the Lighthouse boat. That is a bribe of ten pounds English. The captain is never paid by the Government. The boat comes to Suakin in four days. There will go with thee George, a Greek muleteer. Another bribe of ten pounds. I will pay. They must not know of thy money. George will go with thee as far as he goes with his mules. Then he comes back to me, for his well-beloved is here, and if I do not receive a telegram from Suakin saying that thou art well, the girl answers for George.'

'Thank you.' He felt out sleepily for the cup. 'You are much too kind, Madame.'

'If there were anything that I might do I would say, stay here and be wise; but I do not think that would be best for thee.' She looked at her liquor-stained dress with a sad smile. 'Nay, thou shalt go, in truth, thou shalt go. It is best so. My boy, it is best so.'

She stooped and kissed Dick between the eyes. 'That is for good-morning,' she said, going away. 'When thou art dressed we will speak to George and make everything ready. But first we must open the little trunk. Give me the keys.'

'The amount of kissing lately has been simply scandalous. I shall expect Torp to kiss me next. He is more likely to swear at me for getting in his way, though. Well, it won't last long— Ohé, Madame, help me to my toilette of the guillotine! There will be no chance of dressing properly out yonder.'

He was rummaging among his new campaign-kit, and rowel-ling his hands with the spurs. There are two ways of wearing well-oiled ankle-jacks, spotless blue leg-bands, khaki coat and breeches, and a perfectly pipeclayed helmet. The right' way is the way of the untired man, master of himself, setting out upon an expedition, well pleased.

'Everything must be very correct,' Dick explained. 'It will become dirty afterwards, but now it is good to feel well dressed. Is everything as it should be?'

He patted the revolver neatly hidden under the fullness of the blouse on the right hip and fingered his collar.

'I can do no more,' Madame said, between laughing and crying. 'Look at thyself—but I forgot.'

'I am very content.' He stroked the creaseless spirals of his leggings. 'Now let us go and see the captain and George and the Lighthouse boat. Be quick, Madame.'

'But thou canst not be seen by the harbour walking with *me* in the daylight. Figure to yourself if some English ladies——'

'There are no English ladies; and if there are, I have forgotten them. Take me there.'

In spite of his burning impatience it was nearly evening ere the Lighthouse boat began to move. Madame had said a great deal both to George and the Captain touching the arrangements that were to be made for Dick's benefit. Very few men who had the honour of her acquaintance cared to disregard Madame's advice. That sort of contempt might end in being knifed by a stranger in a gambling-hell upon surprisingly short provocation.

For six days—two of them were wasted in the crowded Canal—the little steamer worked her way to Suakin, where she was to pick up the superintendent of Lighthouses; and Dick made it his business to propitiate George, who was distracted with fears for the safety of his light-of-love and half inclined to make Dick responsible for his own discomfort. When they arrived George took him under his wing, and together they entered the red-hot seaport, encumbered with the material and wastage of the Suakin-Berber line, from locomotives in disconsolate fragments to mounds of chairs and pot-sleepers.

'If you keep with me,' said George, 'nobody will ask for passports or what you do. They are all very busy.'

'Yes; but I should like to hear some of the Englishmen talk. They might remember me. I was known here a long time ago —when I was some one indeed.'

'A long time ago is a very long time ago here. The graveyards are full. Now listen. This new railway runs out so far as Tanai-el-Hassan—that is seven miles. Then there is a camp.

They say that beyond Tanai-el-Hassan the English troops go forward, and everything that they require will be brought to them by this line.'

'Ah! Base camp. I see. That's a better business than fighting Fuzzies in the open.'

'For this reason even the mules go up in the iron-train.'

'Iron what?'

'It is all covered with iron, because it is still being shot at.'

'An armoured train. Better and better! Go on, faithful George.'

'And I go up with my mules to-night. Only those who particularly require to go to the camp go out with the train. They begin to shoot not far from the city.'

'The dears—they always used to!' Dick snuffed the smell of parched dust, heated iron, and flaking paint with delight. Certainly the old life was welcoming him back most generously.

'When I have got my mules together I go up to-night, but you must first send a telegram to Port Said, declaring that I have done you no harm.'

'Madame has you well in hand. Would you stick a knife into me if you had the chance?'

'I have no chance,' said the Greek. '*She* is there with that woman.'

'I see. It's a bad thing to be divided between love of woman and the chance of loot. I sympathise with you, George.'

They went to the telegraph-office unquestioned, for all the world was desperately busy and had scarcely time to turn its head, and Suakin was the last place under sky that would be chosen for holiday-ground. On their return the voice of an English subaltern asked Dick what he was doing. The blue goggles were over his eyes and he walked with his hand on George's elbow as he replied:—

'Egyptian Government—mules. My orders are to give them over to the A. C. G. at Tanai-el-Hassan. Any occasion to show my papers?'

'Oh, certainly not. I beg your pardon. I'd no right to ask, but not seeing your face before I——'

'I go out in the train to-night, I suppose,' said Dick boldly. 'There will be no difficulty in loading up the mules, will there?'

'You can see the horse-platforms from here. You must have them loaded up early.' The young man went away wondering what sort of broken-down waif this might be who talked like a gentleman and consorted with Greek muleteers. Dick felt unhappy. To outface an English officer is no small thing, but the bluff loses relish when one plays it from the utter dark, and stumbles up and down rough ways, thinking and eternally thinking of what might have been if things had fallen out otherwise, and all had been as it was not.

George shared his meal with Dick and went off to the mule-lines. His charge sat alone in a shed with his face in his hands. Before his tight-shut eyes danced the face of Maisie, laughing, with parted lips. There was a great bustle and clamour about him. He grew afraid and almost called for George.

'I say, have you got your mules ready?' It was the voice of the subaltern over his shoulder.

'My man's looking after them. The—the fact is I've a touch of ophthalmia and I can't see very well.'

'By Jove! that's bad. You ought to lie up in hospital for a while. I've had a turn of it myself. It's as bad as being blind.'

'So I find it. When does this armoured train go?'

'At six o'clock. It takes an hour and a half to cover the seven miles.'

'Are the Fuzzies on the rampage—eh?'

'About three nights a week. Fact is I'm in acting command of the night-train. It generally runs back empty to Tanai for the night.'

'Big camp at Tanai, I suppose?'

'Pretty big. It has to feed our desert-column somehow.'

'Is that far off?'

'Between thirty and forty miles—in an infernal thirsty country.'

'Is the country quiet between Tanai and our men?'

'More or less. I shouldn't care to cross it alone, or with a subaltern's command for the matter of that, but the scouts get through in some extraordinary fashion.'

'They always did.'

'Have you been here before, then?'

'I was through most of the trouble when it first broke out.'

'In the Service and cashiered' was the subaltern's first thought, so he refrained from putting any questions.

'There's your man coming up with the mules. It seems rather queer——'

'That I should be mule-leading?' said Dick.

'I didn't mean to say so, but it is. Forgive me—it's beastly impertinence, I know, but you speak like a man who has been at a public school. There's no mistaking the tone.'

'I am a public-school man.'

'I thought so. I say, I don't want to hurt your feelings, but you're a little down on your luck, aren't you? I saw you sitting with your head in your hands, and that's why I spoke.'

'Thanks. I am about as thoroughly and completely broke as a man need be.'

'Suppose—I mean, I'm a public-school man myself. Couldn't I perhaps—take it as a loan, y'know, and——'

'You're much too good, but on my honour I've as much

money as I want. . . . I tell you what you could do for me, though, and put me under an everlasting obligation. Let me come into the bogie truck of the train. There is a fore-truck, isn't there?'

'Yes. How d'you know?'

'I've been in an armoured train before. Only let me see— hear some of the fun, I mean, and I'll be grateful. I go at my own risk as a non-combatant.'

The young man thought for a minute. 'All right,' he said. 'We're supposed to be an empty train, and there's no one to blow me up at the other end.'

George and a horde of yelling amateur assistants had loaded up the mules, and the narrow-gauge armoured train, plated with three-eighths-inch boiler-plate till it looked like one long coffin, stood ready to start.

Two bogie trucks running before the locomotive were completely covered in with plating, except that the leading one was pierced in front for the nozzle of a machine-gun, and the second at either side for lateral fire. The trucks together made one long iron-vaulted chamber in which a score of artillerymen were rioting.

'Whitechapel—last train! Ah, I see yer kissin' in the first class there!' somebody shouted, just as Dick was clambering into the forward truck.

'Lordy! 'Ere's a real live passenger for the Kew, Tanai, Acton, and Ealin' train. *Echo,* sir. Speshul edition! *Star,* sir.'— 'Shall I get you a foot-warmer?' said another.

'Thanks. I'll pay my footing,' said Dick, and relations of the most amicable were established ere silence came with the arrival of the subaltern, and the train jolted out over the rough track.

'This is an immense improvement on shooting the unimpressionable Fuzzy in the open,' said Dick from his place in the corner.

'Oh, but he's still unimpressed. There he goes!' said the subaltern, as a bullet struck the outside of the truck. 'We always have at least one demonstration against the night-train. Generally they attack the rear-truck where my junior commands. He gets all the fun of the fair.'

'Not to-night, though! Listen!' said Dick. A flight of heavy-handed bullets was succeeded by yelling and shouts. The children of the desert valued their nightly amusement, and the train was an excellent mark.

'Is it worth while giving them half a hopper full?' the subaltern asked of the engine, which was driven by a Lieutenant of Sappers.

'I should just think so! This is my section of the line. They'll be playing Old Harry with my permanent way if we don't stop 'em.'

'Right O!'

'*Hrrmph!*' said the machine-gun through all its five noses as the subaltern drew the lever home. The empty cartridges clashed on the floor and the smoke blew back through the truck. There was indiscriminate firing at the rear of the train, a return fire from the darkness without and unlimited howling. Dick stretched himself on the floor, wild with delight at the sounds and the smells.

'God is very good—I never thought I'd hear this again. Give 'em hell, men! Oh, give 'em hell!' he cried.

The train stopped for some obstruction on the line ahead and a party went out to reconnoitre, but came back cursing, for spades. The children of the desert had piled sand and gravel on the rails, and twenty minutes were lost in clearing it away. Then the slow progress recommenced, to be varied with more shots, more shoutings, the steady clack and kick of the machine-guns, and a final difficulty with a half-lifted rail ere the train came under the protection of the roaring camp at Tanai-el-Hassan.

'Now you see why it takes an hour and a half to fetch her through,' said the subaltern, unshipping the cartridge-hopper above his pet gun.

'It was a lark, though. I only wish it had lasted twice as long. How superb it must have looked from outside!' said Dick, sighing regretfully.

'It palls after the first few nights. By the way, when you've settled about your mules, come and see what we can find to eat in my tent. I'm Bennil of the Gunners—in the Artillery lines—and mind you don't fall over my tent-ropes in the dark.'

But it was all dark to Dick. He could only smell the camels, the hay-bales, the cooking, the smoky fires, and the tanned canvas of the tents, as he stood where he had dropped from the train, shouting for George. There was a sound of light-hearted kicking on the iron skin of the rear trucks, with squealing and grunting. George was unloading the mules.

The engine was blowing off steam nearly in Dick's ear; a cold wind of the desert danced between his legs; he was hungry, and felt tired and dirty—so dirty that he tried to brush his coat with his hands. That was a hopeless job; so he thrust his hands into his pockets and began to count over the many times that he had waited in strange or remote places for trains or camels, mules or horses, to carry him to his business. In those days he could see—few men more clearly—and the spectacle of an armed camp at dinner under the stars was an ever fresh pleasure to the eye. There was colour, light, and motion, without which no man has much pleasure in living. This night there remained for him only one more journey through the darkness that never lifts to tell a man how far he has travelled. Then he would grip Torpenhow's hand again—Torpenhow, who was alive and strong, and lived in the midst of the action that had once made the reputation of a man called Dick Heldar: not in the least to be confused with the blind, bewildered vagabond who seemed to answer to the same name. Yes, he would find Torpenhow, and come as near to the old life as might be. Afterwards he would forget everything: Bessie, who had wrecked the Melancolia and so nearly wrecked his life; Beeton, who lived in a strange unreal city full of tin-tacks and gas-plugs, and matters that no men needed; that irrational being who had offered him love and loyalty for nothing, but had not signed her name; and most of all Maisie, who, from her own point of view, was undeniably right in all she did, but oh, at this distance, so tantalisingly fair.

George's hand on his arm pulled him back to the situation. 'And what now?' said George.

'Oh yes, of course. What now? Take me to the camel-men. Take me to where the scouts sit when they come in from the desert. They sit by their camels, and the camels eat grain out of a black blanket, held up at the corners, and the men eat by their side just like camels. Take me there!'

The camp was rough and rutty, and Dick stumbled many times over the stumps of scrub. The scouts were sitting by their beasts, as Dick knew they would. The light of the dung-fires flickered on their bearded faces, and the camels bubbled and mumbled beside them at rest. It was no part of Dick's policy to go into the desert with a convoy of supplies. That would lead to impertinent questions, and since a blind non-combatant is not needed at the Front, he would probably be forced to return to Suakin. He must go up alone, and go immediately.

'Now for one last bluff—the biggest of all,' he said. 'Peace be with you, brethren!' The watchful George steered him to the circle of the nearest fire. The heads of the camel-sheiks bowed gravely, and the camels, scenting a European, looked sideways curiously like brooding hens, half ready to get to their feet.

'A beast and a driver to go to the fighting-line to-night,' said Dick.

'A Mulaid?' said a voice, scornfully naming the best baggage-breed that he knew.

'A Bisharin,' returned Dick with perfect gravity. 'A Bisharin without saddle-galls. Therefore no charge of thine, shock-head.'

Two or three minutes passed. Then:—

'We be knee-haltered for the night. There is no going out from the camp.'

'Not for money?'

'H'm! Ah! English money?'

Another depressing interval of silence.

'How much?'

'Twenty-five pounds English paid into the hand of the driver at my journey's end, and as much more into the hand of the camel-sheik here, to be paid when the driver returns.'

This was royal payment, and the sheik, who knew that he would get his commission on the deposit, stirred in Dick's behalf.

'For scarcely one night's journey—fifty pounds. Land and wells and good trees and wives to make a man content for the rest of his days. Who speaks?' said Dick.

'I,' said a voice. 'I will go—but there is no going from the camp.'

'Fool! I know that a camel can break his knee-halter, and the sentries do not fire if one goes in chase. Twenty-five pounds and another twenty-five pounds. But the beast must be a good Bisharin. I will take no baggage-camel.'

Then the bargaining began, and at the end of half an hour the first deposit was paid over to the sheik, who talked in low tones to the driver. Dick heard the latter say: 'A little way out only. Any baggage-beast will serve. Am I a fool to waste my cattle for a blind man?'

'And though I cannot see'—Dick lifted his voice a little—'yet I carry that which has six eyes, and the driver will sit before me. If we do not reach the English troops in the dawn he will be dead.'

'But where, in God's name, are the troops?'

'Unless thou knowest let another man ride. *Dost* thou know? Remember it will be life or death to thee.'

'I know,' said the driver sullenly. 'Stand back from my beast. I am going to slip him.'

'Not so swiftly. George, hold the camel's head a moment. I want to feel his cheek.' The hands wandered over the hide till they found the branded half-circle that is the mark of the Bisharin, the light-built riding-camel. 'That is well. Cut this one loose. Remember no blessing of God comes on those who try to cheat the blind.'

The men chuckled by the fires at the camel-driver's discomfiture. He had intended to substitute a slow, saddle-galled baggage-colt.

'Stand back!' one shouted, lashing the Bisharin under the belly with a quirt. Dick obeyed as soon as he felt the nose-string tighten in his hand,—and a cry went up, 'Illaha! Aho! He is loose.'

With a roar and a grunt the Bisharin rose to his feet and plunged forward towards the desert, his driver following with shouts and lamentation. George caught Dick's arm and hurried him stumbling and tripping past a disgusted sentry who was used to stampeding camels.

'What's the row now?' he cried.

'Every stitch of my kit on that blasted dromedary,' Dick answered, after the manner of a common soldier.

'Go on, and take care your throat's not cut outside—you and your dromedary's.'

The outcries ceased when the camel had disappeared behind a hillock, and his driver had called him back and made him kneel down.

'Mount first,' said Dick. Then climbing into the second seat and gently screwing the pistol muzzle into the small of his companion's back, 'Go on, in God's name, and swiftly. Goodbye, George. Remember me to Madame, and have a good time with your girl. Get forward, child of the Pit!'

A few minutes later he was shut up in a great silence, hardly broken by the creaking of the saddle and the soft pad of the tireless feet. Dick adjusted himself comfortably to the rock and pitch of the pace, girthed his belt tighter, and felt the darkness slide past. For an hour he was conscious only of the sense of rapid progress.

'A good camel,' he said at last.

'He has never been underfed. He is my own and clean bred,' the driver replied.

'Go on.'

His head dropped on his chest and he tried to think, but the tenor of his thoughts was broken because he was very sleepy. In the half-doze it seemed that he was learning a punishment hymn at Mrs. Jennett's. He had committed some crime as bad as Sabbath-breaking, and she had locked him up in his bedroom. But he could never repeat more than the first two lines of the hymn:—

# THE LIGHT THAT FAILED

*When Israel of the Lord beloved*
*Out of the land of bondage came.*

He said them over and over thousands of times. The driver
turned in the saddle to see if there were any chance of cap-
turing the revolver and ending the ride. Dick roused, struck
him over the head with the butt, and stormed himself wide
awake. Somebody hidden in a clump of camel-thorn shouted
as the camel toiled up rising ground. A shot was fired, and
the silence shut down again, bringing the desire to sleep.
Dick could think no longer. He was too tired and stiff and
cramped to do more than nod uneasily from time to time,
waking with a start and punching the driver with the pistol.

'Is there a moon?' he asked drowsily.

'She is near her setting.'

'I wish that I could see her. Halt the camel. At least let me
hear the desert talk.'

The man obeyed. Out of the utter stillness came one breath
of wind. It rattled the dead leaves of a shrub some distance
away and ceased. A handful of dry earth detached itself from
the edge of a rain-trench and crumbled softly to the bottom.

'Go on. The night is very cold.'

Those who have watched till the morning know how the
last hour before the light lengthens itself into many eternities.
It seemed to Dick that he had never since the beginning of
original darkness done anything at all save jolt through the
air. Once in a thousand years he would finger the nail-heads
on the saddle-front and count them all carefully. Centuries
later he would shift his revolver from his right hand to his
left, and allow the eased arm to drop down at his side. From
the safe distance of London he was watching himself thus employed,—watching critically. Yet whenever he put out his
hand to the canvas that he might paint the tawny yellow des-

ert under the glare of the sinking moon, the black shadow of the camel and the two bowed figures atop, that hand held a revolver and the arm was numb from wrist to collar-bone. Moreover, he was in the dark, and could see no canvas of any kind whatever.

The driver grunted, and Dick was conscious of a change in the air.

'I smell the dawn,' he whispered.

'It is here, and yonder are the troops. Have I done well?'

The camel stretched out its neck and roared as there came down wind the pungent reek of camels in square.

'Go on. We must get there swiftly. Go on.'

'They are moving in their camp. There is so much dust that I cannot see what they do.'

'Am I in better case? Go forward.'

They could hear the hum of voices ahead, the howling and the bubbling of the beasts and the hoarse cries of the soldiers girthing up for the day. Two or three shots were fired.

'Is that at us? Surely they can see that I am English.' Dick spoke angrily.

'Nay, it is from the desert,' the driver answered, cowering in his saddle. 'Go forward, my child! Well it is that the dawn did not uncover us an hour ago.'

The camel headed straight for the column and the shots behind multiplied. The children of the desert had arranged that most uncomfortable of surprises, a dawn attack for the English troops, and were getting their distance by snap-shots at the only moving object without the square.

'What luck! What stupendous and imperial luck!' said Dick. 'It's "just before the battle, mother." Oh, God has been most good to me! Only'—the agony of the thought made him screw up his eyes for an instant—'Maisie . . .'

'Allahu! We are in,' said the man, as he drove into the rearguard and the camel knelt.

'Who the deuce are you? Despatches or what? What's the strength of the enemy behind that ridge? How did you get through?' asked a dozen voices. For all answer Dick took a long breath, unbuckled his belt, and shouted from the saddle at the top of a wearied and dusty voice, 'Torpenhow! Ohé, Torp! Coo-ee, Tor-pen-how.'

A bearded man raking in the ashes of a fire for a light to his pipe moved very swiftly towards that cry, as the rearguard, facing about, began to fire at the puffs of smoke from the hillocks around. Gradually the scattered white cloudlets drew out into long lines of banked white that hung heavily in the stillness of the dawn before they turned over wave-like and glided into the valleys. The soldiers in the square were coughing and swearing as their own smoke obstructed their view, and they edged forward to get beyond it. A wounded camel leaped to its feet and roared aloud, the cry ending in a bubbling grunt. Some one had cut its throat to prevent confusion. Then came the thick sob of a man receiving his death-wound from a bullet; then a yell of agony and redoubled firing.

There was no time to ask any questions.

'Get down, man! Get down behind the camel!'

'No. Put me, I pray, in the forefront of the battle.' Dick turned his face to Torpenhow and raised his hand to set his helmet straight, but, miscalculating the distance, knocked it off. Torpenhow saw that his hair was grey on the temples, and that his face was the face of an old man.

'Come down, you damned fool! Dickie, come off!'

And Dick came obediently, but as a tree falls, pitching sideways from the Bisharin's saddle at Torpenhow's feet. His luck had held to the last, even to the crowning mercy of a kindly bullet through his head.

Torpenhow knelt under the lee of the camel, with Dick's body in his arms.

# THE NAULAHKA

## A STORY OF WEST AND EAST

By

### RUDYARD KIPLING
and
### WOLCOTT BALESTIER

*The Naulahka* was first published in 1892

*There was a strife 'twixt man and maid—*
*Oh, that was at the birth of time!*
*But what befell 'twixt man and maid,*
*Oh, that's beyond the grip of rhyme.*
*'Twas: 'Sweet, I must not bide wi' you,'*
*And: 'Love, I canna bide alone';*
*For baith were young, and baith were true,*
*And baith were hard as the nether stone.*

AUCHINLECK'S RIDE.

NICHOLAS TARVIN sat in the moonlight on the unrailed bridge
that crossed the irrigating ditch above Topaz, dangling his
feet over the stream. A brown, sad-eyed little woman sat
beside him, staring quietly at the moon. She was tanned
with the tan of the girl who does not mind wind and
rain and sun, and her eyes were sad with the settled
melancholy of eyes that know big mountains, and seas of
plain, and care, and life. The women of the West shade such
eyes under their hands at sunset in their cabin-doors, scanning those hills or those grassless, treeless plains for the home-
coming of their men. A hard life is always hardest for the
woman.

Kate Sheriff had lived with her face to the West and with
her smouldering eyes fixed upon the wilderness since she could
walk. She had advanced into the wilderness with the railroad.
Until she had gone away to school, she had never lived where
a railroad ran both ways. She had often stayed long enough
at the end of a section with her family to see the first glim-

245

mering streaks of the raw dawn of civilisation, usually helped out by the electric light; but in the new and still newer lands to which her father's civil engineering orders called them from year to year there were not even arc lamps. There was a saloon under a tent, and there was the section-house, where they lived, and where her mother had sometimes taken to board the men employed by her husband. But it was not these influences alone that had produced the young woman of twenty-three who sat near Tarvin, and who had just told him gently that she liked him, but that she had a duty elsewhere.

This duty, as she conceived it, was, briefly, to spend her life in the East in the effort to better the condition of the women of India. It had come to her as an inspiration and a command two years before, toward the end of her second year at the St. Louis school, where she went to tie up the loose ends of the education she had given herself in lonely camps.

Kate's mission had been laid on her one April afternoon, warmed and sunned with the first breath of spring. The green trees, the swelling buds, and the sunlight outside had tempted her from the prospect of a lecture on India by a Hindu woman; and it was finally because it was a school duty not to be escaped that she listened to Pundita Ramabai's account of the sad case of her sisters at home. It was a heartbreaking story, and the girls, making the offerings begged of them in strange accents, went from it stilled and awed to the measure of their natures, and talked it over in the corridors in whispers, until a nervous giggle broke the tension, and they began chattering again.

Kate made her way from the hall with the fixed, inward-looking eye, the flaming cheek and air-borne limbs of one on whom the mantle of the Spirit has descended. She went quickly out into the school garden, away from everybody, and paced the flower-bordered walks, exalted, rich, sure, happy. She had found herself. The flowers knew it, the tender-leaved trees overhead were aware, the shining sky had word. Her head was high; she wanted to dance, and, much more, she wanted to cry. A pulse in her forehead went beat, beat; the warm blood sang through her veins; she stopped every little while to take a deep draught of the good air. In those moments she dedicated herself.

'All her life should take breath from this hour; she vowed it to the service this day revealed to her, as once to the prophets—vowed all her strength and mind and heart. The angel of the Lord had laid a command upon her. She obeyed joyfully.

And now, after two years spent in fitting herself for her calling, she returned to Topaz, a capable and instructed nurse, on fire for her work in India, to find that Tarvin wished her to stay at Topaz and marry him.

'You can call it what you like,' Tarvin told her, while she gazed at the moon; 'you can call it duty, or you can call it woman's sphere, or you can call it, as that meddling missionary called it at church to-night, "carrying the light to them that sit in darkness." I've no doubt you've got a halo to put to it. They've taught you names enough for things in the East. But for *me*, what I say is, it's a freeze-out.'

'Don't say that, Nick! It's a call.'

'You've got a call to stay at home; and if you haven't heard of it, I'm a committee to notify you,' said Tarvin doggedly. He shied a pebble into the irrigating ditch, and eyed the racing current with lowering brows.

'Dear Nick, how can you bear to urge any one who is free to stay at home and shirk after what we've heard to-night?'

'Well, by the holy smoke, some one has got to urge girls to stand by the old machine, these days! You girls are no good at all under the new regulations until you desert. It's the road to honour.'

'Desert!' gasped Kate. She turned her eyes on him.

'Well, what do you call it? That's what the little girl I used to know on Section 10 of the N. P. and Y. would have called it. Oh, Kate dear, put yourself back in the old days; remember yourself then, remember what we used to be to each other, and see if you don't see it that way. You've got a father and mother, haven't you? You can't say it's the square thing to give them up. And you've got a man sitting beside you on this bridge who loves you for all he's worth—loves you, you dear old thing, for keeps. You used to like him a little bit too. Eh?'

He slid his arm about her as he spoke, and for a moment she let it rest there.

'Does that mean nothing to you either? Don't you seem to see a call here, too, Kate?'

He forced her to turn her face to him, and gazed wistfully into her eyes for a moment. They were brown, and the moonlight deepened their sober depths.

'Do you think you have a claim?' she asked, after a moment.

'I'll think almost anything to keep you. But no; I haven't any claim—or none at least that you are not free to jump. But we all have a claim; hang it, the situation has a claim. If you don't stay, you go back on it. That's what I mean.'

'You don't take a serious view of things, Nick,' she said, putting down his arm.

Tarvin didn't see the connection; but he said good-humouredly, 'Oh yes, I do! There's no serious view of life I won't take in fun to please you.'

248

'You see,—you're not in earnest.'

'There's one thing I'm in earnest about,' he whispered in her ear.

'Is there?' She turned away her head.

'I can't live without you.' He leaned toward her, and added in a lower voice: 'Another thing, Kate—I won't.'

Kate compressed her lips. She had her own will. They sat on the bridge beating out their difference until they heard the kitchen clock in a cabin on the other side of the ditch strike eleven. The stream came down out of the mountains that loomed above them; they were half a mile from the town. The stillness and the loneliness closed on Tarvin with a physical grip as Kate got up and said decisively that she must go home. He knew she meant that she must go to India, and his own will crumpled helplessly for the moment within hers. He asked himself whether this was the will by which he earned his living, the will which at twenty-eight had made him a successful man by Topaz standards, which was taking him to the State Legislature, and which would one day take him much further, unless what ceased to be what. He shook himself scornfully; but he had to add to himself that after all she was only a girl, if he did love her, before he could stride to her side, as she turned her back on him, and say, 'See here, young woman, you're away off!'

She did not answer, but walked on.

'You're not going to throw your life away on this Indian scheme,' he pursued. 'I won't have it. Your father won't have it. Your mother will kick and scream at it, and I'll be there to encourage her. *We* have some use for your life, if you haven't. You don't know the size of your contract. The land isn't fit for rats; it's the Bad Lands—yes, that's just what it is, a great big Bad Lands—morally, physically, and agriculturally, Bad Lands. It's no place for white men, let alone white women; there's no climate, no government, no drainage; and there's cholera, heat, and fighting until you can't rest. You'll find it all in the Sunday papers. You want to stay right where you are, young lady!'

She stopped a moment in the road they were following back to Topaz and glanced at his face in the moonlight. He took her hand, and, for all his masterfulness, awaited her word with parted lips.

'You're a good man, Nick, but'—she drooped her eyes—'I'm going to sail on the 31st for Calcutta.'

# II

*Beware the man who's crossed in love,*
*For pent-up steam must find its vent;*
*Step back when he is on the move,*
*And lend him all the Continent.*

THE BUCK AND THE SAW.

TO SAIL FROM NEW YORK on the 31st she must leave Topaz
by the 27th at latest. It was now the 15th. Tarvin made the
most of the intervening time. He called on her at her home
every evening, and argued it out with her.

Kate listened with the gentlest willingness to be convinced,
but with a dread firmness round the corners of her mouth,
and with a sad wish to be good to him, if she could, battling
in her eyes with a sadder helplessness.

'I'm called!' she cried. 'I'm called. I can't get away from it.
I can't help listening. I can't help going!'

And, as she told him, grieving, how the cry of her sisters
out of that dim misery, that was yet so distinct, tugged at her
heart—how the useless horror and torture of their lives called
on her by night and by day, Tarvin could not refuse to
respect the solemnly felt need that drew her from him. He
could not help begging her in every accent he knew not to
hearken to it, but the painful pull of the cry she heard was
not a strange or incredible thing to his own generous heart.
He only urged hotly that there were other cries, and that
there were other people to attend to this one. He, too, had a
need, the need for her; and she another, if she would stop a
moment to listen to it. They needed each other. That was the

251

supreme need. The women in India could wait; they would go over and look them up later, when the Three C.'s had come to Topaz, and he had made his pile. Meanwhile there was happiness; meanwhile there was love! He was ingenious, he was deeply in love, he knew what he wanted, and he found the most persuasive language for making it seem to be what she wanted in disguise. Kate had to strengthen her resolution often in the intervals between his visits. She could not say much in reply. She had no such gift of communicating herself as Tarvin. Hers was the still, deep, voiceless nature that can only feel and act.

She had the kind of pluck and the capacity for silent endurance which goes with such natures, or she must often have faltered and turned back from the resolve which had come upon her in the school garden that spring day, in the two years that followed it. Her parents were the first obstacle. They refused outright to allow her to study medicine. She had wished to be both physician and nurse, believing that in India she would find use for both callings; but since she could follow only one, she was content to enrol herself as a student at a New York training-school for nurses, and this her parents suffered in the bewilderment of finding that they had forgotten how to oppose her gently resolute will through the lifelong habit of yielding to it.

Her ideas had made her mother wish, when she explained them to her, that she had let her grow up wild, as she had once seemed certain to do. She was even sorry that the child's father had at last found something to do away from the awful railroad. The railroad now ran two ways from Topaz. Kate had returned from school to find the track stretching a hundred miles to the westward, and her family still there. This time the boom had overtaken them before they could get away. Her father had bought city lots in the acre form and was too rich to move. He had given up his calling and had gone into politics.

Sheriff's love for his daughter was qualified by his general flatness; but it was the clinging affection not uncommon with shallow minds, and he had the habit of indulgence toward her which is the portion of an only child. He was accustomed to say that what she did was about right, he guessed, and he was usually content to let it go at that. He was anxious now that his riches should do her some good, and Kate had not the heart to tell him the ways she had found to make them do her good. To her mother she confided all her plan; to her father she only said that she wished to learn to be a trained nurse. Her mother grieved in secret with the grim, philosophic, almost cheerful hopelessness of women whose lives have taught them always to expect the worst. It was a sore trial to Kate to disappoint her mother; and it cut her to the heart to know that she could not do what both her father and mother expected of her. Indefinite as the expectation was—it was simply that she should come home and live, and be a young lady, like the rest of the world—she felt its justice and reason, and she did not weep the less for them because for herself she believed, modestly, that it was ordered otherwise.

This was her first trouble. The dissonance between those holy moments in the garden and the hard prose which was to give them reality and effect, grew deeper as she went on. It was daunting, and sometimes it was heart-sickening; but she went forward—not always strong, not every moment brave, and only a very little wise, but always forward.

The life at the training-school was a cruel disillusion. She had not expected the path she had set before her to bloom with ease; but at the end of her first month she could have laughed bitterly at the difference between her consecrating dreams and the fact. The dreams looked to her vocation; the fact took no account of it. She had hoped to befriend misery, to bring help and healing to pain from the first days of her apprenticeship. What she was actually set to do was to scald babies' milk-cans.

Her further duties in these early days were no more nearly related to the functions of a nurse, and looking about her among the other girls to see how they kept their ideals alight in the midst of work so little connected with their future calling, she perceived that they got on for the most part by not having any. As she advanced, and was trusted first with babies themselves, and later with the actual work of nursing, she was made to feel how her own purpose isolated her. The others were here for business. With one or two exceptions they had apparently taken up nursing as they might have taken up dressmaking. They were here to learn how to make twenty dollars a week, and the sense of this dispirited her even more than the work she was given to do as a preparation for her high calling. The talk of the Arkansas girl, who sat on a table and swung her legs while she discussed her flirtations with the young doctors at the clinics, seemed in itself sometimes a final discouragement. Through all ran the bad food, the scanty sleep, the insufficient hours for recreation, the cruelly long hours assigned for work, the nervous strain of supporting the life from the merely physical point of view.

In addition to the work which she shared with the others, she was taking regular lessons in Hindustani; and she was constantly grateful for the earlier days which had given her robust health and a sound body. Without them she must often have broken down; and soon it began to be a duty not to break down, because it had become possible to help suffering a little. It was this which reconciled her finally to the low and sordid conditions under which the whole affair of her preparation went on.

The repulsive aspects of the nursing itself she did not mind. On the contrary, she found herself liking them as she got into the swing of her work; and when, at the end of her first year, she was placed in charge of a ward at the women's hospital, under another nurse, she began to feel herself drawing in sight of her purpose, and kindled with an interest which made even the surgical operations seem good to her because they helped, and because they allowed her to help a little.

From this time she went on working strongly and efficiently toward her end. Above all, she wanted to be competent— to be wise and thorough. When the time came when those helpless, walled-up women should have no knowledge and no comfort to lean on but hers, she meant that they should lean on the strength of solid intelligence. Her trials were many, but it was her consolation in the midst of them all that her women loved her, and lived upon her comings and goings. Her devotion to her purpose carried her forward. She was presently in full charge, and in that long, bare ward where she strengthened so many sufferers for the last parting, where she lived with death and dealt with it, where she went about softly, soothing unspeakable pain, learning the note of human anguish, hearing no sound but the murmur of suffering or relief, she sounded one night the depths of her own nature, and received from an inward monitor the confirmation of her mission. She consecrated herself to it afresh with a joy beyond her first joy of discovery.

And now, every night at half-past eight, Tarvin's hat hung

on the hat-rack in the hall-way of her home. He removed it gloomily at a little after eleven, spending the interval in talking over her mission with her persuasively, commandingly, imploringly, indignantly. His indignation was for her plan, but it would sometimes irrepressibly transfer itself to Kate. She was capable not only of defending her plan, but of defending herself and keeping her temper; and as this last was an art beyond Nick, these sessions often came to an end suddenly, and early in the evening. But the next night he would come and sit before her in penitence, and with his elbows on his knees, and his head supported moodily in his hands, would entreat her submissively to have some sense. This never lasted long, and evenings of this kind usually ended in his trying to pound sense into her by hammering his chair-arm with a convinced fist.

No tenderness could leave Tarvin without the need to try to make others believe as he did; but it was a good-humoured need, and Kate did not dislike it. She liked so many things about him, that often as they sat thus, facing each other, she let her fancy wander where it had wandered in her school-girl vacations—in a possible future spent by his side. She brought her fancy back again sharply. She had other things to think of now; but there must always be something between her and Tarvin different from her relation to any other man. They had lived in the same house on the prairie at the end of the section, and had risen to take up the same desolate life together morning after morning. The sun brought the morning greyly up over the sad grey plain, and at night left them alone together in the midst of the terrible spaces of silence. They broke the ice together in the muddy river near the section-house, and Tarvin carried her pail back for her. A score of other men lived under the same roof, but it was Tarvin who was kind.

The others ran to do what she asked them to do. Tarvin found things to do, and did them while she slept. There was plenty to do. Her mother had a family of twenty-five, twenty of whom were boarders—the men working in one capacity or another directly under Sheriff. The hands engaged in the actual work of building the railroad lived in huge barracks near by, or in temporary cabins or tents. The Sheriffs had a house; that is, they lived in a structure with projecting eaves, windows that could be raised or lowered, and a veranda. But this was the sum of their conveniences, and the mother and daughter did their work alone with the assistance of two Swedes, whose muscles were firm but whose cookery was vague.

Tarvin helped her, and she learned to lean on him; she let him help her, and Tarvin loved her for it. The bond of work shared, of a mutual dependence, of isolation, drew them to each other; and when Kate left the section-house for school there was a tacit understanding between them. The essence of such an understanding, of course, lies in the woman's recognition of it. When she came back from school for the first holiday, Kate's manner did not deny her obligation, but did not confirm the understanding, and Tarvin, restless and insistent as he was about other things, did not like to force his claim upon her. It wasn't a claim he could take into court.

This kind of forbearance was well enough while he expected to have her always within reach, while he imagined for her the ordinary future of an unmarried girl. But when she said she was going to India she changed the case. He was not thinking of courtesy or forbearance, or of the propriety of waiting to be formally accepted as he talked to her on the bridge, and afterward in the evenings. He ached with his need for her, and with the desire to keep her.

But it looked as if she were going—going in spite of everything he could say, in spite of his love. He had made her believe in that, if it was any comfort; and it was real enough to her to hurt her, which *was* a comfort!

Meanwhile she was costing him much, in one way and another, and she liked him well enough to have a conscience about it. But when she would tell him that he must not waste so much time and thought on her, he would ask her not to bother her little head about him: he saw more in her than he did in real estate or politics just then; he knew what he was about.

'I know,' returned Kate. 'But you forget what a delicate position you put me in. I don't want to be responsible for your defeat. Your party will say I planned it.'

Tarvin made a positive and unguarded remark about his party, to which Kate replied that if he didn't care she must; she couldn't have it said, after the election, that he had neglected his canvass for her, and that her father had won his seat in consequence.

'Of course,' she added frankly, 'I want father to go to the State Legislature, and I don't want you to go, because if you win the election, he can't. But I don't want to help prevent you from getting in.'

'Don't worry about your father getting that seat, young lady!' cried Tarvin. 'If that's all you've got to lie awake about, you can sleep from now until the Three C.'s comes to Topaz. I'm going to Denver myself this fall, and you'd better make your plans to come along. Come! How would it suit you to be the Speaker's wife, and live on Capitol Hill?'

Kate liked him well enough to go half credulously with him in his customary assumption that the difference between his having anything he wanted and his not having it, was the difference between his wanting it and his not wanting it.

'Nick!' she exclaimed, deriding but doubtful, 'you won't be Speaker!'

'I'd undertake to be Governor, if I thought the idea would fetch you. Give me a word of hope, and you'll see what I'd do!'

'No, no!' she said, shaking her head. 'My governors are all Rajahs, and they live a long way from here.'

'But say, India's half the size of the United States. Which State are you going to?'

'Which——?'

'Ward, township, county, section? What's your post-office address?'

'Rhatore, in the province of Gokral Seetarun, Rajputana, India.'

'All that!' he repeated despairingly. There was a horrible definiteness about it; it almost made him believe she was going. He saw her drifting hopelessly out of his life into a land on the nether rim of the world, named out of the *Arabian Nights* and probably populated out of them. 'Nonsense, Kate! You're not going to try to live in any such heathen fairyland. What's it got to do with Topaz, Kate? What's it got to do with home? You can't do it, I tell you. Let them nurse themselves. Leave it to them! Or leave it to me! I'll go over myself, turn some of their pagan jewels into money, and organise a nursing corps on a plan that you shall dictate. Then we'll be married, and I'll take you out to look at my work. I'll make a go of it. Don't say they're poor. That necklace alone would fetch money enough to organise an army of nurses! If your missionary told the truth in his sermon at church the other night, it would pay the national debt. Diamonds the size of hens' eggs, yokes of pearls, coils of sapphires the girth of a man's wrist, and emeralds until you can't rest—and they hang all that around the neck of an idol, or keep it stored in a temple, and then call on decent white girls to come out and help nurse them! It's what I call cheek.'

'As if money could help them! It's not that. There's no charity or kindness or pity in money, Nick. The only real help is to give yourself.'

'All right. Then give me too! I'll go along,' he said, returning to the safer humorous view.

She laughed, but stopped herself suddenly. 'You mustn't come to India, Nick. You won't do that? You won't follow me! You shan't.'

'Well, if I get a place as Rajah, I don't say I wouldn't. There might be a dollar in it.'

'Nick! They wouldn't let an American be a Rajah.'

It is strange that men to whom life is a joke find comfort in women to whom it is a prayer.

'They might let him *run* a Rajah, though,' said Tarvin, undisturbed; 'and it might be the softer snap. Rajahing itself is classed extra hazardous, I think.'

'How?'

'By the accident insurance companies—double premium. None of *my* companies would touch the risk. They might take a Vizier, though,' he added meditatively. 'They come from that *Arabian Nights* section, don't they?'

'Well, you are not to come,' she said definitely. 'You must keep away. Remember that.'

Tarvin got up suddenly. 'Oh, good night! *Good* night!' he cried.

He shook himself together impatiently, and waved her from him with a parting gesture of rejection and cancellation. She followed him into the passage, where he was gloomily taking his hat from its wonted peg; but he would not even let her help him on with his coat.

No man can successfully conduct a love-affair and a political canvass at the same time. It was perhaps the perception of this fact that had led Sheriff to bend an approving eye on the attentions which his opponent in the coming election had lately been paying his daughter. Tarvin had always been interested in Kate, but not so consecutively and intensely. Sheriff was stumping the district and was seldom at home, but in his irregular appearances at Topaz he smiled stolidly on his rival's occupation. In looking forward to an easy victory over him in the joint debate at Cañon City, however, he had perhaps relied too much on the younger man's absorption. Tarvin's consciousness that he had not been playing his party fair had lately chafed against his pride of success. The result was irritation, and Kate's prophecies and insinuations were pepper on an open wound.

The Cañon City meeting was set down for the night following the conversation just recorded, and Tarvin set foot on the shaky dry-goods-box platform at the roller-skating rink that night, with a raging young intention to make it understood that he was still here—if he *was* in love.

Sheriff had the opening, and Tarvin sat in the background dangling a long, restless leg from one knee. The patchily illumined huddle of auditors below him looked up at a nervous, bony, loose-hung man, with a kind, clever, aggressive eye, and a masterful chin. His nose was prominent, and he had the furrowed forehead and the hair thinned about the temples which come to young men in the West. The alert, acute glance which went roving about the hall, measuring the audience to which he was to speak, had the look of sufficiency to the next need, whatever it might be, which, perhaps, more than anything else, commends men to other men beyond the Mississippi. He was dressed in the short sack-coat which is good enough for most Western public functions;

but he had left at Topaz the flannel of everyday wear, and was clad in the white linen of civilisation.

He was wondering, as he listened to Sheriff, how a father could have the heart to get off false views on silver and the tariff to this crowd, while his daughter was hatching that ghastly business at home. The true views were so much mixed up in his own mind with Kate, that when he himself rose at last to answer Sheriff, he found it hard not to ask how the deuce a man expected an intelligent mass meeting to accept the political economy he was trying to apply to the government of a State, when he couldn't so much as run his own family? Why in the world didn't he stop his daughter from making such a hash of her life?—that was what he wanted to know. What were fathers for? He reserved these apt remarks, and launched instead upon a flood of figures, facts, and arguments.

Tarvin had precisely the gift by which the stump orator coils himself into the heart of the stump auditor: he upbraided, he arraigned; he pleaded, insisted, denounced; he raised his lean, long arms, and called the Gods and the statistics and the Republican party to witness, and, when he could make a point that way, he did not scorn to tell a story. 'Why,' he would cry defiantly, in that colloquial shout which the political orator uses for his anecdotes, 'that is like a man I used to know back in Wisconsin, who——' It wasn't very much like the man in Wisconsin; and Tarvin had never been in Wisconsin, and didn't know the man; but it was a good story, and when the crowd howled with delight Sheriff gathered himself together a little and tried to smile, and that was what Tarvin wanted.

There were dissentient voices, and the jointness of the debate was sometimes not confined to the platform; but the deep, relishing groans which would often follow applause or laughter acted as a spur to Tarvin, who had joined the janitor of the rink that afternoon in mixing the dusky brew on the table before him, and who really did not need a spur. Under the inspiration of the mixture in the pitcher, the passionate resolve in his heart, and the groans and hisses, he melted gradually into an ecstasy of conviction which surprised even himself, and he began to feel at last that he had his audience under his hand. Then he gripped them, raised them aloft like a conjuror, patted and stroked them, dropped them to dreadful depths, snatched them back to show that he could, caught them to his heart, and told them a story. And with that audience hugged to his breast he marched victoriously up and down upon the prostrate body of the Democratic party, chanting its requiem. It was a great time. Everybody rose at the end and said so loudly; they stood on benches and shouted it with a bellow that shook the building. They tossed their caps in the air, and danced on one another, and wanted to carry Tarvin around the hall on their shoulders.

But Tarvin, with a choking at the throat, turned his back on it all, and, fighting his way blindly through the crowd which had gathered on the platform, reached the dressing-room behind the stage. He shut and bolted the door behind him, and flung himself into a chair, mopping his forehead.

'And the man who can do that,' he muttered, 'can't make one tiny little bit of a girl marry him.'

*Who are the Rulers of Ind?—to whom shall we bow the
knee?
Make thy peace with the women, and men shall make
thee L. G.*

MAXIMS OF HAFIZ.

IT WAS AN OPINION not concealed in Cañon City the next
morning, that Tarvin had wiped up the floor with his adver-
sary; and it was at least definitely on record, as a result of
Tarvin's speech, that when Sheriff rose half-heartedly to make
the rejoinder set down for him on the programme, he had
been howled back into his seat by a united public opinion.
But Sheriff met Tarvin at the railway station where they were
both to take the train for Topaz with a fair imitation of a nod
and smile, and certainly showed no inclination to avoid him
on the journey up. If Tarvin had really done Kate's father
the office attributed to him by the voice of Cañon City, Sheriff
did not seem to be greatly disturbed by the fact. But Tarvin
reflected that Sheriff had balancing grounds of consolation—
a reflection which led him to make the further one that he
had made a fool of himself. He had indeed had the satisfaction
of explaining publicly to the rival candidate which was the
better man, and had enjoyed the pleasure of proving to his
constituents that he was still a force to be reckoned with, in
spite of the mad missionary notion which had built a nest in
a certain young woman's head. But how did that bring him
nearer Kate? Had it not rather, so far as her father could influence the matter, put him farther away—as far as it had

brought his own election near. He believed he would be elected now. But to what? Even the speakership he had dangled before her did not seem so remote in the light of last night's occurrences. But the only speakership that Tarvin cared to be elected to was the speakership of Kate's heart.

He feared he shouldn't be chosen to fill that high office immediately, and as he glanced at the stumpy, sturdy form standing next him on the edge of the track, he knew whom he had to thank. She would never go to India if she had a man for a father like some men he knew. But a smooth, politic, conciliating, selfish, easy-going rich man—what could you expect? Tarvin could have forgiven Sheriff's smoothness if it had been backed by force. But he had his opinion of a man who had become rich by accident in a town like Topaz.

Sheriff presented the spectacle, intolerable to Tarvin, of a man who had become bewilderingly well-to-do through no fault of his own, and who now wandered vaguely about in his good fortune, seeking anxiously to avoid giving offence. In his politics he carried this far; and he was a treasury of delight just at this time to the committees of railroad engineers' balls, Knight Templars, excursions, and twilight coteries, and to the organisers of church bazaars, theatricals, and oyster suppers, who had tickets to sell. He went indiscriminately to the oyster suppers and bazaars of all denominations in Topaz, and made Kate and her mother go with him; and his collection of Baptist dolls, Presbyterian embroidery, and Roman Catholic sofa-pillows and spatter-work, filled his parlour at home.

But his universal good-nature was not so popular as it deserved to be. The twilight coteries took his money but kept their opinion of him; and Tarvin, as the opposing candidate, had shown what he thought of his rival's system of politics by openly declining to buy a single ticket. This feeble-foolish wish to please everybody was, he understood very well, at the root of Sheriff's attitude toward his daughter's mania. Kitty wanted to go so bad, he supposed he'd better let her, was his slouching version of the situation at home. He declared that he had opposed the idea strongly when she had first suggested it, and Tarvin did not doubt that Sheriff, who he knew was fond of her, had really done what he could. His complaint against him was not on the score of disposition but of capacity. He recognised, however, that this was finally a complaint, like all his others, against Kate; for it was Kate's will which made all pleadings vain.

When the train for Topaz arrived at the station, Sheriff and Tarvin got into the drawing-room car together. Tarvin did not yearn to talk to Sheriff on the way to Topaz, but neither did he wish to seem to shirk conversation. Sheriff offered him a cigar in the smoking-room of the Pullman, and when Dave Lewis, the conductor, came through, Tarvin hailed him as an old friend, and made him come back and join them when he had gone his rounds. Tarvin liked Lewis in the way that he liked the thousand other casual acquaintances in the State with whom he was popular; and his invitation was not altogether a device for avoiding private talk with Sheriff. The conductor told them that he had the president of the Three C.'s on behind in a special car, with his party.

'No!' exclaimed Tarvin, and begged him to introduce him on the spot; he was precisely the man he wanted to see. The conductor laughed, and said he wasn't a director of the road— not himself; but when he had left them to go about his duties, he came back, after a time, to say that the president had been asking whom he could recommend at Topaz as a fair-minded and public-spirited man, able to discuss in a reasonable spirit the question of the Three C.'s coming to Topaz. The conductor told him that he had two such gentlemen on board his train at that moment; and the president sent word to them by him that he would be glad to have a little talk with them if they would come back to his car.

For a year the directorate of the Three C.'s had been talking of running their line through Topaz, in the dispassionate and impartial manner of directorates which await encouragement. The board of trade at Topaz had promptly met and voted the encouragement. It took the shape of town bonds and gifts of land, and finally of an undertaking to purchase shares of stock in the road itself, at an inflated price. This was handsome even for a board of trade; but, under the prick of town ambition and town pride, Rustler had done better. Rustler lay fifteen miles from Topaz, up in the mountains, and by that much nearer the mines; and Topaz recognised it as its rival in other matters than that of the Three C.'s.

The two towns had enjoyed their boom at about the same time; then the boom had left Rustler and had betaken itself to Topaz. This had cost Rustler a number of citizens, who moved to the more prosperous place. Some of the citizens took their houses up bodily, loaded them on a flat car, and sent them over to Topaz as freight, to the desolation of the remaining inhabitants of Rustler. But Topaz now began in her turn to feel that she was losing her clutch. A house or two had been moved back. It was Rustler this time which was gaining. If the railroad went there, Topaz was lost. If Topaz secured the railroad, the town was made. The two towns hated each other as such towns hate in the West—malignantly, viciously, joyously. If a convulsion of nature had obliterated one town, the other must have died from sheer lack of interest in life. If Topaz could have killed Rustler, or if Rustler could have killed Topaz, by more enterprise, push, and go, or by the light-nings of the local press, the surviving town would have organ-ised a triumphal procession and a dance of victory. But the destruction of the other town by any other than the heaven-appointed means of schemes, rustle, and a board of trade, would have been a poignant grief to the survivor.

The most precious possession of a citizen of the West is his town pride. It is the flower of that pride to hate the rival town. Town pride cannot exist without town jealousy, and it was therefore fortunate that Topaz and Rustler lay within convenient hating distance of each other, for this living belief of men in the one spot of all the great Western wilderness on which they have chosen to pitch their tents, contains within itself the future and the promise of the West.

Tarvin cherished this sentiment as a religion. It was nearer to him than anything in the world but Kate, and sometimes it was even nearer than Kate. It did duty with him for all the higher aspirations and ideals which beckon other men. He wished to succeed, he wished to make a figure, but his best wish for himself was one with his best wish for the town. He could not succeed if the town failed; and if the town prospered he must prosper. His ambition for Topaz, his glory in Topaz, were a patriotism—passionate and personal. Topaz was his country; and because it was near and real, because he could put his hand on it, and, above all, because he could buy and sell pieces of it, it was much more recognisably his coun-try than the United States of America, which was his country in time of war.

He had been present at the birth of Topaz. He had known it when his arms could almost encircle it; he had watched and fondled and caressed it; he had pegged down his heart with the first peg of the survey; and now he knew what was good for it. It wanted the Three C.'s.

# THE NAULAHKA

The conductor presented Tarvin and Sheriff to the president when he had led them back to his private car, and the president made them both known to his young wife—a blonde of twenty-five, consciously pretty and conspicuously bridal—by whose side Tarvin placed himself with his instant perception. There were apartments in the private car before and beyond the drawing-room into which they had been shown. The whole was a miracle of compactness and convenience; the decoration was of a specious refinement. In the drawing-room was a smother of plushes, in hues of no kindred, a flicker of tortured nickel-work, and a flash of mirrors. The studied soberness of the woodwork, in a more modern taste, heightened the high pitch of the rest.

The president of the embryo Colorado and California Central made room for Sheriff in one of the movable wicker chairs by tilting out a heap of illustrated papers, and bent two beady black eyes on him from under a pair of bushy eyebrows. His own bulk filled and overflowed another of the frail chairs. He had the mottled cheeks and the flaccid fullness of chin of a man of fifty who has lived too well. He listened to the animated representations which Sheriff at once began making him with an irresponsive, sullen face, while Tarvin engaged Mrs. Mutrie in a conversation which did not imply the existence of railroads. He knew all about the marriage of the president of the Three C.'s, and he found her very willing to let him use his knowledge flatteringly. He made her his compliments; he beguiled her into telling him about her wedding journey. They were just at the end of it; they were to settle in Denver. She wondered how she should like it. Tarvin told her how she would like it. He guaranteed Denver; he gilded and graced it for her; he made it the city of a dream, and peopled it out of an Eastern fairy tale. Then he praised the stores and the theatres. He said they beat New York, but she ought to see their theatre at Topaz. He hoped they meant to stay over a day or two at Topaz.

Tarvin would not praise Topaz crudely, as he praised Denver. He contrived to intimate its unique charm, and when he had managed to make her see it in fancy as the prettiest, and finest, and most prosperous town in the West, he left the subject. But most of their subjects were more personal, and while he discussed them with her he pushed out experimentally in one direction and another, first for a chord of sympathy, then for her weak point. He wanted to know how she could be reached. *That* was the way to reach the president. He had perceived it as soon as he entered the car. He knew her history, and had even known her father, who had once kept the hotel where he stayed when he went to Omaha. He asked her about the old house, and the changes of proprietorship since he had been there. Who had it now? He hoped they had kept the head waiter. And the cook? It made his mouth water to think of that cook. She laughed with instant sociability. Her childhood had been passed about the hotel. She had played in the halls and corridors, drummed on the parlour piano, and consumed candy in the office. She knew that cook—knew him personally. He had given her custards to take to bed with her. Oh yes! *He* was still there.

There was an infectious quality in Tarvin's open and friendly manner, in his willingness to be amused, and in his lively willingness to contribute to the current stock of amusement, and there was something endearing in his hearty, manly way, his confident, joyous air, his manner of taking life strongly, and richly, and happily. He had an impartial kindness for the human species. He was own cousin to the race, and own brother to the members of it he knew, when they would let him be.

He and Mrs. Mutrie were shortly on beautiful terms, and she made him come back with her to the bow-window at the end of the car, and point out the show sights of the Grand Cañon of the Arkansas to her. Theirs was the rearmost carriage, and they looked back through the polished sweep of glass, in which the president's car terminated, at the twisting streak of the receding track, and the awful walls of towering rock between which it found its way. They stooped to the floor to catch sight of the massy heights that hung above them, and peered back at the soaring chaos of rock which, having opened to let them through, closed again immitigably as they left it behind. The train went racketing profanely through the tumbled beauty of this primeval world, miraculously keeping a foothold on the knife-edge of space won for it at the bottom of the cañon from the river on one side, and from the rock on the other. Mrs. Mutrie would sometimes lose her balance as the train swept them around the ceaseless curves, and only saved herself by snatching at Tarvin. It ended in his making her take his arm, and then they stood and rocked together with the motion of the train, Tarvin steadying their position with outstretched legs, while they gazed up at the monster spires and sovereign hills of stone, wavering and dizzying over their heads.

Mrs. Mutrie gave frequent utterance to little exclamations of wonder and applause, which began by being the appropriate feminine response to great expressions of Nature, and ended in an awed murmur. Her light nature was controlled and subdued by the spectacle as it might have been silenced by the presence of death; she used her little arts and coquetries on Tarvin mechanically and half-heartedly, until they were finally out of the cañon, when she gave a gasp of relief, and, taking petulant possession of him, made him return with her to the chairs they had left in the drawing-room. Sheriff was still pouring the story of the advantages of Topaz into the unattending ear of the president, whose eyes were on the window-pane. Mutrie received her pat on the back and her whispered confidence with the air of an embarrassed ogre. She flounced into her former seat, and commanded Tarvin to amuse her; and Tarvin willingly told her of a prospecting expedition he had once made into the country above the cañon. He hadn't found what he was looking for, which was silver, but he had found some rather uncommon amethysts.

'Oh, you don't mean it! You delightful man! Amethysts! Real live ones? I didn't know they found amethysts in Colorado.'

A singular light kindled in her eyes, a light of passion and longing. Tarvin fastened on the look instantly. Was *that* her weak point? If it was— He was full of learning about precious stones. Were they not part of the natural resources of the country about Topaz? He could talk precious stones with her until the cows came home. But would that bring the Three C.'s to Topaz? A wild notion of working complimentary bridal resolutions and an appropriation for a diamond tiara through the board of trade danced through his head, and was dismissed. No public offerings of that kind would help Topaz. This was a case for private diplomacy, for subtle and laborious delicacies, for quiet and friendly manipulation, for the tact of finger-tips—a touch here, a touch there, and then a grip— a case, in fine, for Nicholas Tarvin, and for no one else on top of earth. He saw himself bringing the Three C.'s splendidly, royally, unexpectedly into Topaz, and fixing it there by that same Tarvin's unaided strength. He saw himself the founder of the future of the town he loved. He saw Rustler in the dust, and the owner of a certain twenty-acre plot in Topaz a millionaire.

His fancy dwelt affectionately for a moment on the twenty-acre plot. The money with which he had bought it had not come easily, and business in the last analysis was always business. But the plot, and his plan of selling a portion of it to the Three C.'s for a round-house, when the railroad came, and disposing of the rest as town lots by the front foot, were minor chords in the larger harmony. His dream was of Topaz. If promoters, in accord with the high plan of Providence, usually came in on the ground floor when their plans went right, that was a fact strictly by the way.

He noticed now, as he glanced at Mrs. Mutrie's hands, that she wore unusual rings. They were not numerous, but the stones were superb. He ventured to admire the huge solitaire she wore on her left hand, and, as they fell into a talk about jewels, she drew it off to let him see it. She said the diamond had a history. Her father had bought it from an actor, a tragedian who had met bad business at Omaha, after playing to empty houses at Denver, Topeka, Kansas City, and St. Jo. The money had paid the fares of the company home to New York, a fact which connected the stone with the only real good it had ever done its various owners. The tragedian had won it from a gambler who had killed his man in a quarrel over it; the man who had died for it had bought it at a low price from the absconding clerk of a diamond merchant.

'It ought to have been smuggled out of the mines by the man who found it at Kimberley, or somewhere, and sold to an I.D.B.,' she said, 'to make the story complete. Don't you think so, Mr. Tarvin?'

She asked all her questions with an arch of the eyebrow, and an engaging smile which required the affirmative readily furnished by Tarvin. He would have assented to an hypothesis denying virtue to the discoveries of Galileo and Newton if Mrs. Mutrie had broached it just then. He sat tense and rigid, full of his notion, watching, waiting, like a dog on the scent.

'I look into it sometimes to see if I can't find a picture of the crimes it has seen,' she said. 'They're so nice and shivery, don't you think so, Mr. Tarvin, particularly the murder? But what I like best about it is the stone itself. It *is* a beauty, isn't it? Pa used to say it was the handsomest he'd ever seen, and in a hotel you see lots of good diamonds, you know.' She gazed a moment affectionately into the liquid depths of the brilliant. 'Oh, there's nothing like a beautiful stone—nothing!' she breathed. Her eyes kindled. He heard for the first time in her voice the ring of absolute sincerity and unconsciousness. 'I could look at a perfect jewel for ever, and I don't much care what it is, so it *is* perfect. Pa used to know how I loved stones, and he was always trading them with the people who came to the house. Drummers are great fellows for jewellery, you know, but they don't always know a good stone from a bad one. Pa used to make some good trades,' she said, pursing her pretty lips meditatively; 'but he would never take anything but the best, and then he would trade that, if he could, for something better. He would always give two or three stones with the least flaw in them for one real good one. He knew they were the only ones I cared for. Oh, I do love them! They're better than folks. They're always there, and always just so beautiful!'

'I think I know a necklace you'd like, if you care for such things,' said Tarvin quietly.

'Do you?' she beamed. 'Oh, where?'

'A long way from here.'

'Oh—*Tiffany's*!' she exclaimed scornfully. 'I know you!' she added, with resumed art of intonation.

'No. Further.'

'Where?'

'India.'

She stared at him a moment interestedly. 'Tell me what it's like,' she said. Her whole attitude and accent were changed again. There was plainly one subject on which she could be serious. 'Is it really good?'

'It's the best,' said Tarvin, and stopped.

'Well!' she exclaimed. 'Don't tantalise me. What is it made of?'

'Oh, diamonds, pearls, rubies, opals, turquoises, amethysts, sapphires—a rope of them. The rubies are as big as your fist; the diamonds are the size of hens' eggs. It's worth a king's ransom.'

She caught her breath. Then after a long moment, 'Oh!' she sighed; and then, 'Oh!' she murmured again, languorously, wonderingly, longingly. 'And where is it?' she asked briskly, of a sudden.

'Round the neck of an idol in the province of Rajputana. Do you want it?' he asked grimly.

She laughed. 'Yes,' she answered.

'I'll get it for you,' said Tarvin simply.

'*Yes*, you will!' pouted she.

'I will,' repeated Tarvin.

She threw back her gay blonde head, and laughed to the painted Cupids on the ceiling of the car. She always threw back her head when she laughed; it showed her throat.

# IV

*Your patience, Sirs, the Devil took me up*
*To the burned mountain over Sicily,*
*(Fit place for me), and thence I saw my Earth—*
*Not all Earth's splendour, 'twas beyond my need;*
*And that one spot I love—all Earth to me.*
*And her I love, my Heaven. What said I? . . .*
*My love was safe from all the powers of Hell—*
*For you—e'en you—acquit her of my guilt.*
*But Sula, nestling by our sail-specked sea,*
*My city, child of mine, my heart, my home,*
*Mine and my pride—evil might visit there!*
*It was for Sula and her naked ports,*
*Prey to the galleys of the Algerine,*
*Our city Sula, that I drove my price—*
*For love of Sula and for love of her.*
*The twain were woven, gold on sackcloth, twined*
*Past any sundering—till God shall judge*
*The evil and the good.*
                    THE GRAND-MASTER'S DEFENCE.

THE PRESIDENT ENGAGED ROOMS at the hotel beside the railroad track at Topaz, and stayed over the next day. Tarvin and Sheriff took possession of him, and showed him the town, and what they called its 'natural resources.' Tarvin caused the president to hold rein when he had ridden with him to a point outside the town, and discoursed, in the midst of the open plain, and in the face of the snow-capped mountains, on the reasonableness and necessity of making Topaz the end of a division for the new railroad, and putting the division superintendent, the workshops, and the round-house here.

In his heart he knew the president to be absolutely opposed to bringing the railroad to Topaz at all; but he preferred to assume the minor point. It was much easier, as a matter of fact, to show that Topaz ought to be made a junction, and the end of a division, than it was to show that it ought to be a station on the Three C's. If it was anything it would have to be a junction. The difficulty was to prove that it ought to be anything.

Tarvin knew the whole Topaz situation forward and back, as he might have known the multiplication table. He was not president of the board of trade and the head of a land and improvement company, organised with a capital of a million on a cash basis of $2000, for nothing. Tarvin's company included all the solid men of the town; it owned the open plain from Topaz to the foothills, and had laid it out in streets, avenues, and public parks. One could see the whole thing on a map hung in the company's office on Connecticut Avenue, which was furnished in oak, floored with mosaic, carpeted with Turkish rugs, and draped with silk. There one could buy town lots at any point within two miles of the town; there, in fact, Tarvin had some town lots to sell. The habit of having them to sell had taught him the worst and the best that could be said about the place; and he knew to an exactitude all that he could make a given man believe about it.

He was aware, for example, that Rustler not only had richer mines in its near neighbourhood than Topaz, but that it tapped a mining country behind it of unexplored and fabulous wealth; and he knew that the president knew it. He was equally familiar with other facts—as, for example, that the mines about Topaz were fairly good, though nothing remarkable in a region of great mineral wealth; and that, although the town lay in a wide and well-irrigated valley, and in the midst of an excellent cattle country, these were limited advantages, and easily matched elsewhere. In other words, the natural resources of Topaz constituted no such claim for it as a 'great railroad centre' as he would have liked any one to suppose who heard him talk.

But he was not talking to himself. His private word to himself was that Topaz was created to be a railroad town, and the way to create it was to *make* it a railroad town. This proposition, which could not have been squared to any system of logic, proceeded on the soundest system of reasoning. As thus: Topaz was not an existence at all; Topaz was a hope. Very well! And when one wished to make such hopes realities in the West, what did one do? Why, get some one else to believe in them, of course. Topaz was valueless without the Three C.'s. Then what was its value to the Three C.'s? Obviously the value that the Three C.'s would give it.

Tarvin's pledge to the president amounted to this: that if he would give them the chance, they would be worthy of it; and he contended that, in essence, that was all that any town could say. The point for the president to judge was which place would be most likely to be worthy of such an opportunity—Topaz or Rustler—and he claimed there could be no question about that. When you came to size it up, he said, it was the character of the inhabitants that counted. They were dead at Rustler—dead and buried. Everybody knew that: there was no trade, no industry, no life, no energy, no money there. And look at Topaz! The president could see the character of her citizens at a glance as he walked the streets. They were wide awake down here. They meant business. They believed in their town, and they were ready to put their money on her. The president had only to say what he expected of them. And then he broached to him his plan for getting one of the Denver smelters to establish a huge branch at Topaz;

he said that he had an agreement with one of them in his pocket, conditioned solely on the Three C.'s coming their way. The company couldn't make any such arrangement with Rustler; he knew that. Rustler hadn't the flux, for one thing. The smelter people had come up from Denver at the expense of Topaz, and had proved Topaz's allegation that Rustler couldn't find a proper flux for smelting its ore nearer to her own borders than fifteen miles—in other words, she couldn't find it this side of Topaz.

Tarvin went on to say that what Topaz wanted was an outlet for her products to the Gulf of Mexico, and the Three C.'s was the road to furnish it. The president had, perhaps, listened to such statements before, for the entire and crystalline impudence of this drew no retort from his stolidity. He seemed to consider it as he considered the other representations made to him, without hearing it. A railroad president, weighing the advantages of rival towns, could not find it within his conception of dignity to ask which of the natural products of Topaz sought relief through the Gulf. But if Mutrie could have asked such a question, Tarvin would have answered unblushingly, 'Rustler's.' He implied this freely in the suggestion which he made immediately in the form of a concession. Of course, he said, if the road wanted to tap the mineral wealth of the country behind Rustler it would be a simple matter to run a branch road up there, and bring down the ore to be smelted at Topaz. Rustler had a value to the road as a mining centre; he didn't pretend to dispute that. But a mineral road would bring down all the ore as well as a main line, make the same traffic for the road, and satisfy all proper claims of Rustler to consideration, while leaving the junction where it belonged by virtue of natural position.

He boldly asked the president how he expected to get up

steam and speed for the climb over the Pass, if he made Rustler the end of the division, and changed engines there. The place was already in the mountains; as a practical railroad-man the president must know that his engines could get no start from Rustler. The heavy grade by which the railroad would have to get out of the place, beginning in the town itself, prohibited the idea of making it the end of a division. If his engines, by good luck, weren't stalled on the grade, what did he think of the annual expense involved in driving heavy trains daily at a high mountain from the vantage-ground of a steep slope? What the Three C.'s wanted for the end of their division and their last stop before the climb over the Pass was a place like Topaz, designed for them by nature, built in the centre of a plain, which the railroad could traverse at a level for five miles before attacking the hills.

This point Tarvin made with the fervour and relief born of dealing with one solid and irrefragable fact. It was really his best argument, and he saw that it had reached the president as the latter took up his reins silently, and led the way back to town. But another glance at Mutrie's face told him that he had failed hopelessly in his main contention. The certainty of this would have been heartbreaking if he had not expected to fail. Success lay elsewhere; but before trying that he had determined to use every other means.

Tarvin's eye rested lovingly on his town as they turned their horses again toward the cluster of dwellings scattered irregularly in the midst of the wide valley. She might be sure that he would see her through.

Of course the Topaz of his affections melted in and out of the Topaz of fact, by shadings and subtleties which no measurement could record. The relation of the real Topaz to Tarvin's Topaz, or to the Topaz of any good citizen of the

place, was a matter which no friendly observer could wish
to press. In Tarvin's own case it was impossible to say where
actual belief stopped and willingness to believe went on.
What he knew was that he did believe; and with him the best
possible reason for faith in Topaz would have been that it
needed to be believed in hard. The need would have been
only another reason for liking it.

To the ordered Eastern eye the city would have seemed a
raw, untidy, lonely collection of ragged wooden buildings
sprawling over a level plain. But this was only another proof
that one can see only what one brings to the seeing. It was not
so that Tarvin saw it; and he would not have thanked the
Easterner who should have taken refuge in praise of his snow-
whitened hills, walling the valley in a monstrous circle. The
Easterner might keep his idea that Topaz merely blotted a
beautiful picture; to Tarvin the picture was Topaz's scenery,
and the scenery only an incident of Topaz. It was one of her
natural advantages—her own, like her climate, her altitude,
and her Board of Trade.

He named the big mountains to the president as they rode;
he showed him where their big irrigating ditch led the water
down out of the heights, and where it was brought along
under the shadow of the foothills before it started across the
plain toward Topaz; he told him the number of patients in
their hospital, decently subduing his sense of their numerous-
ness, as a testimony to the prosperity of the town; and as they
rode into the streets he pointed out the opera-house, the post-
office, the public school, and the courthouse, with the modesty
a mother summons who shows her first-born.

It was at least as much to avoid thinking as to exploit the
merits of Topaz that he spared the president nothing.
Through all his advocacy another voice had made itself heard,

and now, in the sense of momentary failure, the bitterness of another failure caught him with a fresh twinge; for since his return he had seen Kate, and knew that nothing short of a miracle would prevent her from starting for India within three days. In contempt of the man who was making this possible, and in anger and desperation, he had spoken at last directly to Sheriff, appealing to him by all he held most dear to stop this wickedness. But there are limp rags which no buckram can stiffen; and Sheriff, willing as he was to oblige, could not take strength into his fibre from the outside, though Tarvin offered him all of his. His talk with Kate, supplemented by his barren interview with her father, had given him a sickening sense of powerlessness from which nothing but a large success in another direction could rescue him. He thirsted for success, and it had done him good to attack the president, even with the foreknowledge that he must fail with him.

He could forget Kate's existence while he fought for Topaz, but he remembered it with a pang as he parted from Mutrie. He had her promise to make one of the party he was taking to the Hot Springs that afternoon. If it had not been for that he could almost have found it in his heart to let Topaz take care of herself for the remainder of the president's stay. As it was, he looked forward to the visit to the Springs as a last opening to hope. He meant to make a final appeal; he meant to have it out with Kate, for he could not believe in defeat, and he could not think that she would go.

The excursion to the Hot Springs was designed to show the president and Mrs. Mutrie what a future Topaz must have as a winter resort, if all other advantages failed her; and they had agreed to go with the party which Tarvin had hastily got together. With a view to a little quiet talk with

Kate, he had invited three men besides Sheriff—Maxim, the postmaster; Heckler, the editor of the *Topaz Telegram* (both his colleagues on the Board of Trade); and a pleasant young Englishman, named Carmathan. He expected them to do some of the talking to the president, and to give him half an hour with Kate, without detriment to Mutrie's impressions of Topaz. It had occurred to him that the president might be ready by this time for a fresh view of the town, and Heckler was the man to give it to him.

Carmathan had come to Topaz two years before in his capacity of colonising younger son, to engage in the cattle business, equipped with a riding-crop, top-boots, and $2000 in money. He had lost the money; but he knew now that riding-crops were not used in punching cattle, and he was at the moment using this knowledge, together with other information gathered on the same subject, in the calling of cowboy on a neighbouring range. He was getting $30 a month, and was accepting his luck with the philosophy which comes to the adoptive as well as to the native-born citizens of the West. Kate liked him for the pride and pluck which did not allow him the easy remedy of writing home, and for other things; and for the first half of their ride to the Hot Springs they rode side by side, while Tarvin made Mr. and Mrs. Mutrie look up at the rocky heights between which they began to pass. He showed them the mines burrowing into the face of the rock far aloft, and explained the geological formation with the purely practical learning of a man who buys and sells mines. The road, which ran alongside the track of the railroad already going through Topaz, wandered back and forth over it from time to time, as Tarvin said, at the exact angle which the three C.'s would be choosing later. Once a train laboured past them, tugging up the heavy grade

that led to the town. The narrowing gorge was the first closing in of the hills, which, after widening again, gathered in
the great cliffs of the cañon twenty miles below, to face each
other across the chasm. The sweep of pictured rock above their
heads lifted itself into strange, gnarled crags, or dipped suddenly and swam on high in straining peaks; but for the most
part it was sheer wall—blue and brown and purplish-red
umber, ochre, and the soft hues between.

Tarvin dropped back, and ranged his horse beside Kate's.
Carmathan, with whom he was in friendly relation, gave place
to him instantly, and rode forward to join the others in
advance.

She lifted her speaking eyes as he drew rein beside her, and
begged him silently to save them both the continuance of a
hopeless contest; but Tarvin's jaw was set, and he would not
have listened to an angel's voice.

'I tire you by talking of this thing, Kate. I know it. But
I've got to talk of it. I've got to save you.'

'Don't try any more, Nick,' she answered gently. 'Please
don't. It's my salvation to go. It is the one thing I want to
do. It seems to me sometimes, when I think of it, that it was
perhaps the thing I was sent into the world to do. We are all
sent into the world to do something, don't you think so, Nick,
even if it's ever so tiny and humble and no account? I've got
to do it, Nick. Make it easy for me.'

'I'll be—hammered if I will! I'll make it hard. That's what
I'm here for. Every one else yields to that vicious little will
of yours. Your father and mother let you do what you like.
They don't begin to know what you are running your precious head into. I can't replace it. Can you? That makes me
positive. It also makes me ugly.'

Kate laughed.

'It does make you ugly, Nick. But I don't mind. I think I

284

like it that you should care. If I could stay at home for any one, I'd do it for you. Believe that, won't you?'

'Oh, I'll believe, and thank you into the bargain. But what good will it do me? I don't want belief. I want *you*.'

'I know, Nick. I know. But India wants me more—or not me, but what I can do, and what women like me can do. There's a cry from Macedonia, "Come over and help us!" While I hear that cry I can find no pleasure in any other good. I could be your wife, Nick. That's easy. But with that in my ears I should be in torture every moment.'

'That's rough on me,' suggested Tarvin, glancing ruefully at the cliffs above them.

'Oh no. It has nothing to do with you.'

'Yes,' returned he, shutting his lips, 'that's just it.'

She could not help smiling a little again at his face.

'I will never marry any one else, if it helps you any to know that, Nick,' she said, with a sudden tenderness in her voice.

'But you won't marry me?'

'No,' she said quietly, firmly, simply.

He meditated this answer a moment in bitterness. They were riding at a walk, and he let the reins drop on his pony's neck as he said, 'Oh, well. Don't matter about me. It isn't all selfishness, dear. I *do* want you to stay for my own sake, I want you for my very own, I want you always beside me, I want you—want you; but it isn't for that I ask you to stay. It's because I can't think of you throwing yourself into the dangers and horrors of that life alone, unprotected, a girl. I can't think of it and sleep nights. I daren't think of it. The thing's monstrous. It's hideous. It's absurd. You won't do it!'

'I must not think of myself,' she answered in a shaken voice. 'I must think of *them*.'

'But *I* must think of *you*. And you shan't bribe me, you shan't tempt me, to think of any one else. You take it all too hard. Dearest girl,' he entreated, lowering his voice, 'are you in charge of the misery of the earth? There is misery elsewhere, too, and pain. Can you stop it? You've got to live with the sound of the suffering of millions in your ears all your life, whatever you do. We're all in for that. We can't get away from it. We pay that price for daring to be happy for one little second.'

'I know, I know. I'm not trying to save myself. I'm not trying to stifle the sound.'

'No, but you are trying to stop it, and you can't. It's like trying to scoop up the ocean with a dipper. You can't do it. But you can spoil your life in trying; and if you've got a scheme by which you can come back and have a spoiled life over again, I know some one who hasn't. Oh, Kate, I don't ask anything for myself—or, at least, I only ask everything—but do think of that a moment sometimes when you are putting your arms around the earth, and trying to lift it up in your soft little hands—you are spoiling more lives than your own. Great Scott, Kate, if you are looking for some misery to set right, you needn't go off this road. Begin on me.'

She shook her head sadly. 'I must begin where I see my duty, Nick. I don't say that I shall make much impression on the dreadful sum of human trouble, and I don't say it is for everybody to do what I'm going to try to do; but it's right for me. I know that, and that's all any of us can know. Oh, to be sure that people are a little better—if *only* a little better—because you have lived,' she exclaimed, the look of exaltation coming into her eyes; 'to know that you have lessened by the slightest bit the sorrow and suffering that must go on all the same, would be good. Even you must feel that, Nick,' she said, gently laying her hand on his arm as they rode.

Tarvin compressed his lips. 'Oh yes, I feel it,' he said desperately.

'But you feel something else. So do I.'

'Then feel it more. Feel it enough to trust yourself to me. I'll find a future for you. You shall bless everybody with your goodness. Do you think I should like you without it? And you shall begin by blessing me.'

'I can't! I can't! she cried in distress.

'You can't do anything else. You must come to me at last. Do you think I could live if I didn't think that? But I want to save you all that lies between. I don't want you to be driven into my arms, little girl. I want you to come—and come now.'

For answer to this she only bowed her head on the sleeve of her riding-habit, and began to cry softly. Nick's fingers closed on the hand with which she nervously clutched the pommel of her saddle.

'You can't, dear?'

The brown head was shaken vehemently. Tarvin ground his teeth.

'All right; don't mind.'

He took her yielding hand into his, speaking gently, as he would have spoken to a child in distress. In the silent moment that lengthened between them Tarvin gave it up—not Kate, not his love, not his changeless resolve to have her for his own, but just the question of her going to India. She could go if she liked. There would be two of them.

When they reached the Hot Springs he took an immediate opportunity to engage the willing Mrs. Mutrie in talk, and to lead her aside, while Sheriff showed the president the water steaming out of the ground, the baths, and the proposed site of a giant hotel. Kate, willing to hide her red eyes from Mrs. Mutrie's sharp gaze, remained with her father.

# THE NAULAHKA

When Tarvin had led the president's wife to the side of the stream that went plunging down past the Springs to find a tomb at last in the cañon below, he stopped short in the shelter of a clump of cottonwoods.

'Do you really want that necklace?' he asked her abruptly.

She laughed again, gurglingly, amusedly, this time, with the little air of spectacle which she could not help lending to all she did.

'Want it?' she repeated. 'Of course I want it. I want the moon, too.'

Tarvin laid a silencing hand upon her arm.

'You shall have this,' he said positively.

She ceased laughing, and grew almost pale at his earnestness.

'What do you mean?' she asked quickly.

'It would please you? You would be glad of it?' he asked. 'What would you do to get it?'

'Go back to Omaha on my hands and knees,' she answered with equal earnestness. 'Crawl to India.'

'All right,' returned Tarvin vigorously. 'That settles it. Listen! I want the Three C.'s to come to Topaz. You want this. Can we trade?'

'But you can never——'

'No matter; I'll attend to my part. Can you do yours?'

'You mean——' she began.

'Yes,' nodded her companion decisively. 'I do. Can you fix it?'

Tarvin, fiercely repressed and controlled, stood before her with clenched teeth, and hands that drove the nails into his palms, awaiting her answer.

She tilted her fair head on one side with deprecation, and regarded him out of the vanishing angle of one eye provocatively, with a lingering, tantalising look of adequacy.

'I guess what I say to Jim goes,' she said at last with a dreamy smile.

'Then it's a bargain?'

'Yes,' she answered.

'Shake hands on it.'

They joined hands. For a moment they stood confronted, penetrating each other's eyes.

'You'll really get it for me?'

'Yes.'

'You won't go back on me?'

'No.'

He pressed her hand so that she gave a little scream.

'Ouch! You hurt.'

'All right,' he said hoarsely, as he dropped her hand. 'It's a trade. I start for India to-morrow.'

# V

*Now it is not good for the Christian's health to hustle*
  *the Aryan brown,*
*For the Christian riles, and the Aryan smiles, and he*
  *weareth the Christian down;*
*And the end of the fight is a tombstone white, with the*
  *name of the late deceased,*
*And the epitaph drear: 'A fool lies here who tried to*
  *hustle the East.'*

  SOLO FROM LIBRETTO OF 'NAULAHKA.'

TARVIN STOOD ON THE PLATFORM of the station at Rawut Junction watching the dust-cloud that followed the retreating Bombay mail. When it had disappeared, the heated air above the stone ballast began its dance again, and he turned blinking to India.

It was amazingly simple to come fourteen thousand miles. He had lain still in a ship for a certain time, and then had transferred himself to stretch at full length, in his shirt-sleeves, on the leather-padded bunk of the train which had brought him from Calcutta to Rawut Junction. The journey was long only as it kept him from sight of Kate, and kept him filled with thought of her. But was this what he had come for—the yellow desolation of a Rajputana desert, and the pinched-off perspective of the track? Topaz was cosier when they had got the church, the saloon, the school, and three houses up; the loneliness made him shiver. He saw that they did not mean to do any more of it. It was a desolation which doubled desolateness, because it was left for done. It was final, intended, abso-

290

lute. The grim solidity of the cut-stone station-house, the solid masonry of the empty platform, the mathematical exactitude of the station name-board looked for no future. No new railroad could help Rawut Junction. It had no ambition. It belonged to the Government. There was no green thing, no curved line, no promise of life that produces, within eyeshot of Rawut Junction. The mauve railroad-creeper on the station had been allowed to die from lack of attention.

Tarvin was saved from the more positive pangs of homesickness by a little healthy human rage. A single man, fat, brown, clothed in white gauze, and wearing a black velvet cap on his head, stepped out from the building. This stationmaster and permanent population of Rawut Junction accepted Tarvin as a feature of the landscape: he did not look at him. Tarvin began to sympathise with the South in the war of the rebellion.

'When does the next train leave for Rhatore?' he asked.

'There is no train,' returned the man, pausing with precise deliberation between the words. He sent his speech abroad with an air of detachment, irresponsibly, like a phonograph.

'No train? Where's your time-table? Where's your railroad guide? Where's your Pathfinder?'

'No train at all of any kind whatever.'

'Then what the devil are you here for?'

'Sir, I am the stationmaster of this station, and it is prohibited using profane language to employees of this company.'

'Oh, are you? Is it? Well, see here, my friend—you stationmaster of the steep-edge of the jumping-off-place, if you want to save your life you will tell me how I get to Rhatore—quick!'

The man was silent.

'Well, what do I do, anyway?' shouted the West.

'What do I know?' answered the East.

Tarvin stared at the brown being in white, beginning at his patent-leather shoes, surmounted by open-work socks, out of which the calf of his leg bulged, and ending with the velvet smoking-cap on his head. The passionless regard of the Oriental, borrowed from the purple hills behind his station, made him wonder for one profane, faithless, and spiritless moment whether Topaz and Kate were worth all they were costing.

'Ticket, please,' said the Babu.

The gloom darkened. This thing was here to take tickets, and would do it though men loved, and fought, and despaired and died at his feet.

'See here,' cried Tarvin, 'you shiny-toed fraud; you agate-eyed pillar of alabaster——' But he did not go on; speech failed in a shout of rage and despair. The desert swallowed all impartially; and the Babu, turning with awful quiet, drifted through the door of the station-house, and locked it behind him.

Tarvin whistled persuasively at the door with uplifted eye-brows, jingling an American quarter against a rupee in his pocket. The window of the ticket-office opened a little way, and the Babu showed an inch of impassive face.

'Speaking now in offeecial capacity, your honour can getting to Rhatore *via* country bullock-cart.'

'Find me the bullock-cart,' said Tarvin.

'Your honour granting commission on transaction?'

'Cert!' It was the tone that conveyed the idea to the head under the smoking-cap.

The window was dropped. Afterward, but not too immediately afterward, a long-drawn howl made itself heard—the howl of a weary warlock invoking a dilatory ghost.

'O mot*ee*! Mot*ee*—O-oh!'

'Ah, there, Moti!' murmured Tarvin, as he vaulted over the low stone wall, gripsack in hand, and stepped out through the ticket-wicket into Rajputana. His habitual gaiety and confidence had returned with the prospect of motion.

Between himself and a purple circle of hills lay fifteen miles of profitless, rolling ground, jagged with laterite rocks, and studded with unthrifty trees—all given up to drought and dust, and all colourless as the sun-bleached locks of a child of the prairies. Very far away to the right the silver gleam of a salt lake showed, and a formless blue haze of heavier forest. Sombre, desolate, oppressive, withering under a brazen sun, it smote him with its likeness to his own prairies, and with its homesick unlikeness.

Apparently out of a crack in the earth—in fact, as he presently perceived, out of a spot where two waves of plain folded in upon each other and contained a village—came a pillar of dust, the heart of which was a bullock-cart. The distant whine of the wheels sharpened, as it drew near, to the full-bodied shriek that Tarvin knew when they put the brakes suddenly on a freight coming into Topaz on the down grade. But this was in no sense a freight. The wheels were sections of tree butts—square for the most part. Four unbarked poles bounded the corners of a flat body; the sides were made of netted rope of cocoanut fibre. Two bullocks, a little larger than Newfoundlands, smaller than Alderneys, drew a vehicle which might have contained the half of a horse's load.

The cart drew up at the station, and the bullocks, after contemplating Tarvin for a moment, lay down. Tarvin seated himself on his gripsack, rested his shaggy head in his hands, and expended himself in mirth.

'Sail in,' he instructed the Babu; 'make your bargain. I'm in no hurry.'

Then began a scene of declamation and riot, to which a quarrel in a Leadville gambling saloon was a poor matter. The impassiveness of the stationmaster deserted him like a wind-blown garment. He harangued, gesticulated, and cursed; and the driver, naked except for a blue loin-cloth, was nothing behind him. They pointed at Tarvin; they seemed to be arguing over his birth and ancestry; for all he knew they were appraising his weight. When they seemed to be on the brink of an amicable solution, the question re-opened itself, and they went back to the beginning, and re-classified him and the journey.

Tarvin applauded both parties, sicking one on the other impartially for the first ten minutes. Then he besought them to stop, and when they would not he discovered that it was hot, and swore at them.

The driver had for the moment exhausted himself, when the Babu turned suddenly on Tarvin, and, clutching him by the arm, cried, almost shouting, 'All arrange, sir! All arrange! This man *most* uneducated man, sir. You giving me the money, I arrange everything.'

Swift as thought, the driver had caught his other arm, and was imploring him in a strange tongue not to listen to his opponent. As Tarvin stepped back they followed him with uplifted hands of entreaty and representation, the stationmaster forgetting his English, and the driver his respect for the white man. Tarvin, eluding them both, pitched his gripsack into the bullock-cart, bounded in himself, and shouted the one Indian word he knew. It happened, fortunately, to be the word that moves all India, '*Challo!*' which, being interpreted, is 'Go on!'

So, leaving strife and desolation behind him, rode out into the desert of Rajputana Nicholas Tarvin of Topaz, Colorado.

*In the State of Kot-Kumharsen, where the wild dacoits*
  *abound,*
  *And the Thakurs live in castles on the hills,*
*Where the bunnia and bunjara in alternate streaks are*
  *found,*
  *And the Rajah cannot liquidate his bills;*
*Where the Agent Sahib Bahadur shoots the blackbuck for*
  *his larder,*
  *From the tonga which he uses as machân,*
*'Twas a white man from the West came expressly to*
  *invest-*
  *igate the natural wealth of Hindustan.*

  SONG FROM LIBRETTO OF 'NAULAHKA.'

UNDER CERTAIN CONDITIONS four days can dwarf eternity. Tarvin had found these circumstances in the bullock-cart from which he crawled ninety-six hours after the bullocks had got up from the dust at Rawut Junction. They stretched behind him—those hours—in a maddening, creaking, dusty, deliberate procession. In an hour the bullock-cart went two and a half miles. Fortunes had been made and lost in Topaz—happy Topaz!—while the cart ploughed its way across a red-hot river-bed, shut in between two walls of belted sand. New cities might have risen in the West and fallen to ruins older than Thebes while, after any of their meals by the wayside, the driver droned over a water-pipe something less wieldy than a Gatling gun. In these waits and in others—it seemed to him that the journey was chiefly made up of waits—Tarvin saw himself distanced in the race of life by every male citizen of the United States, and groaned with the consciousness that he could never overtake them, or make up this lost time.

Great grey cranes with scarlet heads stalked through the high grass of the swamps in the pockets of the hills. The snipe and the quail hardly troubled themselves to move from beneath the noses of the bullocks, and once in the dawn, lying upon a glistening rock, he saw two young panthers playing together like kittens.

A few miles from Rawut Junction his driver had taken from underneath the cart a sword which he hung around his neck, and sometimes used on the bullocks as a goad. Tarvin saw that every man went armed in this country, as in his own. But three feet of clumsy steel struck him as a poor substitute for the delicate and nimble revolver.

Once he stood up in the cart and hallooed, for he thought he saw the white top of a prairie schooner. But it was only a gigantic cotton-wain, drawn by sixteen bullocks, dipping and plunging across the ridges. Through all, the scorching Indian sun blazed down on him, making him wonder how he had ever dared praise the perpetual sunshine of Colorado. At dawn the rocks glittered like diamonds, and at noonday the sands of the rivers troubled his eyes with a million flashing sparks. At eventide a cold, dry wind would spring up, and the hills lying along the horizon took a hundred colours under the light of the sunset. Then Tarvin realised the meaning of 'the gorgeous East,' for the hills were turned to heaps of ruby and amethyst, while between them the mists in the valleys were opal. He lay in the bullock-cart on his back and stared at the sky, dreaming of the Naulahka, and wondering whether it would match the scenery.

'The clouds know what I'm up to. It's a good omen,' he said to himself.

He cherished the definite and simple plan of buying the Naulahka and paying for it in good money to be raised at Topaz by bonding the town—not, of course, ostensibly for any such purpose. Topaz was good for it, he believed, and if the Maharajah wanted too steep a price when they came to talk business he would form a syndicate.

As the cart swayed from side to side, bumping his head, he wondered where Kate was. She might, under favourable conditions, be in Bombay by this time. That much he knew from careful consideration of her route; but a girl alone could not pass from hemisphere to hemisphere as swiftly as an unfettered man, spurred by love of herself and of Topaz. Perhaps she was resting for a little time with the Zenana Mission at Bombay. He refused absolutely to admit to himself that she had fallen ill by the way. She was resting, receiving her orders, absorbing a few of the wonders of the strange lands he had contemptuously thrust behind him in his eastward flight; but in a few days at most she ought to be at Rhatore, whither the bullock-cart was taking him.

He smiled and smacked his lips with pure enjoyment as he thought of their meeting, and amused himself with fancies about her fancies touching his present whereabouts.

He had left Topaz for San Francisco by the night train over the Pass a little more than twenty-four hours after his conference with Mrs. Mutrie, saying good-bye to no one, and telling nobody where he was going. Kate perhaps wondered at the fervour of his 'Good evening' when he left her at her father's house on their return from their ride to the Hot Springs. But she said nothing, and Tarvin contrived by an effort to take himself off without giving himself away. He had made a quiet sale of a block of town lots the next day at a sacrifice, to furnish himself with money for the voyage; but this was too much in the way of his ordinary business to excite comment, and he was finally able to gaze down at the winking lights of Topaz in the valley from the rear platform of his train, as it climbed up over the Continental Divide, with the certainty that the town he was going to India to bless and boom was not 'on to' his beneficent scheme. To make sure that the right story went back to the town, he told the conductor of the train, in strict confidence, while he smoked his usual cigar with him, about a little placer-mining scheme in Alaska which he was going there to nurse for a while.

The conductor embarrassed him for a moment by asking what he was going to do about his election meanwhile; but Tarvin was ready for him here too. He said that he had that fixed. He had to let him into another scheme to show him how it was fixed, but as he bound him to secrecy again, this didn't matter.

He wondered now, however, whether that scheme had worked, and whether Mrs. Mutrie would keep her promise to cable the result of the election to him at Rhatore. It was amusing to have to trust a woman to let him know whether he was a member of the Colorado Legislature or not; but she was the only living person who knew his address, and as the idea had seemed to please her, in common with their whole 'charming conspiracy' (this was what she called it), Tarvin had been content.

When he had become convinced that his eyes would never again be blessed with the sight of a white man, or his ears with the sound of intelligible speech, the cart rolled through a gorge between two hills, and stopped before the counterpart of the station at Rawut Junction. It was a double cube of red sandstone, but—for this Tarvin could have taken it in his arms—it was full of white men. They were undressed excessively; they were lying in the veranda in long chairs, and beside each chair was a well-worn bullock-trunk.

Tarvin got himself out of the cart, unfolding his long stiffened legs with difficulty, and unkinking his muscles one by one. He was a mask of dust—dust beyond sand-storms or cyclones. It had obliterated the creases of his clothing and turned his black American four-button cutaway to a pearly white. It had done away with the distinction between the hem of his trousers and the top of his shoes. It dropped off him and rolled up from him as he moved. His fervent 'Thank God!' was extinguished in a dusty cough. He stepped into the veranda, rubbing his smarting eyes.

'Good evening, gentlemen,' he said. 'Got anything to drink?'

No one rose, but somebody shouted for the servant. A man dressed in thin tussore silk, yellow and ill-fitting as the shuck on a dried cob, and absolutely colourless as to his face, nodded to him and asked languidly:—

'Who are you for?'

'No? Have they got them here too?' said Tarvin to himself, recognising in that brief question the universal shibboleth of the commercial traveller.

He went down the long line and twisted each hand in pure joy and thankfulness before he began to draw comparisons between the East and the West, and to ask himself if these idle, silent lotos-eaters could belong to the profession with which he had swapped stories, commodities, and political opinions this many a year in smoking-cars and hotel offices. Certainly they were debased and spiritless parodies of the alert, aggressive, joyous, brazen animals whom he knew as the drummers of the West. But perhaps—a twinge in his back reminded him—they had all reached this sink of desolation *via* country bullock-cart.

He thrust his nose into twelve inches of whisky and soda, and it remained there till there was no more; then he dropped into a vacant chair and surveyed the group again.

'Did some one ask who I was for? I'm for myself, I suppose, as much as any one—travelling for pleasure.'

He had not time to enjoy the absurdity of this, for all five men burst into a shout of laughter—the laughter of men who have long been estranged from mirth.

'Pleasure!' cried one. 'Oh, Lord! Pleasure! You've come to the wrong place.'

'It's just as well you've come for pleasure. You'd be dead before you did business,' said another.

'You might as well try to get blood out of a stone. I've been here over a fortnight.'

'Great Scot! What for?' asked Tarvin.

'We've all been here over a week,' growled a fourth.

'But what's your lay? What's your racket?'

'Guess you're an American, ain't you?'

'Yes; Topaz, Colorado.' The statement had no effect upon them. He might as well have spoken in Greek. 'But what's the trouble?'

'Why, the King married two wives yesterday. You can hear the gongs going in the city now. He's trying to equip a new regiment of cavalry for the service of the Indian Government, and he's quarrelled with his Political Resident. I've been living at Colonel Nolan's door for three days. He says he can't do anything without authority from the Supreme Government. I've tried to catch the King when he goes out pig-shooting. I write every day to the Prime Minister, when I'm not riding around the city on a camel; and here's a bunch of letters from the firm asking why I don't collect.'

At the end of ten minutes Tarvin began to understand that these washed-out representatives of half-a-dozen firms in Calcutta and Bombay were hopelessly besieging this place on their regular spring campaign to collect a little on account from a King who ordered by the ton and paid by the scruple. He had purchased guns, dressing-cases, mirrors, mantelpiece ornaments, crochet-work, iridescent Christmas-tree glass balls, saddlery, mail-phaetons, four-in-hands, scent-bottles, surgical instruments, chandeliers, and chinaware by the dozen, gross, or score as his royal fancy prompted. When he lost interest in his purchases he lost interest in paying for them; and as few things amused his jaded fancy more than twenty minutes, it sometimes came to pass that the mere purchase was sufficient, and the costly packing-cases from Calcutta were never opened. The ordered peace of the Indian Empire forbade him to take up arms against his fellow-sovereigns, the only lasting delight which he or his ancestors had known for thousands of years; but there remained a certain modified interest of war in battling with bill-collectors. On one side stood the Political Resident of the State, planted there to teach him good government, and, above all, economy; on the other side—that is to say, at the palace gates—might generally be found a commercial traveller, divided between his contempt for an evasive debtor and his English reverence for a king. Between these two his Majesty went forth to take his pleasure in pig-sticking, in racing, in the drilling of his army, in the ordering of more unnecessaries, and in the fitful government of his womankind, who knew considerably more of each commercial traveller's claims than even the Prime Minister. Behind these was the Government of India, explicitly refusing to guarantee payment of the King's debts, and from time to time sending him, on a blue velvet cushion, the jewelled insignia of an Imperial Order to sweeten the remonstrances of the Political Resident.

'Well, I hope you make the King pay for it,' said Tarvin.

'How's that?'

'Why, in my country, when a customer sillies about like

that, promising to meet a man one day at the hotel and not
showing up, and then promising to meet him the next day
at the store and not paying, a drummer says to himself, "Oh,
all right! If you want to pay my board, and my wine, liquor,
and cigar bill, while I wait, don't mind me. I'll mosey along
somehow." And after the second day he charges up his poker
losings to him.'

'Ah, that's interesting. But how does he get those items into
his account?'

'They go into the next bill of goods he sells him, of course.
He makes the prices right for that.'

'Oh, we can make prices right enough. The difficulty is to
get your money.'

'But I don't see how you fellows have the time to monkey
around here at this rate,' urged Tarvin, mystified. 'Where I
come from, a man makes his trip on schedule time, and when
he's a day behind he'll wire to his customer in the town ahead
to come down to the station and meet him, and he'll sell him
a bill of goods while the train waits. He could sell him the
earth while one of your bullock-carts went a mile. And as to
getting your money, why don't you get out an attachment on
the old sinner? In your places I'd attach the whole country
on him. I'd attach the palace, I'd attach his crown. I'd get a
judgment against him, and I'd execute it too—personally, if
necessary. I'd lock the old fellow up and rule Rajputana for
him, if I had to; but I'd have his money.'

A compassionate smile ran around the group. 'That's because you don't know,' said several at once. Then they began
to explain voluminously. There was no languor about them
now. They all spoke together.

The men in the veranda, though they seemed idle, were no
fools, Tarvin perceived after a time. Lying still as beggars at

the gate of greatness was their method of doing business. It wasted time, but in the end some sort of payment was sure to be made, especially, explained the man in the yellow coat, if you could interest the Prime Minister in your needs, and through him wake the interests of the King's women.

A flicker of memory made Tarvin smile faintly, as he thought of Mrs. Mutrie.

The man in the yellow coat went on, and Tarvin learned that the head Queen was a murderess, convicted of poisoning her former husband. She had lain crouching in an iron cage awaiting execution when the King first saw her, and the King had demanded whether she would poison him if he married her, so the tale ran. Assuredly, she replied, if he treated her as her late husband had treated her. Thereupon the King had married her, partly to please his fancy, mainly through sheer delight in her brutal answer.

This gipsy without lineage held in less than a year King and State under her feet—feet which women of the household sang spitefully were roughened by travel of shameful roads. She had borne the King one son, in whom all her pride and ambition centred, and, after his birth, she had applied herself with renewed energy to the maintenance of mastery in the State. The Supreme Government, a thousand miles away, knew that she was a force to be reckoned with, and had no love for her. The white-haired, soft-spoken Political Resident, Colonel Nolan, who lived in the pink house, a bow-shot from the city gates, was often thwarted by her. Her latest victory was peculiarly humiliating to him, for she had discovered that a rock-hewn canal, designed to supply the city with water in summer, would pass through an orange garden under her window, and had used her influence with the Maharajah against it. The Maharajah had thereupon caused it to be taken around by another way at an expense of a quarter of his year's revenue, and in the teeth of the almost tearful remonstrance of the Resident.

Sitabhai, the gipsy, behind her silken curtains, had both heard and seen this interview between the Maharajah and his Political, and had laughed.

Tarvin devoured all this eagerly. It fed his purpose; it was grist to his mill, even if it tumbled his whole plan of attack topsy-turvy. It opened up a new world for which he had no measures and standards, and in which he must be frankly and constantly dependent on the inspiration of the next moment. He couldn't know too much of this world before taking his first step toward the Naulahka, and he was willing to hear all these lazy fellows would tell him. He began to feel as if he should have to go back and learn his A B C's over again. What pleased this strange being they called King? what appealed to him? what tickled him? Above all, what did he fear?

He was thinking much and rapidly.

But he said, 'No wonder your King is bankrupt if he has such a Court to look after.'

'He's one of the richest princes in India,' returned the man in the yellow coat. 'He doesn't know himself what he has.'

'Why doesn't he pay his debts, then, instead of keeping you mooning about here?'

'Because he's a native. He'd spend a hundred thousand pounds on a marriage feast, and delay payment of a bill for two hundred rupees four years.'

'You ought to cure him of that,' insisted Tarvin. 'Send a sheriff after the crown jewels.'

'You don't know Indian princes. They would pay a bill before they would let the crown jewels go. They are sacred. They are part of the government.'.

'Ah, I'd give something to see the Luck of the State!' exclaimed a voice from one of the chairs, which Tarvin afterward learned belonged to the agent of a Calcutta firm of jewellers.

'What's that?' he asked, as casually as he knew how, sipping his whisky and soda.

'The Naulahka. Don't you know?'

Tarvin was saved the need of an answer by the man in yellow. 'Pshaw! All that talk about the Naulahka is invented by the priests.'

'I don't think so,' returned the jeweller's agent judicially. 'The King told me when I was last here that he had once shown it to a Viceroy. But he is the only foreigner who has ever seen it. The King assured me he didn't know where it was himself.'

'Pooh! Do you believe in carved emeralds two inches square?' asked the other, turning to Tarvin.

'That's only the centre-piece,' said the jeweller; 'and I wouldn't mind wagering that it's a tallow-drop emerald. It isn't that that staggers me. My wonder is how these chaps, who don't care anything for water in a stone, could have taken the trouble to get together half-a-dozen perfect gems, much less fifty. They say that the necklace was begun when William the Conqueror came over.'

'That gives them a year or two,' said Tarvin. 'I would undertake to get some jewellery together myself if you gave me eight centuries.'

His face was turned a little away from them as he lay back in his chair. His heart was going quickly. He had been through mining-trades, land-speculations, and cattle-deals in his time. He had known moments when the turn of a hair, the wrinkle of an eyelid, meant ruin to him. But they were not moments into which eight centuries were gathered.

They looked at him with a remote pity in their eyes.

'Five absolutely perfect specimens of the nine precious stones,' began the jeweller; 'the ruby, emerald, sapphire, diamond, opal, cat's-eye, turquoise, amethyst, and——'

'Topaz?' asked Tarvin, with the air of a proprietor.

'No; black diamond—black as night.'

'But how do you know all these things? How do you get on to them?' asked Tarvin curiously.

'Like everything else in a Native State—common talk, but difficult to prove. Nobody can as much as guess where that necklace is.'

'Probably under the foundations of some temple in the city,' said the yellow-coated man.

Tarvin, in spite of the careful guard he was keeping over himself, could not help kindling at this. He saw himself digging up the city.

'Where *is* this city?' inquired he.

They pointed across the sun-glare, and showed him a rock girt by a triple line of wall. It was exactly like one of the many ruined cities that Tarvin had passed in the bullock-cart. A rock of a dull and angry red surmounted that rock. Up to the foot of the rock ran the yellow sands of the actual desert—the desert that supports neither tree nor shrub, only the wild ass, and somewhere in its heart, men say, the wild camel.

Tarvin stared through the palpitating haze of heat, and saw that there was neither life nor motion about the city. It was a little after noonday, and his Majesty's subjects were asleep. This solid block of loneliness, then, was the visible end of his journey—the Jericho he had come from Topaz to overthrow.

And he reflected, 'Now, if a man should come from New York in a bullock-cart to whistle around the Sauguache Range, I wonder what sort of fool I'd call him!'

He rose and stretched his dusty limbs. 'What time does it get cool enough to take in the town?' he asked.

'Do *what* to the town? Better be careful. You might find yourself in difficulties with the Resident,' warned his friendly adviser.

Tarvin could not understand why a stroll through the deadest town he had ever seen should be forbidden. But he held his peace, inasmuch as he was in a strange country, where nothing, save a certain desire for command on the part of women, was as he had known it. He would take in the town thoroughly. Otherwise he began to fear that its monumental sloth—there was still no sign of life upon the walled rock—would swallow him up, or turn him into a languid Calcutta drummer.

Something must be done at once before his wits were numbed. He inquired the way to the telegraph-office, half doubting, even though he saw the wires, the existence of a telegraph in Rhatore.

'By the way,' one of the men called after him, 'it's worth remembering that any telegram you send here is handed all round the Court and shown to the King.'

Tarvin thanked him, and thought this *was* worth remembering, as he trudged on through the sand toward a desecrated Mohammedan mosque near the road to the city which was doing duty as a telegraph-office.

A trooper of the State was lying fast asleep on the threshold, his horse picketed to a long bamboo lance driven into the ground. Other sign of life there was none, save a few doves cooing sleepily in the darkness under the arch.

Tarvin gazed about him dispiritedly for the blue-and-white sign of the Western Union, or its analogue in this queer land. He saw that the telegraph wires disappeared through a hole in the dome of the mosque. There were two or three low wooden doors under the archway. He opened one at random, and stepped upon a warm, hairy body, which sprang up with a grunt. Tarvin had hardly time to draw back before a young buffalo calf rushed out. Undisturbed, he opened another door, disclosing a flight of steps eighteen inches wide. Up these he travelled with difficulty, hoping to catch the sound of the ticker. But the building was as silent as the tomb it had once been. He opened another door, and stumbled into a room, the domed ceiling of which was inlaid with fretted tracery in barbaric colours, picked out with myriads of tiny fragments of mirror. The flood of colour and the glare of the snow-white floor made him blink after the pitchy darkness of the staircase. Still, the place was undoubtedly a telegraph-office, for an antiquated instrument was clamped upon a cheap dressing-table. The sunlight streamed through the gash in the dome which had been made to admit the telegraph wires. It had never been repaired.

Tarvin stood in the sunlight and stared about him. He took off the soft, wide-brimmed Western hat, which he was finding too warm for this climate, and mopped his forehead. As he stood in the sunlight, straight, clean-limbed, and strong, one who lurked in this mysterious spot with designs upon him would have decided that he did not look a wholesome person to attack. He pulled at the long thin moustache which drooped at the corners of his mouth in a curve shaped by the habit of tugging at it in thought, and muttered picturesque remarks in a tongue to which these walls had never echoed. What chance was there of communicating with the United States of America from this abyss of oblivion? Even the 'damn' that came back to him from the depths of the dome sounded foreign and inexpressive.

A sheeted figure lay on the floor. 'It *takes* a dead man to run this place!' exclaimed Tarvin, discovering the body. 'Hallo, you! Get up there!'

The figure rose to its feet with grunts, cast away its covering, and disclosed a very sleepy native in a complete suit of dove-coloured satin.

'Ho!' cried he.

'Yes,' returned Tarvin imperturbably.

'You want to see me?'

'No. I want to send a telegram, if there's any electric fluid in this old tomb.'

'Sir,' said the native affably, 'you have come to right shop. I am telegraph operator and Postmaster-General of this State.'

He seated himself in a decayed chair, opened a drawer of the table, and began to search for something.

'What you looking for, young man? Lost your connection with Calcutta?'

'Most gentlemen bring their own forms,' he said, with a distant note of reproach in his bland manner. 'But here is form. Have you got pencil?'

'Oh, see here, don't let me strain this office. Hadn't you better go and lie down again? I'll tap the message off myself. What's your signal for Calcutta?'

'You, sir, not understanding this instrument.'

'*Don't* I? You ought to see me milk the wires at election time.'

'This instrument require most judeecious handling, sir. You write message. I send. That is proper division of labour. Ha! ha!'

Tarvin wrote his message, which ran thus:—

'Getting there. Remember Three C.'s—TARVIN.'

It was addressed to Mrs. Mutrie at the address she had given him in Denver.

'Rush it!' he said, as he handed it back over the table to the smiling image.

'All right. No feear. I am here for that,' returned the native, understanding in general terms from the cabalistic word that his customer was in haste.

'Will the thing ever get there?' drawled Tarvin, as he leaned over the table and met the gaze of the satin-clothed being with an air of good comradeship, which invited him to let him into the fraud, if there was one.

'Oh yes; to-morrow. Denver is in the United States America,' said the native, looking up at Tarvin with childish glee in the sense of knowledge.

'Shake!' exclaimed Tarvin, offering him a hairy fist. 'You've been well brought up.'

He stayed half an hour fraternising with the man on the foundation of this common ground of knowledge, and saw him work the message off on his instrument, his heart going out on that first click all the way home. In the midst of the conversation the native suddenly dived into the cluttered drawer of the dressing-table, and drew forth a telegram covered with dust, which he offered to Tarvin's scrutiny.

'You knowing any new Englishman coming to Rhatore name Turpin?' he asked.

Tarvin stared at the address a moment, and then tore open the envelope to find, as he expected, that it was for him. It was from Mrs. Mutrie, congratulating him on his election to the Colorado Legislature by a majority of 1518 over Sheriff.

Tarvin uttered an abandoned howl of joy, executed a war-dance on the white floor of the mosque, snatched the astounded operator from behind his table, and whirled him away into a mad waltz. Then, making a low salaam to the now wholly bewildered native, he rushed from the building, waving his cable in the air, and went capering up the road.

When he was back at the rest-house again, he retired to a bath to grapple seriously with the dust of the desert, while the commercial travellers without discussed his comings and goings. He plunged about luxuriously in a gigantic bowl of earthenware, while a brown-skinned water-carrier sluiced the contents of a goat-skin over his head.

A voice in the veranda, a little louder than the others, said, 'He's probably come prospecting for gold, or boring for oil, and won't tell.'

Tarvin winked a wet left eye.

# VII

*There is pleasure in the wet, wet clay,*
  *When the artist's hand is potting it;*
*There is pleasure in the wet, wet lay,*
  *When the poet's pad is blotting it;*
*There is pleasure in the shine of your picture on the line*
  *At the Royal Acade-my;*
*But the pleasure felt in these is as chalk to Cheddar cheese,*
  *When it comes to a well-made Lie:*
    *To a quite unwreckable Lie,*
    *To a most impeccable Lie,*
*To a water-tight, fireproof, angle-iron, sunk-hinge, time-*
  *lock, steel-faced Lie!*
    *Not a private-hansom Lie,*
    *But a pair-and-brougham Lie,*
*Not a little-place-at-Tooting, but a country-house-with-*
  *shooting,*
    *And a ring-fence-deer-park Lie.*
      *—Op. 3.*

A COMMON REST-HOUSE in the desert is not overstocked with furniture or carpets. One table, two chairs, a rack on the door for clothing, and a list of charges, are sufficient for each room; and the traveller brings his own bedding. Tarvin read the tariff with deep interest before falling asleep that night, and discovered that this was only in a distant sense a hotel, and that he was open to the danger of being turned out at twelve hours' notice, after he had inhabited his unhomely apartment for a day and a night.

Before he went to bed he called for pen and ink, and wrote a letter to Mrs. Mutrie on the notepaper of his land and improvement company. Under the map of Colorado, at the top, which confidently showed the railroad system of the State converging at Topaz, was the legend, 'N. Tarvin, Real Estate and Insurance Agent.' The tone of his letter was even more assured than the map.

He dreamed that night that the Maharajah was swapping the Naulahka with him for town lots. His Majesty backed out just as they were concluding the deal, and demanded that Tarvin should throw in his own favourite mine, the 'Lingering Lode,' to boot. In his dream Tarvin had kicked at this, and the Maharajah had responded, 'All right, my boy; no Three C.'s then,' and Tarvin had yielded the point, had hung the Naulahka about Mrs. Mutrie's neck, and in the same breath had heard the Speaker of the Colorado Legislature declaring that since the coming of the Three C.'s he officially recognised Topaz as the metropolis of the West. Then, perceiving that he himself was the Speaker, Tarvin began to doubt the genuineness of these remarks, and awoke, with aloes in his mouth, to find the dawn spreading over Rhatore, and beckoning him out to the conquests of reality.

He was confronted in the veranda by a grizzled, bearded, booted native soldier on a camel, who handed down to him a greasy little brown book, bearing the legend, *Please write 'Seen.'*

Tarvin looked at this new development from the heated landscape with interest, but not with an outward effect of surprise. He had already learned one secret of the East—never to be surprised at anything. He took the book and read, on a thumbed page, the announcement, 'Divine services conducted on Sundays in the drawing-room of the Residency at 7.30 A.M.

Strangers are cordially invited to attend. (Signed) L. R. Estes, American Presbyterian Mission.'

'They don't get up early for nothing in this country,' mused Tarvin. 'Church "at 7.30 A.M." When do they have dinner? Well, what do I do about this?' he asked the man aloud. The trooper and camel looked at him together, and grunted as they went away. It was no concern of theirs.

Tarvin addressed a remark of confused purport to the retreating figures. This was plainly not a country in which business could be done at red heat. He hungered for the moment when, with the necklace in his pocket and Kate by his side, he should again set his face westward.

The shortest way to that was to go over to call on the missionary. He was an American, and could tell him about the Naulahka if anybody could. Tarvin had also a shrewd suspicion that he could tell him something about Kate.

The missionary's home, which was just without the city walls, was also of red sandstone, one storey high, and as bare of vines or any living thing as the station at Rawut Junction. But he presently found that there were living beings inside the house, with warm hearts and a welcome for him. Mrs. Estes turned out to be that motherly and kindly woman, with the instinct for housekeeping, who would make a home of a cave. She had a round, smooth face, a soft skin, and quiet, happy eyes. She may have been forty. Her still untinged brown hair was brushed smoothly back; her effect was sedate and restful.

Their visitor had learned that they came from Bangor, Maine, had founded a tie of brotherhood on the fact that his father had been born on a farm down Portland way, and had been invited to breakfast before he had been ten minutes in the house. Tarvin's gift of sympathy was irresistible. He was the kind of man to whom men confide their heart-secrets, and the cankers of their inmost lives, in hotel smoking-rooms. He was the repository of scores of tales of misery and error which he could do nothing to help, and of a few which he could help, and had helped. Before breakfast was ready he had from Estes and his wife the whole picture of their situation at Rhatore. They told him of their troubles with the Maharajah and with the Maharajah's wives, and of the exceeding unfruitfulness of their work; and then of their children, living in the exile of Indian children, at home. They explained that they meant Bangor; they were there with an aunt, receiving their education at the hands of a public school.

'It's five years since we saw them,' said Mrs. Estes, as they sat down to breakfast. 'Fred was only six when he went, and Laura was eight. They are eleven and thirteen now. Only think! We hope they haven't forgotten us; but how can they remember? They are only children.'

And then she told him stories of the renewal of filial ties in India, after such absences, that made his blood run cold.

The breakfast woke a violent homesickness in Tarvin. After a month at sea, two days of the chance railroad meals between Calcutta and Rawut Junction, and a night at the rest-house, he was prepared to value the homely family meal, and the abundance of an American breakfast. They began with a water-melon, which did not help him to feel at home, because water-melons were next to an unknown luxury at Topaz, and, when known, did not ripen in grocers' windows in the month of April. But the oatmeal brought him home again, and the chops and fried potatoes, the coffee and the hot brown popovers, with their beguiling yellow interiors, were reminders far too deep for tears. Mrs. Estes, enjoying his enjoyment, said they must have out the can of maple syrup, which had been sent them all the way from Bangor; and when the white-robed, silent-moving servant in the red turban came in with the waffles, she sent him for it. They were all very happy together over this, and said pleasant things about the American Republic, while the punkah sang its droning song over their heads.

Tarvin had a map of Colorado in his pocket, of course, and when the talk, swinging to one part of the United States and another, worked westward, he spread it out on the breakfast-table, between the waffles and the chops, and showed them the position of Topaz. He explained to Estes how a new railroad, running north and south, would make the town, and then he had to say affectionately what a wonderful town it really was, and to tell them about the buildings they had put up in the last twelve months, and how they had picked themselves up after the fire and gone to building the next morning. The fire had brought $100,000 into the town in insurance, he said. He exaggerated his exaggerations in unconscious defiance of the hugeness of the empty landscape lying outside the window. He did not mean to let the East engulf him or Topaz.

'We've got a young lady coming to us, I think, from your State,' interrupted Mrs. Estes, to whom all Western towns were alike. 'Wasn't it Topaz, Lucien? I'm almost sure it was.'

She rose and went to her work-basket for a letter, from which he confirmed her statement. 'Yes; Topaz. A Miss Sheriff. She comes to us from the Zenana Mission. Perhaps you know her?'

Tarvin's head bent over the map, which he was refolding. He answered shortly, 'Yes; I know her. When is she likely to be here?'

'Most any day now,' said Mrs. Estes.

'It seems a pity,' said Tarvin, 'to bring a young girl out here all alone, away from her friends—though I'm sure you'll be friends to her,' he added quickly, seeking Mrs. Estes' eyes.

'We shall try to keep her from getting homesick,' said Mrs. Estes, with the motherly note in her voice. 'There's Fred and Laura home in Bangor, you know,' she added after a pause.

'That will be good of you,' said Tarvin, with more feeling than the interests of the Zenana Mission demanded.

'May I ask what your business is here?' inquired the missionary, as he passed his cup to his wife to be refilled. He had a rather formal habit of speech, and his words came muffled from the depths of a dense jungle of beard—iron-grey and unusually long. He had a benevolently grim face, a precise but friendly manner, and a good way of looking one in the eye which Tarvin liked. He was a man of decided opinions, particularly about the native races of India.

'Well, I'm prospecting,' Tarvin said, in a leisurely tone, glancing out of the window as if he expected to see Kate start up out of the desert.

'Ah! For gold?'

'W-e-l-l, yes. As much that as anything.'

Estes invited him out upon the veranda to smoke a cigar with him; his wife brought her sewing and sat with them; and as they smoked Tarvin asked him his questions about the Naulahka. Where was it? What was it? he inquired boldly. But he found that the missionary, though an American, was no wiser about it than the lazy commercial travellers at the rest-house. He knew that it existed, but knew no man who had seen it save the Maharajah. Tarvin got at this through much talk about other things which interested him less; but he began to see an idea in the gold-mining to which the missionary persistently returned. Estes said he meant to engage in placer-mining, of course?

'Of course,' assented Tarvin.

'But you won't find much gold in the Amet River, I fancy. The natives have washed it spasmodically for hundreds of years. There is nothing to be found but what little silt washes down from the quartz rocks of the Gungra Hills. But you will be undertaking work on a large scale, I judge?' said the missionary, looking at him curiously.

'Oh, on a large scale, of course.'

Estes added that he supposed he had thought of the political difficulties in his way. He would have to get the consent of Colonel Nolan, and through him the consent of the British Government, if he meant to do anything serious in the State. In fact, he would have to get Colonel Nolan's consent to stay in Rhatore at all.

'Do you mean that I shall have to make it worth the British Government's while to let me alone?'

'Yes.'

'All right; I'll do that too.'

Mrs. Estes looked up quickly at her husband from under her eyebrows. Woman-like, she was thinking.

# VIII

*When a Lover hies abroad,*
  *Looking for his Love,*
*Azrael smiling sheathes his sword;*
  *Heaven smiles above.*
*Earth and Sea*
*His servants be,*
*And to lesser compass round,*
*That his Love be sooner found.*
        CHORUS FROM LIBRETTO TO 'NAULAHKA.'

TARVIN LEARNED a number of things within the next week; and
with what the West calls 'adaptability,' put on, with the complete suit of white linen which he donned the second day, an
initiation into a whole new system of manners, usages, and
traditions. They were not all agreeable, but they were all in
a good cause, and he took pains to see that his new knowledge
should not go for nothing, by securing an immediate presenta-
tion to the only man in the State of whom it was definitely
assertable that he had seen the object of his hopes. Estes willingly presented him to the Maharajah. The missionary and
he rode one morning up the steep slopes of the rock on which
stood the palace, itself rock-hewn. Passing through a deep archway, they entered a marble-flagged courtyard, and there found
the Maharajah, attended by one ragged and out-at-elbow
menial, discussing the points of a fox-terrier, which was lying
before him on the flags.

Tarvin, unversed in kings, had expected a certain amount
of state from one who did not pay his bills, and might be

reasonably expected to cultivate reserve; but he was not prepared for the slovenly informality of a ruler in his everyday
garb, released from the duty of behaving with restraint in the
presence of a Viceroy, nor for the picturesque mixture of dirt
and decoration about the Court. The Maharajah proved a
large and amiable despot, brown and bush-bearded, arrayed
in a gold-sprigged, green velvet dressing-gown, who appeared
only too delighted to meet a man who had no connection
with the Government of India, and who never mentioned the
subject of money.

The disproportionate smallness of his hands and feet showed
that the ruler of Gokral Seetarun came of the oldest blood in
Rajputana. His fathers had fought hard and ridden far with
sword-hilts and stirrups that would hardly serve an English
child. His face was bloated and sodden, and the dull eyes
stared wearily above deep, rugged pouches. To Tarvin, accustomed to read the motives of Western men in their faces, there
seemed to be neither fear nor desire in those eyes—only everlasting weariness. It was like looking at an extinct volcano—a
volcano that rumbled in good English.

Tarvin had a natural interest in dogs, and the keenest possible desire to ingratiate himself with the ruler of the State.
As a king he considered him something of an imposture, but
as a brother dog-fancier, and the lord of the Naulahka, he
was to Tarvin more than a brother; that is to say, the brother
of one's beloved. He spoke eloquently and to the point.

'Come again,' said the Maharajah, with a light of real interest in his eyes, as Estes, a little scandalised, drew off his
guest. 'Come again this evening after dinner. You have come
from new countries.'

His Majesty, later, carried away by the evening dose of
opium, without which no Rajput can talk or think, taught this

irreverent stranger, who told him tales of white men beyond the seas, the royal game of pachisi. They played it far into the night, in the marble-flagged courtyard, surrounded by green shutters from behind which Tarvin could hear, without turning his head, the whisper of watching women and the rustle of silken robes. The palace, he saw, was all eyes.

Next morning, at dawn, he found the King waiting at the head of the main street of his city for a certain notorious wild boar to come home. The game laws of Gokral Seetarun extended to the streets of walled towns, and the wild pig rooted unconcerned at night in the alley-ways. The pig came, and was dropped, at a hundred yards, by his Majesty's new Express rifle. It was a clean shot, and Tarvin applauded cordially. Had his Majesty the King ever seen a flying coin hit by a pistol bullet? The weary eyes brightened with childish delight. The King had not seen this feat, and had not the coin. Tarvin flung an American quarter skyward, and clipped it with his revolver as it fell. Thereupon the King begged him to do it again, which Tarvin, valuing his reputation, politely declined to do unless one of the Court officials would set the example.

The King was himself anxious to try, and Tarvin threw the coin for him. The bullet whizzed unpleasantly close to Tarvin's ear, but the quarter on the grass was dented when he picked it up. The King liked Tarvin's dent as well as if it had been his own, and Tarvin was not the man to undeceive him.

The following morning the royal favour was completely withdrawn, and it was not until he had conferred with the disconsolate drummers in the rest-house that Tarvin learned that Sitabhai had been indulging one of her queenly rages. On this he transferred himself and his abundant capacity for interesting men off-hand to Colonel Nolan, and made that weary white-haired man laugh as he had not laughed since he had been a subaltern over an account of the King's revolver practice. Tarvin shared his luncheon, and discovered from him in the course of the afternoon the true policy of the Government of India in regard to the State of Gokral Seetarun. The Government hoped to elevate it; but as the Maharajah would not pay for the means of civilisation, the progress was slow. Colonel Nolan's account of the internal policy of the palace, given with official caution, was absolutely different from the missionary's, which again differed entirely from the profane versions of the men in the rest-house.

At twilight the Maharajah pursued Tarvin with a mounted messenger, for the favour of the royal countenance was restored, and he required the presence of the tall man who clipped coins in the air, told tales, and played pachisi. There was more than pachisi upon the board that night, and his Majesty the King grew pathetic, and confided to Tarvin a long and particular account of his own and the State's embarrassments, which presented everything in a fourth new light. He concluded with an incoherent appeal to the President of the United States, on whose illimitable powers and far-reaching authority Tarvin dwelt, with a patriotism extended for the moment to embrace the nation to which Topaz belonged. For many reasons he did not conceive that this was an auspicious time to open negotiations for the transfer of the Naulahka. The Maharajah would have given away half his kingdom, and appealed to the Resident in the morning.

The next day, and many succeeding days, brought to the door of the rest-house, where Tarvin was still staying, a procession of rainbow-clad Orientals, ministers of the Court each one, who looked with contempt on the waiting commercial travellers, and deferentially made themselves known to Tar-

vin, whom they warned in fluent and stilted English against
trusting anybody except themselves. Each confidence wound
up with, 'And I am your true friend, sir'; and each man ac-
cused his fellows to the stranger of every crime against the
State, or ill-will toward the Government of India, that it had
entered his own brain to conceive.

Tarvin could only faintly conjecture what all this meant. It
seemed to him no extraordinary mark of Court favour to play
pachisi with the King, and the mazes of Oriental diplomacy
were dark to him. The ministers were equally at a loss to
understand him. He had walked in upon them from out of
the skyline, utterly self-possessed, utterly fearless, and, so far as
they could see, utterly disinterested; the greater reason, therefore, for suspecting that he was a veiled emissary of the Government, whose plans they could not fathom. That he was
barbarously ignorant of everything pertaining to the Government of India only confirmed their belief. It was enough for
them to know that he went to the King in secret, was closeted
with him for hours, and possessed, for the time being, the
royal ear.

These smooth-voiced, stately, mysterious strangers filled Tarvin with weariness and disgust, and he took out his revenge
upon the commercial travellers, to whom he sold stock in his
land and improvement company between their visits. The
yellow-coated man, as his first friend and adviser, he allowed
to purchase a very few shares in the 'Lingering Lode,' on the
dead quiet. It was before the days of the gold boom in Lower
Bengal, and there was still faith in the land.

These transactions took him back in fancy to Topaz, and
made him long for some word about the boys at home, from
whom he had absolutely cut himself off by this secret expedition, in which he was playing, necessarily alone, for the high

stake common to them both. He would have given all the rupees in his pocket at any moment for a sight of the *Topaz Telegram,* or even for a look at a Denver daily. What was happening to his mines—to the 'Mollie K.,' which was being worked on a lease; to the 'Mascot,' which was the subject of a legal dispute; to the 'Lingering Lode,' where they had been on the point of striking it very rich when he left; and to his 'Garfield' claim, which Fibby Winks had jumped? What had become of the mines of all his friends; of their cattle-ranches; of their deals? What, in fine, had become of Colorado and of the United States of America? They might have legislated silver out of existence at Washington, for all he knew, and turned the Republic into a monarchy at the old stand.

His single resource from these pangs was his visits to the house of the missionary, where they talked Bangor, Maine, in the United States. To that house he knew that every day was bringing nearer the little girl he had come half-way round the world to keep in sight.

In the splendour of a yellow and violet morning, ten days after his arrival, he was roused from his sleep by a small, shrill voice in the veranda demanding the immediate attendance of the new Englishman. The Maharaj Kunwar, heir-apparent to the throne of Gokral Seetarun, a wheat-coloured child, aged nine, had ordered his miniature Court, which was held quite distinct from his father's, to equip his C-spring barouche, and to take him to the rest-house.

Like his jaded father, the child required amusement. All the women of the palace had told him that the new Englishman made the King laugh. The Maharaj Kunwar could speak English much better than his father—French, too, for the matter of that—and he was anxious to show off his accomplishments to a Court whose applause he had not yet commanded.

Tarvin obeyed the voice because it was a child's, and came out to find an apparently empty barouche, and an escort of ten gigantic troopers.

'How do you do? *Comment vous portez-vous?* I am the prince of this State. I am the Maharaj Kunwar. Some day I shall be King. Come for drive with me.'

A tiny mittened hand was extended in greeting. The mittens were of the crudest magenta wool, with green stripes at the wrist; but the child was robed in stiff gold brocade from head to foot, and in his turban was set an aigrette of diamonds six inches high, while emeralds in a thick cluster fell over his eyebrow. Under all this glitter the dark onyx eyes looked out, and they were full of pride and of the loneliness of childhood.

Tarvin obediently took his seat in the barouche. He was beginning to wonder whether he should ever wonder at anything again.

'We will drive beyond the racecourse on the railway road,' said the child. 'Who are you?' he asked, softly laying his hand on Tarvin's wrist.

'Just a man, sonny.'

The face looked very old under the turban, for those born to absolute power, or those who have never known a thwarted desire, and reared under the fiercest sun in the world, age even more swiftly than the other children of the East, who are self-possessed men when they should be bashful babes.

'They say you come here to see things.'

'That's true,' said Tarvin.

'When I'm King I shall allow nobody to come here—not even the Viceroy.'

'That leaves me out,' remarked Tarvin, laughing.

'You shall come,' returned the child, measuredly, 'if you make me laugh. Make me laugh now.'

# THE NAULAHKA

'Shall I, little fellow? Well—there was once—I wonder what *would* make a child laugh in this country. I've never seen one do it yet. W-h-e-w!' Tarvin gave a low, long-drawn whistle. 'What's that over there, my boy?'

A little puff of dust rose very far down the road. It was made by swiftly moving wheels, consequently it had nothing to do with the regular traffic of the State.

'That is what I came out to see,' said the Maharaj Kunwar. 'She will make me well. My father, the Maharajah, said so. I am not well now.' He turned imperiously to a favourite groom at the back of the carriage. 'Soor Singh'—he spoke in the vernacular—'what is it when I become without sense? I have forgotten the English.' The groom leaned forward.

'Heaven-born, I do not remember,' he said.

'Now I remember,' said the child suddenly. 'Mrs. Estes says it is fits. What are fits?'

Tarvin put his hand tenderly on the child's shoulder, but his eyes were following the dust-cloud. 'Let us hope she'll cure them, anyway, young 'un, whatever they are. But who is *she*?'

'I do not know the name, but she will make me well. See! My father has sent a carriage to meet her.'

An empty barouche was drawn up by the side of the road as the rickety, straining mail-cart drew nearer, with frantic blasts upon a battered key-bugle.

'It's better than a bullock-cart anyway,' said Tarvin to himself, standing up in the carriage, for he was beginning to choke.

'Young man, don't you know who she is?' he asked huskily again.

'She was sent,' said the Maharaj Kunwar.

'Her name's Kate,' said Tarvin in his throat, 'and don't you forget it.' Then to himself in a contented whisper, '*Kate!*'

The child waved his hand to his escort, who, dividing, lined either side of the road, with all the ragged bravery of irregular cavalry. The mail-cart halted, and Kate, crumpled, dusty, dishevelled from her long journey, and red-eyed from lack of sleep, drew back the shutters of the palanquin-like affair, and stepped dazed into the road. Her numbed limbs would have doubled under her, but Tarvin, leaping from the barouche, caught her to him, regardless of the escort and of the calm-eyed child in the golden drapery, who was shouting, 'Kate! Kate!'

'Run along home, bub,' said Tarvin. 'Well, Kate?'

But Kate had only her tears for him, and a gasping 'You! You! *You!*'

## IX

*We meet in an evil land*
*    That is near to the gates of Hell—*
*I wait for thy command,*
*To serve, to speed, or withstand;*
*    And thou sayest I do not well?*

*Oh, love, the flowers so red*
*    Be only blossoms of flame.*
*The earth is full of the dead,*
*The new-killed, restless dead.*
*There is danger beneath and o'erhead;*
*    And I guard at thy gates in fear*
*        Of peril and jeopardy,*
*    Of words thou canst not hear,*
*        Of signs thou canst not see—*
*And thou sayest 'tis ill that I came?*

IN SHADOWLAND.

TEARS STOOD AGAIN in Kate's eyes as she uncoiled her hair before the mirror in the room Mrs. Estes had prepared against her coming—tears of vexation. It was an old story with her that the world wants nothing done for it, and visits with displeasure those who must prod up its lazy content. But in landing at Bombay she had supposed herself at the end of outside hindrances and obstacles. What was now to come would belong to the wholesome difficulties of real work. And here was Nick!

She had made the journey from Topaz in a long mood of exaltation. She was launched; it made her giddy and happy,

like the boy's first taste of the life of men. She was free at last.
No one could stop her. Nothing could keep her from the life
to which she had promised herself. A little moment and she
might stretch forth her hand and lay it fast upon her work.
A few days and she should stoop eye to eye above the pain
that had called to her across seas. In her dreams piteous hands
of women were raised in prayer to her, and dry, sick palms
were laid in hers. The steady urge of the ship was too slow for
her; she counted the throbs of the screw. Standing far in the
prow, with wind-blown hair, straining her eyes toward India,
her spirit went longingly forth toward those to whom she was
going; and her life seemed to release itself from her, and sped
far, far over the waves, until it reached them and gave itself
to them. For a moment, as she set foot on land, she trembled
with a revulsion of feeling. She drew near her work; but was
it for her? These old fears, which had gone doubtfully with
her purpose from the beginning, she put behind her with a
stern refusal to question them. She was for so much of her
work as Heaven would let her do; and she went forward with
a new, strong, humble impulse of devotion filling and uplifting
her.

It was in this mood that she stepped out of the coach at
Rhatore into Tarvin's arms.

She did justice to the kindness that had brought him over
all these leagues, but she heartily wished that he had not come.
The existence of a man who loved her, and for whom she
could do nothing, was a sad and troubling fact enough fourteen thousand miles away. Face to face with it, alone in India,
it enlarged itself unbearably, and thrust itself between her and
all her hopes of bringing serious help to others. Love literally
did not seem to her the most important thing in the world at
that moment, and something else did; but that didn't make

Nick's trouble unimportant, or prevent it, while she braided her hair, from getting in the way of her thoughts. On the morrow she was to enter upon the life which she meant should be a help to those whom it could reach; and here she was thinking of Nicholas Tarvin!

It was because she foresaw that she would keep on thinking of him that she wished him away. He was the tourist wandering about behind the devotee in the cathedral at prayers. He was the other thought. In his person he represented and symbolised the life she had left behind; much worse, he represented a pain she could not heal. It was not with the haunting figure of Love attendant that one carried out large purposes. Nor was it with a divided mind that men conquered cities. The intent with which she was aflame needed all of her. She could not divide herself even with Nick. And yet it was good of him to come, and like him. She knew that he had not come merely in pursuit of a selfish hope. It was as he had said—he couldn't sleep nights, knowing what might befall her. That was *really* good of him.

Mrs. Estes had invited Tarvin to breakfast the day before, when Kate was not expected, but Tarvin was not the man to decline an invitation at the last moment on that account, and he faced Kate across the breakfast-table next morning with a smile which evoked an unwilling smile from her. In spite of a sleepless night she was looking very fresh and pretty in the white muslin frock which had replaced her travelling dress, and when he found himself alone with her after breakfast on the veranda (Mrs. Estes having gone to look after the morning affairs of a housekeeper, and Estes having betaken himself to his mission-school, inside the city walls), he began to make her his compliments upon the cool white, unknown to the West. But Kate stopped him.

'Nick,' she said, facing him, 'will you do something for me?'

Seeing her much in earnest, Tarvin attempted the parry humorous; but she broke in—

'No; it is something I want very much, Nick. Will you do it for me?'

'Is there anything I wouldn't do for you?' he asked seriously.

'I don't know; this, perhaps. But you must do it.'

'What is it?'

'Go away.'

He shook his head.

'But you must.'

'Listen, Kate,' said Tarvin, thrusting his hands deep into the big pockets of his white coat; 'I can't. You don't know the place you've come to. Ask me the same question a week hence. I won't agree to go. But I'll agree to talk it over with you then.'

'I know now everything that counts,' she answered. 'I want to do what I've come here for. I shan't be able to do it if you stay. You understand, don't you, Nick? Nothing can change that.'

'Yes, it can. *I* can. I'll behave.'

'You needn't tell me you'll be kind. I know it. But even you can't be kind enough to help hindering me. Believe that, now, Nick, and go. It isn't that I want you to go, you know.'

'Oh!' observed Tarvin, with a smile.

'Well—you know what I mean,' returned Kate, her face unrelaxed.

'Yes; I know. But if I'm good it won't matter. I know that too. You'll see,' he said gently. 'Awful journey, isn't it?'

'You promised me not to take it.'

'I didn't take it,' returned Tarvin, smiling, and spreading a seat for her in the hammock, while he took one of the deep veranda chairs himself. He crossed his legs and fixed the white

*331*

pith helmet he had lately adopted on his knee. 'I came round the other way on purpose.'

'What do you mean?' asked Kate, dropping tentatively into the hammock.

'San Francisco and Yokohama, of course. You told me not to follow you.'

'*Nick!*' She gathered into the single syllable the reproach and reproof, the liking and despair, with which the least and the greatest of his audacities alike affected her.

Tarvin had nothing to say for once, and in the pause that fell she had time to reassure herself of her abhorrence of his presence here, and time to still the impulse of pride, which told her that it was good to be followed over half the earth's girdle for love, and the impulse of admiration for that fine devotion—time, above all—for this was worst and most shameful—to scorn the sense of loneliness and far-awayness that came rolling in on her out of the desert like a cloud, and made the protecting and homelike presence of the man she had known in the other life seem for a moment sweet and desirable.

'Come, Kate, you didn't expect me to stay at home, and let you find your way out here to take the chances of this old sandheap, did you? It would be a cold day when I let you come to Gokral Seetarun all by your lone, little girl—freezing cold. I've thought since I've been here, and I've seen what sort of camp it is.'

'Why didn't you tell me you were coming?'

'You didn't seem particularly interested in what I did, when I last saw you.'

'Nick! I didn't want you to come here, and I had to come myself.'

'Well, you've come. I hope you'll like it,' said he, grimly.

'Is it so bad?' she asked. 'Not that I shall mind.'

'Bad! Do you remember Mastodon?'

Mastodon was one of those Western towns which have their future behind them—a city without an inhabitant, abandoned and desolate.

'Take Mastodon for deadness, and fill it with ten Leadvilles for wickedness—Leadville the first year—and you've got a tenth of it.'

He went on to offer her an exposition of the history, politics, and society of Gokral Seetarun, from his own point of view, dealing with the dead East from the standpoint of the living West, and dealing with it vividly. It was a burning theme, and it was a happiness to him to have a listener who could understand his attitude, even if she could not entirely sympathise with it. His tone besought her to laugh at it with him a little, if only a little, and Kate consented to laugh; but she said it all seemed to her more mournful than amusing.

Tarvin could agree to this readily enough, but he told her that he laughed to avoid weeping. It made him tired to see the fixedness, the apathy, and lifelessness of this rich and populous world, which should be up and stirring by rights—trading, organising, inventing, building new towns, making the old ones keep up with the procession, laying new railroads, going in for fresh enterprises, and keeping things humming.

'The've got resources enough,' he said. 'It isn't as if they had the excuse that the country's poor. It's a good country. Move the population of a lively Colorado town to Rhatore, set up a good local paper, organise a board of trade, and let the world know what there is here, and we'd have a boom in six months that would shake the Empire. But what's the use? They're dead. They're mummies. They're wooden images. There isn't enough real, old-fashioned downright rustle and razzle-dazzle and "git up and git" in Gokral Seetarun to run a milk-cart.'

'Yes, yes,' she murmured, half to herself, with illumined eyes. 'It's for that I've come.'

'How's that?'

'Because they are *not* like us,' she answered, turning her lustrous face on him. 'If they were clever, if they were wise, what could we do for them? It is because they are lost, stumbling, foolish creatures that they need us.' She heaved a deep sigh. 'It is good to be here.'

'It's good to have you,' said Tarvin.

She started. 'Don't say such things any more, please, Nick,' she said.

'Oh, well!' he groaned.

'But it's this way, Nick,' she said earnestly, but kindly. 'I don't belong to such things any more—not even to the possibility of them. Think of me as a nun. Think of me as having renounced all such happiness, and all other kinds of happiness but my work.'

'H'm. May I smoke?' At her nod he lighted a cigar. 'I'm glad I'm here for the ceremony.'

'What ceremony?' she asked.

'Seeing you take the veil. But you won't take it.'

'Why not?'

He grumbled inarticulately over his cigar a moment. Then he looked up. 'Because I've got big wealth that says you won't. I know you, I know Rhatore, and I know——'

'What? Who?'

'Myself,' he said, looking up.

She clasped her hands in her lap. 'Nick,' she said, leaning toward him, 'you know I like you. I like you too well to let you go on thinking— You talk of not being able to sleep. How do you suppose I can sleep with the thought always by me that you are laying up a pain and disappointment for yourself—

*334*

one that I can't help, unless I can help it by begging you to go away now. I do beg it. *Please* go!'

Tarvin pulled at his cigar musingly for some seconds. 'Dear girl, I'm not afraid.'

She sighed, and turned her face away toward the desert. 'I wish you were,' she said hopelessly.

'Fear is not for legislators,' he retorted oracularly.

She turned back to him with a sudden motion. 'Legislators! Oh, Nick, are you——?'

'I'm afraid I am—by a majority of 1518.' He handed her the cable-despatch.

'Poor father!'

'Well, I don't know.'

'Oh! Well, I congratulate you, of course.'

'Thanks.'

'But I'm not sure it will be a good thing for you.'

'Yes; that's the way it had struck me. If I spend my whole term out here, like as not my constituents won't be in a mood to advance my political career when I get back.'

'All the more reason——'

'No; the more reason for fixing the real thing first. I can make myself solid in politics any time. But there isn't but one time to make myself solid with you, Kate. It's here. It's now.' He rose and bent over her. 'Do you think I can postpone that, dear? I can adjourn it from day to day, and I do cheerfully, and you shan't hear any more of it until you're ready to. But you like me, Kate. I know that. And I—well, I like you. There isn't but one end to that sort of thing.' He took her hand. 'Good-bye. I'll come and take you for a look at the city tomorrow.'

Kate gazed long after his retreating figure, and then took herself into the house, where a warm, healthful chat with Mrs.

Estes, chiefly about the children at Bangor, helped her to a
sane view of the situation she must face with the reappearance
of Tarvin. She saw that he meant to stay, and if she didn't
mean to go, it was for her to find the brave way of adjusting
the fact to her hopes. His perversity complicated an undertaking which she had never expected to find simple in itself;
and it was finally only because she trusted all that he said im-
plicitly that she was able to stay herself upon his promise to
'behave.' Liberally interpreted, this really meant much from
Tarvin. Perhaps it meant all that she need ask.

When all was said, there remained the impulse to flight; but
she was ashamed to find, when he came in the morning, that a
formidable pang of homesickness drew her toward him, and
made his definite and cheerful presence a welcome sight. Mrs.
Estes had been kind. The two women had made friends, and
found each other's heart with instant sympathy. But a home
face was different, and perhaps Nick's was even more different.
At all events, she willingly let him carry out his plan of showing her the city.

In their walk about it Tarvin did not spare her the advantage of his ten days' residence in Rhatore preceding her
coming. He made himself her guide, and stood on rocks overlooking things and spouted his second-hand history with an
assurance that the oldest Political Resident might have envied.
He was interested in the problems of the State, if not responsible for their solution. Was he not a member of a governing
body? His ceaseless and fruitful curiosity about all new things
had furnished him, in ten days, with much learning about
Rhatore and Gokral Seetarun, enabling him to show to Kate,
with eyes scarcely less fresh than her own, the wonders of the
narrow, sand-choked streets, where the footfalls of camels and
men alike fell dead. They lingered by the royal menagerie of

starved tigers, and the cages of the two tame hunting-leopards, hooded like hawks, that slept, and yawned, and scratched on their two bedsteads by the main gate of the city; and he showed her the ponderous door of the great gate itself, studded with foot-long spikes against the attacks of that living battering-ram, the elephant. He led her through the long lines of dark shops planted in and among the ruins of palaces, whose builders had been long since forgotten, and about the straggling barracks, past knots of fantastically attired soldiers, who hung their day's marketing from the muzzle of their Brown Bess or flint-lock. And then he showed her the mausoleum of the kings of Gokral Seetarun, under the shadow of the great temple where the children of the Sun and Moon went to worship, and where the smooth, black stone bull glared across the main square at the cheap bronze statue of Colonel Nolan's predecessor—an offensively energetic and very plain Yorkshireman. Lastly, they found beyond the walls the clamouring caravansary of traders by the Gateway of the Three Gods, whence the caravans of camels filed out with their burdens of glistening rock-salt for the railroad, and where by day and by night cloaked and jaw-bound riders of the desert, speaking a tongue that none could understand, rode in from God knows what fastness beyond the white hillocks of Jeysulmir.

As they went along, Tarvin asked her about Topaz. How had she left it? How was the dear old town looking? Kate said she had only left it three days after his departure.

'Three days! Three days is a long time in the life of a growing town.'

Kate smiled. 'I didn't see any changes,' she said.

'No? Peters was talking about breaking ground for his new brick saloon on G Street the day after I left; Parsons was getting in a new dynamo for the city's electric light plant. They were just getting to work on the grading of Massachusetts Avenue, and they had planted the first tree in my twenty-acre plot. Kearney, the druggist, was putting in a plate-glass window, and I shouldn't wonder if Maxim had got his new post-office boxes from Meriden before you left. Didn't you notice?'

Kate shook her head. 'I was thinking of something else just then.'

'Pshaw! I'd like to know. But no matter. I suppose it *is* asking too much to expect a woman to play her own hand, and keep the run of improvements in the town,' he mused. 'Women aren't built that way. And yet I used to run a political canvass and a business or two, and something else in that town.' He glanced humorously at Kate, who lifted a warning hand. 'Forbidden subject? All right. I *will* be good. But they had to get up early in the morning to do anything to it without letting me into it. What did your father and mother say at the last?'

'Don't speak of that,' begged Kate.

'Well, I won't.'

'I wake up at night, and think of mother. It's dreadful. At the last I suppose I should have stayed behind and shirked if some one had said the right word—or the wrong one—as I got on board the train, and waved my handkerchief to them.'

'Good Heavens! Why didn't I stay!' he groaned.

'You couldn't have said it, Nick,' she told him quietly.

'You mean your father could. Of course he could, and if he had happened to be some one else he would. When I think of that I want to——!'

'Don't say anything against father, please,' she said, with a tightening of the lips.

'Oh, dear child!' he murmured contritely, 'I didn't mean that. But I have to say something against somebody. Give me somebody to curse, and I'll be quiet.'

'Nick!'

'Well, I'm not a block of wood,' he growled.

'No; you are only a very foolish man.'

Tarvin smiled. 'Now you're shouting.'

She asked him about the Maharaj Kunwar, to change the subject, and Tarvin told her that he was a little brick. But he added that the society of Rhatore wasn't all as good.

'You ought to see Sitabhai!'

He went on to tell her about the Maharajah and the people of the palace with whom she would come in contact. They talked of the strange mingling of impassiveness and childishness in the people, which had already impressed Kate, and spoke of their primitive passions and simple ideas—simple as the massive strength of the Orient is simple.

'They aren't what we should call cultured. They don't know Ibsen a little bit, and they don't go in for Tolstoi for sour apples,' said Tarvin, who did not read three newspapers a day at Topaz for nothing. 'If they really knew the modern young woman, I suppose her life wouldn't be worth an hour's purchase. But they've got some rattling good old-fashioned ideas, all the same—the sort I used to hear once upon a time at my dear old mother's knee, away back in the State of Maine. Mother believed in marriage, you know; and that's where she agreed with me and with the fine old-style natives of India. The venerable, ramshackle, tumble-down institution of matrimony is still in use here, you know.'

'But I never said I sympathised with Nora, Nick,' exclaimed Kate, leaping all the chasms of connection.

'Well, then, that's where you are solid with the Indian Empire. The *Doll's House* glanced right off this blessed old-timey country. You wouldn't know where it had been hit.'

'But I don't agree with all your ideas either,' she felt bound to add.

'I can think of one,' retorted Tarvin, with a shrewd smile. 'But I'll convert you to my views there.'

Kate stopped short in the street along which they were walking. 'I trusted you, Nick!' she said reproachfully.

He stopped, and gazed ruefully at her for a moment. 'Oh, Lord!' he groaned. 'I trusted myself! But I'm always thinking of it. What can you expect? But I tell you what, Kate, this shall be the end—last, final, ultimate. I'm done. From this out I'm a reformed man. I don't promise not to think, and I'll have to go on feeling, just the same. But I'll be quiet. Shake on it.' He offered his hand, and Kate took it.

They walked on for some moments in silence until Tarvin said mournfully, 'You didn't see Heckler just before you came away, did you?'

She shook her head.

'No. Jim and you never did get along much together. But I wish I knew what he's thinking about me. Didn't hear any rumour, any report, going around about what had become of me, I suppose?'

'They thought in town that you had gone to San Francisco to see some of the Western directors of the Colorado and California Central, I think. They thought that because the conductor of your train brought back word that you said you were going to Alaska, and they didn't believe that. I wish you had a better reputation for truth-telling at Topaz, Nick.'

'So do I, Kate. So do I,' exclaimed Tarvin heartily. 'But if I had, how would I ever get the right thing believed? That's just what I wanted them to think—that I was looking after their interests. But where would I be if I had sent that story back? They would have had me working a land-grab in Chile before night. That reminds me—don't mention that I'm here in writing home, please. Perhaps they'll figure that out, too, by the rule of contraries, if I give them the chance. But I don't want to give them the chance.'

'I'm not likely to mention it,' said Kate, flushing.

A moment later she recurred to the subject of her mother. In the yearning for home that came upon her anew in the midst of all the strangeness through which Tarvin was taking her, the thought of her mother, patient, alone, looking for some word from her, hurt her as if for the first time. The memory was for the moment intolerable to her; but when Tarvin asked her why she had come at all if she felt that way, she answered with the courage of better moments—'Why do men go to war?'

Kate saw little of Tarvin during the next few days. Mrs. Estes made her known at the palace, and she had plenty to occupy her mind and heart. There she stepped bewilderedly into a land where it was always twilight—a labyrinth of passages, courtyards, stairs, and hidden ways, all overflowing with veiled women, who peered at her and laughed behind her back, or childishly examined her dress, her helmet, and her gloves. It seemed impossible that she should ever know the smallest part of the vast warren, or distinguish one pale face from another in the gloom, as the women led her through long lines of lonely chambers where the wind sighed alone under the glittering ceilings, to hanging gardens two hundred feet above the level of the ground, but still jealously guarded by high walls, and down again by interminable stairways, from the glare and the blue of the flat roofs to silent subterranean chambers hewn against the heat of the summer sixty feet into the heart of the living rock. At every step she found women and children, and yet more women and children. The palace was reported to hold within its walls four thousand living, and no man knew how many buried, dead.

There were many women—how many she did not know—worked upon by intrigues she could not comprehend, who refused her ministrations absolutely. They were not ill, they said, and the touch of the white woman meant pollution. Others there were who thrust their children before her and bade her bring colour and strength back to these pale buds born in the darkness; and terrible, fierce-eyed girls who leaped upon her out of the dark, overwhelming her with passionate complaints that she did not and dared not understand. Monstrous and obscene pictures glared at her from the walls of the little rooms, and the images of shameless gods mocked her from their greasy niches above the doorways. The heat and the smell of cooking, faint fumes of incense, and the indescribable taint of overcrowded humanity, caught her by the throat. But what she heard and what she guessed sickened her more than any visible horror. Plainly it was one thing to be stirred to generous action by a vivid recital of the state of the women of India, and another to face the unutterable facts in the isolation of the women's apartments of the palace of Rhatore.

Tarvin meanwhile was going about spying out the land on a system which he had contrived for himself. It was conducted on the principle of exhaustion of the possibilities in the order of their importance—every movement which he made having the directest, though not always the most obvious, relation to the Naulahka.

He was free to come and go through the royal gardens, where innumerable and very seldom paid gardeners fought with water-skin and well-wheel against the destroying heat of the desert. He was welcomed in the Maharajah's stables, where eight hundred horses were littered down nightly, and was allowed to watch them go out for their morning exercise, four hundred at a time, in a whirlwind of dust. In the outer courts

of the palace it was open to him to come and go as he chose—
to watch the toilets of the elephants when the Maharajah went
out in state, to laugh with the quarter-guard, and to unearth
dragon-headed, snake-throated pieces of artillery, invented by
native artificers, who, here in the East, had dreamed of the
*mitrailleuse*. But Kate could go where he was forbidden to
venture. He knew the life of a white woman to be as safe in
Rhatore as in Topaz; but on the first day she disappeared,
untroubled and unquestioning, behind the darkness of the
veiled door leading to the apartments of the women of the
palace, he found his hand going instinctively to the butt of
his revolver.

The Maharajah was an excellent friend, and no bad hand
at pachisi; but as Tarvin sat opposite him, half an hour later,
he reflected that he should not recommend the Maharajah's
life for insurance if anything happened to his love while she
remained in those mysterious chambers from which the only
sign that came to the outer world was a ceaseless whispering
and rustling. When Kate came out, the little Maharaj Kunwar
clinging to her hand, her face was white and drawn, and her
eyes full of indignant tears. She had seen.

Tarvin hastened to her side, but she put him from her with
the imperious gesture that women know in deep moments, and
fled to Mrs. Estes.

Tarvin felt himself for the moment rudely thrust out of her
life. The Maharaj Kunwar found him that evening pacing up
and down the veranda of the rest-house, almost sorry that he
had not shot the Maharajah for bringing that look into Kate's
eyes. With deep-drawn breath he thanked his God that he was
there to watch and defend, and, if need were, to carry off, at
the last, by force. With a shudder he fancied her here alone,
save for the distant care of Mrs. Estes.

'I have brought this for Kate,' said the child, descending from his carriage cautiously, with a parcel that filled both his arms. 'Come with me there.'

Nothing loth, Tarvin came, and they drove over to the house of the missionary.

'All the people in my palace,' said the child as they went, 'say that she's your Kate.'

'I'm glad they know that much,' muttered Tarvin to himself savagely. 'What's this you have got for her?' he asked the Maharaj aloud, laying his hand on the parcel.

'It is from my mother, the Queen—the real Queen, you know, because I am the Prince. There is a message, too, that I must not tell.' He began to whisper, child-like, to himself, to keep the message in mind. Kate was in the veranda when they arrived, and her face brightened a little at sight of the child.

'Tell my guard to stand back out of the garden. Go, and wait in the road.'

The carriage and troopers withdrew. The child, still holding Tarvin's hand, held out the parcel to Kate.

'It is from my mother,' he said. 'You have seen her. This man need not go. He is'—he hesitated a little—'of your heart, is he not? Your speech is his speech.'

Kate flushed, but did not attempt to set the child right. What could she say?

'And I am to tell this,' he continued, 'first before every-thing, till you quite understand.' He spoke hesitatingly, trans-lating out of his own vernacular as he went on, and drawing himself to his full height, as he cleared the cluster of emeralds from his brow. 'My mother, the Queen—the real Queen—says, "I was three months at this work. It is for you, because I have seen your face. That which has been made may be unravelled against our will, and a gipsy's hands are always picking. For the love of the Gods look to it that a gipsy unravels nothing that I have made, for it is my life and soul to me. Protect this work of mine that comes from me—a cloth nine years upon the loom." I know more English than my mother,' said the child, dropping into his ordinary speech.

Kate opened the parcel, and unrolled a crude yellow and black comforter, with a violent crimson fringe, clumsily knitted. With such labours the queens of Gokral Seetarun were wont to beguile their leisure.

'That is all,' said the child. But he seemed unwilling to go. There was a lump in Kate's throat, as she handled the pitiful gift. Without warning, the child, never loosening for a moment his grip on Tarvin's hand, began to repeat the message word by word, his little fingers tightening on Tarvin's fist as he went on.

'Say I am very grateful indeed,' said Kate, a little puzzled, and not too sure of her voice.

'That was not the answer,' said the child; and he looked appealingly at his tall friend, the new Englishman.

The idle talk of the commercial travellers in the veranda of the rest-house flashed through Tarvin's mind. He took a quick pace forward, and laid his hand on Kate's shoulder, whispering huskily:—

'Can't you see what it means? It's the boy—the cloth nine years on the loom.'

'But what can I do?' cried Kate, bewildered.

'Look after him. Keep on looking after him. You are quick enough in most things. Sitabhai wants his life. See that she doesn't get it.'

Kate began to understand a little. Everything was possible in that awful palace, even child-murder. She had already guessed the hate that lives between childless and mother queens. The Maharaj Kunwar stood motionless in the twilight, twinkling in his jewelled robes.

'Shall I say it again?' he asked.

'No, no, no, child! No!' she cried, flinging herself on her knees before him, and snatching his little figure to her breast, with a sudden access of tenderness and pity. 'Oh, Nick! what shall we do in this horrible country?' She began to cry.

'Ah!' said the Maharaj, utterly unmoved, 'I was to go when I saw that you cried.' He lifted up his voice for the carriage and troopers, and departed, leaving the shabby comforter on the floor.

Kate was sobbing in the half darkness. Neither Mrs. Estes nor her husband was within just then. That little 'we' of hers went through Tarvin with a sweet and tingling ecstasy. He stooped and took her in his arms, and for that which followed Kate did not rebuke him.

'We'll pull through together, little girl,' he whispered to the shaken head on his shoulder.

# X

*Ye know the Hundred Danger Time when, gay with paint and flowers,*
*Your household gods are bribed to help the bitter, helpless hours;*
*Ye know the worn and rotten mat whereon your daughter lies,*
*Ye know the Sootak-room unclean, the cell wherein she dies;*

*Dies with the babble in her ear of midwife's muttered charm,*
*Dies, spite young life that strains to stay, the suckling on her arm—*
*Dies in the fourfold heated room, parched by the Birth-Fire's breath—*
*Foredoomed, ye say, lest anguish lack, to haunt her home in death.*

A Song of the Women.

'Dear Friend—That was very unkind of you, and you have made my life harder. I know I was weak. The child upset me. But I must do what I came for, and I want you to strengthen me, Nick, not hinder me. Don't come for a few days, please. I need all I am or hope to be for the work I see opening here. I think I can really do some good. Let me, please.
Kate.'

Tarvin read fifty different meanings into this letter, received the following morning, and read them out again. At

347

the end of his conjectures he could be sure only of one thing
—that in spite of that moment's weakness, Kate was fixed
upon her path. He could not yet prevail against her stead-
fast gentleness, and perhaps it would be better not to try.
Talks in the veranda, and sentinel-like prowlings about her
path when she went to the palace, were pleasant enough, but
he had not come to Rhatore to tell her that he loved her.
Topaz, in whose future the other half of his heart was bound
up, knew that secret long ago, and—Topaz was waiting for
the coming of the Three C.'s, even as Nick was waiting on
Kate's comings and goings. The girl was unhappy, overstrained, and despairing, but since—he thanked God always
—he was at hand to guard her from the absolute shock of
evil fate, she might well be left for the moment to Mrs. Estes'
comfort and sympathy.

She had already accomplished something in the guarded
courts of the women's quarters, for the Marahaj Kunwar's
mother had entrusted her only son's life to her care (who
could help loving and trusting Kate?); but for his own part,
what had he done for Topaz beyond—he looked toward the
city—playing pachisi with the Maharajah? The low morning
sun flung the shadow of the rest-house before him. The commercial travellers came out one by one, gazed on the walled
bulk of Rhatore, and cursed it. Tarvin mounted his horse,
of which much more hereafter, and ambled toward the city
to pay his respects to the Maharajah. It was through him, if
through any one, that he must possess himself of the Naulahka; he had been anxiously studying him, and shrewdly
measuring the situation, and he now believed that he had
formed a plan through which he might hope to make himself solid with the Maharajah—a plan which, whether it
brought him the Naulahka or not, would at least allow him

the privilege of staying at Rhatore. This privilege certain broad hints of Colonel Nolan's had seemed to Tarvin of late plainly to threaten, and it had become clear to him that he must at once acquire a practical and publishable object for his visit, if he had to rip up the entire State to find it. To stay, he must do something in particular. What he had found to do was particular enough; it should be done forthwith, and it should bring him first the Naulahka, and then—if he was at all the man he took himself for—Kate!

As he approached the gates he saw Kate, in a brown habit, riding with Mrs. Estes out of the missionary's garden.

'You needn't be afraid, dear. I shan't bother you,' he said to himself, smiling at the dust-cloud rising behind her, as he slackened his pace. 'But I wonder what's taking you out so early.'

The misery within the palace walls which had sent her half weeping to Mrs. Estes represented only a phase of the work for which Kate had come. If the wretchedness was so great under the shadow of the throne, what must the common folk endure? Kate was on her way to the hospital.

'There is only one native doctor at the hospital,' Mrs. Estes was saying, as they went along, 'and, of course, he's only a native; that is to say, he is idle.'

'How can any one be idle here?' her companion cried, as the stored heat from under the city gates beat across their temples.

'Every one grows idle so soon in Rhatore,' returned Mrs. Estes, with a little sigh, thinking of Lucien's high hopes and strenuous endeavours, long since subdued to a mild apathy.

Kate sat her horse with the assured seat of a Western girl who has learned to ride and to walk at the same time. Her well-borne little figure had advantages on horseback. The glow of resolve lighting her simply framed face at the moment lent it a spiritual beauty; and she was warmed by the consciousness that she drew near her purpose and the goal of two years' working and dreaming. As they rounded a curve in the main street of the city, a crowd was seen waiting at the foot of a flight of red sandstone steps rising to the platform of a whitewashed house three storeys in height, on which appeared the sign, 'State Dispensary.' The letters leaned against one another, and drooped down over each side of the door.

A sense of the unreality of it all came over Kate as she surveyed the crowd of women, clad in vermilion, dull-red, indigo, saffron, blue, pink, and turquoise garments of raw silk. Almost every woman held a child on her hip, and a low wailing cry rose up as Kate drew rein. The women clustered about her stirrup, caught at her foot, and thrust their babies into her arms. She took one little one to her breast, and hushed it tenderly. It was burnt and dry with fever.

'Be careful,' said Mrs. Estes; 'there is smallpox in the hills behind us, and these people have no notion of precautions.'

Kate, listening to the cry of the women, did not answer. A portly, white-bearded native, in a brown camel's-hair dressing-gown and patent leather boots, came out of the dispensary, thrusting the women right and left, and bowing profoundly.

'You are new Lady Doctor?' he said. 'Hospital is quite ready for inspection. Stand back from the Miss Sahib!' he shouted in the vernacular, as Kate slipped to the ground, and the crowd closed about her. Mrs. Estes remained in the saddle, watching the scene.

A woman of the desert, very tall, gold-coloured, and scarlet-lipped, threw back her face-cloth, caught Kate by the wrist, and made as if she would drag her away, crying aloud fiercely in the vernacular. The trouble in her eyes was not to be denied. Kate followed unresisting, and, as the crowd parted, saw a camel kneeling in the roadway. On its back a gaunt skeleton of a man was muttering, and picking aimlessly at the nail-studded saddle. The woman drew herself up to full height, and, without a word, flung herself down upon the ground, clasping Kate's feet. Kate stooped to raise her, her underlip quivering, and the doctor from the steps shouted cheerfully:—

'Oh, that is all right. He is confirmed lunatic, her husband. She is always bringing him here.'

'Have you done nothing, then?' cried Kate, turning on him angrily.

'What *can* do? She will not leave him here for treatment so I may blister him.'

'Blister him!' murmured Kate to herself, appalled, as she caught the woman's hands and held them firmly. 'Tell her that I say he must be left here,' she said aloud. The doctor conveyed the command. The woman took a deep breath, and stared at Kate under level brows for a full half-minute. Then she carried Kate's hand to the man's forehead, and sat down in the dust, veiling her head.

Kate, dumb under these strange expressions of the workings of the Eastern mind, stared at her for a moment, with an impulse of the compassion which knows no race, before she bent and kissed her quietly on the forehead.

'Carry this man up,' she said, pointing; and he was carried up the steps and into the hospital, his wife following like a dog. Once she turned and spoke to her sisters below, and there went up a little chorus of weeping and laughter.

'She says,' said the doctor, beaming, 'that she will kill any one who is impolite to you. Also, she will be the nurse of your son.'

Kate paused to say a word to Mrs. Estes, who was bound on an errand further into the city. Then she mounted the steps with the doctor.

'Now, will you see the hospital?' he asked. 'But first let me introduce. I am Lalla Dhunpat Rai, Licentiate Medicine, from the Duff College. I was first native my province that took that degree. That was twenty years ago.'

Kate looked at him wonderingly. 'Where have you been since?' she asked.

'Some time I stayed in my father's house. Then I was clerk in medical stores in British India. But his Highness have graciously given me this appointment, which I hold now.'

Kate lifted her eyebrows. This, then, was to be her colleague. They passed into the hospital together in silence, Kate holding the skirt of her riding-habit clear of the accumulated grime of the floor.

Six roughly made pallets, laced with hide and string, stood in the filthy central courtyard of the house, and on each cot a man, swathed in a white sheet, tossed and moaned and jabbered. A woman entered with a pot full of rancid native sweetmeats, and tried vainly to make one of the men eat of her delicacies. In the full glare of the sunlight stood a young man almost absolutely unclothed, his hands clasped behind his head, trying to outstare the sun. He began a chant, broke off, and hurried from bed to bed, shouting to each words that Kate could not understand. Then he returned to his place in the centre, and took up his interrupted song.

'He is confirmed lunatic, also,' said the doctor. 'I have blistered and cupped him very severely, but he will not go away. He is quite harmless, except when he does not get his opium.'

'Surely you don't allow the patients opium!' exclaimed Kate.

'Of *course* I allow opium. Otherwise they would die. All Rajputs eat opium.'

'And you?' asked Kate, with horror.

'Once I did not—when I first came. But now——' He drew a smooth-worn tin tobacco-box from his waist, and took from it what appeared to Kate a handful of opium pills.

Despair was going over her in successive waves. 'Show me the women's ward,' she said wearily.

'Oh, they are all upstairs and downstairs and roundabout,' returned the doctor casually.

'And the maternity cases?' she asked.

'They are in casual ward.'

'Who attends to them?'

'They do not like me. But there is very clever woman from the outside. She comes in.'

'Has she any training—any education?'

'She is much esteemed in her own village,' said the doctor. 'She is here now, if you wish to see.'

'Where?' demanded Kate.

Dhunpat Rai, somewhat uneasy in his mind, made haste to lead the way up a narrow staircase to a closed door, from behind which came the wail of a new life.

Kate flung the door open wrathfully. In that particular ward of the State Hospital were the clay and cow-dung images of two gods, which the woman in charge was besprinkling with marigold buds. Every window, every orifice that might admit a breath of air, was closed, and the birth-fire blazed fiercely in one corner, its fumes nearly asphyxiating Kate as she entered.

What happened between Kate and the much-esteemed woman will never be known. The girl did not emerge for half an hour. But the woman came out much sooner, dishevelled, and cackling feebly.

After this Kate was prepared for anything, even for the neglected condition of the drugs in the dispensary—the mortar was never cleaned, and every prescription carried to the patient many more drugs than were written for him—and for the foul, undrained, uncleaned, unlighted, and unventilated rooms which she entered one after another hopelessly. The patients were allowed to receive their friends as they would, and to take from their hands whatever misguided kindness offered. When death came, the mourners howled in chorus about the cot, and bore the naked body through the courtyard, amid the jeers of the lunatic, to carry through the city what infection Heaven willed.

There was no isolation of infectious cases during the progress of the disease, and children scourged with ophthalmia played light-heartedly with the children of the visitors or among the diphtheria beds. At one point, and one point only, the doctor was strong; he was highly successful in dealing with the very common trouble entered on the day-book as 'loin-bite.' The woodcutters and small traders who had occasion to travel through the lonely roads of the State were not infrequently struck down by tigers, and in these cases the doctor, discarding the entire English pharmacopoeia, fell back on simples of proved repute in the neighbouring villages, and wrought wonders. None the less, it was necessary to convey to him that in future there would be only one head of the State Hospital, that her orders must be obeyed without question, and that her name was Miss Kate Sheriff.

The doctor, reflecting that she attended on the women of the Court, offered no protest. He had been through many such periods of reform and reorganisation, and knew that his own inertia and a smooth tongue would carry him through many more. He bowed and assented, allowing Kate's reproaches to pass over his head, and parrying all questions with the statement:—

'This hospital only allowed one hundred and fifty rupees per mensem from State revenues. How can get drugs *all* the way from Calcutta for that?'

'*I* am paying for this order,' said Kate, writing out a list of needed drugs and appliances on the desk in the bath-room, which was supposed to serve as an office; 'and I shall pay for whatever else I think necessary.'

'Order going through me offeecially?' suggested Dhunpat Rai, with his head on one side.

Unwilling to raise unnecessary obstacles, Kate assented. With those poor creatures lying in the rooms about her unwatched, untended, at the mercy of this creature, it was not a time to argue about commissions.

'Yes,' she said decidedly; 'of course.' And the doctor, when he saw the size and scope of the order, felt that he could endure much at her hands.

At the end of the three hours Kate came away, fainting with weariness, want of food, and bitter heartache.

# XI

*Who speaks to the King carries his life in his hand.*
                                           NATIVE PROVERB.

TARVIN FOUND THE MAHARAJAH, who had not yet taken his morning allowance of opium, sunk in the deepest depression. The man from Topaz gazed at him shrewdly, filled with his purpose.

The Maharajah's first words helped him to declare it. 'What have you come here for?' he asked.

'To Rhatore?' inquired Tarvin, with a smile that embraced the whole horizon.

'Yes; to Rhatore,' grunted the Maharajah. 'The Agent Sahib says you do not belong to any Government, and that you have come here only to see things and write lies about them. Why have you come?'

'I have come to turn your river. There is gold in it,' he said steadily.

The Maharajah answered him with brevity. 'Go and speak to the Government,' he said sulkily.

'It's your river, I guess,' returned Tarvin cheerfully.

'Mine! Nothing in the State is mine. The shop-keeper people are at my gates day and night. The Agent Sahib won't let me collect taxes as my fathers used to do. I have no Army.'

'That's perfectly true,' assented Tarvin, under his breath. 'I'll run off with it some morning.'

'And if I had,' continued the Maharajah, 'I have no one

to fight against. I am only an old wolf, with all my teeth drawn. Go away!'

They were talking in the flagged courtyard immediately outside that wing of the palace occupied by Sitabhai. The Maharajah was sitting in a broken Windsor chair, while his grooms brought up successive files of horses, saddled and bridled, in the hope that one of the animals might be chosen for his Majesty's ride. The stale, sick air of the palace drifted across the marble flags before the morning wind, and it was not a wholesome smell.

Tarvin, who had drawn rein in the courtyard without dismounting, flung his right leg over the pony's withers, and held his peace. He had seen something of the effect of opium upon the Maharajah. A servant was approaching with a small brass bowl full of opium and water. The Maharajah swallowed the draught with many wry faces, dashed the last brown drops from his moustache and beard, and dropped back into the chair, staring with vacant eyes. In a few minutes he sprang to his feet, erect and smiling.

'Are you here, Sahib?' said he. 'You are here, or I should not feel ready to laugh. Do you go riding this morning?'

'I'm your man.'

'Then we will bring out the Foxhall colt. He will throw you.'

'Very good,' said Tarvin leisurely.

'And I will ride my own Cutch mare. Let us get away before the Agent Sahib comes,' said the Maharajah.

The blast of a bugle was heard without the courtyard, and a clatter of wheels, as the grooms departed to saddle the horses.

The Maharaj Kunwar ran up the steps and pattered toward

the Maharajah, his father, who picked him up in his lap, and fondled him.

'What brings thee here, Lalji?' asked the Maharajah. Lalji, the Beloved, was the familiar name by which the Prince was known within the palace.

'I came to exercise my guard. Father, they are giving me bad saddlery for my troopers from the State arsenal. Jeysingh's saddle-peak is mended with string, and Jeysingh is the best of my soldiers. Moreover, he tells me nice tales,' said the Maharaj Kunwar, speaking in the vernacular, with a friendly little nod toward Tarvin.

'Hai! Hai! Thou art like all the rest,' said the King. 'Always some fresh demand upon the State. And what is it now?'

The child joined his little hands together, and caught his father fearlessly by his monstrous beard, which, in the manner of a Rajput, was brushed up over his ears. 'Only ten little new saddles,' said the child. 'They are in the big saddle-rooms. I have seen them. But the keeper of the horses said that I was first to ask the King.'

The Maharajah's face darkened, and he swore a great oath by his gods.

'The King is a slave and a servant,' he growled—'the servant of the Agent Sahib and this woman-talking English Raj; but, by Indur! the King's son is at least a King's son. What right had Saroop Singh to stay thee from anything that thou desiredst, Prince?'

'I told him,' said the Maharaj Kunwar, 'that my father would not be pleased. But I said no more, because I was not very well, and thou knowest'—the boy's head drooped under its turban—'I am only a little child. I may have the saddles?'

Tarvin, to whom no word of this conversation was intelligible, sat at ease on his pony, smiling at his friend the Maharaj. The interview had begun in the dead dawn-silence of the courtyard—a silence so intense that he could hear the doves cooing on a tower a hundred and fifty feet above his head. But now all four sides of the green-shuttered courtyard were alive. awake, and intent about him. He could hear muffled breathings, the rustle of draperies, and the faintest possible jarring of shutters, cautiously opened from within. A heavy smell of musk and jasmine came to his nostrils and filled him with uneasiness, for he knew, without turning his head or his eyes, that Sitabhai and her women were watching all that went on. But neither the King nor the Prince heeded. The Maharaj Kunwar was very full of his English lessons, learned at Mrs. Estes' knee, and the King was as interested as he. Lest Tarvin should fail to understand, the Prince began to speak in English again, but very slowly and distinctly, that his father also might comprehend.

'And this is a new verse,' he said, 'which I learned only yesterday.'

'Is there any talk of their Gods in it?' asked the Maharajah suspiciously. 'Remember thou art a Rajput.'

'No; oh no! said the Prince. 'It is only English, and I learned it very quickly.'

'Let me hear, little Pundit. Some day thou wilt become a scribe, and go to the English colleges, and wear a long black gown.'

The child slipped quickly back into the vernacular. 'The flag of our State has five colours,' he said. 'When I have fought for that, perhaps I will become an Englishman.'

'There is no leading of armies afield any more, little one; but say thy verses.'

The subdued rustle of unseen hundreds grew more intense. Tarvin leaned forward with his chin in his hand, as the

Prince slid down from his father's lap, put his hands behind him, and began, without pauses or expression—

> *'Tiger, tiger, burning bright*
> *In the forests of the night,*
> *What immortal hand or eye*
> *Framed thy fearful symmetry?*
> *When thy heart began to beat*
> *What dread hand made thy dread feet?*

'There is more that I have forgotten,' he went on, 'but the last line is—

> *'Did He who made the lamb make thee?*

I learned it all very quickly.' And he began to applaud himself with both hands, while Tarvin followed suit.

'I do not understand; but it is good to know English. Thy friend here speaks such English as I never knew,' said the Maharajah in the vernacular.

'Ay,' rejoined the Prince. 'But he speaks with his face and his hands alive—so; and I laugh before I know why. Now Colonel Nolan Sahib speaks like a buffalo, with his mouth shut. I cannot tell whether he is angry or pleased. But, father, what does Tarvin Sahib do here?'

'We go for a ride together,' returned the King. 'When we return, perhaps I will tell thee. What do the men about thee say of him?'

'They say he is a man of clean heart; and he is always kind to me.'

'Has he said aught to thee of me?'

'Never in language that I could understand. But I do not doubt that he is a good man. See, he is laughing now.'

# THE NAULAHKA

Tarvin, who had pricked up his ears at hearing his own name, now resettled himself in the saddle, and gathered up his reins, as a hint to the King that it was time to be moving.

The grooms brought up a long, switch-tailed English thoroughbred and a lean, mouse-coloured mare. The Maharajah rose to his feet.

'Go back to Saroop Singh and get the saddles, Prince,' said he.

'What are you going to do to-day, little man?' asked Tarvin.

'I shall go and get new equipment,' answered the child, 'and then I shall come to play with the Prime Minister's son here.'

Again, like the hiss of a hidden snake, the rustle behind the shutters increased. Evidently some one there understood the child's words.

'Shall you see Miss Kate to-day?'

'Not to-day. 'Tis holiday for me. I do not go to Mrs. Estes to-day.'

The King turned on Tarvin swiftly, and spoke under his breath.

'Must he see that Doctor Lady every day? All my people lie to me, in the hope of winning my favour. Even Colonel Nolan says that the child is very strong. Speak the truth. He is my first son.'

'He is not strong,' answered Tarvin calmly. 'Perhaps it would be better to let him see Miss Sheriff this morning. You don't lose anything by keeping your weather eye open, you know.'

'I do not understand,' said the King; 'but go to the missionary's house to-day, my son.'

'I am to come here and play,' answered the Prince petulantly.

'You don't know what Miss Sheriff's got for you to play with,' said Tarvin.

'What is it?' asked the Maharaj sharply.

'You've got a carriage and ten troopers,' replied Tarvin. 'You've only got to go there and find out.'

He drew a letter from his breast-pocket, glancing with liking at the two-cent American stamp, and scribbled a note to Kate on the envelope, which ran thus:—

'Keep the little fellow with you to-day. There's a wicked look about things this morning. Find something for him to do; get up games for him; do anything, but keep him away from the palace. I got your note. All right. I understand.'

He called the Maharaj to him, and handed him the note. 'Take this to Miss Kate, like a little man, and say I sent you,' he said.

'My son is not an orderly,' said the King surlily.

'Your son is not very well, and I'm the first to speak the truth to you about him, it seems to me,' said Tarvin. 'Gently on that colt's mouth—you.' The Foxhall colt was dancing between his grooms.

'You'll be thrown,' said the Maharaj Kunwar, in an ecstasy of delight. 'He throws all his grooms.'

At that moment a shutter in the courtyard clicked distinctly three times in the silence.

One of the grooms passed to the off-side of the plunging colt deftly. Tarvin put his foot into the stirrup to spring up, when the saddle turned completely round. Some one let go of the horse's head, and Tarvin had just time to kick his foot free as the animal sprang forward.

'I've seen slicker ways of killing a man than that,' he said quietly. 'Bring my friend back,' he added to one of the grooms; and when the Foxhall colt was under his hands again he cinched him up as the beast had not been girt since he had first felt the bit. 'Now!' he said, and leaped into the saddle, as the King clattered out of the courtyard.

The colt reared on end, landed stiffly on his forefeet, and lashed out. Tarvin, sitting him with the cowboy seat, said quietly to the child, who was still watching his movements, 'Run along, Maharaj. Don't hang around here. Let me see you started for Miss Kate.'

The boy obeyed, with a regretful glance at the prancing horse. Then the Foxhall colt devoted himself to unseating his rider. He refused to quit the courtyard, though Tarvin argued with him, first behind the saddle, and then between the indignant ears. Accustomed to grooms who slipped off at the first sign of rebellion, the Foxhall colt was wrathful. Without warning, he dashed through the archway, wheeled on his haunches, and bolted in pursuit of the Maharajah's mare. Once in the open, sandy country, he felt that he had a field worthy of his powers. Tarvin also saw his opportunity. The Maharajah, known in his youth as a hard rider among a nation of perhaps the hardest riders on earth, turned in his saddle and watched the battle with interest.

'You ride like a Rajput,' he shouted, as Tarvin flew past him. 'Breathe him on a straight course in the open.'

'Not till he's learned who's boss,' replied Tarvin, and he wrenched the colt around.

'*Shabash! Shabash!* Oh, well done! Well done!' cried the Maharajah, as the colt answered the bit. 'Tarvin Sahib, I'll make you Colonel of my regular cavalry.'

'Ten million irregular devils!' said Tarvin impolitely. 'Come back, you brute! Back!'

The horse's head was bowed on his lathering chest under the pressure of the curb; but before obeying he planted his forefeet, and bucked as viciously as one of Tarvin's own broncos. 'Both feet down and chest extended,' he murmured gaily to himself, as the creature see-sawed up and down. He was in his element, and dreamed himself back in Topaz.

'*Maro! Maro!*' exclaimed the King. 'Hit him hard! Hit him well!'

'Oh, let him have his little picnic,' said Tarvin easily. 'I like it.'

When the colt was tired he was forced to back for ten yards. 'Now we'll go on,' said Tarvin, and fell into a trot by the side of the Maharajah. 'That river of yours is full of gold,' he said, after a moment's silence, as if continuing an uninterrupted conversation.

'When I was a young man,' said the King, 'I rode pig here. We chased them with the sword in the springtime. That was before the English came. Over there, by that pile of rock, I broke my collarbone.'

'Full of gold, Maharajah Sahib. How do you propose to get it out?'

Tarvin knew something already of the King's discursiveness, and did not mean to give way to it.

'What do I know?' answered the King solemnly. 'Ask the Agent Sahib.'

'But, look here, who *does* run this State, you or Colonel Nolan?'

'You know,' returned the Maharajah. 'You have seen.' He pointed north and south. 'There,' he said, 'is one railway line. Yonder is another. I am a goat between two wolves.'

'Well, anyway, the country between is your own. Surely you can do what you like with that.'

They had ridden some two or three miles beyond the city, parallel with the course of the Amet River, their horses sinking fetlock-deep in the soft sand. The King looked along the chain of shining pools, the white, scrub-tipped hillocks of the desert, and the far-distant line of low granite-topped hills, whence the Amet sprang. It was not a prospect to delight the heart of a King.

'Yes; I am lord of all this country,' he said. 'But look you, one-fourth of my revenue is swallowed up by those who collect it; one-fourth those black-faced camel-breeders in the sand there will not pay, and I must not march troops against them; one-fourth I myself, perhaps, receive; but the people who should pay the other fourth do not know to whom it should be sent. Yes; I am very rich King.'

'Well, any way you look at it, the river ought to treble your income.'

The Maharajah looked at Tarvin intently.

'What would the Government say?' he asked.

'I don't quite see where the Government comes in. You can lay out orange-gardens and take canals around them.' (There was a deep-set twinkle of comprehension in his Majesty's eye.) 'Working the river would be much easier. You've tried placer-mining here, haven't you?'

'There was some washing in the bed of the river one summer. My jails were too full of convicts, and I feared rebellion. But there was nothing to see, except those black dogs digging in the sand. That year I won the Poona cup with a bay pony.'

Tarvin brought his hand down on his thigh with an unguarded smack. What was the use of talking business to this wearied man, who would pawn what the opium had left to him of soul for something to see? He shifted his ground instantly.

'Yes; that sort of mining is nothing to look at. What you want is a little dam up Gungra way.'

'Near the hills?'

'Yes.'

'No man has ever dammed the Amet,' said the King. 'It comes out of the ground, and sinks back into the ground, and when the rain falls it is as wide as the Indus.'

'We'll have the whole bed of it laid bare before the Rains begin—bare for twelve miles,' said Tarvin, watching the effect on his companion.

'No man has dammed the Amet,' was the stony reply.

'No *man* has ever tried. Give me all the labour I want, and *I* will dam the Amet.'

'Where will the water go?' inquired the King.

'I'll take it around another way, same as you took the canal around the orange-garden, of course.'

'Ah! *Then* Colonel Nolan talked to me as if I were a child.'

'You know why, Maharajah Sahib,' said Tarvin placidly.

The King was frozen for a moment by this audacity. He knew that all the secrets of his domestic life were common talk in the mouths of the city, for no man can bridle three hundred women; but he was not prepared to find them so frankly hinted at by this irreverent stranger, who was and was not an Englishman.

'Colonel Nolan will say nothing this time,' continued Tarvin. 'Besides, it will help your people.'

'Who are also his,' said the King.

The opium was dying out of his brain, and his head fell forward upon his chest.

'Then I shall begin to-morrow,' said Tarvin. 'It will be something to see. I must find the best place to dam the river, and I daresay you can lend me a few hundred convicts.'

'But why have you come here at all,' asked the King, 'to dam my rivers, and turn my State upside down?'

'Because it's good for you to laugh, Maharajah Sahib. You know that as well as I do. I will play pachisi with you every night until you are tired, and I can speak the truth—a rare commodity in these parts.'

'Did you speak truth about the Maharaj Kunwar? Is he indeed not well?'

'I have told you he isn't quite strong. But there's nothing the matter with him that Miss Sheriff can't put right.'

'Is that the truth?' demanded the King. 'Remember, he has my throne after me.'

'If I know Miss Sheriff, he'll have that throne. Don't you fret, Maharajah Sahib!'

'You are a great friend of hers?' pursued his companion. 'You both come from one country?'

'Yes,' assented Tarvin; 'and one town.'

'Tell me about that town,' said the King curiously.

Tarvin, nothing loth, told him—told him at length, in detail, and with his own touches of verisimilitude, forgetting in the heat of admiration and affection that the King could understand, at best, not more than one word in ten of his vigorous Western colloquialisms. Half-way through his rhapsody the King interrupted.

'If it was so good, why did you not stay there?'

'I came to see you,' said Tarvin quickly. 'I heard about you there.'

'Then it is true, what my poets sing to me, that my fame is known in the four corners of the earth? I will fill Bussant Rao's mouth with gold if it is so.'

'You can bet your life. Would you like me to go away, though? Say the word!' Tarvin made as if to check his horse.

The Maharajah remained sunk in deep thought, and when he spoke it was slowly and distinctly, that Tarvin might catch every word. 'I hate all the English,' he said. 'Their ways are not my ways, and they make such trouble over the killing of a man here and there. *Your* ways are not my ways; but you do not give so much trouble, and you are a friend of the Doctor Lady.'

'Well, I hope I'm a friend of the Maharaj Kunwar's too,' said Tarvin.

'Are you true friend to him?' asked the King, eyeing him closely.

'That's all right. I'd like to see the man who tried to lay a hand on the little one. He'd vanish, King; he'd disappear; he wouldn't be. I'd mop up Gokral Seetarun with him.'

'I have seen you hit that rupee. Do it again.'

Without thinking for a moment of the Foxhall colt, Tarvin drew his revolver, tossed a coin into the air, and fired. The coin fell beside them—a fresh one this time—marked squarely in the centre. The colt plunged furiously, and the Cutch mare curveted. There was a thunder of hoofs behind him. The escort, which, till now, had waited respectfully a quarter of a mile behind, were racing up at full speed, with levelled lances. The King laughed a little contemptuously.

'They are thinking you have shot me,' he said. 'So they will kill you, unless I stop them. Shall I stop them?'

Tarvin thrust out his under-jaw with a motion peculiar to himself, wheeled the colt, and waited without answering, his empty hands folded on the pommel of his saddle. The troop swept down in an irregular mob, each man crouching, lance in rest, over his saddle-bow, and the captain of the troop flourishing a long, straight Rajput sword. Tarvin felt rather than saw the lean, venomous lance-heads converging on the breast of the colt. The King drew off a few yards, and watched him where he stood alone in the centre of the plain, waiting. For that single moment, in which he faced death, Tarvin thought to himself that he preferred any customer to a Maharajah.

Suddenly his Majesty shouted once, the lance-butts fell as though they had been smitten down, and the troop, opening out, whirled by on each side of Tarvin, each man striving as nearly as might be to brush the white man's boot.

The white man stared in front of him without turning his head, and the King gave a little grunt of approval.

'Would you have done that for the Maharaj Kunwar?' he asked, wheeling his mare in again beside him, after a pause.

'No,' said Tarvin placidly. 'I should have begun shooting long before.'

'What! Fifty men?'

'No. The captain.'

The King shook in his saddle with laughter, and held up his hand. The commandant of the troop trotted up.

'*Ohé*, Pertab Singh-Ji, he says he would have shot thee.' Then, turning to Tarvin, smiling, 'That is my cousin.'

The burly Rajput captain grinned from ear to ear, and, to Tarvin's surprise, answered in perfect English:—

'That would do for irregular cavalry—to kill the subalterns, you understand—but we are drilled exclusively on English model, and I have my commission from the Queen. Now, in the German army——'

Tarvin looked at him in blank amazement.

'But you are not connected with the military,' said Pertab Singh-Ji politely. 'I have heard how you shoot, and I saw what you were doing. But you must please excuse. When a shot is fired near his Highness it is our order always to come up.'

He saluted, and withdrew to his troop.

The sun was growing unpleasantly hot, and the King and Tarvin trotted back toward the city.

'How many convicts can you lend me?' asked Tarvin, as they went.

'All my jails full, if you want them,' was the enthusiastic answer. 'By God, Sahib, I never saw anything like that. I would give you anything.'

Tarvin took off his hat, and mopped his forehead, laughing.

'Very good, then. I'll ask for something that will cost you nothing.'

The Maharajah grunted doubtfully. People generally demanded of him things he was not willing to part with.

'That talk is new to me, Tarvin Sahib,' said he.

'You'll see I'm in earnest when I say I only want to look at the Naulahka. I've seen all your State diamonds and gold carriages, but I haven't seen that.'

The Maharajah trotted fifty yards without replying. Then:—

'Do they speak of it where you come from?'

'Of course. All Americans know that it's the biggest thing in India. It's in all the guide-books,' said Tarvin brazenly.

'Do the books say where it is? The English people are so wise.' The Maharajah stared straight in front of him, and almost smiled.

'No; but they say you know, and I'd like to see it.'

'You must understand, Tarvin Sahib'—the Maharajah spoke meditatively—'that this is not *a* State jewel, but *the* State jewel—the jewel of the State. It is a holy thing. Even I do not keep it, and I cannot give you any order to see it.'

Tarvin's heart sank.

'But,' the Maharajah continued, 'if I say where it is, you can go at your own risk, without Government interfering. I have seen you are not afraid of risk, and I am a very grateful man. Perhaps the priests will show you; perhaps they will not. Or perhaps you will not find the priests at all. Oh, I forgot; it is not in *that* temple that I was thinking of. No; it must be in the Gye-Mukh—the Cow's Mouth. But there are no priests there, and nobody goes. Of *course* it is in the Cow's Mouth. I thought it was in this city,' resumed the Maharajah. He spoke as if he were talking of a dropped horse-shoe or a mislaid turban.

'Oh, of course. The Cow's Mouth,' repeated Tarvin, as if this also were in the guide-books.

Chuckling with renewed animation, the King went on: 'By God, only a very brave man would go to the Gye-Mukh; such a brave man as yourself, Tarvin Sahib,' he added, giving his companion a shrewd look. 'Ho, ho! Pertab Singh-Ji would not go. No; not with all his riders that you conquered to-day.'

'Keep your praise until I've earned it, Maharajah Sahib,' said Tarvin. 'Wait until I've dammed that river.' He was silent for a while, as if digesting this newest piece of information.

'Now, you have a city like this city, I suppose?' said the Maharajah interrogatively, pointing to Rhatore.

Tarvin had overcome, in a measure, his first feeling of contempt for the State of Gokral Seetarun and the city of Rhatore. He had begun to look upon them both, as was his nature in the case of people and things with which he dwelt, with a certain kindness.

'Topaz is going to be bigger,' he explained.

'And when you are there what is your offeecial position?' asked the Maharajah.

Tarvin, without answering, drew from his breastpocket the cable from Mrs. Mutrie, and handed it in silence to the King.

Where an election was concerned even the sympathy of an opium-soaked Rajput was not indifferent to him.

'What does it mean?' asked the King, and Tarvin threw up his hands in despair.

He explained his connection with the government of his State, making the Colorado Legislature appear as one of the parliaments of America. He owned up to being the Hon. Nicholas Tarvin, if the Maharajah really wanted to give him his full title.

'Such as the members of Provincial Councils that come here?' suggested the Maharajah, remembering the grey-headed men who visited him from time to time, charged with authority only little less than that of a Viceroy. 'But still you will not write letters to that Legislature about my government,' queried he suspiciously, recalling again over-curious emissaries from the British Parliament overseas, who sat their horses like sacks, and talked interminably of good government when he wished to go to bed. 'And above all,' he added slowly, as they drew near to the palace, 'you are most true friend of the Maharaj Kunwar? And your friend, the Doctor Lady, will make·him well?'

'That,' said Tarvin, with a sudden inspiration, 'is what we are both here for!'

## XII

*This I saw when the rites were done,*
*And the lamps were dead and the Gods alone,*
*And the grey snake coiled on the altar-stone—*
*Ere I fled from a Fear that I could not see,*
*And the Gods of the East made mouths at me.*

IN SEEONEE.

WHEN HE LEFT THE KING'S SIDE, Tarvin's first impulse was to set the Foxhall colt into a gallop, and forthwith depart in search of the Naulahka. He mechanically drove his heels home, and shortened his rein under the impulse of the thought; but the colt's leap beneath him recalled him to his senses, and he restrained himself and his mount with the same motion.

His familiarity with the people's grotesque nomenclature left him unimpressed by the Cow's Mouth as a name for a spot, but he gave some wonder to the question why the thing should be *in* the Cow's Mouth. This was a matter to be laid before Estes.

'These heathen,' he said to himself, 'are just the sort to hide it away in a salt-lick, or bury it in a hole in the ground. Yes; a hole is about their size. They put the State diamonds in cracker-boxes tied up with boot-laces. The Naulahka is probably hanging on a tree.'

As he trotted toward the missionary's house, he looked at the hopeless landscape with new interest, for any spur of the low hills, or any roof in the jumbled city, might contain his treasure.

Estes, who had outlived many curiosities, and knew Rajpu-

*373*

tana as a prisoner knows the bricks of his cell, turned on Tarvin, in reply to the latter's direct question, a flood of information. There were mouths of all kinds in India, from the Burning Mouth in the north, where a jet of natural gas was worshipped by millions as the incarnation of a divinity, to the Devil's Mouth among some forgotten Buddhist ruins in the furthest southern corner of Madras.

There was also a Cow's Mouth some hundreds of miles away, in the courtyard of a temple at Benares, much frequented by devotees; but as far as Rajputana was concerned, there was only one Cow's Mouth, and that was to be found in a dead city.

The missionary launched into a history of wars and rapine, extending over hundreds of years, all centring round one rock-walled city in the wilderness, which had been the pride and the glory of the kings of Mewar. Tarvin listened with patience as infinite as his weariness—ancient history had no charm for the man who was making his own town—while Estes enlarged upon the past, and told stories of voluntary immolation on the pyre in subterranean palaces by thousands of Rajput women who, when the city fell before a Mohammedan, and their kin had died in the last charge of defence, cheated the conquerors of all but the empty glory of conquest. Estes had a taste for archaeology, and it was a pleasure to him to speak of it to a fellow-countryman.

By retracing the ninety-six miles to Rawut Junction, Tarvin might make connection with a train that would carry him sixty-seven miles westward to yet another junction, where he would change and go south by rail for a hundred and seven miles; and this would bring him within four miles of this city, its marvellous nine-storeyed tower of glory, which he was to note carefully, its stupendous walls and desolate palaces. The journey would occupy at least two days. At this point Tarvin suggested a map, and a glance at it showed him that Estes proposed an elaborate circus round three sides of a square, whereas a spider-like line ran more or less directly from Rhatore to Gunnaur.

'This seems shorter,' he said.

'It's only a country road, and you have had some experience of roads in this State. Fifty-seven miles on a *kutcha* road in this sun would be fatal.'

Tarvin smiled to himself. He had no particular dread of the sun, which, year by year, had stolen from his companion something of his vitality.

'I think I'll ride, anyhow. It seems a waste to travel half round India to get at a thing across the road, though it *is* the custom of the country.'

He asked the missionary what the Cow's Mouth was like, and Estes explained archaeologically, architecturally, and philologically to such good purpose that Tarvin understood that it was some sort of a hole in the ground—an ancient, a remarkably ancient, hole of peculiar sanctity, but nothing more than a hole.

Tarvin decided to start without an hour's delay. The dam might wait until he returned. It was hardly likely that the King's outburst of generosity would lead him to throw open his jails on the morrow. Tarvin debated for a while whether he should tell him of the excursion he was proposing to himself, and then decided that he would look at the necklace first, and open negotiations later. This seemed to suit the customs of the country. He returned to the rest-house with Estes' map in his pocket to take stock of his stable. Like other men of the West, he reckoned a horse a necessity before all necessities, and had purchased one mechanically immediately after his arrival. It had been a comfort to him to note all the tricks of all the men he had ever traded horses with faithfully reproduced in the lean, swarthy Kabuli trader, who had led his kicking, plunging horse up to the veranda one idle evening; and it had been a greater comfort to battle with them as he had battled in the old days. The result of the skirmish, fought out in broken English and expressive American, was an unhandsome, doubtful-tempered, mouse-coloured Kathiawar stallion, who had been dismissed for vice from the service of his Majesty, and who weakly believed that, having eaten pieces of the troopers of the Deoli Irregular Horse, ease and idleness awaited him. Tarvin had undeceived him leisurely, in such moments as he most felt the need of doing something, and the Kathiawar, though never grateful, was at least civil. He had been christened Fibby Winks in recognition of ungentlemanly conduct and a resemblance which Tarvin fancied he detected between the beast's lean face and that of the man who had jumped his claim.

Tarvin threw back the loin-cloth as he came upon Fibby drowsing in the afternoon sun behind the rest-house.

'We're going for a little walk down town, Fibby,' he said.

The Kathiawar squealed and snapped.

'Yes. You always were a loafer, Fibby.'

Fibby was saddled by his nervous native attendant, while Tarvin took a blanket from his room and rolled up into it an imaginative assortment of provisions. Fibby was to find his rations where Heaven pleased. Then he set out as light-heartedly as though he were going for a canter round the city. It was now about three in the afternoon. All Fibby's boundless reserves of ill-temper and stubborn obstinacy Tarvin resolved should be devoted, by the aid of his spurs, to covering the fifty-seven miles to Gunnaur in the next ten hours, if the road were fair. If not, he should be allowed another two hours. The return journey would not require spurs. There was a moon that night, and Tarvin knew enough of native roads in Gokral Seetarun, and rough trails elsewhere, to be certain that he would not be confused by cross-tracks.

It being borne into Fibby's mind that he was required to advance, not in three directions at once, but in one, he clicked his bit comfortably in his mouth, dropped his head, and began to trot steadily. Then Tarvin pulled him up, and addressed him tenderly.

'Fib, my boy, we're not out for exercise—you'll learn that before sundown. Some galoot has been training you to waste your time over the English trot. I'll be discussing other points with you in the course of the campaign; but we'll settle this now. We don't begin with crime. Drop it, Fibby, and behave like a man-horse.'

Tarvin was obliged to make further remarks on the same subject before Fibby returned to the easy native lope, which is also a common Western pace, tiring neither man nor beast. By this he began to understand that a long journey was demanded of him, and, lowering his tail, buckled down to it.

At first he moved in a cloud of sandy dust with the cotton-wains and the country carts that were creaking out to the far distant railway at Gunnaur. As the sun began to sink, his gaunt shadow danced like a goblin across low-lying volcanic rock tufted with shrubs, and here and there an aloe.

The carters unyoked their cattle on the roadside, and prepared to eat their evening meal by the light of dull red fires. Fibby cocked one ear wistfully toward the flames, but held on through the gathering shadows, and Tarvin smelt the acrid juice of bruised camel-thorn beneath his horse's hoofs. The moon rose in splendour behind him, and, following his lurching shadow, he overtook a naked man who bore over his shoulder a stick loaded with jingling bells, and fled panting and perspiring from one who followed him armed with a naked sword. This was the mail-carrier and his escort running to Gunnaur. The jingling died away on the dead air, and Fibby was ambling between interminable lines of thorn-bushes that threw mad arms to the stars, and cast shadows as solid as themselves across the road. Some beast of the night plunged through the thicket alongside, and Fibby snorted in panic. Then a porcupine crossed under his nose with a rustle of quills, and left an evil stench to poison the stillness for a moment. A point of light gleamed ahead, where a bullock-cart had broken down, and the drivers were sleeping peacefully till daylight should show the injury. Here Fibby stopped, and Tarvin, through the magic of a rupee, representing fortune to the rudely awakened sleepers, procured food and a little water for him, eased the girths, and made as much of him as he was disposed to permit. On starting again, Fibby found his second wind, and with it there woke the spirit of daring and adventure inherited from his ancestors, who were accustomed to take their masters thirty leagues in a day for the sacking of a town, to sleep by a lance driven into the earth as a picket, and to return whence they had come before the ashes of the houses had lost heat. So Fibby lifted his tail valiantly, neighed, and began to move.

The road descended for miles, crossing the dry beds of many water-courses and once a broad river, where Fibby stopped for another drink, and would have lain down to roll in a melon-bed but that his rider spurred him on up the slope. The country grew more fertile at every mile, and rolled in broader waves. Under the light of the setting moon, the fields showed silver-white with opium-poppy, or dark with sugar-cane.

Poppy and sugar ceased together, as Fibby topped a long,

slow ascent, and with distended nostrils snuffed for the wind of the morning. He knew that the day would bring him rest. Tarvin peered forward where the white line of the road disappeared in the gloom of velvety scrub. He commanded a vast level plain flanked by hills of soft outline—a plain that in the dim light seemed as level as the sea. Like the sea, too, it bore on its breast a ship, like a gigantic monitor with a sharp bow, cutting her way from north to south; such a ship as man never yet has seen—two miles long, with three or four hundred feet freeboard, lonely, silent, mastless, without lights, a derelict of the earth.

'We are nearly there, Fib, my boy,' said Tarvin, drawing rein, and scanning the monstrous thing by the starlight. 'We'll get as close as we can, and then wait for the daylight before going aboard.'

They descended the slope, which was covered with sharp stones and sleeping goats. Then the road turned sharply to the left, and began to run parallel to the ship. Tarvin urged Fibby into a more direct path, and the good horse blundered piteously across the scrub-covered ground, cut up and channelled by the rains into a network of six-foot ravines and gulches.

Here he gave out with a despairing grunt. Tarvin took pity on him, and, fastening him to a tree, bade him think of his sins till breakfast-time, and dropped from his back into a dry and dusty water-hole. Ten steps further, and the scrub was all about him, whipping him across the brows, hooking thorns into his jacket, and looping roots in front of his knees as he pushed on up an ever-steepening incline.

At last Tarvin was crawling on his hands and knees, grimed from head to foot, and hardly to be distinguished from the wild pig that passed like slate-coloured shadows through the tangle of the thickets on their way to their rest. Too absorbed to hear them grunt, he pulled and screwed himself up the slope, tugging at the roots as though he would rend the Naulahka from the bowels of the earth, and swearing piously at every step. When he stopped to wipe the sweat from his face, he found, more by touch than by eye, that he knelt at the foot of a wall that ran up into the stars. Fibby, from the tangle below, was neighing dolefully.

'You're not hurt, Fibby,' he gasped, spitting out some fragments of dry grass. 'You aren't on in this scene. Nobody's asking *you* to fly to-night,' he said, looking hopelessly up at the wall again, and whistling softly in response to an owl's hooting overhead.

He began to pick his way between the foot of the wall and the scrub that grew up to it, pressing one hand against the huge cut stones, and holding the other before his face. A figseed had found foothold between two of the gigantic slabs, and, undisturbed through the centuries, had grown into an arrogant, gnarled tree, that writhed between the fissures and heaved the stonework apart. Tarvin considered for a while whether he could climb into the crook of the lowest branch, then moved on a few steps, and found the wall rent from top to bottom through the twenty feet of its thickness, allowing passage for the head of an army.

'Like them, exactly like them!' he mused. 'I might have expected it. To build a wall sixty feet high, and put an eighty-foot hole in it! The Naulahka must be lying out on a bush, or a child's playing with it, and—I can't get it!'

He plunged through the gap, and found himself amid scattered pillars, slabs of stone, broken lintels, and tumbled tombs, and heard a low, thick hiss almost under his riding-boots. No man born of woman needs to be instructed in the Voice of the Serpent.

Tarvin jumped, and stayed still. Fibby's neigh came faintly now. The dawn-wind blew through the gap in the wall, and Tarvin wiped his forehead with a deep sigh of relief. He would do no more till the light came. This was the hour to eat and drink; also to stand very still, because of that voice from the ground.

He pulled food and a flask from his pocket, and, staring before him in every direction, ate hungrily. The loom of the night lifted a little, and he could see the outline of some great building a few yards away. Beyond this were other shadows, faint as the visions in a dream—the shadows of yet more temples and lines of houses; the wind, blowing among them, brought back a rustle of tossing hedges.

The shadows grew more distinct. He could see that he was standing with his face to some decayed tomb. Then his jaw fell, for, without warning or presage, the red dawn shot up behind him, and there leaped out of the night the city of the dead. Tall-built, sharp-domed palaces, flushing to the colour of blood, revealed the horror of their emptiness, and glared at the day that pierced them through and through.

The wind passed singing down the empty streets, and, finding none to answer, returned, chasing before it a muttering cloud of dust, which presently whirled itself into a little cyclone-funnel, and lay down with a sigh.

A screen of fretted marble lay on the dry grass, where it had fallen from some window above, and a gecko crawled over it to sun himself. Already the dawn flush had passed. The hot light was everywhere, and a kite had poised himself in the parched blue sky. The day, new-born, might have been as old as the city. It seemed to Tarvin that he and it were standing still to hear the centuries race by on the wings of the purposeless dust.

As he took his first step into the streets, a peacock stepped from the threshold of a lofty red house, and spread his tail in the splendour of the sun. Tarvin halted, and with perfect gravity took off his hat to the royal bird, where it blazed against the sculptures on the wall, the sole living thing in sight.

The silence of the place and the insolent nakedness of the empty ways lay on him like a dead weight. For a long time he did not care to whistle, but rambled aimlessly from one wall to another, looking at the gigantic reservoirs, dry and neglected, the hollow guard-houses that studded the battlements, the time-riven arches that spanned the streets, and, above all, the carven tower with a shattered roof that sprang a hundred and fifty feet into the air, for a sign to the countryside that the royal city of Gunnaur was not dead, but would one day hum with men.

It was from this tower, encrusted with figures in high relief of beast and man, that Tarvin, after a heavy climb, looked out on the vast sleeping land in the midst of which the dead city lay. He saw the road by which he had come in the night, dipping and reappearing again over thirty miles of country, saw the white poppy-fields, the dull-brown scrub, and the unending plain to the northward, cut by the shining line of the rail. From his eyrie he peered forth as a man peers from a crow's-nest at sea; for, once down there below in the city, all view was cut off by the battlements that rose like bulwarks. On the side nearest to the railroad, sloping causeways, paved with stone, ran down to the plain under many gates, as the gangway of a ship when it is let down, and through the gaps in the walls—time and the trees had torn their way to and fro—there was nothing to be seen except the horizon, which might have been the deep sea.

He thought of Fibby waiting in the scrub for his breakfast, and made haste to descend to the streets again. Remembering the essentials of his talk with Estes as to the position of the Cow's Mouth, he passed up a side lane, disturbing the squirrels and monkeys that had taken up their quarters in the cool dark of the rows of empty houses. The last house ended in a heap of ruins among a tangle of mimosa and tall grass, through which ran a narrow foot-track.

Tarvin marked the house as the first actual ruin he had seen. His complaint against all the others, the temples and the palaces, was that they were not ruined, but dead—empty, swept, and garnished, with the seven devils of loneliness in riotous possession. In time—in a few thousand years perhaps— the city would crumble away. He was distinctly glad that one house at least had set the example.

The path dropped beneath his feet on a shelf of solid rock that curved over like the edge of a waterfall. Tarvin took only one step, and fell, for the rock was worn into deep gutters, smoother than ice, by the naked feet of millions who had trodden that way for no man knew how many years. When he rose he heard a malignant chuckle, half suppressed, which ended in a choking cough, ceased, and broke out anew. Tarvin registered an oath to find that scoffer when he had found the necklace, and looked to his foothold more carefully. At this point it seemed that the Cow's Mouth must be some sort of disused quarry fringed to the lips with rank vegetation.

All sight of what lay below him was blocked by the thick foliage of trees that leaned forward, bowing their heads together as night-watchers huddle over a corpse. Once upon a time there had been rude steps leading down the almost sheer descent, but the naked feet had worn them to glassy knobs and lumps, and blown dust had made a thin soil in their chinks. Tarvin looked long and angrily, because the laugh came from the bottom of this track, and then, digging his heel into the mould, began to let himself down step by step, steadying himself by the tufts of grass. Before he had realised it, he was out of reach of the sun, and neck-deep in tall grass. Still there was a sort of pathway under his feet, down the almost perpendicular side. He gripped the grass, and went on. The earth beneath his elbows grew moist, and the rock where it cropped out showed rotten with moisture and coated with moss. The air grew cold and damp. Another plunge downward revealed to him what the trees were guarding, as he drew breath on a narrow stone ledge. They sprang from the masonry round the sides of a square tank of water so stagnant that it had corrupted past corruption, and lay dull blue beneath the blackness of the trees. The drought of summer had shrunk it, and a bank of dried mud ran round its sides. The head of a sunken stone pillar, carved with monstrous and obscene gods, reared itself from the water like the head of a tortoise swimming to land. The birds moved in the sunlit branches of the trees far overhead. Little twigs and berries dropped into the water, and the noise of their fall echoed from side to side of the tank that received no sunlight.

The chuckle that had so annoyed Tarvin broke out again as he listened. This time it was behind him, and wheeling sharply, he saw that it came from a thin stream of water that spurted fitfully from the rudely carved head of a cow, and dripped along a stone spout into the heavy blue pool. Behind that spout the moss-grown rock rose sheer. This, then, was the Cow's Mouth!

The tank lay at the bottom of a shaft, and the one way down to it was that by which Tarvin had come—a path that led from the sunlight to the chill and mould of a vault.

'Well, this is kind of the King, anyhow,' he said, pacing the ledge cautiously, for it was almost as slippery as the pathway on the rocks. 'Now, what's the use of this?' he continued, returning. The ledge ran only round one side of the tank, and, unless he trusted to the mud-banks on the other three, there was no hope of continuing his exploration further. The Cow's Mouth chuckled again, as a fresh jet of water forced its way through the formless jaws.

'Oh, dry up!' he muttered impatiently, staring through the half-light that veiled all.

He dropped a piece of rock on the mud under the lip of the ledge, then tested it with a cautious foot, found that it bore, and decided to walk round the tank. As there were more trees to the right of the ledge than to the left, he stepped off on the mud from the right, holding cautiously to the branches and the tufts of grass in case of any false step.

When the tank was first made its rock walls had been perfectly perpendicular, but time and weather and the war of the tree-roots had broken and scarred the stone in a thousand places, giving a scant foothold here and there.

Tarvin crept along the right side of the tank, resolved, whatever might come, to go round it. The gloom deepened as he came directly under the largest fig-tree, throwing a thousand arms across the water, and buttressing the rock with snake-like roots as thick as a man's body. Here, sitting on a root, he rested and looked at the ledge. The sun, shooting down the path that he had trampled through the tall grass, threw one patch of light on the discoloured marble of the ledge and on the blunt muzzle of the cow's head; but where Tarvin rested under the fig-tree there was darkness, and an intolerable scent of musk. The blue water was not inviting to watch. He turned his face inward to the rock and the trees, and, looking up, caught the emerald-green of a parrot's wing moving among the upper branches. Never in his life had Tarvin so acutely desired the blessed sunshine. He was cold and damp, and conscious that a gentle breeze was blowing in his face from between the snaky tree-roots.

It was the sense of space more than actual sight that told him that there was a passage before him shrouded by the roots on which he sat, and it was his racial instinct of curiosity rather than any love of adventure that led him to throw himself at the darkness, which parted before and closed behind him. He could feel that his feet were treading on cut stone overlaid with a thin layer of dried mud, and, extending his arms, found masonry on either side. Then he lighted a match, and congratulated himself that his ignorance of cows' mouths had not led him to bring a lantern with him. The first match flickered in the draught and went out, and before the flame had died he heard a sound in front of him like the shivering backward draw of a wave on a pebbly beach. The noise was not inspiriting, but Tarvin pressed on for a few steps, looking back to see that the dull glimmer of the outer day was still behind him, and lighted another match, guarding it with his hands. At his next step he shuddered from head to foot. His heel had crashed through a skull on the ground.

The match showed him that he had quitted the passage, and was standing in a black space of unknown dimensions. He fancied that he saw the outline of a pillar, or rows of pillars, flickering drunkenly in the gloom, and was all too sure that the ground beneath him was strewn with bones. Then he became aware of pale emerald eyes watching him fixedly, and perceived that there was deep breathing in the place other than his own. He flung the match down, the eyes retreated, there was a wild rattle and crash in the darkness, a howl that might have been bestial or human, and Tarvin, panting between the tree-roots, swung himself to the left, and fled back over the mud-banks to the ledge, where he stood, his back to the Cow's Mouth and his revolver in his hand.

In that moment of waiting for what might emerge from the hole in the side of the tank, Tarvin tasted all the agonies of pure physical terror. Then he noted with the tail of his eye that a length of mud-bank to his left—half the mud-bank, in fact—was moving slowly into the water. It floated slowly across the tank, a long welt of filth and slime. Nothing came out of the hole between the fig-tree roots, but the mud-bank grounded under the ledge almost at Tarvin's feet, and opened horny eyelids, heavy with green slime.

The Western man is familiar with many strange things, but the alligator does not come within the common range of his experiences. A second time Tarvin moved from point to point without being able to explain the steps he took between. He found himself sitting in the sunshine at the head of the slippery path that led downwards. His hands were full of the wholesome jungle grass and the clean dry dust. He could see the dead city about him, and he felt that it was home.

The Cow's Mouth chuckled and choked out of sight as it had chuckled since the making of the tank, and that was at the making of Time. A man, old, crippled, and all but naked, came through the high grass leading a little kid, and calling mechanically from time to time, '*Ao, Bhai! Ao!*' 'Come, brother! Come!' Tarvin marvelled first at his appearance on earth at all, and next that he could so unconcernedly descend the path to the darkness and the horror below. He did not know that the sacred crocodile of the Cow's Mouth was waiting for his morning meal, as he had waited in the days when Gunnaur was peopled, and its queens never dreamed of death.

# XIII

*Beat off in our last fight were we?*
*The greater need to seek the sea;*
*For Fortune changeth as the moon*
*To caravel and picaroon.*
*Then, Eastward Ho! or Westward Ho!*
*Whichever wind may meetest blow.*
*Our quarry sails on either sea,*
*Fat prey for such bold lads as we.*
*And every sun-dried buccaneer*
*Must hand and reef and watch and steer,*
*And bear great wrath of sea and sky*
*Before the plate-ships wallow by.*
*Now, as our tall bow takes the foam,*
*Let no man turn his heart to home,*
*Save to desire land the more,*
*And larger warehouse for his store,*
*When treasure won from Santos Bay*
*Shall make our sea-washed village gay.*

BLACKBEARD.

FIBBY AND TARVIN ate their breakfast together, half an hour later, in the blotched shadows of the scrub below the wall. The horse buried his nose into his provender, and said nothing. The man was equally silent. Once or twice he rose to his feet, scanned the irregular line of wall and bastion, and shook his head. He had no desire to return there. As the sun grew fiercer he found a resting-place in the heart of a circle of thorn, tucked the saddle under his head, and lay down to

388

sleep. Fibby, rolling luxuriously, followed his master's example. The two took their rest while the air quivered with heat and the hum of insects, and the browsing goats clicked and pattered through the water-channels.

The shadow of the Tower of Glory lengthened, fell across the walls, and ran far across the plain; the kites began to drop from the sky by twos and threes; and naked children, calling one to another, collected the goats and drove them to the smoky villages before Tarvin roused himself for the homeward journey.

He halted Fibby once for a last look at Gunnaur as they reached the rising ground. The sunlight had left the walls, and they ran black against the misty levels and the turquoise-blue of the twilight. Fires twinkled from a score of huts about the base of the city, but along the ridge of the desolation itself there was no light.

'Mum's the word, Fibby,' said Tarvin, picking up his reins. 'We don't think well of this picnic, and we won't mention it at Rhatore.'

He chirruped, and Fibby went home as swiftly as he could lay hoof to stone, only once suggesting refreshment. Tarvin said nothing till the end of the long ride, when he heaved a deep sigh of relief as he dismounted in the fresh sunlight of the morning.

Sitting in his room, it seemed to him a waste of a most precious opportunity that he had not manufactured a torch in Gunnaur and thoroughly explored the passage. But the memory of the green eyes and the smell of musk came back to him, and he shivered. The thing was not to be done. Never again, for any consideration, under the wholesome light of the sun, would he, who feared nothing, set foot in the Cow's Mouth.

It was his pride that he knew when he had had enough. He

had had enough of the Cow's Mouth; and the only thing for which he still wished in connection with it was to express his mind about it to the Maharajah. Unhappily, this was impossible. That idle monarch, who, he now saw plainly, had sent him there either in a mood of luxurious sportiveness or to throw him off the scent of the necklace, remained the only man from whom he could look for final victory. It was not to the Maharajah that he could afford to say all that he thought.

Fortunately the Maharajah was too much entertained by the work which Tarvin immediately instituted on the Amet River to inquire particularly whether his young friend had sought the Naulahka at the Gye-Mukh. Tarvin had sought an audience with the King the morning after his return from that black spot, and, with the face of a man who had never known fear and who lacks the measure of disappointments, gaily demanded the fulfilment of the King's promise. Having failed in one direction on a large scale, he laid the first brick on the walls of a new structure without delay, as the people of Topaz had begun to build their town anew the morning after the fire. His experience at the Gye-Mukh only sharpened his determination, adding to it a grim willingness to get even with the man who had sent him there.

The Maharajah, who felt in especial need of amusement that morning, was very ready to make good his promise, and ordered that the long man who played pachisi should be granted all the men he could use. With the energy of disgust, and with a hot memory of the least assured and comfortable moments of his life burning in his breast, Tarvin flung himself on the turning of the river and the building of his dam. It was necessary, it seemed, in the land upon which he had fallen, to raise a dust to hide one's ends. He would raise a dust, and it should be on the same scale as the catastrophe which he had just encountered—thorough, businesslike, un-compromising.

He raised it, in fact, in a stupendous cloud. Since the State was founded no one had seen anything like it. The Maharajah lent him all the convict labour of his jails, and Tarvin marched the little host of leg-ironed *kaidies* into camp at a point five miles beyond the city walls, and solemnly drew up his plans for the futile damming of the barren Amet. His early training as a civil engineer helped him to lay out a reasonable plan of operations, and to give a semblance of reality to his work. His notion was to back up the river by means of a dam at a point where it swept around a long curve, and to send it straight across the plain by excavating a deep bed for it. When this was completed the present bed of the river would lie bare for several miles, and if there were any gold there, as Tarvin said to himself, then would be the time to pick it up. Meanwhile his operations vastly entertained the King, who rode out every morning and watched him directing his small army for an hour or more. The marchings and counter-marchings of the mob of convicts with baskets, hoes, shovels, and pannier-laden donkeys, the prodigal blasting of rocks, and the general bustle and confusion, drew the applause of the King, for whom Tarvin always reserved his best blasts. This struck him as only fair, as the King was paying for the powder, and, indeed, for the entire entertainment.

Among the unpleasant necessities of his position was the need of giving daily to Colonel Nolan, to the King, and to all the drummers at the rest-house, whenever they might choose to ask him, his reasons for damming the Amet. The great Indian Government itself also presently demanded his reasons, in writing, for damming the Amet; Colonel Nolan's reasons, in writing, for allowing the Amet to be dammed; and the

King's reasons for allowing anybody but a duly authorised agent of the Government to dam the Amet. This was accompanied by a request for further information. To these inquiries Tarvin, for his part, returned an evasive answer, and felt that he was qualifying himself for his political career at home. Colonel Nolan explained officially to his superiors that the convicts were employed in remunerative labour, and, unofficially, that the Maharajah had been so phenomenally good for some time past (being kept amused by this American stranger) that it would be a thousand pities to interrupt the operations. Colonel Nolan was impressed by the fact that Tarvin was the Hon. Nicholas Tarvin, and a member of the Legislature of one of the United States.

The Government, knowing something of the irrepressible race who stride booted into the council-halls of kings, and demand concessions for oil-boring from Arakan to the Peshin, said no more, but asked to be supplied with information from time to time as to the progress of the stranger's work. When Tarvin heard this he sympathised with the Indian Government. He understood this thirst for information; he wanted some himself as to the present whereabouts of the Naulahka; also touching the time it would take Kate to find out that she wanted him more than the cure of any misery whatever.

At least twice a week, in fancy, he gave up the Naulahka definitely, returned to Topaz, and resumed the business of a real estate and insurance agent. He drew a long breath after each of these decisions, with the satisfying recollection that there was still one spot on the earth's surface where a man might come directly at his desires if he possessed the sand and the hustle; where he could walk a straight path to his ambition; and where he did not by preference turn five corners to reach an object a block away.

Sometimes, as he grilled patiently in the river bed under the blighting rays of the Indian sun, he would heretically blaspheme the Naulahka, refusing to believe in its existence, and persuading himself that it was as grotesque a lie as the King's parody of a civilised government, or as Dhunpat Rai's helpful surgery. Yet from a hundred sources he heard of the existence of that splendour, only never in reply to a direct question.

Dhunpat Rai, in particular (once weak enough to complain of the new Lady Doctor's 'excessive zeal and surplusage administration'), had given him an account that made his mouth water. But Dhunpat Rai had not seen the necklace since the crowning of the present King, fifteen years before. The very convicts on the works, squabbling over the distribution of food, spoke of millet as being as costly as the Naulahka. Twice the Maharaj Kunwar, babbling vaingloriously to his big friend of what he would do when he came to the throne, concluded his confidences with, 'and *then* I shall wear the Naulahka in my turban all day long.'

But when Tarvin asked him where that precious necklace lived, the Maharaj Kunwar shook his head, answering sweetly, 'I do not know.'

The infernal thing seemed to be a myth, a word, a proverb—anything rather than the finest necklace in the world. In the intervals of blasting and excavation he would make futile attempts to come upon its track. He took the city ward by ward, and explored every temple in each. He rode, under pretence of archaeological study, to the outlying forts and ruined palaces that lay beyond the city in the desert, and roved restlessly through the mausoleums that held the ashes of the dead kings of Rhatore. He told himself a hundred times that he knew each quest to be hopeless; but he needed the consolation of persistent search. And the search was always vain.

# THE NAULAHKA

Tarvin fought his impatience when he rode abroad with the Maharajah. At the palace, which he visited at least once a day under pretence of talking about the dam, he devoted himself more sedulously than ever to pachisi. It pleased the Maharajah in those days to remove himself from the white marble pavilion in the orange garden, where he usually spent the spring months, to Sitabhai's wing of the red-stone palace, and to sit in the courtyard watching trained parrots firing little cannons, and witnessing combats between fighting quail or great grey apes dressed in imitation of English officers. When Colonel Nolan appeared the apes were hastily dismissed; but Tarvin was allowed to watch the play throughout, when he was not engaged on the dam. He was forced to writhe in inaction and in wonder about his necklace, while these childish games went forward; but he constantly kept the corner of an eye upon the movements of the Maharaj Kunwar. There, at least, his wit could serve some one.

The Maharajah had given strict orders that the child should obey all Kate's instructions. Even his heavy eyes noted an improvement in the health of the little one, and Tarvin was careful that he should know that the credit belonged to Kate alone. With impish perversity the young Prince, who had never received an order in his life before, learned to find joy in disobedience, and devoted his wits, his escort, and his barouche to gambolling in the wing of the palace belonging to Sitabhai. There he found grey-headed flatterers by the score, who abased themselves before him, and told him what manner of King he should be in the years to come. There also were pretty dancing-girls, who sang him songs, and would have corrupted his mind but that it was too young to receive corruption. There were, besides, apes and peacocks and jugglers—new ones every day—together with dancers on the slack-rope, and wonderful pack-

ing-cases from Calcutta, out of which he was allowed to choose
ivory-handled pistols and little gold-hilted swords with seed
pearls set in a groove along the middle, and running musically
up and down as he waved the blade round his head. Finally,
the sacrifice of a goat in an opal and ivory temple in the heart
of the women's quarters, which he might watch, allured him
that way. Against these enticements Kate, moody, grave, distracted, her eyes full of the miseries on which it was her daily
lot to look, and her heart torn with the curelessness of it all,
could offer only little childish games in the missionary's drawing-room. The heir-apparent to the throne did not care for
leap-frog, which he deemed in the highest degree undignified;
nor yet for puss-in-the-corner, which seemed to him over-active;
nor for tennis, which he understood was played by his brother
princes, but which to him appeared no part of a Rajput's
education. Sometimes, when he was tired (and on rare occasions when he escaped to Sitabhai's wing it was observable
that he returned very tired indeed), he would listen long and
intently to the stories of battle and siege which Kate read to
him, and would scandalise her at the end of the tale by an-
nouncing, with flashing eye:—

'When I am King I will make my army do *all* those things.'

It was not in Kate's nature—she would have thought it in
the highest degree wrong—to refrain from some little attempt
at religious instruction. But here the child retreated into the
stolidity of the East, and only said:—

'All these things are very good for you, Kate, but all my Gods
are very good for me; and if my father knew, he would be
angry.'

'And what *do* you worship?' asked Kate, pitying the young
pagan from the bottom of her heart.

'My sword and my horse,' answered the Maharaj Kunwar;

and he half drew the jewelled sabre that was his inseparable companion, returning it with a resolute clank that closed the discussion.

But it was impossible, he discovered, to evade the long man Tarvin as he evaded Kate. He resented being called 'bub,' nor did he approve of 'little man.' But Tarvin could drawl the word 'Prince' with a quiet deference that made the young Rajput almost suspect himself the subject of a jest. And yet Tarvin Sahib treated him as a man, and allowed him, under due precautions, to handle his mighty 'gun,' which was not a gun, but a pistol. And once, when the Prince had coaxed the keeper of the horse into allowing him to bestride an unmanageable mount, Tarvin, riding up, had picked him out of the depths of the velvet saddle, set him on his own saddle-bow, and, in the same cloud of dust, shown him how, in his own country, they laid the reins on one side or the other of the neck of their cattle-ponies to guide them in pursuit of a steer broken from the herd.

The trick of being lifted from his saddle, appealing to the 'circus' latent in the boy breast even of an Eastern prince, struck the Maharaj as so amusing that he insisted on exhibiting it before Kate; and as Tarvin was a necessary figure in the performance, he allured him into helping him with it one day before the house of the missionary. Mr. and Mrs. Estes came out upon the veranda with Kate and watched the exhibition, and the missionary pursued it with applause and requests for a repetition, which having been duly given, Mrs. Estes asked Tarvin if he would not stay to dinner with them since he was there. Tarvin glanced doubtfully at Kate for permission, and, by a process of reasoning best known to lovers, construed the veiling of her eyes and the turning of her head into assent.

After dinner, as they sat on the veranda in the starlight, 'Do you really mind?' he asked.

'What?' asked she, lifting her sober eyes and letting them fall upon him.

'My seeing you sometimes. I know you don't like it; but it will help me to look after you. You must see by this time that you need looking after.'

'Oh no.'

'Thank you,' said Tarvin, almost humbly.

'I mean I don't need looking after.'

'But you don't dislike it?'

'It's good of you,' she said impartially.

'Well, then, it will be bad of you not to like it.'

Kate had to smile. 'I guess I like it,' she replied.

'And you will let me come once in a while? You can't think what the rest-house is. Those drummers will kill me yet. And the coolies at the dam are not in my set.'

'Well, since you're here. But you ought *not* to be here. Do me a real kindness, and go away, Nick.'

'Give me an easier one.'

'But *why* are you here? You can't show any rational reason.'

'Yes; that's what the British Government says. But I brought my reason along.'

He confessed his longing for something homely and natural and American after a day's work under a heathen and raging sun; and when he put it in this light, Kate responded on another side. She had been brought up with a sense of responsibility for making young men feel at home; and he certainly felt at home when she was able to produce, two or three evenings later, a Topaz paper sent her by her father. Tarvin pounced on it, and turned the flimsy four pages inside out, and then back again.

He smacked his lips. 'Oh, good, good, *good!*' he murmured relishingly. 'Don't the advertisements look nice? What's the matter with Topaz?' cried he, holding the sheet from him at arm's length, and gazing ravenously up and down its columns. 'Oh, *she*'s all right.' The cooing, musical sing-song in which he uttered this consecrated phrase was worth going a long way to hear. 'Say, we're coming on, aren't we? We're not lagging nor loafing, nor fooling our time away, if we *haven't* got the Three C.'s *yet*. We're keeping up with the procession. Hi-yi! look at the "Rustler Rootlets"—just about a stickful! Why, the poor old worm-eaten town is going sound, sound asleep in her old age, isn't she? Think of taking a railroad there! Listen to this:—

' "Milo C. Lambert, the owner of 'Lambert's Last Ditch,' has a car-load of good ore on the dump, but, like all the rest of us, don't find it pays to ship without a railroad line nearer than fifteen miles. Milo says Colorado won't be good enough for him after he gets his ore away."

'I should think not. Come to Topaz, Milo! And this:—

' "When the Three C.'s comes into the city in the fall we shan't be hearing this talk about hard times. Meantime it's an injustice to the town, which all honest citizens should resent and do their best to put down, to speak of Rustler as taking a back seat to any town of its age in the State. As a matter of fact, Rustler was never more prosperous. With mines which produced last year ore valued at a total of $1,200,000, with six churches of different denominations, with a young but prosperous and growing academy which is destined to take a front rank among American schools, with a record of new buildings erected during the past year equal if not superior to any town in the mountains, and with a population of lively and determined business men, Rustler bids fair in the coming year to be worthy of her name."

'Who said "afraid"? We're not hurt. Hear us whistle. But I'm sorry Heckler let that into his correspondence,' he added, with a momentary frown. 'Some of our Topaz citizens might miss the fun of it, and go over to Rustler to wait for the Three C.'s. Coming in the fall, is it? Oh, dear! Oh, dear, dear, dear! This is the way they amuse themselves while they dangle their legs over Big Chief Mountain and wait for it:—

' "Our merchants have responded to the recent good feeling which has pervaded the town since word came that President Mutrie, on his return to Denver, was favourably considering the claims of Rustler. Robbins has his front windows prettily decorated and filled with fancy articles. His store seems to be the most popular for the youngsters who have a nickel or two to spend."

'I should murmur! Won't you like to see the Three C.'s come sailing into Topaz one of these fine mornings, little girl?' asked Tarvin suddenly, as he seated himself on the sofa beside her, and opened out the paper so that she could look over his shoulder.

'Would you like it, Nick?'

'*Would* I!'

'Then, of course, I should. But I think you will be better off if it doesn't. It will make you too rich. See father.'

'Well, I'd put on the brakes if I found myself getting real rich. I'll stop just after I've passed the Genteel Poverty Station. Isn't it good to see the old heading again—Heckler's name as large as life just under "oldest paper in Divide County," and Heckler's fist sticking out all over a rousing editorial on the prospects of the town? Homelike, isn't it? He's got two columns of new advertising; that shows what the town's doing. And look at the good old "ads." from the Eastern agencies. How they take you back! I never expected to thank Heaven for a Castoria advertisement; did you, Kate? But I swear it makes me feel good all over. I'll read the patent inside if you say much.'

Kate smiled. The paper gave her a little pang of homesickness too. She had her own feeling for Topaz; but what reached her through the *Telegram's* lively pages was the picture of her mother sitting in her kitchen in the long afternoons (she had sat in the kitchen so long in the poor and wandering days of the family that she did it now by preference), gazing sadly out at white-topped Big Chief, and wondering what her daughter was doing at that hour. Kate remembered well that afternoon hour in the kitchen when the work was done. She recalled from the section-house days the superannuated rocker, once a parlour chair, which her mother had hung with skins and told off for kitchen service. Kate remembered with starting tears that her mother had always wanted her to sit in it, and how good it had been to see from her own hassock next the oven the little mother swallowed up in its deeps. She heard the cat purring under the stove, and the kettle singing; the clock ticked in her ear, and the cracks between the boards in the floor of the hastily built section-house blew the cold prairie air against her heels.

She gazed over Tarvin's shoulder at the two cuts of Topaz which appeared in every issue of the *Telegram*—the one representing the town in its first year, the other the town of to-day—and a lump rose in her throat.

'Quite a difference, isn't there?' said Tarvin, following her eye. 'Do you remember where your father's tent used to stand, and the old section-house, just here by the river?' He pointed, and Kate nodded without speaking. 'Those were good days, weren't they? Your father wasn't as rich as he is now, and neither was I; but we were all mighty happy together.'

# THE NAULAHKA

Kate's thought drifted back to that time, and called up other visions of her mother expending her slight frame in many forms of hard work. The memory of the little characteristic motion with which she would shield with raised hand the worn young-old face when she would be broiling above an open fire, or frying doughnuts, or lifting the stove lid, forced her to gulp down the tears. The simple picture was too clear, even to the light of the fire on the face, and the pink light shining through the frail hand.

'Hello!' said Tarvin, casting his eye up and down the columns, 'they've had to put another team on to keep the streets clean. We had one. Heckler don't forget the climate either. And they are doing well at the Mesa House. That's a good sign. The tourists will all have to stop over at Topaz when the new line comes through, and we have the right hotel. Some towns might think we had a little tourist traffic now. Here's Loomis dining fifty at the Mesa the other day—through express. They've formed a new syndicate to work the Hot Springs. Do you know, I shouldn't wonder if they made a town down there. Heckler's right. It *will* help Topaz. We don't mind a town that near. It makes a suburb of it.'

He marked his sense of the concession implied in letting him stay that evening by going early; but he did not go so early on the following evening, and as he showed no inclination to broach forbidden subjects, Kate found herself glad to have him there, and it became a habit of his to drop in, in the evenings, and to join the group that gathered, with open doors and windows, about the family lamp. In the happiness of seeing visible effects from her labours blossoming under her eyes, Kate regarded his presence less and less. Sometimes she would let him draw her out upon the veranda under the sumptuous Indian night—nights when the heat-lightning played like a drawn sword on the horizon, and the heavens hovered near the

401

earth, and the earth was very still. But commonly they sat within, with the missionary and his wife, talking of Topaz, of the hospital, of the Maharaj Kunwar, of the dam, and sometimes of the Estes children at Bangor. For the most part, however, when the talk was among the group, it fell upon the infinitesimal gossip of a sequestered life, to the irritation and misery of Tarvin.

When the conversation lagged in these deeps he would fetch up violently with a challenge to Estes on the subject of the tariff or silver legislation, and after that the talk was at least lively. Tarvin was, by his training, largely a newspaper-educated man. But he had also been taught at first hand by life itself, and by the habit of making his own history; and he used the hairy fist of horse-sense in dealing with the theories of newspaper politics and the systems of the schools.

Argument had no allurements for him, however; it was with Kate that he talked when he could, and oftenest, of late, of the hospital, since her progress there had begun to encourage her. She yielded at last to his entreaties to be allowed to see this paragon, and to look for himself upon the reforms she had wrought.

Matters had greatly improved since the days of the lunatic and the 'much-esteemed woman,' but only Kate knew how much remained to be done. The hospital was at least clean and sweet if she inspected it every day, and the people in their fashion were grateful for kinder tending and more skilful treatment than they had hitherto dreamed of. Upon each cure a rumour went abroad through the countryside of a new power in the land, and other patients came; or the convalescent herself would bring back a sister, a child, or a mother with absolute faith in the power of the White Fairy to make all whole. They could not know all the help that Kate brought in the train of her quiet movements, but for what they knew they blessed her as they lay. Her new energy swept even Dhunpat Rai along the path of reform. He became curious in the limewashing of stone-work, the disinfecting of wards, the proper airing of bed-linen, and even the destruction by fire of the bedsteads, once his per-quisite, on which smallpox patients had died. Native-like, he worked best for a woman with the knowledge that there was an energetic white man in the background. Tarvin's visits, and a few cheery words addressed to him by that capable outsider, supplied him with this knowledge.

Tarvin could not understand the uncouth talk of the out-patients, and did not visit the women's wards; but he saw enough to congratulate Kate unreservedly. She smiled con-tentedly. Mrs. Estes was sympathetic, but in no way enthu-siastic; and it was good to be praised by Nick, who had found so much to blame in her project.

'It's clean and it's wholesome, little girl,' he said, peering and sniffing; 'and you've done miracles with these jellyfish. If you'd been on the opposition ticket instead of your father I shouldn't be a member of the Legislature.'

Kate never talked to him about that large part of her work which lay among the women of the Maharajah's palace. Little by little she learned her way about such portions of the pile as she was permitted to traverse. From the first she had under-stood that the palace was ruled by one Queen, of whom the women spoke under their breath, and whose lightest word, conveyed by the mouth of a grinning child, set the packed mazes humming. Once only had she seen this Queen, glim-mering like a tiger-beetle among a pile of *kinkob* cushions—a lithe, black-haired young girl, it seemed, with a voice as soft as running water at night, and with eyes that had no shadow of fear in them. She turned lazily, the jewels clinking on ankle, arm, and bosom, and looked at Kate for a long time without speaking.

'I have sent that I may see you,' she said at last. 'You have come here across the water to help these cattle?'

Kate nodded, every instinct in her revolting at the silver-tongued splendour at her feet.

'You are not married?' The Queen put her hands behind her head and looked at the painted peacocks on the ceiling.

Kate did not reply, but her heart was hot.

'Is there any sickness here?' she asked at last sharply. 'I have much to do.'

'There is none, unless it may be that you yourself are sick. There are those who sicken without knowing it.'

The eyes turned to meet Kate's, which were blazing with indignation. This woman, lapped in idleness, had struck at the life of the Maharaj Kunwar; and the horror of it was that she was younger than herself.

'*Achcha*,' said the Queen, still more slowly, watching her face. 'If you hate me so, why do you not say so? You white people love truth.'

Kate turned on her heel to leave the room. Sitabhai called her back for an instant, and, moved by some royal caprice, would have caressed her, but she fled indignant, and was careful never again to venture into that wing of the palace. None of the women there called for her services, and not once but several times, when she passed the mouth of the covered way that led to Sitabhai's apartments, she saw a little naked child flourishing a jewelled knife, and shouting round the headless carcass of a goat whose blood was flooding the white marble. 'That,' said the women, 'is the gipsy's son. He learns to kill daily. A snake is a snake, and a gipsy is a gipsy, till they are dead.'

There was no slaughter of goats, singing of songs, or twangling of musical instruments in the wing of the palace that made itself specially Kate's own. Here lived, forgotten by the Maharajah and mocked by Sitabhai's maidens, the mother of the Maharaj Kunwar. Sitabhai had taken from her—by the dark arts of the gipsies, so the Queen's adherents said—by her own beauty and knowledge in love, they sang in the other wing of the palace—all honour and consideration due to her as the Queen-Mother. There were scores of empty rooms where once there had been scores of waiting-women, and those who remained with the fallen Queen were forlorn and ill-favoured. She herself was a middle-aged woman, by Eastern standards; that is to say, she had passed twenty-five, and had never been more than ordinarily comely.

Her eyes were dull with much weeping, and her mind was full of superstitions—fears for every hour of the night and the day, and vague terrors, bred of loneliness, that made her tremble at the sound of a footfall. In the years of her prosperity she had been accustomed to perfume herself, put on her jewels, and with braided hair await the Maharajah's coming. She would still call for her jewels, attire herself as of old, and wait amid the respectful silence of her attendants till the long night gave way to the dawn, and the dawn showed the furrows on her cheeks. Kate had seen one such vigil, and perhaps showed in her eyes the wonder that she could not repress, for the Queen-Mother fawned on her timidly after the jewels had been put away, and begged her not to laugh.

'You do not understand, Miss Kate,' she pleaded. 'There is one custom in your country and another in ours; but still you are a woman, and you will know.'

'But you know that no one will come,' Kate said tenderly.

'Yes, I know; but—no, you are not a woman, only a fairy that has come across the water to help me and mine.'

Here again Kate was baffled. Except in the message sent by

the Maharaj Kunwar, the Queen-Mother never referred to the danger that threatened her son's life. Again and again Kate had tried to lead up to the subject—to gain some hint, at least, of the nature of the plot.

'I know nothing,' the Queen would reply. 'Here behind the curtain no one knows anything. Miss Kate, if my own women lay dead out there in the sun at noon'—she pointed downwards through the tracery of her window to the flagged path below—'I should know nothing. Of what I said I know nothing; but surely it is allowed'—she lowered her voice to a whisper—'oh, surely it is allowed to a mother to bid another woman to look to her son. He is so old now that he thinks himself a man, and wanders far, and so young that he thinks the world will do him no harm. *Ahi!* And he is so wise that he knows a thousand times more than I. He speaks English like an Englishman. How can I control him with my little learning and my very great love? I say to you, Be good to my son. That I can say aloud, and write it upon a wall, if need were. There is no harm in that. But if I said more, look you, the plaster between the stones beneath me would gape to suck it in, and the wind would blow all my words across to the villages. I am a stranger here—a Raputni from Kulu, a thousand thousand miles away. They bore me here in a litter to be married—in the dark they bore me for a month; and except that some of my women have told me, I should not know which way the home wind blows when it goes to Kulu. What can a strange cow do in the byre? May the Gods witness!'

'Ah, but tell me what you think?'

'I think nothing,' the Queen would answer sullenly. 'What have women to do with thinking? They love and they suffer. I have said all that I may say. Miss Kate, some day you will bear a little son. As you have been good to my son, so may the Gods be good to yours when that time comes, and you know how the heart is full of love.'

'If I am to protect him, I *must* know. You leave me in the dark.'

'And I also am in the dark—and the darkness is full of danger.'

Tarvin himself was much about the palace, not only because he perceived that it was there he might most hopefully keep his ear to the ground for news of the Naulahka, but because it enabled him to observe Kate's comings and goings, and with his hand ready for a rapid movement to his pistol-pocket.

His gaze followed her at these times, as at others, with the longing look of the lover; but he said nothing, and Kate was grateful to him. It was a time, as it seemed to him, to play the part of the Tarvin who had carried water for her long ago at the end of the section; it was a time to stand back, to watch, to guard, but not to trouble her.

The Maharaj Kunwar came often under his eye, and he was constantly inventing amusing things for him to do remote from Sitabhai's courtyard; but the boy would occasionally break away, and then it was Tarvin's task to go after him and make sure that he came to no harm. One afternoon when he had spent some time in coaxing the child away, and had finally resorted to force, much to the child's disgust, a twelve-foot baulk of teakwood, as he was passing out under an arch in process of repair, crashed down from the scaffolding just in front of Fibby's nose. The horse retired into the courtyard on his hind legs, and Tarvin heard the rustle of the women behind the shutters.

He reflected on the incurable slackness of these people,

stopped to swear at the workmen crouched on the scaffolding in the hollow of the arch, and went on. They were no less careless about the dam—it was in the blood, he supposed,— for the headman of a coolie gang who must have crossed the Amet twenty times showed him a new ford across a particularly inviting channel, which ended in a quicksand; and when Tarvin had flung himself clear, the gang spent half the day in hauling Fibby out with ropes. They could not even build a temporary bridge without leaving the boards loose, so that a horse's hoof found its way between; and the gangs seemed to make a point of letting bullock-carts run down the steep embankments into the small of Tarvin's back, when, at infrequent intervals, that happened to be turned.

Tarvin was filled with great respect for the British Government, which worked on these materials, and began to understand the mild-faced melancholy and decisive views of Lucien Estes about the native population, as well as to sympathise more keenly than ever with Kate.

This curious people were now, he learned with horror, to fill the cup of their follies by marrying the young Maharaj Kunwar to a three-year-old babe, brought from the Kulu hills, at vast expense, to be his bride. He sought out Kate at the missionary's, and found her quivering with indignation. She had just heard.

'It's like them to waste a wedding where it isn't wanted,' said Tarvin soothingly. Since he saw Kate excited, it became his part to be calm. 'Don't worry your overworked head about it, Kate. You are trying to do too much, and you are feeling too much. You will break down before you know it, from sheer exhaustion of the chord of sympathy.'

'Oh no!' said Kate. 'I feel quite strong enough for anything that may come. I mustn't break down. Think of this marriage coming on. The Maharaj will need me more than ever. He has just told me that he won't get any sleep for three days and three nights while their priests are praying over him.'

'Crazy! Why, it's a quicker way of killing him than Sitabhai's. Heavens! I daren't think of it. Let's talk of something else. Any papers from your father lately? This kind of thing makes Topaz taste sort of good.'

She gave him a package received by the last post, and he fell silent as he ran his eye hastily over a copy of the *Telegram* six weeks old; but he seemed to find little comfort in it. His brows knitted.

'Pshaw!' he exclaimed with irritation. 'This won't do!'

'What is it?'

'Heckler bluffing about the Three C.'s, and not doing it well. That isn't like Jim. He talks about it as a sure thing as hard as if he didn't believe in it, and had a private tip from somewhere that it wasn't coming after all. I've no doubt he has. But he needn't give it away to Rustler like that. Let's look at the real estate transfers. Ah! that tells the story,' he exclaimed excitedly, as his eye rested on the record of the sale of a parcel of lots on G Street. 'Prices are going down—away, 'way down. The boys are caving. They're giving up the fight.' He leaped up and marched about the room nervously. 'Heavens! if I could only get word to them!'

'Why—what, Nick? What word do you want to send them?'

He pulled himself up instantly.

'To let them know that *I* believe in it,' he said. 'To get them to hold on.'

'But suppose the road doesn't come to Topaz after all. How can you know, away off here in India?'

'Come to Topaz, little girl!' he shouted. 'Come to Topaz! It's coming if I have to lay the rails!'

But the news about the temper of the town vexed and disconcerted him notwithstanding, and after he left Kate that night he sent a cable to Heckler, through Mrs. Mutrie, desiring her to forward the despatch from Denver, as if that were the originating office of the message.

'HECKLER, TOPAZ.—Take a brace, for God's sake. Got dead cinch on Three C's. Trust me, and boom like——. TARVIN.'

*Because I sought it far from men,*
*In deserts and alone,*
*I found it burning overhead,*
*The jewel of a throne.*

*Because I sought—I sought it so*
*And spent my days to find—*
*It blazed one moment ere it left*
*The blacker night behind.*

THE CRYSTALS OF ISWARA

A CITY OF TENTS had grown up in three days without the walls of Rhatore—a city greened with far-brought lawns of turf, and stuck about with hastily transplanted orange-trees, wooden lamp-posts painted in gaudy colours, and a cast-iron fountain of hideous design. Many guests were expected at Rhatore to grace the marriage of the Maharaj Kunwar—barons, princes, thakurs, lords of waste fortresses and of hopeless crags of the north and the south, fiefs from the fat, poppy-blazoned plains of Mewar, and brother Rajahs of the King. They came accompanied by their escorts, horse and foot.

In a land where genealogies, to be respectable, must run back without a break for eight hundred years, it is a delicate matter not to offend; and all were desperately jealous of the place and precedence of their neighbours in the camp. Lest the task should be too easy, the household bards of the princes came with them, and squabbled with the Court officials of Gokral Seetarun. Behind the tents stretched long lines of horse-pickets, where the fat pink-and-blue-spotted stallions neighed and squealed at one another, under their heavy velvet trappings, all day long; and the ragged militia of twenty tiny Native States smoked and gambled among their saddles, or quarrelled at the daily distribution of food furnished by the generosity of the Maharajah. From hundreds of miles about, vagrant and mendicant priests of every denomination had flocked into the city, and their salmon-coloured raiment, black blankets, or ash-smeared nudity gave Tarvin many minutes of untrammelled entertainment as he watched them roaming fearlessly from tent to tent, their red eyes rolling in their heads, alternately threatening or fawning for gifts. The rest-house, as Tarvin discovered, was crammed with fresh contingents of commercial travellers. His Highness was not likely to pay at such a season, but fresh orders would be plentiful. The city itself was brilliant with coats of pink-and-white limewash, and the main streets were obstructed with the bamboo scaffoldings of fireworks. Every house-front was swept and newly luted with clean mud, and the doorways were hung with marigolds and strings of jasmine-buds. Through the crowds tramped the sweating sweetmeat-dealers, vendors of hawks, dealers in cheap jewellery 'and glass bracelets and little English mirrors, while camels, loaded with wedding gifts of far-off kings, ploughed through the crowd, or the mace-bearers of the State cleared a path with their silver staves for the passage of the Maharajah's carriages. Forty barouches were in use, and, as long as horse-flesh held out, or harness could be patched with string, it did not beseem the dignity of the State to provide less than four horses to each. As these horses were untrained, and as the little native boys, out of sheer lightness of heart, touched off squibs and crackers at high noon, the streets were animated.

The hill on which the palace stood seemed to smoke like

a volcano, for the little dignitaries came without cessation, each expecting the salute of cannon due to his rank. Between the roars of the ordnance, strains of uncouth music would break from the red walls, and presently some officer of the Court would ride out of one of the gates, followed by all his retinue, each man gorgeous as a cock-pheasant in spring, his moustache fresh oiled and curled fiercely over his ears; or one of the royal elephants, swathed in red velvet and bullion from shoulder to ankle, would roll out under the weight of his silver howdah, and trumpet till the streets were cleared for his passage. Seventy elephants were fed daily by the King—no mean charge, since each beast consumed as much green fodder daily as he could carry on his back, as well as thirty or forty pounds of flour. Now and again one of the monsters, maddened by the noise and confusion, and by the presence of strange rivals, would be overtaken with paroxysms of blind fury. Then he would be hastily stripped of his trappings, bound with ropes and iron chains, hustled out of the city between two of his fellows, and tied down half a mile away by the banks of the Amet, to scream and rage till the horses in the neighbouring camps broke their pickets and stampeded wildly among the tents. Pertab Singh, commandant of his Highness's bodyguard, was in his glory. Every hour of the day gave him excuse for charging with his troop on mysterious but important errands between the palace and the tents of the princes. The formal interchange of visits alone occupied two days. Each prince with his escort would solemnly drive to the palace, and half an hour later the silver state barouche and the Maharajah himself, jewelled from head to heel, would return the visit, while the guns gave word of the event to the city of houses and to the city of tents.

When night fell on the camp there was no silence till near

the dawn, for strolling players, singers of songs, and tellers of stories, dancing-girls, brawny Oudh wrestlers, and camp-followers beyond counting, wandered from tent to tent, making merry. When these had departed, the temples in the city sent forth the hoarse cries of conchs, and Kate, listening, seemed to hear in every blast the wail of the little Maharaj Kunwar, who was being prepared for his marriage by interminable prayers and purifications. She saw as little of the boy as Tarvin did of the King. In those days every request for an audience was met with, 'He is with the priests.' Tarvin cursed all the priests of Rhatore, and condemned to every variety of perdition the hang-dog fakirs that prowled about his path.

'I wish to goodness they'd come to a point with this fool business,' he said to himself. 'I haven't got a century to spend in Rhatore.'

After nearly a week of uninterrupted clamour, blazing sunshine, and moving crowds clad in garments, the colours of which made Tarvin's eyes ache, there arrived, by the same road that had borne Kate to the city, two carriages containing five Englishmen and three Englishwomen, who, later, walked about the city with lack-lustre eyes, bored by the official duty which compelled them to witness in the hot weather a crime which it was not only beyond them to hinder, but to which they were obliged to lend their official patronage.

The Agent to the Governor-General—that is to say, the official representative of the Viceroy in Rajputana—had some time before represented to the Maharajah that he might range himself in the way of progress and enlightenment by ordering that his son should not be given in marriage for another ten years. The Maharajah, pleading the immemorial custom of his land and the influence of the priests, gilded his refusal by a generous donation to a women's hospital in Calcutta which was not in want of funds.

For his own part, Tarvin could not comprehend how any Government could lend its countenance to this wicked farce, calling itself a marriage, which was presently to be played out with the assistance of two children. He was presently introduced to the Agent of the Governor-General, who was anxious to learn more about the damming of the Amet. To be asked about the damming of the Amet, when he was making no more progress than at present with the Naulahka, seemed to Tarvin, however, the last touch of insult, and he was not communicative, asking the Agent, instead, a number of urgent questions about the approaching infamy at the palace. The Agent declaring the marriage to be a political necessity, the destination suggested by Tarvin for political necessities of this sort caused the official to stiffen, and to look this wild American up and down with startled curiosity. They parted on poor terms.

With the rest of the party Tarvin was more at ease. The Agent's wife, a tall brunette, belonging to one of those families which from the earliest days of the East India Company have administered the fortunes of India, solemnly inspected Kate's work at the hospital; and being only a woman, and not an official, was attracted, and showed that she was attracted, by the sad-eyed little woman who did not talk about her work. Therefore Tarvin devoted himself to the amusement and entertainment of the Agent's wife, and she pronounced him an extraordinary person. 'But then, all Americans are extraordinary, you know, though they're so clever.'

Not forgetting in the midst of this tumultuous pageant that he was a citizen of Topaz, Tarvin told her about that blessed city of the plain, away off there under the Sauguache Range, where half his heart lay. He called it 'the magic city,' implying that the dwellers of the Western continent had agreed to call it so by general consent. She was not bored; she enjoyed it. Talk of land and improvement companies, boards of trade, town lots, and the Three C.'s was fresh to her, and it became easy to lead up to what Tarvin actually had in mind. What about the Naulahka? Had she ever seen it? He asked these questions boldly.

No; she knew nothing of the Naulahka. Her thoughts were bounded by the thought of going home in the spring. Home for her meant a little house near Sydenham, close to the Crystal Palace, where her three-year-old boy was waiting for her; and the interests of the other English men and women seemed equally remote from Rajputana—not to mention the Naulahka. It was only inferentially that Tarvin could gather that they had spent the greater part of their working lives within the limits of the country. They talked as gipsies might talk by the roadside a little before the horses are put into the caravan. The ways were hot, they implied, and very dusty; and they hoped one day to be able to rest. The wedding was only one more weary incident on the line of march, and they devoutly wished it over. One of them even envied Tarvin for coming to the State with his fresh eye and his lively belief in the possibility of getting something out of the land besides a harvest of regrets.

The last day of the marriage ceremonies began and ended with more cannon, more fireworks, more clattering of hoofs, more trumpeting of elephants, and with the clamour of bands trying to play 'God Save the Queen.' The Maharaj Kunwar was to appear in the evening (in an Indian state wedding the bride is neither mentioned nor seen) at a banquet, where the Agent of the Governor-General would propose his health and that of his father. The Maharaj was to make a speech in his best English. A Court scribe had already composed a long oration to be used by his father. Tarvin was beginning seriously to doubt whether he should ever see the child alive again; and, before the banquet, rode out into the seething city to reconnoitre. It was twilight, and the torches were flaring between the houses. Wild outlanders from the desert, who had never seen a white man before, caught his horse by the bridle, examined him curiously, and with a grunt let him pass. The many-coloured turbans showed under the flickering light like the jewels of a broken necklace, and all the white housetops were crowded with the veiled figures of women. In half an hour the Maharaj Kunwar would make his way from the royal temple to the banqueting-tent at the head of a procession of caparisoned elephants.

Tarvin forced his way inch by inch through the dense crowd that waited at the foot of the temple steps. He merely wished to satisfy himself that the child was well; he wanted to see him come from the temple. As he looked about him he saw that he was the only white man in the crowd, and pitied his jaded acquaintances, who could find no pleasure in the wild scene under his eyes.

The temple doors were closed, and the torchlight flashed back from the ivory and silver with which they were inlaid. Somewhere out of sight stood the elephants, for Tarvin could hear their deep breathing and an occasional squeal above the hum of the crowd. Half a troop of cavalry, very worn and dusty with the day's labours, were trying to clear an open space before the temple, but they might as well have tried to divide a rainbow. From the roofs of the houses the women were throwing flowers, sweetmeats, and coloured rice into the crowd, while small bards, not yet attached to the house of any prince, chanted aloud in praise of the Maharajah, the Maharaj Kunwar, the Viceroy, the Agent of the Governor-General, Colonel Nolan, and any one else who might possibly reward praise with pence. One of these men, recognising Tarvin, struck up a chant in his honour. He had come, said the song, from a far country to dam an ungovernable river, and fill the countryside with gold; his step was like the step of a dromedary in the spring; his eye terrible as that of an elephant; and the graces of his person such that the hearts of all the women of Rhatore turned to water when he rode upon the public way. Lastly, he would reward the singer of this poor song with untold generosity, and his name and fame should endure in the land so long as the flag of Gokral Seetarun had five colours, or as long as the Naulahka adorned the throat of kings.

Then, with an ear-splitting shriek of conchs, the temple doors opened inward, and the voices of the crowd were hushed into a whisper of awe. Tarvin's hands tightened on the reins of his horse, and he leaned forward to stare. The opened doors of the temple framed a square of utter darkness, and to the screeching of the conchs was added a throbbing of innumerable drums. A breath of incense, strong enough to make him cough, drifted across the crowd, which was absolutely silent now.

The next moment the Maharaj Kunwar, alone and unattended, came out of the darkness, and stood in the torchlight with his hands on the hilt of his sword. The face beneath the turban, draped with loops of diamonds under an emerald aigrette, was absolutely colourless. There were purple circles about his eyes, and his mouth was half open; but the pity Tarvin felt for the child's weariness was silenced by a sudden thrill and leap of his heart, for on the gold cloth of the Maharaj Kunwar's breast lay the Naulahka.

There was no need, this time, to ask any questions. It was not he who saw it; its great deep eyes seemed to fall on him. It blazed with the dull red of the ruby, the angry green of the emerald, the cold blue of the sapphire, and the white-hot glory of the diamond. But dulling all these glories was the superb radiance of one gem that lay above the great carved emerald on the central clasp. It was the black diamond—black as the pitch of the infernal lake, and lighted from below by the fires of Hell.

The thing lay on the boy's shoulders, a yoke of flame. It outshone the silent Indian stars above, turned the tossing torches to smears of dull yellow, and sucked the glitter from the cloth of gold on which it lay.

There was no time to think, to estimate, to appraise, scarcely a moment even to realise, for the conchs suddenly wailed again, the Maharaj stepped back into the darkness, and the doors of the temple were shut.

# XV

*From smallpox and the Evil Eye, a wasteful marriage-feast, and the kindness of my co-wife, may the Gods protect my son.*—HINDU PROVERB.

TARVIN MADE HIS WAY to the banquet with his face aflame and his tongue dry between his teeth. He had seen it. It existed. It was not a myth. And he would have it; he would take it back with him. Mrs. Mutrie should hang it about the sculptured neck that looked so well when she laughed; and the Three C.'s should come to Topaz. He would be the saviour of his town; the boys at home would take the horses out of his carriage and drag him up Pennsylvania Avenue with their own hands; and town lots would sell next year in Topaz by the running inch.

It was worth all the waiting, worth the damming of a hundred rivers, worth a century of pachisi-playing, and a thousand miles of bullock-cart. As he drained a glass to the health of the young Maharaj Kunwar at the banquet that evening, he renewed his pledge to himself to fight it out on this line if it took all summer. His pride of success had lain low of late, and taken many hurts; but now that he had seen his prize he esteemed it already within his grasp, as he had argued at Topaz that Kate must be his because he loved her.

Next morning he woke with a confused notion that he stood on the threshold of great deeds; and then, in his bath, he wondered whence he had plucked the certainty and exultation of the night before. He had, indeed, seen the Naulahka. But the temple doors had closed on the vision. He found himself asking whether either temple or necklace had been real, and in the midst of his wonder and excitement was half-way to the city before he knew that he had left the rest-house. When he came to himself, however, he knew well whither he was going and what he was going for. If he had seen the Naulahka, he meant to keep it in sight. It had disappeared into the temple. To the temple, therefore, he would go.

Fragments of burnt-out torches lay on the temple steps among trampled flowers and spilt oil, and the marigold garlands hung limp and wilted on the fat shoulders of the black stone bulls that guarded the inner court. Tarvin took off his white pith helmet (it was very hot, though it was only two hours after dawn), pushed back the scanty hair from his high forehead, and surveyed the remnants of yesterday's feast. The city was still asleep after its holiday. The doors of the building were wide open, and he ascended the steps and walked in, with none to hinder.

The formless, four-faced god Iswara, standing in the centre of the temple, was smeared and discoloured with stains of melted butter, and the black smoke of exhausted incense. Tarvin looked at the figure curiously, half expecting to find the Naulahka hung about one of its four necks. Behind him, in the deeper gloom of the temple, stood other divinities, many-handed and many-headed, tossing their arms aloft, protruding their tongues, and grinning at one another. The remains of many sacrifices lay about them, and in the half-light Tarvin could see that the knees of one were black with dried blood. Overhead the dark roof ran up into a Hindu dome, and there was a soft rustle and scratching of nesting bats.

Tarvin, with his hat on the back of his head and his hands in his pockets, gazed at the image, looking about him and whistling softly. He had been a month in India, but he had not yet penetrated to the interior of a temple. Standing there, he recognised with fresh force how entirely the life, habits, and traditions of this strange people alienated them from all that seemed good and right to him; and he was vaguely angered to know that it was the servants of these horrors who possessed a necklace which had power to change the destiny of a Christian and civilised town like Topaz.

He knew that he would be expelled without ceremony for profanation, if discovered, and made haste to finish his investigations, with a half-formed belief that the slovenliness of the race might have caused them to leave the Naulahka about somewhere, as a woman might leave her jewels on her dressing-table after a late return from a ball the night before. He peered about and under the gods, one by one, while the bats squeaked above him. Then he returned to the central image of Iswara, and in his former attitude regarded the idol.

It occurred to him that, though he was on level ground, most of his weight was resting on his toes, and he stepped back to recover his balance. The slab of sandstone he had just quitted rolled over slowly, as a porpoise rolls in the still sea, revealing for an instant a black chasm below. Then it shouldered up into its place again without a sound, and Tarvin wiped the cold sweat from his forehead. If he had found the Naulahka at that instant he would have smashed it in pure rage. He went out into the sunlight once more, devoting the country where such things were possible to its own Gods; he could think of nothing worse.

A priest, sprung from an unguessable retreat, came out of the temple immediately afterward, and smiled upon him.

Tarvin, willing to renew his hold on the wholesome world in which there were homes and women, betook himself to the missionary's cottage, where he invited himself to breakfast. Mr. and Mrs. Estes had kept themselves strictly aloof from the marriage ceremony, but they could enjoy Tarvin's account of it, delivered from the Topaz point of view. Kate was un-feignedly glad to see him. She was full of the discreditable desertion of Dhunpat Rai and the hospital staff from their posts. They had all gone to watch the wedding festivities, and for three days had not appeared at the hospital. The entire work of the place had devolved on herself and the wild woman of the desert who was watching her husband's cure. Kate was very tired, and her heart was troubled with misgivings for the welfare of the little Prince, which she communicated to Tarvin when he drew her out upon the veranda after breakfast.

'I'm sure he wants absolute rest now,' she said, almost tear-fully. 'He came to me at the end of the dinner last night—I was in the women's wing of the palace—and cried for half an hour. Poor little baby! It's cruel.'

'Oh, well, he'll be resting to-day. Don't worry.'

'No; to-day they take his bride back to her own people again, and he has to drive out with the procession or some-thing—in this sun, too. It's very wicked. Doesn't it ever make your head ache, Nick? I sometimes think of you sitting out on that dam of yours, and wonder how you can bear it.'

'I can bear a good deal for you, little girl,' returned Tarvin, looking down into her eyes.

'Why, how is that for me, Nick?'

'You'll see if you live long enough,' he assured her; but he was not anxious to discuss his dam, and returned to the safer subject of the Maharaj Kunwar.

Next day and the day after he rode aimlessly about in the neighbourhood of the temple, not caring to trust himself within its walls again, but determined to keep his eye upon the first and last spot where he had seen the Naulahka. There was no chance at present of getting speech with the only living person, save the King, whom he definitely knew to have touched the treasure. It was maddening to await the reappearance of the Maharaj Kunwar in his barouche, but he summoned what patience he could. He hoped much from him; but meanwhile he often looked in at the hospital to see how Kate fared. The traitor Dhunpat Rai and his helpers had returned; but the hospital was crowded with cases from the furthest portions of the State—fractures caused by the King's reckless barouches, and one or two cases, new in Kate's experience, of men drugged, under the guise of friendship, for the sake of the money they carried with them, and left helpless in the public ways.

Tarvin, as he cast his shrewd eye about the perfectly kept men's ward, humbly owned to himself that, after all, she was doing better work in Rhatore than he. She at least did not run a hospital to cover up deeper and darker designs, and she had the inestimable advantage over him of having her goal in sight. It was not snatched from her after one maddening glimpse; it was not the charge of a mysterious priesthood, or of an impalpable State; it was not hidden in treacherous temples, nor hung round the necks of vanishing infants.

One morning, before the hour at which he usually set out for the dam, Kate sent a note over to him at the rest-house asking him to call at the hospital as soon as possible. For one rapturous moment he dreamed of impossible things. But smiling bitterly at his readiness to hope, he lighted a cigar, and obeyed the order.

Kate met him on the steps, and led him into the dispensary.

She laid an eager hand on his arm. 'Do you know anything about the symptoms of hemp-poisoning?' she asked him.

He caught her by both hands quickly, and stared wildly into her face. 'Why? Why? Has any one been daring——?'

She laughed nervously. 'No, no. It isn't me. It's him.'

'Who?'

'The Maharaj—the child. I'm certain of it now.' She went

on to tell him how, that morning, the barouche, the escort, and a pompous native had hurried up to the missionary's door bearing the almost lifeless form of the Maharaj Kunwar; how she had at first attributed the attack, whatever it might be, to exhaustion consequent upon the wedding festivities; how the little one had roused from his stupor, blue-lipped and hollow-eyed, and had fallen from one convulsion into another, until she had begun to despair; and how, at the last, he had dropped into a deep sleep of exhaustion, when she had left him in the care of Mrs. Estes. She added that Mrs. Estes had believed that the young Prince was suffering from a return of his usual malady; she had seen him in paroxysms of this kind twice before Kate came.

'Now look at this,' said Kate, taking down the chart of her hospital cases, on which were recorded the symptoms and progress of two cases of hemp-poisoning that had come to her within the past week.

'These men,' she said, 'had been given sweetmeats by a gang of travelling gipsies, and all their money was taken from them before they woke up. Read for yourself.'

Tarvin read, biting his lips. At the end he looked up at her sharply.

'Yes,' he said, with an emphatic nod of his head—'yes. Sitabhai?'

'Who else would dare?' answered Kate passionately.

'I know. I know. But how to stop her going on? How to bring it home to her?'

'Tell the Maharajah,' responded Kate decidedly.

Tarvin took her hand. 'Good! I'll try it. But there's no shadow of proof, you know.'

'No matter. Remember the boy. Try. I must go back to him now.'

The two returned to the house of the missionary together,

saying very little on the way. Tarvin's indignation that Kate should be mixed up in this miserable business almost turned to anger at Kate herself, as he rode beside her; but his wrath was extinguished at sight of the Maharaj Kunwar. The child lay on a bed in an inner room at the missionary's, almost too weak to turn his head. As Kate and Tarvin entered, Mrs. Estes rose from giving him his medicine, said a word to Kate by way of report, and returned to her own work. The child was clothed only in a soft muslin coat; but his sword and jewelled belt lay across his feet.

'Salaam, Taravin Sahib,' he murmured. 'I am very sorry that I was ill.'

Tarvin bent over him tenderly. 'Don't try to talk, little one.'

'Nay; I am well now,' was the answer. 'Soon we will go riding together.'

'Were you very sick, little man?'

'I cannot tell. It is all dark to me. I was in the palace laughing with some of the dance-girls. Then I fell. And after that I remember no more till I came here.'

He gulped down the cooling draught that Kate gave him, and resettled himself on the pillows, while one wax-yellow hand played with the hilt of his sword. Kate was kneeling by his side, an arm under the pillow supporting his head; and it seemed to Tarvin that he had never before done justice to the beauty latent in her good, plain, strong features. The trim little figure took softer outlines, the firm mouth quivered, the eyes were filled with a light that Tarvin had never seen before.

'Come to the other side—so,' said the child, beckoning Tarvin in the native fashion, by folding all his tiny fingers into his palms rapidly and repeatedly. Tarvin knelt obediently on the other side of the couch. 'Now I am a King, and this is my Court.'

Kate laughed musically in her delight at seeing the boy recovering strength. Tarvin slid his arm under the pillow, found Kate's hand there, and held it.

The portière at the door of the room dropped softly. Mrs. Estes had stolen in for a moment, and imagined that she saw enough to cause her to steal out again. She had been thinking a great deal since the days when Tarvin first introduced himself.

The child's eyes began to grow dull and heavy, and Kate would have withdrawn her arm to give him another draught.

'Nay; stay so,' he said imperiously; and relapsing into the vernacular, muttered thickly: 'Those who serve the King shall not lack their reward. They shall have villages free of tax— three, five villages; Sujjain, Amet, and Gungra. Let it be entered as a free gift when they marry. They shall marry, and be about me always—Miss Kate and Tarvin Sahib.'

Tarvin did not understand why Kate's hand was withdrawn swiftly. He did not know the vernacular as she did.

'He is getting delirious again,' said Kate, under her breath. 'Poor, poor little one!'

Tarvin ground his teeth, and cursed Sitabhai between them. Kate was wiping the damp forehead, and trying to still the head as it was thrown restlessly from side to side. Tarvin held the child's hands, which closed fiercely on his own, as the boy was racked and convulsed by the last effects of the hemp.

For some minutes he fought and writhed, calling upon the names of many Gods, striving to reach his sword, and ordering imaginary regiments to hang those white dogs to the beams of the palace gate, and to smoke them to death.

Then the crisis passed, and he began to talk to himself and to call for his mother.

The vision of a little grave dug in the open plain sloping

to the river, where they had laid out the Topaz cemetery, rose before Tarvin's memory. They were lowering Heckler's first baby into it, in its pine coffin; and Kate, standing by the grave-side, was writing the child's name on the finger's length of smoothed pine which was to be its only headstone.

'Nay, nay, nay!' wailed the Maharaj Kunwar. 'I am speaking the truth; and oh, I was so tired at that *pagal* dance in the temple, and I only crossed the courtyard. . . . It was a new girl from Lucknow; she sang the song of "The Green Pulse of Mundore." . . . Yes; but only some almond curd. I was hungry, too. A little white almond curd, mother. Why should I not eat when I feel inclined? Am I a sweeper's son, or a prince? Pick me up! pick me up! It is very hot inside my head. . . . Louder. I do not understand. Will they take me over to Kate? She will make all well. What was the message?' The child began to wring his hands despairingly. 'The message! The message! I have forgotten the message. No one in the State speaks English as I speak English. But I have forgotten the message.

> 'Tiger, tiger, burning bright
> In the forests of the night,
> What immortal hand or eye
> Framed thy fearful symmetry?

Yes, mother; till she cries. I am to say the whole of it till she cries. I will not forget. I did not forget the first message. By the great God Har! I have forgotten this message.' And he began to cry.

Kate, who had watched so long by bedsides of pain, was calm and strong; she soothed the child, speaking to him in a low, quieting voice, administering a sedative draught, doing the right thing, as Tarvin saw, surely and steadily, undisturbed. It was he who was shaken by the agony that he could not alleviate.

The Maharaj Kunwar drew a long, sobbing breath, and contracted his eyebrows.

'*Mahadeo ki jai!*' he shouted. 'It has come back. A gipsy has done this. A gipsy has done this. And I was to say it until she cried.'

Kate half rose, with an awful look at Tarvin. He returned it, and, nodding, strode from the room, dashing the tears from his eyes.

# XVI

*Heart of my heart, is it meet or wise*
*To warn a King of his enemies?*
*We know what Heaven or Hell may bring,*
*But no man knoweth the mind of the King.*
THE BALLAD OF THE KING'S JEST.

'WANT TO SEE THE MAHARAJAH.'

'He cannot be seen.'

'I shall wait until he comes.'

'He will not be seen all day.'

'Then I shall wait all day.'

Tarvin settled himself comfortably in his saddle, and drew up in the centre of the courtyard, where he was wont to confer with the Maharajah.

The pigeons were asleep in the sunlight, and the little fountain was talking to itself, as a pigeon coos before settling to its nest. The white marble flagging glared like hot iron, and waves of heat flooded him from the green-shaded walls. The guardian of the gate tucked himself up in his sheet again and slept. And with him slept, as it seemed, the whole world in a welter of silence as intense as the heat. Tarvin's horse champed his bit, and the echoes of the ringing iron tinkled from side to side of the courtyard. The man himself whipped a silk handkerchief round his neck as some slight protection against the peeling sunbeams, and, scorning the shade of the archway, waited in the open that the Maharajah might see there was an urgency in his visit.

In a few minutes there crept out of the stillness a sound

like the far-off rustle of wind across a wheat-field on a still
autumn day. It came from behind the green shutters, and
with its coming Tarvin mechanically straightened himself in
the saddle. It grew, died down again, and at last remained
fixed in a continuous murmur, for which the ear strained
uneasily—such a murmur as heralds the advance of a loud
racing tide in a nightmare, when the dreamer cannot flee nor
declare his terror in any voice but a whisper. After the rustle
came the smell of jasmine and musk that Tarvin knew well.

The palace wing had wakened from its afternoon siesta,
and was looking at him with a hundred eyes. He felt the
glances that he could not see, and they filled him with wrath
as he sat immovable, while the horse swished at the flies.
Somebody behind the shutters yawned a polite little yawn.
Tarvin chose to regard it as an insult, and resolved to stay
where he was till he or the horse dropped. The shadow of the
afternoon sun crept across the courtyard inch by inch, and
wrapped him at last in stifling shade.

There was a muffled hum—quite distinct from the rustle—
of voices within the palace. A little ivory inlaid door opened,
and the Maharajah rolled into the courtyard. He was in the
ugliest muslin undress, and his little saffron-coloured Rajput
turban was set awry on his head, so that the emerald plume
tilted drunkenly. His eyes were red with opium, and he
walked as a bear walks when he is overtaken by the dawn in
the poppy-field, where he has gorged his fill through the night
watches.

Tarvin's face darkened at the sight, and the Maharajah,
catching the look, bade his attendants stand back out of ear-
shot.

'Have you been waiting long, Tarvin Sahib?' he asked
huskily, with an air of great good-will. 'You know I see no

man at this afternoon hour, and—and they did not bring me the news.'

'I can wait,' said Tarvin composedly.

The King seated himself in the broken Windsor chair, which was splitting in the heat, and eyed Tarvin suspiciously.

'Have they given you enough convicts from the jails? Why are you not on the dam, then, instead of breaking my rest? By God! is a King to have no peace because of you and such as you?'

Tarvin let this outburst go by without comment.

'I have come to you about the Maharaj Kunwar,' he said quietly.

'What of him?' said the Maharajah quickly. 'I—I—have not seen him for some days.'

'Why?' asked Tarvin bluntly.

'Affairs of state and urgent political necessity,' murmured the King, evading Tarvin's wrathful eyes. 'Why should I be troubled by these things, when I know that no harm has come to the boy?'

'No harm!'

'How could harm arrive?' The voice dropped into an almost conciliatory whine. 'You yourself, Tarvin Sahib, promised to be his true friend. That was on the day you rode so well, and stood so well against my bodyguard. Never have I seen such riding, and *therefore* why should I be troubled? Let us drink.'

He beckoned to his attendants. One of them came forward with a long silver tumbler concealed beneath his flowing garments, and poured into it an allowance of liqueur brandy that made Tarvin, used to potent drinks, open his eyes. The second man produced a bottle of champagne, opened it with a skill born of long practice, and filled up the tumbler with the creaming wine.

The Maharajah drank deep, and wiped the foam from his

beard, saying apologetically: 'Such things are not for Political Agents to see; but you, Sahib, are true friend of the State. Therefore I let you see. Shall they mix you one like this?'

'Thanks. I didn't come here to drink. I came to tell you that the Maharaj has been very ill.'

'I was told there was a little fever,' said the King, leaning back in his chair. 'But he is with Miss Sheriff, and she will make all well. Just a little fever, Tarvin Sahib. Drink with me.'

'A little hell! Can you understand what I am saying? The little chap has been half poisoned.'

'Then it was the English medicines,' said the Maharajah, with a bland smile. 'Once they made me very sick, and I went back to the native *hakims*. You are always making funny talks, Tarvin Sahib.'

With a mighty effort Tarvin choked down his rage, and tapped his foot with his riding-whip, speaking very clearly and distinctly: 'I haven't come here to make funny talk to-day. The little chap is with Miss Sheriff now. He was driven over there; and somebody in the palace has been trying to poison him with hemp.'

'Bhang!' said the Maharajah stupidly.

'I don't know what you call the mess, but he has been poisoned. But for Miss Sheriff he would have died—your first son would have died. He has been poisoned—do you hear, Maharajah Sahib?—and by some one in the palace.'

'He has eaten something bad, and it has made him sick,' said the King surlily. 'Little boys eat anything. By God! no man would dare to lay a finger on my son.'

'What would you do to prevent it?'

The Maharajah half rose to his feet, and his red eyes filled with fury. 'I would tie him to the forefoot of my biggest elephant, and kill him through an afternoon!' Then he relapsed, foaming, into the vernacular, and poured out a list of the hideous tortures that were within his will but not in his power to inflict. 'I would do all these things to any man who touched him,' he concluded.

Tarvin smiled incredulously.

'I know what you think,' stormed the King, maddened by the liquor and the opium. 'You think that because there is an English Government I can make trials only by law, and all that nonsense. Stuff! What do I care for the law that is in books? Will the walls of my palace tell anything that I do?'

'They won't. If they did, they might let you know that it is a woman inside the palace who is at the bottom of this.'

The Maharajah's face turned grey under its brown. Then he burst forth anew, almost huskily: 'Am I a King or a potter that I must have the affairs of my zenana dragged into the sunlight by any white dog that chooses to howl at me? Go out, or the guard will drive you out like a jackal.'

'That's all right,' said Tarvin calmly. 'But what has it to do with the Prince, Maharajah Sahib? Come over to Mr. Estes's and I'll show you. You've had some experience of drugs, I suppose. You can decide for yourself. The boy has been poisoned.'

'It was an accursed day for my State when I first allowed the missionaries to come, and a worse day when I did not drive you out.'

'Not in the least. I'm here to look after the Maharaj Kunwar, and I'm going to do it. You prefer leaving him to be killed by your women.'

'Tarvin Sahib, do you know what you say?'

'Shouldn't be saying it if I didn't. I have all the proof in my hands.'

'But when there is a poisoning there are no proofs of any kind, least of all when a woman poisons! One does justice on suspicion, and by the English law it is a *most* illiberal policy to kill on suspicion. Tarvin Sahib, the English have taken away from me everything that a Rajput desires, and I and the others are rolling in idleness like horses that never go to exercise. But at least I am master *there!*'

He waved a hand toward the green shutters, and spoke in a lower key, dropping back into his chair, and closing his eyes.

Tarvin looked at him despairingly.

'No one man would dare—no man would dare,' murmured the Maharajah more faintly. 'And as for the other thing that you spoke of, it is not in your power. By God! I am a Rajput and a King. I do not talk of the life behind the curtain.'

Then Tarvin took his courage in both hands and spoke.

'I don't want you to talk,' he said; 'I merely want to warn you against Sitabhai. She's poisoning the Prince.'

The Maharajah shuddered. That a European should mention the name of his Queen was in itself sufficient insult, and one beyond all his experience. But that a European should cry aloud in the open courtyard a charge such as Tarvin had just made surpassed imagination. The Maharajah had just come from Sitabhai, who had lulled him to rest with songs and endearments sacred to him alone; and here was this lean outlander assailing her with vile charges. But for the drugs he would, in the extremity of his rage, have fallen upon Tarvin, who was saying, 'I can prove it quite enough to satisfy Colonel Nolan.'

The Maharajah stared at Tarvin with shiny eyes, and Tarvin thought for a moment that he was going to fall in a fit; but it was the drink and the opium reasserting their power upon him. He mumbled angrily. The head fell forward, the words ceased, and he sat in his chair breathing heavily, as senseless as a log.

Tarvin gathered up his reins, and watched the sodden

monarch for a long time in silence, as the rustle behind the shutters rose and fell. Then he turned to go, and rode out through the arch, thinking.

Something sprang out of the darkness where the guard slept, and where the King's fighting apes were tethered; and the horse reared as a grey ape, its chain broken at the waistband, flung itself on the pommel of the saddle, chattering. Tarvin felt and smelt the beast. It thrust one paw into the horse's mane, and with the other encircled his own throat. Instinctively he reached back, and before the teeth under the grimy blue gums had time to close he had fired twice, pressing the muzzle of the pistol into the hide. The creature rolled off to the ground, moaning like a human being, and the smoke of the two shots drifted back through the hollow of the arch and dissolved in the open courtyard.

## XVII

*Strangers drawn from the ends of the earth, jewelled and
  plumed were we;*
*I was the Lord of the Inca Race, and she was the Queen
  of the Sea.*
*Under the stars beyond our stars, where the reinless
  meteors glow,*
*Hotly we stormed Valhalla, a million years ago.*

*Dust of the stars was under our feet, glitter of stars
  above—*
*Wrecks of our wrath dropped reeling down as we fought
  and we spurned and we strove;*
*Worlds upon worlds we tossed aside, and scattered them
  to and fro,*
*The night that we stormed Valhalla, a million years ago.*

*She with the star I had marked for my own—I with my
  set desire—*
*Lost in the loom of the Night of Nights, 'wildered by
  worlds afire—*
*Met in a war 'twixt love and hate where the reinless
  meteors glow,*
*Hewing our way to Valhalla, a million years ago.*

                                   THE SACK OF THE GODS.

IN SUMMER the nights of the desert are hotter than the days,
for when the sun goes down, earth, masonry, and marble give

forth their stored heat, and the low clouds, promising rain and never bringing it, allow nothing to escape.

Tarvin was lying at rest in the veranda of the rest-house, smoking a cheroot and wondering how far he had bettered the case of the Maharaj Kunwar by appealing to the Maharajah. His reflections were not disturbed; the last of the commercial travellers had gone back to Calcutta and Bombay, grumbling up to the final moment of their stay, and the rest-house was all his own. Surveying his kingdom, he meditated, between the puffs of his cheroot, on the desperate and apparently hopeless condition of things. They had got to the precise point where he liked them. When a situation looked as this one did, only Nicholas Tarvin could put it through and come out on top. Kate was obdurate; the Naulahka was damnably coy; the Maharajah was ready to turn him out of the State. Sitabhai had heard him denounce her. His life was likely to come to a sudden and mysterious end, without so much as the satisfaction of knowing that Heckler and the boys would avenge him; and if it went on, it looked as though it would have to go on without Kate, and without the gift of new life to Topaz—in others words, without being worth the trouble of living.

The moonlight, shining on the city beyond the sands, threw fantastic shadows on temple spires and the watch-towers along the walls. A dog in search of food snuffed dolefully about Tarvin's chair, and withdrew to howl at him at a distance. It was a singularly melancholy howl. Tarvin smoked till the moon went down in the thick darkness of an Indian night. She had scarcely set when he was aware of something blacker than the night between him and the horizon.

'Is it you, Tarvin Sahib?' the voice inquired in broken English.

Tarvin sprang to his feet before replying. He was beginning to be a little suspicious of fresh apparitions. His hand went to his hip-pocket. Any horror, he argued, might jump out at him from the darkness in a country managed on the plan of a Kiralfy trick spectacle.

'Nay; do not be afraid,' said the voice. 'It is I—Juggut Singh.'

Tarvin pulled thoughtfully at his cigar. 'The State is full of Singhs,' he said. 'Which?'

'I, Juggut Singh, of the household of the Maharajah.'

'H'm. Does the King want to see me?'

The figure advanced a pace nearer.

'No, Sahib; the Queen.'

'Which?' repeated Tarvin.

The figure was in the veranda at his side, almost whispering in his ear. 'There is only one who would dare to leave the palace. It is the Gipsy.'

Tarvin snapped his fingers blissfully and soundlessly in the dark, and made a little click of triumph with his tongue. 'Pleasant calling hours the lady keeps,' he said.

'This is no place for speaking, Sahib. I was to say, "Come, unless you are afraid of the dark."'

'Oh, were you? Well, now, look here, Juggut; let's talk this thing out. I'd like to see your friend Sitabhai. Where are you keeping her? Where do you want me to go?'

'I was to say, "Come with me." Are you afraid?' The man spoke this time at his own prompting.

'Oh, I'm *afraid* fast enough,' said Tarvin, blowing a cloud of smoke from him. 'It isn't that.'

'There are horses—very swift horses. It is the Queen's order. Come with me.'

Tarvin smoked on, unhurrying; and when he finally picked

himself out of the chair it was muscle by muscle. He drew
his revolver from his pocket, turned the chambers slowly one
after another to the vague light, under Juggut Singh's watchful eye, and returned it to his pocket again, giving his companion a wink as he did so.

'Well, come on, Juggut,' he said, and they passed behind
the rest-house to a spot where two horses, their heads enveloped in cloaks to prevent them from neighing, were waiting
at their pickets. The man mounted one, and Tarvin took the
other silently, satisfying himself before getting into the saddle
that the girths were not loose this time. They left the city
road at a walking pace by a cart-track leading to the hills.

'Now,' said Juggut Singh, after they had gone a quarter of
a mile in this fashion, and were alone under the stars, 'we
can ride.'

He bowed forward, struck his stirrups home, and began
lashing his animal furiously. Nothing short of the fear of
death would have made the pampered eunuch of the palace
ride at this pace. Tarvin watched him roll in the saddle,
chuckled a little, and followed.

'You wouldn't make much of a cow-puncher, Juggut, would
you?'

'Ride!' gasped Juggut Singh. 'For the cleft between the two
hills—ride!'

The dry sand flew behind their horses' hoofs, and the hot
winds whistled about their ears as they headed up the easy
slope toward the hills, three miles from the palace. In the
old days, before the introduction of telegraphs, the opium
speculators of the desert were wont to telegraph the rise and
fall in the price of the drug from little beacon-towers on the
hills. It was toward one of these disused stations that Juggut

Singh was straining. The horses fell into a walk as the slope grew steeper, and the outline of the squat-domed tower began to show clear against the sky. A few moments later Tarvin heard the hoofs of their horses ring on solid marble, and saw that he was riding near the edge of a great reservoir, full of water to the lip.

Eastward, a few twinkling lights in the open plain showed the position of Rhatore, and took him back to the night when he had said good-bye to Topaz from the rear platform of a Pullman. Night-fowl called to one another from the weeds at the far end of the tank, and a great fish leaped at the reflection of a star.

'The watch-tower is at the further end of the dam,' said Juggut Singh. 'The Gipsy is there.'

'Will they never have done with that name?' uttered an incomparably sweet voice out of the darkness. 'It is well that I am of a gentle temper, or the fish would know more of thee, Juggut Singh.'

Tarvin checked his horse with a jerk, for almost under his bridle stood a figure enveloped from head to foot in a mist of pale yellow gauze. It had started up from behind the red tomb of a once famous Rajput cavalier who was supposed by the countryside to gallop nightly round the dam he had built. This was one of the reasons why the Dungar Talao was not visited after nightfall.

'Come down, Tarvin Sahib,' said the voice mockingly in English. 'I, at least, am not a grey ape. Juggut Singh, go wait with the horses below the watch-tower.'

'Yes, Juggut; and don't go to sleep,' enjoined Tarvin—'we might want you.' He alighted, and stood before the veiled form of Sitabhai.

'Shekand,' she said, after a little pause, putting out a hand that was smaller even than Kate's. 'Ah, Sahib, I knew that you would come. I knew that you were not afraid.'

She held his hand as she spoke, and pressed it tenderly. Tarvin buried the tiny hand deep in his engulfing paw, and, pressing it in a grip that made her give an involuntary cry, shook it with a hearty motion.

'Happy to make your acquaintance,' he said, as she murmured under her breath, 'By Indur, he has a hold!'

'And I am pleased to see you, too,' she answered aloud. Tarvin noted the music of the voice. He wondered what the face behind the veil might look like.

She sat down composedly on the slab of the tomb, motioning him to a seat beside her.

'All white men like straight talk,' she said, speaking slowly, and with uncertain mastery of English pronunciation. 'Tell me, Tarvin Sahib, how much you know.'

She withdrew her veil as she spoke, and turned her face toward him. Tarvin saw that she was beautiful. The perception thrust itself insensibly between him and his other perceptions about her.

'You don't want me to give myself away, do you, Queen?'

'I do not understand. But I know you do not talk like the other white men,' she said sweetly.

'Well, then, you don't expect me to tell you the truth?'

'No,' she replied. 'Else you would tell me why you are here. Why do you give me so much trouble?'

'*Do* I trouble you?'

Sitabhai laughed, throwing back her head, and clasping her hands behind her neck. Tarvin watched her curiously in the starlight. All his senses were alert; he was keenly on his guard, and he cast a wary eye about and behind him from time to time. But he could see nothing but the dull glimmer of the water that lapped at the foot of the marble steps, and hear nothing save the cry of the night-owls.

'Oh, Tarvin Sahib,' she said. 'You know! After the first time I was sorry.'

'Which time was that?' inquired Tarvin vaguely.

'Of course it was when the saddle turned. And then when the timber fell from the archway I thought at least that I had maimed your horse. Was he hurt?'

'No,' said Tarvin, stupefied by her engaging frankness.

'Surely you knew,' she said almost reproachfully.

He shook his head. 'No, Sitabhai, my dear,' he said slowly and impressively. 'I wasn't on to you, and it's my eternal shame. But I'm beginning to sabe. You worked the little business at the dam, too, I suppose, and the bridge and the bullock-carts. And I thought it was their infernal clumsiness! Well, I'll be——' He whistled melodiously, and the sound was answered by the hoarse croak of a crane across the reeds.

The Queen leaped to her feet, thrusting her hand into her bosom. 'A signal!' Then sinking back upon the slab of the tomb, 'But you have brought no one with you. I know you are not afraid to go alone.'

'Oh, I'm not trying to do *you* up, young lady,' he answered. 'I'm too busy admiring your picturesque and systematic deviltry. So you're at the bottom of all my troubles? That quicksand trick was a pretty one. Do you often work it?'

'Oh, on the dam!' exclaimed the Queen, waving her hands lightly. 'I only gave them orders to do what they could. But they are very clumsy people—only coolie people. They told me what they had done, and I was angry.'

'Kill any one?'

'No; why should I?'

'Well, if it comes to that, why should you be so hot on killing me?' inquired Tarvin drily.

'I do not like any white men to stay here, and I knew that you had come to stay.' Tarvin smiled at the unconscious Americanism. 'Besides,' she went on, 'the Maharajah was fond of you, and I had never killed a white man. Then, too, I like you.'

'Oh!' responded Tarvin expressively.

'By Malang Shah, and you never knew!' She was swearing by the God of her own clan—the God of the Gipsies.

'Well, don't rub it in,' said Tarvin.

'And you killed my big pet ape,' she went on. 'He used to salaam to me in the mornings like Luchman Rao, the Prime Minister. Tarvin Sahib, I have known many Englishmen. I have danced on the slack-rope before the mess-tents of the officers on the line of march, and taken my little begging-gourd up to the big bearded Colonel when I was no higher than his knee.' She lowered her hand to within a foot of the ground. 'And when I grew older,' she continued, 'I thought that I knew the hearts of all men. But, by Malang Shah, Tarvin Sahib, I never saw a man like unto you! Nay,' she went on almost beseechingly, 'do not say that you did not know. There is a love song in my tongue, "I have not slept between moon and moon because of you"; and indeed for me that song is quite true. Sometimes I think that I did not quite wish to see you die. But it would be better that you were dead. I, and I alone, command this State. And now, after that which you have told the King——'

'Yes? You heard, then?'

She nodded. 'After that I cannot see that there is any other way—unless you go away.'

'I'm not going,' said Tarvin.

'That is good,' said the Queen, with a little laugh. 'And so I shall not miss seeing you in the courtyard day by day. I thought the sun would have killed you when you waited for the Maharajah. Be grateful to me, Tarvin Sahib, for I made the Maharajah come out. And you did me an ill turn.'

'My dear young lady,' said Tarvin earnestly, 'if you'd pull in your wicked little fangs, no one wants to hurt you. But I can't let you beat me about the Maharaj Kunwar. I'm here to see that the young man stays with us. Keep off the grass, and I'll drop it.'

'Again I do not understand,' said the Queen, bewildered. 'But what is the life of a little child to you who are a stranger here?'

'What is it to me? Why, it's fair-play; it's the life of a little child. What more do you want? Is nothing sacred to you?'

'I also have a son,' returned the Queen, 'and he is not weak. Nay, Tarvin Sahib, the child always was sickly from his birth. How can he govern men? *My* son will be a Rajput; and in the time to come—— But that is no concern of the white men. Let this little one go back to the Gods!'

'Not if I know it,' responded Tarvin decisively.

'Otherwise,' swept on the Queen, 'he will live infirm and miserable for ninety years. I know the bastard Kulu stock that he comes from. Yes; I have sung at the gate of his mother's palace when she and I were children—I in the dust, and she in her marriage-litter. To-day she is in the dust. Tarvin Sahib'—her voice melted appealingly—'I shall never bear another son; but I may at least mould the State from behind the curtain, as many queens have done. I am not a palace-bred woman. Those'—she pointed scornfully toward the lights of Rhatore—'have never seen the wheat wave, or heard the wind blow, or sat in a saddle, or talked face to face with men in the streets. They call me the Gipsy, and they cower under their robes like fat slugs when I choose to lift my hand to the Maharajah's beard. Their bards sing of their ancestry for twelve hundred years. They are noble, forsooth! By Indur and Allah—yea, and the God of your missionaries too—their children and the British Government shall remember me for twice twelve hundred years. *Ahi,* Tarvin Sahib, you do not know how wise my little son is. I do not let him go to the missionary's. All that he shall need afterward—and indeed it is no little thing to govern this State—he shall learn from me; for I have seen the world, and I know. And until you came all was going so softly, so softly, to its end! The little one would have died—yes; and there would have been no more trouble. And never man nor woman in the palace would have breathed to the King one word of what you cried aloud before the sun in the courtyard. Now suspicion will never cease in the King's mind, and I do not know—I do not know——' She bent forward earnestly. 'Tarvin Sahib, if I have spoken one word of truth this night, tell me how much is known to you.'

Tarvin preserved absolute silence. She stole one hand pleadingly on his knee. 'And none would have suspected. When the ladies of the Viceroy came last year, I gave out of my own treasures twenty-five thousand rupees to the nursing hospital, and the Lady Sahib kissed me on both cheeks, and I talked English, and showed them how I spent my time knitting—I who knit and unknit the hearts of men.'

This time Tarvin did not whistle; he merely smiled and murmured sympathetically. The large and masterly range of her wickedness, and the coolness with which she addressed herself to it, gave her a sort of distinction. More than this, he respected her for the personal achievement which of all feats most nearly appeals to the breast of the men of the West—she had done him up. It was true her plans had failed; but she had played them all on him without his knowledge. He almost revered her for it.

'Now you begin to understand,' said Sitabhai; 'there is something more to think of. Do you mean to go to Colonel Nolan, Sahib, with all your story about me?'

'Unless you keep your hands off the Maharaj Kunwar—yes,' said Tarvin, not allowing his feelings to interfere with business.

'That is very foolish,' said the Queen; 'because Colonel Nolan will give much trouble to the King, and the King will turn the palace into confusion, and every one of my hand-maids, except a few, will give witness against me; and I perhaps shall come to be much suspected. Then you would think, Tarvin Sahib, that you had prevented me. But you cannot stay here for ever. You cannot stay here until I die. And so soon as you are gone——' She snapped her fingers.

'You won't get the chance,' said Tarvin unshakenly. 'I'll fix that. What do you take me for?'

The Queen bit the back of her forefinger irresolutely. There was no saying what this man, who strode unharmed through her machinations, might or might not be able to do. Had she been dealing with one of her own race she would have played threat against threat. But the perfectly composed and loose-knit figure by her side, watching every movement, chin in hand, ready, alert, confident, was an unknown quantity that baffled and distressd her.

There was a sound of a discreet cough, and Juggut Singh waddled toward them, bowing abjectly, to whisper something to the Queen. She laughed scornfully, and motioned him back to his post.

'He says the night is passing,' she explained, 'and it is death for him and for me to be without the palace.'

'Don't let me keep you,' said Tarvin, rising. 'I think we understand each other.' He looked into her eyes. 'Hands off!'

'Then I may not do what I please?' she said. 'And you will go to Colonel Nolan to-morrow?'

'That depends,' said Tarvin, shutting his lips. He thrust his hands into his pockets as he stood looking down at her.

'Seat yourself again a moment, Tarvin Sahib,' said Sitabhai, patting the slab of the tomb invitingly with her little palm. Tarvin obeyed. 'Now, if I let no more timber fall, and keep the grey apes tied fast——'

'And dry up the quicksands in the Amet River,' pursued Tarvin grimly. 'I see. My dear little spitfire, you are at liberty to do what you like. Don't let me interfere with your amusements.'

'I was wrong. I should have known that nothing would make you afraid,' said she, eyeing him thoughtfully out of the corner of her eye; 'and, excepting you, Tarvin Sahib, there is no man that I fear. If you were a king as I a queen, we would hold Hindustan between our two hands.'

She clasped his locked fist as she spoke, and Tarvin remembering that sudden motion to her bosom when he had whistled, laid his own hand quickly above hers, and held them fast.

'Is there nothing, Tarvin Sahib, that would make you leave me in peace? What is it you care for? You did not come here to keep the Maharaj Kunwar alive.'

'How do you know I didn't?'

'You are very wise,' she said, with a little laugh, 'but it is not good to pretend to be too wise. Shall I tell you why you came?'

'Well, why did I? Speak up.'

'You came here, as you came to the temple of Iswara, to find that which you will never find, unless'—she leaned toward him—'I help you. Was it very cold in the Cow's Mouth, Tarvin Sahib?'

Tarvin drew back, frowning, but not betraying himself further.

'I was afraid that the snakes would have killed you there?'

'*Were* you?'

'Yes,' she said softly. 'And I was afraid, too, that you might not have stepped swiftly enough for the turning stone in the temple.'

Tarvin glanced at her. 'No?'

'Yes. Ah! I knew what was in your mind, even before you spoke to the King—when the bodyguard charged.'

'See here, young woman, do you run a private inquiry agency?'

She laughed. 'There is a song in the palace now about your bravery. But the boldest thing was to speak to the King about the Naulahka. He told me all you said. But he—even he did not dream that any *feringhi* could dare to covet it. And I was so good—I did not tell him. But I knew men like you are not made for little things. Tarvin Sahib,' she said, leaning close, releasing her hand and laying it softly on his shoulder, 'you and I are kin indeed! For it is more easy to govern this State —ay, and from this State to recapture all Hindustan from these white dogs, the English—than to do what you have dreamed of. And yet a stout heart makes all things easy. Was it for yourself, Tarvin Sahib, that you wanted the Naulahka, or for another—even as I desire Gokral Seetarun for my son? We are not little people. It is for another, is it not?'

'Look here,' said Tarvin reverently, as he took her hand

from his shoulder and held it firmly in his clutch again, 'are there many of you in India?'

'But one. I am like yourself—alone.' Her chin dropped against his shoulder, and she looked up at him out of her eyes as dark as the lake. The scarlet mouth and the quivering nostrils were so close to his own that the fragrant breath swept his cheek.

'Are you making States, Tarvin Sahib, like me? No; surely it is a woman. Your government is decreed for you, and you do what it orders. I turned the canal which the Government said should run through my orange-garden, even as I will bend the King to my will, even as I will kill the boy, even as I will myself rule in Gokral Seetarun through my child. But you, Tarvin Sahib—you wish only a woman! Is it not so? And she is too little to bear the weight of the Luck of the State. She grows paler day by day.' She felt the man quiver, but he said nothing.

From the tangle of scrub and brushwood at the far end of the lake broke forth a hoarse barking cough that filled the hills with desolation as water brims a cup. Tarvin leaped to his feet. For the first time he heard the angry complaint of the tiger going home to his lair after a fruitless night of ranging.

'It is nothing,' said the Queen, without stirring. 'It is only the tiger of the Dungar Talao. I have heard him howling many times when I was a gipsy, and even if he came you would shoot him, would you not, as you shot the ape?'

She nestled close to him, and, as he sank beside her on the stone again, his arm slipped unconsciously about her waist.

The shadow of the beast drifted across an open space by the lake-shore as noiselessly as thistledown draws through the air of summer, and Tarvin's arm tightened in its resting-place

—tightened on a bossed girdle that struck cold on his palm through many folds of muslin.

'So little and so frail—how could she wear it?' resumed the Queen.

She turned a little in his embrace, and Tarvin's arm brushed against one, and another, and then another, strand of the girdle, studded like the first with irregular bosses, till under his elbow he felt a great square stone.

He started, and tightened his hold about her waist, with paling lips.

'But we two,' the Queen went on, in a low voice, regarding him dreamily, 'could make the kingdoms fight like the water-buffaloes in spring. Would you be my Prime Minister, Tarvin Sahib, and advise me through the curtain?'

'I don't know whether I could trust you,' said Tarvin briefly.

'I do not know whether I could trust myself,' responded the Queen; 'for after a time it might be that I should be servant who have always been queen. I have come near to casting my heart under the hoofs of your horse—not once, but many times.' She put her arms around his neck and joined them there, gazing into his eyes, and drawing his head down to hers. 'Is it a little thing,' she cooed, 'if I ask you to be my king? In the old days, before the English came, Englishmen of no birth stole the hearts of Begums, and led their armies. They were kings in all but the name. We do not know when the old days may return, and we might lead our armies together.'

'All right. Keep the place open for me. I might come back and apply for it one of these days when I've worked a scheme or two at home.'

'Then you are going away—you will leave us soon?'

'I'll leave you when I've got what I want, my dear,' he answered, pressing her closer.

She bit her lip. 'I might have known,' she said softly. 'I, too, have never turned aside from anything I desired. Well, and what is it?'

The mouth drooped a little at the corners, as the head fell on his shoulder. Glancing down, he saw the ruby-jewelled jade handle of a little knife at her breast.

He disengaged himself from her arms with a quick movement, and rose to his feet. She was very lovely as she stretched her arms appealingly out to him in the half-light; but he was there for other things.

Tarvin looked at her between the eyes, and her glance fell.

'I'll take what you have around your waist, please.'

'I might have known that the white man thinks only of money!' she cried scornfully.

She unclasped a silver belt from her waist and threw it from her, clinking, upon the marble.

Tarvin did not give it a glance.

'You know me better than that,' he said quietly. 'Come, hold up your hands. Your game is played.'

'I do not understand,' she said. 'Shall I give you some rupees?' she asked scornfully. 'Be quick, Juggut Singh is bringing the horses.'

'Oh, I'll be quick enough. Give me the Naulahka.'

'The Naulahka?'

'The same. I'm tired of tipsy bridges and ungirt horses and uneasy arches and dizzy quicksands. I want the necklace.'

'And I may have the boy?'

'No; neither boy nor necklace.'

'And will you go to Colonel Nolan in the morning?'

'The morning is here now. You'd better be quick.'

'Will you go to Colonel Nolan?' she repeated, rising and facing him.

'Yes; if you don't give me the necklace.'

'And if I do?'

'No. Is it a trade?' It was his question to Mrs. Mutrie.

The Queen looked desperately at the day-star that was beginning to pale in the East. Even her power over the King could not save her from death if the day discovered her beyond the palace walls.

The man spoke as one who held her life in the hollow of his hand; and she knew he was right. If he had proof he would not scruple to bring it before the Maharajah; and if the Maharajah believed—— Sitabhai could feel the sword at her throat. She would be no founder of a dynasty, but a nameless disappearance in the palace. Mercifully, the King had not been in a state to understand the charges Tarvin had brought against her in the courtyard. But she lay open now to anything this reckless and determined stranger might choose to do against her. At the least he could bring upon her the formless suspicion of an Indian Court, worse than death to her plans, and set the removal of Maharaj Kunwar beyond her power, through the interposition of Colonel Nolan; and at the worst—— But she did not pursue this train of thought.

She cursed the miserable weakness of liking for him which had prevented her from killing him just now as he lay in her arms. She had meant to kill him from the first moment of their interview; she had let herself toy too long with the fascination of being dominated by a will stronger than her own, but there was still time.

'And if I do not give you the Naulahka?' she asked.

'I guess you know best about that.'

As her eye wandered out on the plain she saw that the stars

no longer had fire in them; the black water of the reservoir paled and grew grey, and the wild-fowl were waking in the reeds. The dawn was upon her, as merciless as the man. Juggut Singh was leading up the horses, motioning to her in an agony of impatience and terror. The sky was against her; and there was no help on earth.

She put her hands behind her. Tarvin heard the snap of a clasp, and the Naulahka lay about her feet in ripples of flame.

Without looking at him or the necklace, she moved toward the horses. Tarvin stooped swiftly and possessed himself of the treasure. Juggut Singh had released his horse. Tarvin strode forward and caught at the bridle, cramming the necklace into his breast-pocket.

He bent to make sure of his girth. The Queen, standing behind her horse, waited an instant to mount.

'Good-bye, Tarvin Sahib; and remember the Gipsy,' she said, flinging her arm out over the horse's withers. *'Heh!'*

A flicker of light passed his eye. The jade handle of the Queen's knife quivered in the saddle-flap, half an inch above his right shoulder. His horse plunged forward at the Queen's stallion, with a snort of pain.

'Kill him, Juggut Singh!' gasped the Queen, pointing to Tarvin, as the eunuch scrambled into his saddle. 'Kill him!'

Tarvin caught her tender wrist in his fast grip. 'Easy there, girl! Easy!' She returned his gaze, baffled. 'Let me put you up,' he said.

He put his arms about her and swung her into the saddle. 'Now give us a kiss,' he said, as she looked down at him.

She stooped. 'No, you don't! Give me your hands.' He prisoned both wrists, and kissed her full upon the mouth. Then he smote the horse resoundingly upon the flank, and the animal blundered down the path and leaped out into the plain.

He watched the Queen and Juggut Singh disappear in a cloud of dust and flying stones, and turned with a deep sigh of relief to the lake. Drawing the Naulahka from its resting-place, and laying it fondly out upon his hands, he fed his eyes upon it.

The stones kindled with the glow of the dawn, and mocked the shifting colours of the hills. The shining ropes of gems put to shame the red glare that shot up from behind the reeds, as they had dulled the glare of the torches on the night of the little Prince's wedding. The tender green of the reeds themselves, the intense blue of the lake, the beryl of the flashing kingfishers, and the blinding ripples spreading under the first rays of the sun, as a bevy of coots flapped the water from their wings—the necklace abashed them all. Only the black diamond took no joy from the joy of the morning, but lay among its glorious fellows as sombre and red-hearted as the troublous night out of which Tarvin had snatched it.

Tarvin ran the stones through his hands one by one, and there were forty-five of them—each stone perfect and flawless of its kind; nipped, lest any of its beauty should be hidden, by a tiny gold clasp, each stone swinging all but free from the strand of soft gold on which it was strung, and each stone worth a King's ransom or a Queen's good name.

It was a good moment for Tarvin. His life gathered into it. Topaz was safe!

The wild duck were stringing to and fro across the lake, and the cranes called to one another, stalking through reeds almost as tall as their scarlet heads. From some temple hidden among the hills a lone priest chanted sonorously as he made the morning sacrifice to his God, and from the city in the plain came the boom of the first ward-drums, telling that the gates were open and the day was born.

Tarvin lifted his head from the necklace. The jade-handled knife was lying at his feet. He picked up the delicate weapon and threw it into the lake.

'And now for Kate,' he said.

# XVIII

*Now we are come to our Kingdom,*
*And the State is thus and thus:*
*Our legions wait at the palace gate—*
*Little it profits us,*
   Now we are come to our Kingdom.

*Now we are come to our Kingdom,*
*The crown is ours to take—*
*With a naked sword at the council board,*
*And under the throne the snake,*
   Now we are come to our Kingdom.

*Now we are come to our Kingdom,*
*But my love's eyelids fall,*
*All that I wrought for, all that I fought for,*
*Delight her nothing at all.*
*My crown is withered leaves,*
*For she sits in the dust and grieves,*
   Now we are come to our Kingdom.
                                    KING ANTHONY.

THE PALACE ON ITS RED ROCK seemed to be still asleep as he
cantered across the empty plain. A man on a camel rode out
of one of the city gates at right angles to his course, and
Tarvin noted with interest how swiftly a long-legged camel
of the desert can move. Familiar as he had now become with
the ostrich-necked beasts, he could not help associating them
with Barnum's Circus and boyhood memories. The man drew

near and crossed in front of him. Then, in the stillness of the morning, Tarvin heard the dry click of a voice he understood. It was the sound made by bringing up the cartridge of a repeating rifle. Mechanically he slipped from the saddle, and was on the other side of the horse as the rifle spoke, and a puff of blue smoke drifted up and hung motionless above the camel.

'I might have known she'd get in her work early,' he muttered, peering over his horse's withers. 'I can't drop him at this distance with a revolver. What's the fool waiting for?'

Then he perceived that, with characteristic native inaptitude, the man had contrived to jam his lever, and was beating it furiously on the forepart of the saddle. He remounted hastily, and galloped up, revolver in hand, to cover the blanched visage of Juggut Singh.

'*You!* Why, Juggut, old man, this isn't kind of you.'

'It was an order,' said Juggut, quivering with apprehension. 'It was no fault of mine. I—I do not understand these things.'

'I should smile. Let me show you.' He took the rifle from the trembling hand. 'The cartridge is jammed, my friend; it don't shoot as well that way. It only needs a little knack—so! You ought to learn it, Juggut.' He jerked the empty shell over his shoulder.

'What will you do to me?' cried the eunuch. 'She would have killed me if I had not come.'

'Don't you believe it, Juggut. She's a Jumbo at theory, but weak in practice. Go on ahead, please.'

They started back toward the city, Juggut leading the way on his camel, looking back apprehensively every minute. Tarvin smiled at him drily but reassuringly, balancing on his hip the captured rifle. He observed that it was a very good rifle if properly used.

At the entrance to Sitabhai's wing of the palace, Juggut Singh dismounted and slunk into the courtyard, the livid image of fear and shame. Tarvin clattered after him, and as the eunuch was about to disappear through a door, called him back.

'You have forgotten your gun, Juggut,' he said. 'Don't be afraid of it.' Juggut was putting up a doubtful hand to take it from him. 'It won't hurt anybody this trip. Take yourself back to the lady, and tell her you are returned, with thanks.'

No sound came to his ear from behind the green shutters as he rode away, leaving Juggut staring after him. Nothing fell upon him from out of the arch, and the apes were tied securely. Sitabhai's next move was evidently yet to be played.

His own next move he had already reckoned with. It was a case for bolting.

He rode to the mosque outside the city, routed out his old friend in dove-coloured satin, and made him send this message:—

'MRS. MUTRIE, DENVER.—Necklace is yours. Get throat ready and lay that track into Topaz.—TARVIN.'

Then he turned his horse's head toward Kate. He buttoned his coat tightly across his chest, and patted the resting-place of the Naulahka fondly, as he strode up the path to the missionary's veranda, when he had tethered Fibby outside. His high good humour with himself and the world spoke through his eyes as he greeted Mrs. Estes at the door.

'You have been hearing something pleasant,' she said. 'Won't you come in?'

'Well, either the pleasantest, or next to the pleasantest; I'm not sure which,' he answered with a smile, as he followed her

into the familiar sitting-room. 'I'd like to tell you all about it,
Mrs. Estes. I feel almightily like telling somebody. But it isn't
a healthy story for this neighbourhood.' He glanced about
him. 'I'd hire the town crier and a few musical instruments
and advertise it, if I had my way; and we'd all have a little
Fourth of July celebration and a bonfire, and I'd read the
Declaration of Independence over the natives with a relish.
But it won't do. There *is* a story I'd like to tell you, though,'
he added, with a sudden thought. 'You know why I come here
so much, don't you, Mrs. Estes—I mean outside of your kindness to me, and my liking you all so much, and our always
having such good times together? You know, don't you?'

Mrs. Estes smiled. 'I suppose I do,' she said.

'Well; that's right! That's right. I thought you did. Then
I hope you're my friend!'

'If you mean that I wish you well, I do. But you can understand that I feel responsible for Miss Sheriff. I have sometimes thought I ought to let her mother know.'

'Oh, her mother knows! She's full of it. You might say she
liked it. The trouble isn't there, you know, Mrs. Estes.'

'No. She's a singular girl; very strong, very sweet. I've grown
to love her dearly. She has wonderful courage. But I should
like it better for her if she would give it up, and all that goes
with it. She would be better married,' she said meditatively.

Tarvin gazed at her admiringly. 'How wise you are, Mrs.
Estes! How wise you are!' he murmured. 'If I've told her that
once I've told her a dozen times. Don't you think, also, that
it would be better if she were married at once—right away,
without too much loss of time?'

His companion looked at him to see if he was in earnest.
Tarvin was sometimes a little perplexing to her. 'I think if
you are clever you will leave it to the course of events,' she

replied, after a moment. 'I have watched her work here, hoping that she might succeed where every one else has failed. But I know in my heart that she won't. There's too much against her. She's working against thousands of years of traditions, and training, and habits of life. Sooner or later they are certain to defeat her; and then, whatever her courage, she must give in. I've thought sometimes lately that she might have trouble very soon. There's a good deal of dissatisfaction at the hospital. Lucien hears some stories that make me anxious.'

'Anxious! I should say so. That's the worst of it. It isn't only that she won't come to me, Mrs. Estes—that you can understand—but she is running her head meanwhile into all sorts of impossible dangers. I haven't time to wait until she sees that point. I haven't time to wait until she sees any point at all but that this present moment, now and here, would be a good moment in which to marry Nicholas Tarvin. I've got to get out of Rhatore. That's the long and the short of it, Mrs. Estes. Don't ask me why. It's necessary. And I must take Kate with me. Help me if you love her.'

To this appeal Mrs. Estes made the handsomest response in her power, by saying that she would go up and tell her that he wished to see her. This seemed to take some time; and Tarvin waited patiently, with a smile on his lips. He did not doubt that Kate would yield. In the glow of another success it was not possible to him to suppose that she would not come around now. Had he not the Naulahka? She went with it; she was indissolubly connected with it. Yet he was willing to impress into his service all the help he could get, and he was glad to believe that Mrs. Estes was talking to her.

It was an added prophecy of success when he found from a copy of a recent issue of the *Topaz Telegram*, which he picked up while he waited, that the 'Lingering Lode' had justified his expectations. The people he had left in charge had struck a true fissure vein, and were taking out $500 a week. He crushed the paper into his pocket, restraining an inclination to dance. It was perhaps safest, on reflection, to postpone that exercise until he had seen Kate. The little congratulatory whistle that he struck up instead, he had to sober a moment later into a smile as Kate opened the door and came in to him. There could be no two ways about it with her now. His smile, do what he would, almost said as much.

A single glance at her face showed him, however, that the affair struck her less simply. He forgave her; she could not know the source of his inner certitude. He even took time to like the grey house-dress, trimmed with black velvet, that she was wearing in place of the white which had become habitual to her.

'I'm glad you've dropped white for a moment,' he said, as he rose to shake hands with her. 'It's a sign. It represents a general abandonment and desertion of this blessed country; and that's just the mood I want to find you in. I want you to drop it, chuck it, throw it up.' He held her brown little hand in the swarthy fist he pushed out from his own white sleeve, and looked down into her eyes attentively.

'What?'

'India—the whole business. I want you to come with me.' He spoke gently.

She looked up, and he saw in the quivering lines about her mouth signs of the contest on this theme she had passed through before coming down to him.

'You are going? I'm so glad.' She hesitated a moment. 'You know why!' she added, with what he saw was an intention of kindness.

Tarvin laughed as he seated himself. 'I like that. Yes; I'm going,' he said. 'But I'm not going alone. You're in the plan,' he assured her, with a nod.

She shook her head.

'No; don't say that, Kate. You musn't. It's serious this time.'

'Hasn't it always been?' She sank into a chair. 'It's always been serious enough for me—that I couldn't do what you wish, I mean. Not doing it—that is, doing something else; the one thing I want to do—is the most serious thing in the world to me. Nothing has happened to change me, Nick. I would tell you in a moment if it had. How is it different for either of us?'

'Lots of ways. But that I've got to leave Rhatore for a sample. You don't think I'd leave you behind, I hope.'

She studied the hands she had folded in her lap for a moment. Then she looked up and faced him with her open gaze.

'Nick,' she said, 'let me try to explain as clearly as I can how all this seems to me. You can correct me if I'm wrong.'

'Oh, you're sure to be wrong!' he cried; but he leaned forward.

'Well, let me try. You ask me to marry you!'

'I do,' answered Tarvin solemnly. 'Give me a chance of saying that before a clergyman, and you'll see.'

'I am grateful, Nick. It's a gift—the highest, the best, and I'm grateful. But what is it you really want? Shall you mind my asking that, Nick? You want me to round out your life; you want me to complete your other ambitions. Isn't that so? Tell me honestly, Nick; isn't that so?'

'No!' roared Tarvin.

'Ah, but it is! Marriage is that way. It is right. Marriage means that—to be absorbed into another's life: to live your own, not as your own but another's. It is a good life. It's a woman's life. I can like it; I can believe in it. But I can't see myself in it. A woman gives the whole of herself in marriage—in all happy marriages. I haven't the whole of myself to give. It belongs to something else. And I couldn't offer you a part; it is all the best men give to women, but from a woman it would do no man any good.'

'You mean that you have the choice between giving up your work and giving up me, and that the last is easiest.'

'I don't say that; but suppose I did, would it be so strange? Be honest, Nick. Suppose I asked you to give up the centre and meaning of *your* life? Suppose I asked you to give up *your* work? And suppose I offered in exchange—marriage! No, no!' She shook her head. 'Marriage is good; but what man would pay that price for it?'

'My dearest girl, isn't that just the opportunity of women?'

'The opportunity of the happy women—yes; but it isn't given to every one to see marriage like that. Even for women there is more than one kind of devotion.'

'Oh, look here, Kate! A man isn't an Orphan Asylum or a Home for the Friendless. You take him too seriously. You talk as if you had to make him your leading charity, and give up everything to the business. Of course you have to pretend something of the kind at the start, but in practice you only have to eat a few dinners, attend a semi-annual board meeting, and a strawberry festival or two to keep the thing going. It's just a general agreement to drink your coffee with a man in the morning, and be somewhere around, not too far from the fire, in not too ugly a dress, when he comes home in the evening. Come! It's an easy contract. Try me, Kate, and you'll see how simple I'll make it for you. I know about the other things. I understand well enough that you would never care for a life which didn't allow you to make a lot of people happy besides your husband. I recognise that. I begin with it. And I say that's just what I want. You have a talent for making folks happy. Well, I secure you on a special agreement to make me happy, and after you've attended to that, I want you to sail in and make the whole world bloom with your kindness. And you'll do it, too. Confound it, Kate, *we'll* do it! No one knows how good *two* people could be if they formed a syndicate and made a business of it. It hasn't been tried. Try it with me! Oh, Kate, I love you, I need you, and if you'll let me, I'll make a life for you!'

'I know, Nick, you would be kind. You would do all that a man can do. But it isn't the man who makes marriages happy or possible; it's the woman, and it must be. I should either do my part and shirk the other, and then I should be miserable; or I should shirk *you* and be more miserable. Either way such happiness is not for me.'

Tarvin's hand found the Naulahka within his breast, and clutched it tight. Strength seemed to go out of it into him—strength to restrain himself from losing all by a dozen savage words.

'Kate, my girl,' he said quietly, 'we haven't time to conjure dangers. We have to face a real one. You are not safe here. I can't leave you in this place, and I've got to go. That is why I ask you to marry me at once!'

'But I fear nothing. Who would harm me?'

'Sitabhai,' he answered grimly. 'But what difference does it make? I tell you, you are not safe. Be sure that I know.'

'And you?'

'Oh, I don't count.'

'The truth, Nick!' she demanded.

'Well, I always said that there was nothing like the climate of Topaz.'

'You mean you are in danger—great danger, perhaps.'

'Sitabhai isn't going round hunting for ways to save my precious life, that's a fact.' He smiled at her.

'Then you must go away at once; you mustn't lose an hour. Oh, Nick, you won't wait!'

'That's what I say. I can do without Rhatore; but I can't do without you. You must come.'

'Do you mean that if I don't you will stay?' she asked desperately.

'No; that would be a threat. I mean I'll wait for you.' His eyes laughed at her.

'Nick, is this because of what I asked you to do?' she demanded suddenly.

'You didn't ask me,' he defended.

'Then it is, and I am much to blame.'

'What, because I spoke to the King? My dear girl, that isn't more than the introductory walk-around of this circus. Don't run away with any question of responsibility. The only thing you are responsible for at this moment is to run with me—flee, vamoose, get out! Your life isn't worth an hour's purchase here. I'm convinced of that. And mine isn't worth a minute's.'

'You see what a situation you put me in,' she said accusingly.

'I don't put you in it; but I offer you a simple solution.'

'Yourself!'

'Well, yes; I said it was simple. I don't claim it's brilliant. Almost any one could do more for you; and there are millions of better men, but there isn't one who could love you better. Oh, Kate, Kate,' he cried, rising, 'trust yourself to my love, and I'll back myself against the world to make you happy.'

'No, no,' she exclaimed eagerly; 'you must go away.'

He shook his head. 'I can't leave you. Ask that of some one else. Do you suppose a man who loves you can abandon you

in this desert wilderness to take your chances? Do you suppose
any man could do that? Kate, my darling, come with me. You
torment me, you kill me, by forcing me to allow you a single
moment out of my sight. I tell you, you are in imminent,
deadly peril. You won't stay, knowing that? Surely you won't
sacrifice your life for these creatures?'

'Yes,' she cried, rising, with the uplifted look on her face.
'Yes! If it is good to live for them, it is good to die for them.
I do not believe my life is necessary; but if it is necessary,
that too!'

Tarvin gazed at her, baffled, disheartened, at a loss. 'And you
won't come?'

'I can't. Good-bye, Nick. It's the end.'

He took her hand. 'Good afternoon,' he responded. 'It's end
enough for to-day.'

She pursued him anxiously with her eye as he turned away;
suddenly she started after him. 'But you will go?'

'Go! No! No!' he shouted. 'I'll stay now if I have to organise
a standing army, declare myself King, and hold the rest-house
as the seat of government. *Go!*'

She put forth a detaining, despairing hand, but he was gone.

Kate returned to the little Maharaj Kunwar, who had been
allowed to lighten his convalescence by bringing down from
the palace a number of his toys and pets. She sat down by the
side of the bed, and cried for a long time silently.

'What is it, Miss Kate?' asked the Prince, after he had
watched her for some minutes, wondering. 'Indeed, I am quite
well now, so there is nothing to cry for. When I go back to the
palace I will tell my father all that you have done for me, and
he will give you a village. We Rajputs do not forget.'

'It's not that, Lalji,' she said, stooping over him, drying her
tear-stained eyes.

'Then my father will give you *two* villages. No one must cry when I am getting well, for I am a king's son. Where is Moti? I want him to sit upon a chair.'

Kate rose obediently, and began to call for the Maharaj Kunwar's latest pet—a little grey monkey, with a gold collar, who wandered at liberty through the house and garden, and at night did his best to win a place for himself by the young Prince's side. He answered the call from the boughs of a tree in the garden, where he was arguing with the wild parrots, and entered the room, crooning softly in the monkey tongue.

'Come here, little Hanuman,' said the Prince, raising one hand. The monkey bounded to his side. 'I have heard of a king,' said the Prince, playing with his golden collar, 'who spent three lakhs in marrying two monkeys. Moti, wouldst thou like a wife? No, no—a gold collar is enough for thee. We will spend our three lakhs in marrying Miss Kate to Tarvin Sahib, when we get well, and thou shalt dance at the wedding.' He was speaking in the vernacular, but Kate understood too well the coupling of her name with Tarvin's.

'Don't, Lalji, don't!'

'Why not, Kate? Why, even I am married.'

'Yes, yes. But it is different. Kate would rather you didn't, Lalji.'

'Very well,' answered the Maharaj, with a pout. 'Now I am only a little child. When I am well I will be a king again, and no one can refuse my gifts. Listen. Those are my father's trumpets. He is coming to see me.'

A bugle-call sounded in the distance. There was a clattering of horses' feet, and a little later the Maharajah's carriage and escort thundered up to the door of the missionary's house. Kate looked anxiously to see if the noise irritated her young charge; but his eyes brightened, his nostrils quivered, and he whispered, as his hand tightened on the hilt of the sword always by his side:—

'That is very good! My father has brought *all* his sowars.'

Before Kate could rise, Mr. Estes had ushered the Maharajah into the room, which was dwarfed by his bulk and by the bravery of his presence. He had been assisting at a review of his bodyguard, and came therefore in his full uniform as commander-in-chief of the army of the State, which was no mean affair. The Maharaj Kunwar ran his eyes delightedly up and down the august figure of his father, beginning with the polished gold-spurred jack-boots, and ascending to the snowy-white doeskin breeches, the tunic blazing with gold, and the diamonds of the Order of the Star of India, ending with the saffron turban and its nodding emerald aigrette. The King drew off his gauntlets and shook hands cordially with Kate. After an orgy it was noticeable that his Majesty became more civilised.

'And is the child well?' he asked. 'They told me that it was a little fever, and I, too, have had some fever.'

'The Prince's trouble was much worse than that, I am afraid, Maharajah Sahib,' said Kate.

'Ah, little one,' said the King, bending over his son very tenderly, and speaking in the vernacular, 'this is the fault of eating too much.'

'Nay, father, I did not eat, and I am quite well.'

Kate stood at the head of the bed stroking the boy's hair.

'How many troops paraded this morning?'

'Both squadrons, my General,' answered the father, his eye lighting with pride. 'Thou art all a Rajput, my son.'

'And my escort—where were they?'

'With Pertab Singh's troop. They led the charge at the end of the fight.'

'By the Sacred Horse,' said the Maharaj Kunwar, 'they shall lead in true fight one day. Shall they not, my father? Thou on the right flank, and I on the left.'

'Even so. But to do these things a prince must not be ill, and he must learn many things.'

'I know,' returned the Prince reflectively. 'My father, I have lain here some nights, thinking. Am I a little child?' He looked at Kate a minute, and whispered, 'I would speak to my father. Let no one come in.'

Kate left the room quickly, with a backward smile at the boy, and the King seated himself by the bed.

'No, I am not a little child,' said the Prince. 'In five years I shall be a man, and many men will obey me. But how shall I know the right or the wrong in giving an order?'

'It is necessary to learn many things,' repeated the Maharajah vaguely.

'Yes, I have thought of that, lying here in the dark,' said the Prince. 'And it is in my mind that these things are not all learned within the walls of the palace, or from women. My father, let me go away to learn how to be a prince!'

'But whither wouldst thou go? Surely my kingdom is thy home, beloved?'

'I know, I know,' returned the boy. 'And I will come back again, but do not let me be a laughing-stock to the other princes. At the wedding the Rawut of Bunnaul mocked me because my school-books were not as many as his. And *he* is only the son of an ennobled lord. He is without ancestry. But he has been up and down Rajputana as far as Delhi and Agra, ay, and Abu; and he is in the upper class of the Princes' School at Ajmir. Father, all the sons of the kings go there. They do not play with the women; they ride with men. And the air and the water are good at Ajmir. And I should like to go!'

The face of the Maharajah grew troubled, for the boy was very dear to him.

'But an evil might befall thee, Lalji. Think again.'

'I *have* thought,' responded the Prince. 'What evil can come to me under the charge of the Englishmen there? The Rawut of Bunnaul told me that I should have my own rooms,. my own servants, and my own stables, like the other princes—and that I should be much considered there.'

'Yes,' said the King soothingly. 'We be children of the sun —thou and I, my Prince.'

'Then it concerns me to be as learned and as strong and as valiant as the best of my race. Father, I am sick of running about the rooms of the women, of listening to my mother, and to the singing of the dance-girls; and they are always pressing their kisses on me. Let me go to Ajmir. Let me go to the Princes' School. And in a year, even in a year—so says the Rawut of Bunnaul—I shall be fit to lead my escort, as a King should lead them. Is it a promise, my father?'

'When thou art well,' answered the Maharajah, 'we will speak of it again—not as a father to a child, but as a man to a man.'

The Maharaj Kunwar's eyes grew bright with pleasure. 'That is good,' he said—'as a man to a man.'

The Maharajah fondled him in his arms for a few minutes, and told him the small news of the palace—such things as would interest a little boy. Then he said laughing, 'Have I your leave to go?'

'Oh! my father!' The Prince buried his head in his father's beard and threw his arms around him. The Maharajah disengaged himself gently, and as gently went out into the veranda. Before Kate returned he had disappeared in a cloud of dust and a flourish of trumpets. As he was going, a messenger came to the house bearing a grass-woven basket, piled high with shaddock, banana, and pomegranate—emerald, gold, and copper, which he laid at Kate's feet, saying, 'It is a present from the Queen.'

The little Prince within heard the voice, and cried joyfully, 'Kate, my mother has sent you those. Are they big fruits? Oh, give me a pomegranate,' he begged, as she came back into his room. 'I have tasted none since last winter.'

Kate set the basket on the table, and the Prince's mood changed. He wanted pomegranate sherbet, and Kate must mix the sugar and the milk and the syrup and the plump red seeds. Kate left the room for an instant to get a glass, and it occurred to Moti, who had been foiled in an attempt to appropriate the Prince's emeralds, and had hidden under the bed, to steal forth and seize upon a ripe banana. Knowing well that the Maharaj Kunwar could not move, Moti paid no attention to his voice, but settled himself deliberately on his haunches, chose his banana, stripped off the skin with his little black fingers, grinned at the Prince, and began to eat.

'Very well, Moti,' said the Maharaj Kunwar, in the vernacular; 'Kate says you are not a God, but only a little grey monkey, and *I* think so too. When she comes back you will be beaten, Hanuman.'

Moti had half eaten the banana when Kate returned, but he did not try to escape. She cuffed the marauder lightly, and he fell over on his side.

'Why, Lalji, what's the matter with Moti?' she asked, regarding the monkey curiously.

'He has been stealing, and now I suppose he is playing dead man. Hit him!'

Kate bent over the limp little body; but there was no need to chastise Moti. He was dead.

She turned pale, and, rising, took the basket of fruit quickly to her nostrils, and sniffed delicately at it. A faint, sweet, cloying odour rose from the brilliant pile. It was overpowering. She set the basket down, putting her hand to her head. The odour dizzied her.

'Well?' said the Prince, who could not see his dead pet. 'I want my sherbet.'

'The fruit is not quite good, I'm afraid, Lalji,' she said, with an effort. As she spoke she tossed into the garden, through the open window, the uneaten fragment of the banana that Moti had clasped so closely to his wicked little breast.

A parrot swooped down on the morsel instantly from the trees, and took it back to his perch in the branches. It was done before Kate, still unsteadied, could make a motion to stop it, and a moment later a little ball of green feathers fell from the covert of leaves, and the parrot also lay dead on the ground.

'No, the fruit is not good,' she said mechanically, her eyes wide with terror, and her face blanched. Her thoughts leaped to Tarvin. Ah, the warnings and the entreaties that she had put from her! He had said she was not safe. Was he not right? The awful subtlety of the danger in which she stood was a thing to shake a stronger woman than she. From where would it come next? Out of what covert might it not leap? The very air might be poisoned. She scarcely dared to breathe.

The audacity of the attack daunted her as much as its design. If this might be done in open day, under cover of friendship, immediately after the visit of the King, what might not the gipsy in the palace dare next? She and the Maharaj Kunwar were under the same roof; if Tarvin was right in supposing that Sitabhai could wish her harm, the fruit was evidently intended for them both. She shuddered to think how she herself might have given the fruit to the Maharaj innocently.

The Prince turned in his bed and regarded Kate. 'You are not well?' he asked, with grave politeness. 'Then do not trouble about the sherbet. Give me Moti to play with.'

'Oh, Lalji! Lalji!' cried Kate, tottering to the bed. She dropped beside the boy, cast her arms defendingly about him, and burst into tears.

'You have cried twice,' said the Prince, watching her heaving shoulders curiously. 'I shall tell Tarvin Sahib.'

The word smote Kate's heart, and filled her with a bitter and fruitless longing. Oh, for a moment of the sure and saving strength she had just rejected! Where was he? she asked herself reproachfully. What had happened to the man she had sent from her to take the chances of life and death in this awful land?

At that hour Tarvin was sitting in his room at the resthouse, with both doors open to the stifling wind of the desert, that he might command all approaches clearly, his revolver on the table in front of him, and the Naulahka in his pocket, yearning to be gone, and loathing this conquest that did not include Kate.

# XIX

*We be the Gods of the East—*
*    Older than all—*
*Masters of mourning and feast,*
*    How shall we fall?*

*Will they gape to the husks that ye proffer,*
*    Or yearn to your song?*
*And we, have we nothing to offer*
*    Who ruled them so long*
*In the fume of the incense, the clash of the cymbal, the*
*    blare of the conch and the gong?*

*Over the strife of the schools*
*    Low the day burns—*
*Back with the kine from the pools*
*    Each one returns*
*To the life that he knows where the altar-flame glows*
*    And the tulsi is trimmed in the urns.*
IN SEEONEE.

THE EVENING AND THE LONG NIGHT gave Kate ample time for
self-examination after she had locked up the treacherous fruit,
and consoled the Maharaj, through her tears, for the mysterious death of Moti. One thing only seemed absolutely clear to
her, when she rose red-eyed and unrefreshed the next morning:
her work was with the women so long as life remained, and
the sole refuge for her present trouble was in the portion of
that work which lay nearest to her hand. Meanwhile the man

475

who loved her remained in Gokral Seetarun, in deadly peril of his life, that he might be within call of her; and she could not call him, for to summon him was to yield, and she dared not.

She took her way to the hospital. The dread for him that had assailed her yesterday had become a horror that would not let her think.

The woman of the desert was waiting as usual at the foot of the steps, her hands clasped over her knee, and her face veiled. Behind her was Dhunpat Rai, who should have been among the wards; and she could see that the courtyard was filled with people—strangers and visitors, who, by her new regulations, were allowed to come only once a week. This was not their visiting day, and Kate, strained and worn by all that she had passed through since the day before, felt an angry impulse in her heart go out against them, and spoke wrathfully.

'What is the meaning of this, Dhunpat Rai?' she demanded, alighting.

'There is commotion of popular bigotry within,' said Dhunpat Rai. 'It is nothing. I have seen it before. Only do not go in.'

She put him aside without a word, and was about to enter when she met one of her patients, a man in the last stage of typhoid fever, being borne out by half-a-dozen clamouring friends, who shouted at her menacingly. The woman of the desert was at her side in an instant, raising her hand, in the brown hollow of which lay a long, broad-bladed knife.

'Be still, dogs!' she shouted, in their own tongue. 'Dare not to lay hands on this *peri* [fairy], who has done all for you!'

'She is killing our people,' shouted a villager.

'Maybe,' said the woman, with a flashing smile; 'but I know

who will be lying here dead if you do not suffer her to pass. Are you Rajputs, or Bhils from the hills, hunters of fish, and diggers after grubs, that you run like cattle because a lying priest from nowhere troubles your heads of mud? Is she killing your people? How long can *you* keep that man alive with your charms and your *mantras*?' she demanded, pointing to the stricken form on the stretcher. 'Out—go out! Is this hospital your own village to defile? Have you paid one penny for the roof above you or the drugs in your bellies? Get hence before I spit upon you!' She brushed them aside with a regal gesture.

'It is best not to go in,' said Dhunpat Rai in Kate's ear. 'There is local holy man in the courtyard, and he is agitating their minds. Also, I myself feel much indisposed.'

'But what does all this mean?' demanded Kate again.

For the hospital was in the hands of a hurrying crowd, who were strapping up bedding and cooking-pots, lamps and linen, calling to one another up and down the staircases in subdued voices, and bringing the sick from the upper wards as ants bring eggs out of a broken hill, six or eight to each man— some holding bunches of marigold flowers in their hands, and pausing to mutter prayers at each step, others peering fearfully into the dispensary, and yet others drawing water from the well and pouring it out around the beds.

In the centre of the courtyard, as naked as the lunatic who had once lived there, sat an ash-smeared, long-haired, eagletaloned, half-mad, wandering, native priest, and waved above his head his buckshorn staff, sharp as a lance at one end, while he chanted in a loud monotonous voice some song that drove the men and women to work more quickly.

As Kate faced him, white with wrath, her eyes blazing, the song turned to a yelp of fierce hatred.

She dashed among the women swiftly—her own women,

who she thought had grown to love her. But their relatives were about them, and Kate was thrust back by a bare-shouldered, loud-voiced dweller of the out-villages in the heart of the desert.

The man had no intention of doing her harm, but the woman of the desert slashed him across the face with her knife, and he withdrew howling.

'Let me speak to them,' said Kate, and the woman beside her quelled the clamour of the crowd with uplifted hands. Only the priest continued his song. Kate strode toward him, her little figure erect and quivering, crying in the vernacular, 'Be silent, thou, or I will find means to close thy mouth!'

The man was hushed, and Kate, returning to her women, stood amongst them, and began to speak impassionedly.

'Oh, my women, what have I done?' she cried, still in the vernacular. 'If there is any fault here, who should right it but your friend? Surely you can speak to me day or night!' She threw out her arms. 'Listen, my sisters! Have you gone mad, that you wish to go abroad now, half-cured, sick, or dying? You are free to go at any hour. Only, for your own sake, and for the sake of your children, do not go before I have cured you, if God so please. It is summer in the desert now, and many of you have come from many miles distant.'

'She speaks truth! She speaks truth,' said a voice in the crowd.

'Ay, I *do* speak truth. And I have dealt fairly by ye. Surely it is upon your heads to tell me the cause of this flight, and not to run away like mice. My sisters, ye are weak and ill, and your friends do not know what is best for you. But *I* know.'

'*Arré!* But what can we do?' cried a feeble voice. 'It is no fault of ours. I, at least, would fain die in peace, but the priest says——'

Then the clamour broke out afresh. 'There are charms written upon the plasters——'

'Why should we become Christians against our will? The wise woman that was sent away asks it.'

'What are the meanings of the red marks on the plasters?'

'Why should we have strange devil-marks stamped upon our bodies? And they burn, too, like the fires of Hell.'

'The priest came yesterday—that holy man yonder—and he said it had been revealed to him, sitting among the hills, that this devil's plan was on foot to make us lose our religion——'

'And to send us out of the hospital with marks upon our bodies—ay, and all the babies we should bear in the hospital should have tails like camels, and ears like mules. The wise woman says so. The priest says so.'

'Hush! hush!' cried Kate, in the face of these various words. 'What plasters? What child's talk is this of plasters and devils? Not one child, but many have been born here, and all were comely. Ye know it! This is the word of the worthless woman whom I sent away because she was torturing you.'

'Nay, but the priest said——'

'What care I for the priest? Has he nursed you? Has he watched by you of nights? Has he sat by your bedside, and smoothed your pillow, and held your hands in pain? Has he taken your children from you and put them to sleep, when ye needed an hour's rest?'

'He is a holy man. He has worked miracles. We dare not face the anger of the Gods.'

One woman, bolder than the rest, shouted, 'Look at this'; and held before Kate's face one of the prepared mustard-leaves lately ordered from Calcutta, which bore upon the back, in red ink, the maker's name and trade-mark.

'What is this devil's thing?' demanded the woman fiercely.

The woman of the desert caught her by the shoulder, and forced her to her knees.

'Be still, woman without a nose!' she cried, her voice vibrating with passion. 'She is not of thy clay, and thy touch would defile her. Remember thine own dunghill, and speak softly.'

Kate picked up the plaster, smiling.

'And who says there is devil's work in this?' she demanded.

'The holy man, the priest. Surely he should know!'

'Nay, *ye* should know,' said Kate patiently. She understood now, and could pity. 'Ye have worn it. Did it work *thee* any harm, Pithira?' she pointed directly toward her. 'Thou hast thanked me not once but many times for giving thee relief through this charm. If it was the devil's work, why did it not consume thee?'

'Indeed it burnt very much indeed,' responded the woman, with a nervous laugh.

Kate could not help laughing. 'That is true. I cannot make my drugs pleasant. But ye know that they do good. What do these people, your friends—villagers, camel-drivers, goat-herds —know of English drugs? Are they so wise among their hills, or is the priest so wise, that they can judge for thee here, fifty miles away from them? Do not listen. Oh, do not listen! Tell them that ye will stay with me, and I will make you well. I can do no more. It was for that I came. I heard of your misery ten thousand miles away, and it burnt into my heart. Would I have come so far to work you harm? Go back to your beds, my sisters, and bid these foolish people depart.'

There was a murmur among the women, as if of assent and doubt. For a moment the decision swayed one way and the other.

Then the man whose face had been slashed shouted, 'What is the use of talking? Let us take our wives and sisters away!

We do not wish to have sons like devils. Give us your voice, O father!' he cried to the priest.

The holy man drew himself up, and swept away Kate's appeal with a torrent of abuse, imprecation, and threats of damnation; and the crowd began to slip past Kate by twos and threes, half carrying and half forcing their kinsfolk with them.

Kate called on the women by name, beseeching them to stay —reasoning, arguing, expostulating. But to no purpose. Many of them were in tears; but the answer from all was the same. They were sorry, but they were only poor women, and they feared the wrath of their husbands.

Minute after minute the wards were depopulated of their occupants, as the priest resumed his song, and began to dance frenziedly in the courtyard. The stream of colours broke out down the steps into the street, and Kate saw the last of her carefully swathed women borne out into the pitiless sun-glare —only the woman of the desert remaining by her side.

Kate looked on with stony eyes. Her hospital was empty.

# XX

Our sister sayeth such and such,
  And we must bow to her behests;
Our sister toileth overmuch,
  Our little maid that hath no breasts.

A field untilled, a web unwove,
  A bud withheld from sun or bee,
An alien in the courts of Love,
  And priestess of his shrine is she.

We love her, but we laugh the while;
  We laugh, but sobs are mixed with laughter;
Our sister hath no time to smile,
  She knows not what must follow after.

Wind of the South, arise and blow,
  From beds of spice thy locks shake free;
Breathe on her heart that she may know,
  Breathe on her eyes that she may see.

Alas! we vex her with our mirth,
  And maze her with most tender scorn,
Who stands beside the gates of Birth,
  Herself a child—a child unborn!

Our sister sayeth such and such,
  And we must bow to her behests;
Our sister toileth overmuch,
  Our little maid that hath no breasts.
            FROM LIBRETTO OF 'NAULAHKA.'

482

'HAS THE MISS SAHIB any orders?' asked Dhunpat Rai, with Oriental calmness, as Kate turned toward the woman of the desert, staying herself against her massive shoulder.

Kate simply shook her head with closed lips.

'It is very sad,' said Dhunpat Rai thoughtfully, as though the matter were one in which he had no interest; 'but it is on account of religious bigotry and intolerance which is prevalent mania in these parts. Once—twice before I have seen the same thing. About powders, sometimes; and once they said that the graduated glasses were holy vessels, and zinc ointment was cow-fat. But I have never seen all the hospital disembark simultaneously. I do not think they will come back; but my appointment is State appointment,' he said, with a bland smile, 'and so I shall draw my offeecial income as before.'

Kate stared at him. 'Do you mean that they will never come back?' she asked falteringly.

'Oh yes—in time—one or two; two or three of the men when they are hurt by tigers, or have ophthalmia; but the women— no. Their husbands will never allow. Ask that woman!'

Kate bent a piteous look of inquiry upon the woman of the desert, who, stooping down, took up a little sand, let it trickle through her fingers, brushed her palms together, and shook her head. Kate watched these movements despairingly.

'You see it is all up—no good,' said Dhunpat Rai, not unkindly, but unable to conceal a certain expression of satisfaction in a defeat which the wise had already predicted. 'And now what will your honour do? Shall I lock up dispensary, or will you audit drug accounts now?'

Kate waved him off feebly. 'No, no! Not now. I must think. I must have time. I will send you word. Come, dear one,' she added in the vernacular to the woman of the desert, and hand in hand they went out from the hospital together.

The sturdy Rajput woman caught her up like a child when they were outside, and set her upon her horse, and tramped doggedly alongside, as they set off together toward the house of the missionary.

'And whither wilt thou go?' asked Kate, in the woman's own tongue.

'I was the first of them all,' answered the patient being at her side; 'it is fitting therefore that I should be the last. Where thou goest I will go—and afterward what will fall will fall.'

Kate leaned down and took the woman's hand in hers with a grateful pressure.

At the missionary's gate she had to call up her courage not to break down. She had told Mrs. Estes so much of her hopes for the future, had dwelt so lovingly on all that she meant to teach these helpless creatures, had so constantly conferred with her about the help she had fancied herself to be daily bringing to them, that to own that her work had fallen to this ruin was unspeakably bitter. The thought of Tarvin she fought back. It went too deep.

But, fortunately, Mrs. Estes seemed not to be at home, and a messenger from the Queen-Mother awaited Kate to demand her presence at the palace with the Maharaj Kunwar.

The woman of the desert laid a restraining hand on her arm, but Kate shook it off.

'No, no, no! I must go. I must do something,' she exclaimed almost fiercely, 'since there is still some one who will let me. I must have work. It is my only refuge, kind one. Go you on to the palace.'

The woman yielded silently, and trudged on up the dusty road, while Kate sped into the house and to the room where the young Prince lay.

'Lalji,' she said, bending over him, 'do you feel well enough to be lifted into the carriage and taken over to see your mother?'

'I would rather see my father,' responded the boy from the sofa, to which he had been transferred as a reward for the improvement he had made since yesterday. 'I wish to speak to my father upon a most important thing.'

'But your mother hasn't seen you for so long, dear.'

'Very well; I will go.'

'Then I will tell them to get the carriage ready.'

Kate turned to leave the room.

'No, please; I will have my own. Who is without there?'

'Heaven-born, it is I,' answered the deep voice of a trooper.

'*Achcha!* Ride swiftly, and tell them to send down my barouche and escort. If it is not here in ten minutes, tell Saroop Singh that I will cut his pay and blacken his face before all my men. This day I go abroad again.'

'May the mercy of God be upon the Heaven-born for ten thousand years!' responded the voice from without, as the trooper heaved himself into the saddle and clattered away.

By the time that the Prince was ready, a lumbering equipage, stuffed with many cushions, waited at the door. Kate and Mrs. Estes half helped and half carried the child into it, though he strove to stand on his feet in the veranda and acknowledge the salute of his escort as befitted a man.

'*Ahi!* I am very weak,' he said, with a little laugh, as they drove to the palace. 'Certainly it seems to myself that I shall never get well in Rhatore.'

Kate put her arm about him and drew him closer to her.

'Kate,' he continued, 'if I ask anything of my father, will you say that that thing is good for me?'

Kate, whose thoughts were still bitter and far away, patted his shoulder vaguely as she lifted her tear-stained eyes toward the red height on which the palace stood. 'How can I tell, Lalji?' she smiled down into his upturned face.

'But it is a most wise thing.'

'Is it?' asked she fondly.

'Yes; I have thought it out by myself. I am myself a Raj Kumar, and I would go to the Raj Kumar College, where they train the sons of princes to become kings. That is only at Ajmir; but I must go and learn, and fight, and ride with the other princes of Rajputana, and then I shall be altogether a man. I am going to the Raj Kumar College at Ajmir, that I may learn about the world. But you shall see how it is wise. The world looks very big since I have been ill. Kate, how big is the world which you have seen across the Black Water? Where is Tarvin Sahib? I have wished to see him too. Is Tarvin Sahib angry with me or with you?'

He plied her with a hundred questions till they halted before one of the gates in the flank of the palace that led to his mother's wing. The woman of the desert rose from the ground beside it, and held out her arms.

'I heard the message come,' she said to Kate, 'and I knew what was required. Give me the child to carry in. Nay, my Prince, there is no cause for fear. I am of good blood.'

'Women of good blood walk veiled, and do not speak in the streets,' said the child doubtfully.

'One law for thee and thine, and another for me and mine,' the woman answered, with a laugh. 'We who earn our bread by toil cannot go veiled, but our fathers lived before us for many hundred years, even as did thine, Heaven-borne. Come then, the white fairy cannot carry thee so tenderly as I can.'

She put her arms about him, and held him to her breast as easily as though he had been a three-year-old child. He leaned back luxuriously, and waved a wasted hand; the grim gate grated on its hinges as it swung back, and they entered together—the woman, the child, and the girl.

There was no lavish display of ornament in that part of the palace. The gaudy tilework on the walls had flaked and crumbled away in many places, the shutters lacked paint and hung awry, and there was litter and refuse in the courtyard behind the gates. A Queen who has lost the King's favour loses much else as well in material comforts.

A door opened and a voice called. The three plunged into half-darkness, and traversed a long, upward-sloping passage, floored with shining white stucco as smooth as marble, which communicated with the Queen's apartments. The Maharaj Kunwar's mother lived by preference in one long, low room that faced to the north-east, that she might press her face against the marble tracery and dream of her home across the sands, eight hundred miles away, among the Kulu hills. The hum of the crowded palace could not be heard there, and the footsteps of her few waiting-women alone broke the silence.

The woman of the desert, with the Prince hugged more closely to her breast, moved through the labyrinth of empty rooms, narrow staircases, and roofed courtyards with the air of a caged panther. Kate and the Prince were familiar with the dark and the tortuousness, the silence and the sullen mystery. To the one it was part and parcel of the horrors amid which she had elected to move; to the other it was his daily life.

At last the journey ended. Kate lifted a heavy curtain, as the Prince called for his mother; and the Queen, rising from a pile of white cushions by the window, cried passionately:—

'Is it well with the child?'

The Prince struggled to the floor from the woman's arms, and the Queen hung sobbing over him, calling him a thousand endearing names, and fondling him from head to foot. The child's reserve melted—he had striven for a moment to carry himself as a man of the Rajput race: that is to say, as one shocked beyond expression at any public display of emotion —and he laughed and wept in his mother's arms. The woman of the desert drew her hand across her eyes, muttering to herself, and Kate turned to look out of the window.

'How shall I give you thanks?' said the Queen at last. 'Oh, my son—my little son—child of my heart, the Gods and she have made thee well again. But who is that yonder?'

Her eyes fell for the first time on the woman of the desert, where the latter stood by the doorway draped in dull red.

'She carried me here from the carriage,' said the Prince, 'saying that she was a Rajput of good blood.'

'I am of Chohan blood—a Rajput and a mother of Rajputs,' said the woman simply, still standing. 'The white fairy worked a miracle upon my man. He was sick in the head and did not know me. It is true that he died, but before the passing of the breath he knew me and called me by my name.'

'And *she* carried thee!' said the Queen, with a shiver, drawing the Prince closer to her, for, like all Indian women, she counted the touch and glance of a widow things of evil omen.

The woman fell at the Queen's feet. 'Forgive me, forgive me,' she cried. 'I had borne three little ones, and the Gods took them all and my man at the last. It was good—it was so good—to hold a child in my arms again. Thou canst forgive,' she wailed; 'thou art so rich in thy son, and I am only a widow.'

'And I widowed in life,' said the Queen, under her breath. 'Of a truth, I should forgive. Rise thou.'

The woman lay still where she had fallen, clutching at the Queen's naked feet.

'Rise, then, my sister,' the Queen whispered.

'We of the fields,' murmured the woman of the desert, 'we do not know how to speak to the great people. If my words are rough, does the Queen forgive me?'

'Indeed I forgive. Thy speech is softer than that of the hill-women of Kulu, but some of the words are new.'

'I am of the desert—a herder of camels, a milker of goats. What should I know of the speech of Courts? Let the white fairy speak for me.'

Kate listened with an alien ear. Now that she had discharged her duty, her freed mind went back to Tarvin's danger and the shame and overthrow of an hour ago. She saw the women in her hospital slipping away one by one, her work unravelled, and all hope of good brought to wreck; and she saw Tarvin dying atrocious deaths, and, as she felt, by her hand.

'What is it?' she asked wearily, as the woman plucked at her skirt. Then to the Queen, 'This is a woman who alone of all those whom I tried to benefit remained at my side to-day, Queen.'

'There has been a talk in the palace,' said the Queen, her arm round the Prince's neck, 'a talk that trouble had come to your hospital, Sahiba.'

'There is no hospital now,' Kate answered grimly.

'You promised to take me there, Kate, some day,' the Prince said in English.

'The women were fools,' said the woman of the desert quietly, from her place on the ground. 'A mad priest told them a lie—that there was a charm among the drugs——'

'Deliver us from all evil spirits and exorcisms!' the Queen murmured.

'A charm among her drugs that she handles with her own hands, and so forsooth, Sahiba, they must run out shrieking that their children will be misborn apes and their chicken-souls given to the devils. *Aho!* They will know in a week, not one or two, but many, whither their souls go: for they will die—the corn and the corn in the ear together.

Kate shivered. She knew too well that the woman spoke the truth.

'But the drugs!' began the Queen. 'Who knows what powers there may be in the drugs?' She laughed nervously, glancing at Kate.

'*Dekko!* Look at her!' said the woman, with quiet scorn. 'She is a girl and naught else. What could she do to the Gates of Life?'

'She has made my son whole; therefore she is my sister,' said the Queen.

'She caused my man to speak to me before the death hour; therefore I am her servant as well as thine, Sahiba,' said the other.

The Prince looked up in his mother's face curiously. 'She calls thee "thou," ' he said, as though the woman did not exist. 'That is not seemly between a villager and a Queen, thee and thou!'

'We be both women, little son. Stay still in my arms. Oh, it is good to feel thee here again, worthless one.'

'The Heaven-born looks as frail as dried maize,' said the woman quickly.

'A dried monkey, rather,' returned the Queen, dropping her lips on the child's head. Both mothers spoke aloud and with emphasis, that the Gods, jealous of human happiness, might hear and take for truth the disparagement that veils deepest love.

'*Aho,* my little monkey is dead,' said the Prince, moving restlessly. 'I need another one. Let me go into the palace and find another monkey.'

'He must not wander into the palace from this chamber,' said the Queen passionately, turning to Kate. 'Thou art all too weak, beloved. O Miss Sahib, he must not go.' She knew by experience that it was fruitless to cross her son's will.

'It is my order,' said the Prince, without turning his head. 'I will go.'

'Stay with us, beloved,' said Kate. She was wondering whether the hospital could be dragged together again, after three months, and whether it was possible she might have overrated the danger to Nick.

'I go,' said the Prince, breaking from his mother's arms. 'I am tired of this talk.'

'Does the Queen give leave?' asked the woman of the desert under her breath. The Queen nodded, and the Prince found himself caught between two brown arms, against whose strength it was impossible to struggle.

'Let me go, *widow*!' he shouted furiously.

'It is not good for a Rajput to make light of a mother of Rajputs, my king,' was the unmoved answer. 'If the young calf does not obey the cow, he learns obedience from the yoke. The Heaven-born is not strong. He will fall among those passages and stairs. He will stay here. When the rage has left his body he will be weaker than before. Even now'—the large bright eyes bent themselves on the face of the child—'even now,' the calm voice continued, 'the rage is going. One moment more, Heaven-born, and thou wilt be a Prince no longer, but only a little, little child, such as I have borne. *Ahi!* such as I shall never bear again.'

With the last words the Prince's head nodded forward on her shoulder. The gust of passion had spent itself, leaving him, as she had foreseen, weak to sleep.

'Shame—oh, shame!' he muttered thickly. 'Indeed I do not wish to go. Let me sleep.'

She began to pat him on the shoulder, till the Queen put forward hungry arms, and took back her own again, and laying the child on a cushion at her side, spread the skirt of her long muslin robe over him, and looked long at her treasure. The woman crouched down on the floor. Kate sat on a cushion, and listened to the ticking of the cheap American clock in a niche in the wall. The voice of a woman singing a song came muffled and faint through many walls. The dry wind of noon sighed through the fretted screens of the window, and she could hear the horses of the escort swishing their tails and champing their bits in the courtyard a hundred feet below. She listened, thinking ever of Tarvin in growing terror. The Queen leaned over her son more closely, her eyes humid with mother-love.

'He is asleep,' she said at last. 'What was the talk about his monkey, Miss Sahib?'

'It died,' Kate said, and spurred herself to the lie. 'I think it had eaten bad fruit in the garden.'

'In the garden?' said the Queen quickly.

'Yes, in the garden.'

The woman of the desert turned her eyes from one woman to the other. These were matters too high for her, and she began timidly to rub the Queen's feet.

'Monkeys often die,' she observed. 'I have seen as it were a pestilence among the money-folk over there at Banswarra.'

'In what fashion did it die?' insisted the Queen.

'I—I do not know,' Kate stammered, and there was another long silence as the hot afternoon wore on.

'Miss Kate, what do you think about my son?' whispered the Queen. 'Is he well, or is he not well?'

'He is not very well. In time he will grow stronger, but it would be better if he could go away for a while.'

The Queen bowed her head quietly. 'I have thought of

that also many times, sitting here alone; and it was the tearing out of my own heart from my breast. Yes, it would be well if he were to go away. But'—she stretched out her hands despairingly toward the sunshine—'what do I know of the world where he will go, and how can I be sure that he will be safe? Here—even here' . . . She checked herself suddenly. 'Since you have come, Miss Kate, my heart has known a little comfort, but I do not know when you will go away again.'

'I cannot guard the child against every evil,' Kate replied, covering her face with her hands; 'but send him away from this place as swiftly as may be. In God's name let him go away.'

'*Such hai! Such hai!* It is the truth, the truth!' The Queen turned from Kate to the woman at her feet.

'Thou hast borne three?' she said.

'Yea, three, and one other that never drew breath. They were all men-children,' said the woman of the desert.

'And the Gods took them?'

'Of smallpox one, and fever the two others.'

'Art thou certain that it was the Gods?'

'I was with them always till the end.'

'Thy man, then, was all thine own?'

'We were only two, he and I. Among our villages the men are poor, and one wife suffices.'

'*Arré!* They are rich among the villages. Listen now. If a co-wife had sought the lives of those three of thine——'

'I would have killed her. What else?' The woman's nostrils dilated and her hand went swiftly to her bosom.

'And if in place of three there had been one only, the delight of thy eyes, and thou hadst known that thou shouldst never bear another, and the co-wife working in darkness had sought for that life? What then?'

'I would have slain her—but with no easy death. At her

man's side and in his arms I would have slain her. If she died before my vengeance arrived I would seek for her in Hell.'

'Thou canst go out in the sunshine and walk in the streets and no man turns his head,' said the Queen bitterly. 'Thy hands are free and thy face is uncovered. What if thou wert a slave among slaves, a stranger among stranger people, and'— the voice dropped—'dispossessed of the favour of thy lord?'

The woman, stooping, kissed the pale feet under her hands.

'Then I would not wear myself with strife, but, remembering that a man-child may grow into a king, would send that child away beyond the power of the co-wife.'

'Is it so easy to cut away the hand?' said the Queen, sobbing.

'Better the hand than the heart, Sahiba. Who could guard such a child in this place?'

The Queen pointed to Kate. 'She came from far off, and she has once already brought him back from death.'

'Her drugs are good and her skill is great, but—thou knowest she is but a maiden, who has known neither gain nor loss. It may be that I am luckless, and that my eyes are evil—thus did not my man say last autumn—but it may be. Yet I know the pain at the breast and the yearning over the child new-born—as thou hast known it.'

'As I have known it!'

'My house is empty and I am a widow and childless, and never again shall a man call me to wed.'

'As I am—as I am!'

'Nay, the little one is left, whatever else may go; and the little one must be well guarded. If there is any jealousy against the child it were not well to keep him in this hotbed. Let him go out.'

'But whither? Miss Kate, dost thou know? The world is all dark to us who sit behind the curtain.'

'I know that the child of his own motion desires to go to

the Princes' School in Ajmir. He has told me that much,' said Kate, who had lost no word of the conversation from her place on the cushion, bowed forward with her chin supported in her hands. 'It will be only for a year or two.'

The Queen laughed a little through her tears. 'Only a year or two, Miss Kate. Dost thou know how long is one night when he is not here?'

'And he can return at call; but no cry will bring back mine own. Only a year or two. The world is dark also to those who do not sit behind the curtain, Sahiba. It is no fault of hers. How should she know?' said the woman of the desert under her breath to the Queen.

Against her will, Kate began to feel annoyed at this persistent exclusion of herself from the talk, and the assumption that she, with her own great trouble upon her, whose work was pre-eminently to deal with sorrow, must have no place in this double grief.

'How should I *not* know?' said Kate impetuously. 'Do I not know pain? Is it not my life?'

'Not yet,' said the Queen quietly. 'Neither pain nor joy. Miss Kate, thou art very wise, and I am only a woman who has never stirred beyond the palace walls. But I am wiser than thou, for I know that which thou dost not know, though thou hast given back my son to me, and to this woman her husband's speech. How shall I repay thee all I owe?'

'Let her hear truth,' said the woman, under her breath. 'We be all three women here, Sahiba—dead leaf, flowering tree, and the blossom unopened.'

The Queen caught Kate's hands and gently pulled her forward till her head fell on the Queen's knees. Wearied with the emotions of the morning, unutterably tired in body and spirit, the girl had no desire to lift it. The small hands put her hair back from her forehead, and the full dark eyes, worn with much weeping, looked into her own. The woman of the desert flung an arm round her waist.

'Listen, my sister,' began the Queen, with an infinite tenderness. 'There is a proverb among my own people, in the mountains of the North, that a rat found a piece of turmeric, and opened a druggist's shop. Even so with the pain that thou dost know and heal, beloved. Thou art not angry? Nay, thou must not take offence. Forget that thou art white, and I black, and remember only that we three be sisters. Little sister, with us women, 'tis thus, and no other way. From all, except such as have borne a child, the world is hid. I make my prayers trembling to such and such a God, who thou sayest is black stone, and I tremble at the gusts of the night because I believe that the devils ride by my windows at such hours; and I sit here in the dark knitting wool and preparing sweetmeats that come back untasted from my lord's table. And thou coming from ten thousand leagues away, very wise and fearing nothing, hast taught me, oh, ten thousand things. Yet thou art the child, and I am still the mother, and what I know thou canst not know, and the wells of my happiness thou canst not fathom, nor the bitter waters of my sorrow till thou hast tasted happiness and grief alike. I have told thee of the child—all and more than all, thou sayest? Little sister, I have told thee less than the beginning of my love for him, because I knew that thou couldst not understand. I have told thee my sorrows —all and more than all, thou sayest, when I laid my head against thy breast? How could I tell thee all? Thou art a maiden, and the heart in thy bosom, beneath my heart, betrayed in its very beat that it did not understand. Nay, that woman there, coming from without, knows more of me than thou? And they taught thee in a school, thou hast told me, all manner of healing, and there is no disease in life that thou dost not understand? Little sister, how couldst thou understand life that hast never given it? Hast thou ever felt the tug of the child at the breast? Nay, what need to blush? Hast thou? I know thou hast not. Though I heard thy speech for the first time, and looking from the window saw thee walking, I should know. And the others—my sisters in the world— know also. But they do not all speak to thee as I do. When the life quickens under the breast, they, waking in the night, hear all the earth walking to that measure. Why should they tell thee? To-day the hospital has broken from under thee. Is it not so? And the women went out one by one? And what didst thou say to them?'

The woman of the desert, answering for her, spoke. 'She said, "Come back, and I will make ye well." '

'And by what oath did she affirm her words?'

'There was no oath,' said the woman of the desert; 'she stood in the gate and called.'

'And upon what should a maiden call to bring wavering women back again? The toil that she has borne for their sake? They cannot see it. But of the pains that a woman has shared with them, a woman knows. There was no child in thine arms. The mother-look was not in thine eyes. By what magic, then, wouldst thou speak to women? There was a charm among the drugs, they said, and their children would be misshapen. What didst thou know of the springs of life and death to teach them otherwise? It is written in the books of thy school, I know, that such things cannot be. But we women do not read books. It is not from them that we learn of life. How should such an one prevail, unless the Gods help her—and the Gods are very far away. Thou hast given thy life to the helping of women. Little sister, when wilt thou also be a woman?'

The voice ceased. Kate's head was buried deep in the Queen's lap. She let it lie there without stirring.

'Ay!' said the woman of the desert. 'The mark of coverture

has been taken from my head, my glass bangles are broken on my arm, and I am unlucky to meet when a man sets forth on a journey. Till I die I must be alone, earning my bread alone, and thinking of the dead. But though I knew that it was to come again, at the end of one year instead of ten, I would still thank the Gods that have given me love and a child. Will the Miss Sahib take this in payment for all she did for my man? "A wandering priest, a childless woman, and a stone in the water are of one blood." So says the talk of our people. What will the Miss Sahib do now? The Queen has spoken the truth. The Gods and thine own wisdom, which is past the wisdom of a maid, have helped thee so far, as I, who was with thee always, have seen. The Gods have warned thee that their help is at an end. What remains? Is this work for such as thou? Is it not as the Queen says? She, sitting here alone, and seeing nothing, has seen that which I, moving with thee among the sick day by day, have seen and known. Little sister, is it not so?'

Kate lifted her head slowly from the Queen's knee, and rose.

'Take the child, and let us go,' she said hoarsely.

The merciful darkness of the room hid her face.

'Nay,' said the Queen, 'this woman shall take him. Go thou back alone.'

Kate vanished.

## XXI

*The Law whereby my lady moves*
*Was never Law to me,*
*But 'tis enough that she approves*
*Whatever Law it be.*

*For in that Law, and by that Law,*
*My constant course I'll steer;*
*Not that I heed or deem it dread,*
*But that she holds it dear.*

*Tho' Asia sent for my content*
*Her richest argosies,*
*Those would I spurn, and bid return,*
*If that should give her ease.*

*With equal heart I'd watch depart*
*Each splicèd sail from sight,*
*Sans bitterness, desiring less*
*Great gear than her delight.*

*Yet such am I, yea, such am I—*
*Sore bond and freest free,—*
*The Law that sways my lady's ways*
*Is mystery to me!*

To sit still, and to keep sitting still, is the first lesson that the young jockey must learn. Tarvin was learning it in bitterness of spirit. For the sake of his town, for the sake of his love, and, above all, for the sake of his love's life, he must go. The town was waiting, his horse was saddled at the door, but his love would not come. He must sit still.

The burning desert wind blew through the open veranda as remorselessly as Sitabhai's hate. Looking out, he saw nothing but the city asleep in the sunshine and the wheeling kites above it. Yet when evening fell, and a man might be able by bold riding to escape to the railway, certain shrouded figures would creep from the walls and take up their position within easy gunshot of the rest-house. One squatted at each point of the compass, and between them, all night long, came and went a man on horseback. Tarvin could hear the steady beat of the hoofs as he went his rounds, and the sound did not give him fresh hope. But for Kate—but for Kate, he repeated to himself, he would have been long since beyond reach of horse or bullet. The hours were very slow, and as he sat and watched the shadows grow and shorten it seemed to him, as it had seemed so often before, that this and no other was the moment that Topaz would choose to throw her chances from her.

He had lost already, he counted, eight-and-forty precious hours, and, so far as he could see, the remainder of the year might be spent in an equally unprofitable fashion.

Meantime Kate lay exposed to every imaginable danger. Sitabhai was sure to assume that he had wrested the necklace from her for the sake of the 'frail white girl'; she had said as much on the dam. It *was* for Kate's sake, in a measure; but Tarvin reflected bitterly that an Oriental had no sense of proportion, and, like the snake, strikes first at that which is nearest. And Kate? How in the world was he to explain the case to her? He had told her of danger about her path as well as his own, and she had decided to face that danger. For her courage and devotion he loved her; but her obstinacy made him grit his teeth. There was but one grimly comical element in the terrible jumble. What would the King say to Sitabhai when he discovered that she had lost the Luck of the State? In what manner would she veil that loss; and, above all, into what sort of royal rage would she fall? Tarvin shook his head meditatively. 'It's quite bad enough for me,' he said, 'just about as bad as it can possibly be made; but I have a wandering suspicion that it may be unwholesome for Juggut. Yes! I can spare time to be very sorry for Juggut. My fat friend, you should have held straight that first time, outside the city walls!'

He rose and looked out into the sunlight, wondering which of the scattered vagrants by the roadside might be an emissary from the palace. A man lay apparently asleep by the side of his camel near the road that ran to the city. Tarvin stepped out casually from the veranda, and saw, as soon as he was fairly in the open, that the sleeper rolled round to the other side of his beast. He strolled forward a few paces. The sunlight glinted above the back of the camel on something that shone like silver. Tarvin marched straight toward the glitter, his pistol in his hand. The man, when he came up to him, was buried in innocent slumber. Under the fold of his garment peered the muzzle of a new and very clean rifle.

'Looks as if Sitabhai was calling out the militia, and supplying them with outfits from her private armoury. Juggut's gun was new, too,' said Tarvin, standing over the sleeper. 'But this man knows more about guns than Juggut. Hi!' He stooped down and stirred the man up with the muzzle of his revolver. 'I'm afraid I must trouble you for that gun. And tell the lady to drop it, will you? It won't pay.'

The man understood the unspoken eloquence of the pistol, and nothing more. He gave up his gun sullenly enough, and moved away, lashing his camel spitefully.

'Now, I wonder how many more of her army I shall have to

disarm,' said Tarvin, retracing his steps, the captured gun over his shoulder. 'I wonder—no, I won't believe that she would dare to do anything to Kate! She knows enough of me to be sure that I'd blow her and her old palace into to-morrow. If she's half the woman she pretends to be, she'll reckon with me before she goes much further.'

In vain he attempted to force himself into this belief. Sitabhai had shown him what sort of thing her mercy might be, and Kate might have tasted it ere this. To go to her now—to be maimed or crippled at the least if he went to her now—was impossible. Yet, he decided that he would go. He returned hastily to Fibby, whom he had left not three minutes before flicking flies off in the sunshine at the back of the rest-house. But Fibby lay on his side groaning piteously, ham-strung and dying.

Tarvin could hear his groom industriously polishing a bit round the corner, and when the man came up in response to his call he flung himself down by the side of the horse, howling with grief.

'An enemy hath done this, an enemy hath done this!' he clamoured. 'My beautiful brown horse that never did harm except when he kicked through fullness of meat! Where shall I find a new service if I let my charge die thus?'

'I wish I knew! I wish I knew!' said Tarvin, puzzled, and almost despairing. 'There'd be a bullet through one black head, if I were just a little surer. Get up, you! Fibby, old man, I forgive you all your sins. You were a good old boy, and—here's luck.'

The blue smoke enveloped Fibby's head for an instant, the head fell like a hammer, and the good horse was out of his pain. The groom, rising, rent the air with grief, till Tarvin kicked him out of the pickets and bade him begone. Then it was noticeable that his cries ceased suddenly, and, as he retreated into his mud house to tie up his effects, he smiled and dug up some silver from a hole under his bedstead.

Tarvin, dismounted, looked east, west, north, south for help, as Sitabhai had looked on the dam. A wandering gang of gipsies with their lean bullocks and yelping dogs turned an angle of the city wall, and rested like a flock of unclean birds by the city gate. The sight in itself was not unusual, but city regulations forbade camping within a quarter of a mile of the walls.

'Some of the lady's poor relatives, I suppose. They have blocked the way through the gate pretty well. Now, if I were to make a bolt of it to the missionary's they'd have me, wouldn't they?' muttered Tarvin to himself. 'On the whole, I've seen prettier professions than trading with Eastern Queens. They don't seem to understand the rules of the game.'

At that moment a cloud of dust whirled through the gipsy camp, as the escort of the Maharaj Kunwar, clearing the way for the barouche, scattered the dark band to the left and right. Tarvin wondered what this might portend. The escort halted with the customary rattle of accoutrements at the rest-house door, the barouche behind them. A single trooper, two hundred yards or more in the rear, lifted his voice in a deferential shout as he pursued the carriage. He was answered by a chuckle from the escort, and two shrill screams of delight from the occupants of the barouche.

A child whom Tarvin had never before seen stood upright in the back of the carriage, and hurled a torrent of abuse in the vernacular at the outpaced trooper. Again the escort laughed.

'Tarvin Sahib! Tarvin Sahib!' piped the Maharaj Kunwar. 'Come and look at us.'

For a moment Tarvin fancied this a fresh device of the enemy; but reassured by the sight of his old and trusted ally, the Maharaj, he stepped forward.

'Prince,' he said, as he took his hand, 'you ought not to be out.'

'Oh, it is all right,' said the young man hastily, though his little pale face belied it. 'I gave the order and we came. Miss Kate gives me orders; but she took me over to the palace, and there *I* give orders. This is Umr Singh—my brother, the little Prince; but *I* shall be King.'

The second child raised his eyes slowly and looked full at Tarvin. The eyes and the low broad forehead were those of Sitabhai, and the mouth closed firmly over the little pearl-like teeth, as his mother's mouth had closed in the conflict on the Dungar Talao.

'He is from the other side of the palace,' continued the Maharaj, still in English. 'From the other side, where I must not go. But when I was in the palace I went to him—ha, ha, Tarvin Sahib!—and he was killing a goat. Look! His hands are all red now.'

Umr Singh opened a tiny palm at a word from the Maharaj in the vernacular, and flung it outward at Tarvin. It was dark with dried blood, and a bearded whisper ran among the escort. The commandant turned in his saddle, and, nodding at Tarvin, muttered, '*Sitabhai.*' Tarvin caught the word, and it was sufficient for him. Providence had sent him help out of a clear sky. He framed a plan instantly.

'But how did you come here, you young imps?' he demanded.

'Oh, there are only women in the palace yonder, and I am a Rajput and a man. He cannot speak any English at all,' he added, pointing to his companion; 'but when we have played together I have told him about you, Tarvin Sahib, and about the day you picked me out of my saddle, and he wished to come too, to see all the things you show me; so I gave the order very quietly, and we came out of the little door together. And so we are here! *Salaam, baba,*' he said patronisingly to the child at his side, and the child, slowly and gravely, raised his hand to his forehead, still gazing with fixed, incurious eyes on the stranger. Then he whispered something that made the Maharaj Kunwar laugh. 'He says,' said the Maharaj Kunwar, 'that you are not so big as he thought. His mother told him that you were stronger than any man, but some of these troopers are bigger than you.'

'Well, what do you want me to do?' asked Tarvin.

'Show him your gun, and how you shoot rupees, and what you do that makes horses quiet when they kick, and all those things.'

'All right,' said Tarvin. 'But I can't show them here. Come over to Mr. Estes with me.'

'I do not like to go there. My monkey is dead. And I do not think Kate would like to see us. She is always crying now. She took me up to the palace yesterday, and this morning I went to her again; but she would not see me.'

Tarvin could have hugged the child for the blessed assurance that Kate at least still lived. 'Isn't she at the hospital, then?' he asked thickly.

'Oh, the hospital has all gone *phut*. There are no women now. They all ran away.'

'No!' cried Tarvin. 'Say that again, little man. What for?'

'Devils,' said the Maharaj Kunwar briefly. 'What do I know? It was some women's talk. Show him how you ride, Tarvin Sahib.'

Again Umr Singh whispered to his companion, and put one

leg over the side of the barouche. 'He says he will ride in front of you, as I told him I did,' interpreted the Prince. 'Gurdit Singh, dismount!'

A trooper flung himself out of the saddle on the word, and stood to attention at the horse's head. Tarvin, smiling to himself at the perfection of his opportunity, said nothing, but leapt into the saddle, picked Umr Singh out of his barouche, and placed him carefully before him.

'Sitabhai would be rather restless if she could see me,' he murmured to himself, as he tucked his arm round the lithe little figure. 'I don't think there will be any Juggutting while I carry this young man in front of me.'

As the escort opened to allow Tarvin to take his place at their head, a wandering priest, who had been watching the episode from a little distance, turned and shouted with all the strength of his lungs across the plain, in the direction of the city. The cry was taken up by unseen voices, passed on to the city walls, and died away on the sands beyond.

Umr Singh smiled, as the horse began to trot, and urged Tarvin to go faster. This the Maharaj forbade. He wished to see the sight comfortably from his seat in the barouche. As he passed the gipsy camp, men and women threw themselves down on the sands, crying '*Jai! Jungle da Badshah jai!*' and the faces of the troopers darkened.

'That means,' cried the Maharaj Kunwar, 'Victory to the King of the Desert. I have no money to give them. Have you, Tarvin Sahib?'

In his joy at being now safely on his way to Kate, Tarvin could have flung everything he possessed to the crowd—almost the Naulahka itself. He emptied a handful of copper and small silver among them, and the cry rose again, but bitter laughter was mingled with it, and the gipsy folk called to each other, mocking. The Maharaj Kunwar's face turned scarlet. He leaned forward listening for an instant, and then shouted, 'By Indur, it is for *him*! Scatter their tents!' At a wave of his hand the escort, wheeling, plunged through the camp in line, driving the light ash of the fires up in clouds, slashing the donkeys with the flat of their swords until they stampeded, and carrying away the frail brown tents on the butts of their reversed lances.

Tarvin looked on contentedly at the dispersal of the group, which he knew would have stopped him if he had been alone.

Umr Singh bit his lip. Then, turning to the Maharaj Kunwar, he smiled, and put forward from his belt the hilt of his sword in sign of fealty.

'It is just, my brother,' he said in the vernacular. 'But I'— here he raised his voice a little—'would not drive the gipsy folk too far. They always return.'

'Ay,' cried a voice from the huddled crowd, watching the wreck of the camp, significantly, 'gipsies always return, my King.'

'So does a dog,' said the Maharaj, between his teeth. 'Both are kicked. Drive on.'

And a pillar of dust came to Estes' house, Tarvin riding in safety in the midst of it.

Telling the boys to play until he came out, he swept into the house, taking the steps two at a time, and discovered Kate in a dark corner of the parlour with a bit of sewing in her hand. As she looked up he saw that she was crying.

'Nick!' she exclaimed voicelessly. *'Nick!'* He had stopped, hesitating on the threshold; she dropped her work, and rose breathless. 'You have come back! It is you! You are alive!'

Tarvin smiled, and held out his arms. 'Come and see!' She took a step forward.

'Oh, I was afraid——'

'Come!'

She went doubtfully toward him. He caught her fast, and held her in his arms.

For a long minute she let her head lie on his breast. Then she looked up. 'This isn't what I meant,' she protested.

'Oh, don't try to improve on it!' Tarvin said hastily.

'She tried to poison me. I was sure when I heard nothing that she must have killed you. I fancied horrible things.'

'Poor child! And your hospital has gone wrong! You have been having a hard time. But we will change all that. We must leave as soon as you can get ready. I've nipped her claws for a moment. I'm holding a hostage. But we can't keep that up for ever. We must get away.'

'We!' she repeated feebly.

'Well, do you want to go alone?'

She smiled as she released herself. 'I want you to.'

'And you?'

'I'm not worth thinking of. I have failed. Everything I meant to do has fallen about me in a heap. I feel burnt out, Nick—burnt out!'

'All right! We'll put in new works and launch you on a fresh system. That's what I want. There shall be nothing to remind you that you ever saw Rhatore, dear.'

'It was a mistake,' she said.

'What?'

'Everything. My coming. My thinking I could do it. It's not a girl's work. It's my work, perhaps; but it's not for me. I have given it up, Nick. Take me home.'

Tarvin gave an unbecoming shout of joy, and folded her in his arms again. He told her that they must be married at once, and start that night, if she could manage it; and Kate, dreading what might befall him, assented doubtfully. She spoke of preparations; but Tarvin said that they would prepare after they had done it. They could buy things at Bombay —stacks of things. He was sweeping her forward with the onrush of his extempore plans, when she said suddenly, 'But what of the dam, Nick? You can't leave that.'

'Shucks!' exclaimed Tarvin heartily. 'You don't suppose there's any gold in the old river, do you?'

She recoiled quickly from his arms, staring at him in accusation and reproach.

'Do you mean that you have always known that there was no gold there?' she asked.

Tarvin pulled himself together quickly; but not so quickly that she did not catch the confession in his eye.

'I see you have,' she said coldly.

Tarvin measured the crisis which had suddenly descended on him out of the clouds. He achieved an instantaneous change of front, and met her smiling.

'Certainly,' he said; 'I have been working it as a blind.'

'A blind?' she repeated. 'To cover what?'

'You.'

'What do you mean?' she inquired, with a look in her eyes which made him uncomfortable.

'The Indian Government allows no one to remain in the State without a definite purpose. I couldn't tell Colonel Nolan that I had come courting you, could I?'

'I don't know. But you could have avoided taking the Maharajah's money to carry out this—this plan. An honest man would have avoided that.'

'Oh, look here!' exclaimed Tarvin.

'How could you cheat the King into thinking that there was a reason for your work? How could you let him give you the labour of a thousand men, how could you take his money? Oh, Nick!'

He gazed at her for a vacant and hopeless minute. 'Why, Kate,' he exclaimed, 'do you know you are talking of the most stupendous joke the Indian Empire has witnessed since the birth of time?'

This was pretty good, but it was not good enough. He plunged for a stronger hold as she answered, with a perilous little note of breakdown in her voice, 'You make it worse.'

'Well, your sense of humour never was your strongest point, you know, Kate.' He took the seat next her, leaned over and took her hand, as he went on. 'Doesn't it strike you as rather amusing, though, after all, to rip up half a State to be near a very small little girl—a very sweet, very extra lovely little girl, but still a rather tiny little girl in proportion to the size of the Amet valley? Come—doesn't it?'

'Is that all you have to say?' asked she. Tarvin turned pale. He knew the tone of finality he heard in her voice; it went with a certain look of scorn when she spoke of any form of moral baseness that moved her. He recognised his condemnation in it and shuddered. In the moment that passed, while he still kept silence, he recognised this for the crisis of his life. Then he took strong hold of himself, and said quietly, easily, unscrupulously:—

'Why, you don't suppose that I'm not going to ask the Maharajah for his bill, do you?'

She gasped a little. Her acquaintance with Tarvin did not help her to follow his dizzying changes of front. His bird's skill to make his level flight, his reeling dips and circling returns upon himself, all seem part of a single impulse, must ever remain confusing to her. But she rightly believed in his central intention to do the square thing, if he could find out what it was; and her belief in his general strength helped her not to see at this moment that he was deriving his sense of the square thing from herself. She could not know, and probably could not have imagined, how little his own sense of the square thing had to do with any system of morality, and how entirely he must always define morality as what pleased Kate. Other women liked confections; she preferred morality; and he meant she should have it, if he had to turn pirate to get it for her.

'You didn't think I wasn't paying for the show?' he pursued bravely; but in his heart he was saying, 'She loathes it. She hates it. Why didn't I think; why didn't I think?' He added aloud, 'I had my fun, and now I've got you. You're both cheap at the price, and I'm going to step up and pay it like a little man. You must know that.'

His smile met no answering smile. He mopped his forehead and stared anxiously at her. All the easiness in the world couldn't make him sure what she would say next. She said nothing, and he had to go on desperately, with a cold fear gathering about his heart. 'Why, it's just like me, isn't it, Kate, to work a scheme on the old Maharajah? It's like a man who owns a mine that's turning out $2000 a month, to rig a game out in this desert country to do a confiding Indian Prince out of a few thousand rupees?' He advanced this recently inspired conception of his conduct with an air of immemorial familiarity, born of desperation.

'What mine?' she asked, with dry lips.

'The "Lingering Lode," of course. You've heard me speak of it?'

'Yes, but I didn't know——'

'That it was doing that? Well, it is—right along. Want to see the assay?'

'No,' she answered. 'No. But that makes you—— Why, but, Nick, that makes you——'

'A rich man? Moderately, while the lead holds out. Too rich for petty larceny, I guess.'

He was joking for his life. The heart-sickening seriousness of his unseriousness was making a hole in his head. The tension was too much for him. In the mad fear of that moment his perceptions doubled their fineness. Something went through him as he said 'larceny.' Then his heart stopped. A sure, awful, luminous perception leaped upon him, and he knew himself for lost.

If she hated this, what would she say to the other? Innocent, successful, triumphant, even gay, it seemed to him; but what to her? He turned sick.

Kate or the Naulahka. He must choose. The Naulahka or Kate?

'Don't make light of it,' she was saying. 'You would be just as honest if you couldn't afford it, Nick. Ah,' she went on, laying her hand on his lightly, in mute petition for having even seemed to doubt him, 'I know you, Nick! You like to make the better seem the worse reason; you like to pretend to be wicked. But who is so honest? Oh, Nick! I knew you had to be true. If you weren't, everything else would be wrong.'

He took her in his arms. 'Would it, little girl?' he asked, looking down at her. 'We must keep the other things right, then, at any expense.'

He heaved a deep sigh as he stooped and kissed her.

'Have you such a thing as a box?' he asked, after a long pause.

'Any sort of box?' asked Kate bewilderedly.

'No—well, it ought to be the finest box in the world, but

I suppose one of those big grape-boxes will do. It isn't every day that one sends presents to a Queen.'

Kate handed him a large chip box in which long green grapes from Kabul had been packed. Discoloured cotton-wool lay at the bottom.

'That was sold at the door the other day,' she said. 'Is it big enough?'

Tarvin turned away without answering, emptied something that clicked like a shower of pebbles upon the wool, and sighed deeply. Topaz was in that box. The voice of the Maharaj Kunwar lifted itself from the next room.

'Tarvin Sahib—Kate, we have eaten all the fruit, and now we want to do something else.'

'One moment, little man,' said Tarvin. With his back still toward Kate, he drew his hand caressingly, for the last time, over the blazing heap at the bottom of the box, fondling the stones one by one. The great green emerald pierced him, he thought, with a reproachful gaze. A mist crept into his eyes: the diamond was too bright. He shut the lid down upon the box hastily, and put it into Kate's hands with a decisive gesture; he made her hold it while he tied it in silence. Then, in a voice not his, he asked her to take the box to Sitabhai with his compliments. 'No,' he continued, seeing the alarm in her eyes. 'She won't—she daren't hurt you now. Her child's coming along with us; and I'll go with you, of course, as far as I can. Glory be, it's the last journey that you'll ever undertake in this infernal land. The last but one, that's to say. We live at high pressure in Rhatore—too high pressure for me. Be quick, if you love me.'

Kate hastened to put on her helmet, while Tarvin amused the two princes by allowing them to inspect his revolver, and

promising at some more fitting season to shoot as many coins
as they should demand. The lounging escort at the door was
suddenly scattered by a trooper from without, who flung his
horse desperately through their ranks, shouting, 'A letter for
Tarvin Sahib!'

Tarvin stepped into the veranda, took a crumpled half-
sheet of paper from the outstretched hand, and read these
words, traced painfully and laboriously in an unformed round
hand:—

'DEAR MR. TARVIN—Give me the boy and keep the other
thing. Your affectionate                                    FRIEND.'

Tarvin chuckled and thrust the note into his waistcoat
pocket. 'There is no answer,' he said—and to himself: 'You're
a thoughtful girl, Sitabhai, but I'm afraid you're just a little
too thoughtful. That boy's wanted for the next half-hour. Are
you ready, Kate?'

The Princes lamented loudly when they were told that
Tarvin was riding over to the palace at once, and that, if they
hoped for further entertainment, they must both go with him.
'We will go into the great Durbar Hall,' said the Maharaj
Kunwar consolingly to his companion at last, 'and make all
the music-boxes play together.'

'I want to see that man shoot,' said Umr Singh. 'I want to
see him shoot something dead. I do not wish to go to the
palace.'

'You'll ride on my horse,' said Tarvin, when the answer had
been interpreted, 'and I'll make him gallop all the way. Say,
Prince, how fast do you think your carriage can go?'

'As fast as Miss Kate dares.'

Kate stepped in, and the cavalcade galloped to the palace,

Tarvin riding always a little in front with Umr Singh clapping his hands on the saddle-bow.

'We must pull up at Sitabhai's wing, dear,' Tarvin cried. 'You won't be afraid to walk in under the arch with me?'

'I trust you, Nick,' she answered simply, getting out of the carriage.

'Then go in to the women's wing. Give the box into Sitabhai's hands, and tell her that I sent it back. You'll find she knows my name.'

The horse trampled under the archway, Kate at its side, and Tarvin holding Umr Singh very much in evidence. The courtyard was empty, but as they came out into the sunshine by the central fountain the rustle and whisper behind the shutters rose, as the tiger-grass rustles when the wind blows through it.

'One minute, dear,' said Tarvin, halting, 'if you can bear this sun on your head.'

A door opened and a eunuch came out, beckoning silently to Kate. She followed him and disappeared, the door closing behind her. Tarvin's heart rose into his mouth, and unconsciously he clasped Umr Singh so closely to his breast that the child cried out.

The whisper rose, and it seemed to Tarvin as if some one were sobbing behind the shutters. Then followed a peal of low, soft laughter, and the muscles at the corner of Tarvin's mouth relaxed. Umr Singh began to struggle in his arms.

'Not yet, young man. You must wait until—ah! thank God.'

Kate reappeared, her little figure framed against the darkness of the doorway. Behind her came the eunuch, crawling fearfully to Tarvin's side. Tarvin smiled affably, and dropped the amazed young Prince into his arms. Umr Singh was borne away kicking, and ere they left the courtyard Tarvin heard the dry roar of an angry child, followed by an unmistakable yelp of pain. Tarvin smiled.

'They spank young princes in Rajputana. That's one step on the path to progress. What did she say, Kate?'

'She said I was to be sure and tell you that she knew you were not afraid. "Tell Tarvin Sahib that I knew he was not afraid."'

'Where's Umr Singh?' asked the Maharaj Kunwar from the barouche.

'He's gone to his mother. I'm afraid I can't amuse you just now, little man. I've forty thousand things to do, and no time to do them in. Tell me where your father is.'

'I do not know. There has been trouble and crying in the palace. The women are always crying, and that makes my father angry. I shall stay at Mr. Estes', and play with Kate.'

'Yes. Let him stay,' said Kate quickly. 'Nick, do you think I ought to leave him?'

'That's another of the things I must fix,' said Tarvin. 'But first I must find the Maharajah, if I have to dig up Rhatore for him. What's that, little one?'

A trooper whispered to the young Prince.

'This man says that he is there,' said the Maharaj Kunwar. 'He has been there since two days. I also have wished to see him.'

'Very good. Drive home, Kate. I'll wait here.'

He re-entered the archway, and reined up. Again the whisper behind the shutter rose; and a man from a doorway demanded his business.

'I must see the Maharajah,' said Tarvin.

'Wait,' said the man. And Tarvin waited for a full five minutes, using his time for concentrated thought.

Then the Maharajah emerged, and amiability sat on every hair of his newly-oiled moustache.

For some mysterious reason Sitabhai had withdrawn the
light of her countenance from him for two days, and had sat
raging in her own apartments. Now the mood had passed,
and the gipsy would see him again. Therefore the Maharajah's
heart was glad within him; and wisely, as befitted the husband
of many wives, he did not inquire too closely into the reasons
that had led to the change.

'Ah, Tarvin Sahib,' said he, 'I have not seen you for long.
What is the news from the dam? Is there anything to see?'

'Maharajah Sahib, that's what I've come to talk about.
There is nothing to see, and I think that there is no gold to
be got at.'

'That is bad,' said the King lightly.

'But there is a good deal to be seen, if you care to come
along. I don't want to waste your money any more, now I'm
sure of the fact; but I don't see the use of saving all the powder
on the dam. There must be five hundred pounds of it.'

'I do not understand,' said the Maharajah, whose mind was
occupied with other things.

'Do you want to see the biggest explosion that you've ever
seen in your life? Do you want to hear the earth shake, and
see the rocks fly?'

The Maharajah's face brightened.

'Will it be seen from the palace?' he said; 'from the top of
the palace?'

'Oh yes. But the best place to watch it will be from the side
of the river. I shall put the river back at five o'clock. It's three
o'clock now. Will you be there, Maharajah Sahib?'

'I will be there. It will be a big *tamasha*. Five hundred
pounds of powder! The earth will be rent in two.'

'I should remark. And after that, Maharajah Sahib, I am
going to be married; and then I am going away. Will you
come to the wedding?'

The Maharajah shaded his eyes from the sun-glare, and peered up at Tarvin under his turban.

'By God, Tarvin Sahib,' said he, 'you are quick man! So you will marry the Doctor Lady, and then you will go away? I will come to the wedding. I and Pertab Singh.'

The next two hours in the life of Nicholas Tarvin will never be adequately chronicled. There was a fierce need upon him to move mountains and shift the poles of the earth; there was a strong horse beneath him, and in his heart the knowledge that he had lost the Naulahka and gained Kate. When he appeared, a meteor amid the coolies on the dam, they understood, and a word was spoken that great things were toward. The gang foreman turned to his shouts, and learned that the order of the day was destruction—the one thing that the Oriental fully comprehends.

They dismantled the powder-shed with outcries and fierce yells, hauled the bullock-carts from the crown of the dam, and dropped the derrick after them, and tore down the mat-and-grass coolie-lines. Then, Tarvin urging them always, they buried the powder-casks in the crown of the half-built dam, piled the wrapped charges upon them, and shovelled fresh sand atop of all.

It was a hasty onslaught, but the powder was at least all in one place; and it should be none of Tarvin's fault if the noise and smoke at least did not delight the Maharajah.

A little before five he came with his escort, and Tarvin, touching fire to a many-times-lengthened fuse, bade all men run back. The fire ate slowly the crown of the dam. Then with a dull roar the dam opened out its heart in a sheet of white flame, and the masses of flying earth darkened the smoke above.

The ruin closed on itself for an instant ere the waters of the Amet plunged forward into the gap, made a boiling rapid, and then spread themselves lazily along their accustomed levels.

The rain of things descending pitted the earth of the banks and threw the water in sheets and spurts. Then only the smoke and the blackened flanks of the dam, crumbling each minute as the river sucked them down, remained to tell of the work that had been.

'And now, Maharajah Sahib, what do I owe you?' said Tarvin, after he had satisfied himself that none of the more reckless coolies had been killed.

'That was very fine,' said the Maharajah. 'I never saw that before. It is a pity that it cannot come again.'

'What do I owe you?' repeated Tarvin.

'For that? Oh, they were my people. They ate a little grain, and many were from my jails. The powder was from the arsenal. What is the use to talk of paying? Am I a *bunnia* that I can tell what there is to pay? It was a fine *tamasha*. By God, there is no dam left at all.'

'You might let me put it right.'

'Tarvin Sahib, if you waited one year, or perhaps two years, you would get a bill; and besides, if anything was paid, the men who pay the convicts would take it all, and I should not be richer. They were my people, and the grain was cheap, and they have seen the *tamasha*. Enough. It is not good to talk of payment. Let us return to the city. By God, Tarvin Sahib, you are quick man! Now there will be no one to play pachisi with me or to make me laugh. And the Maharaj Kunwar will be sorry also. But it is good that a man should marry. Yes, it is good. Why do you go, Tarvin Sahib? Is it an order of the Government?'

'Yes—the American Government. I am wanted there to help govern my State.'

'No telegram has come for you,' said the King simply. 'But you are so quick.'

Tarvin laughed lightly, wheeled his horse, and was gone, leaving the King interested but unmoved. He had finally learned to accept Tarvin and his ways as a natural phenomenon beyond control. As he drew rein instinctively opposite the missionary's door and looked for an instant at the city, the sense of the otherness of things daily seen that heralds swift coming change smote the mind of the American, and he shivered. 'It was a bad dream—a very bad dream,' he muttered, 'and the worst of it is, not one of the boys in Topaz would ever believe half of it.' Then the eyes that swept the arid landscape twinkled with many reminiscences. 'Tarvin, my boy, you've played with a kingdom, and for results it lays over monkeying with the buzz-saw. You were left when you sized this State up for a played-out hole in the ground; badly left. If you have been romping around six months after something you hadn't the sabe to hold when you'd got it you've learned that much. . . . Topaz! Poor old Topaz!' Again his eyes ran round the tawny horizon, and he laughed aloud. The little town under the shadow of Big Chief, ten thousand miles away and all ignorant of the mighty machinery that had moved on its behalf, would have resented that laugh; for Tarvin, fresh from events that had shaken Rhatore to its heart, was almost patronising the child of his ambition.

He brought his hand down on his thigh with a smack, and turned his horse toward the telegraph-office. 'How in the name of all that's good and holy,' said he, 'am I to clear up this business with the Mutrie? Even a copy of the Naulahka in glass would make her mouth water.' The horse cantered on steadily, and Tarvin dismissed the matter with a generous sweep of his free hand. 'If I can stand it she can. But I'll prepare her by electricity.'

The dove-coloured telegraph-operator and Postmaster-General of the State remembers even to-day how the Englishman who was not an Englishman, and, therefore, doubly incomprehensible, climbed for the last time up the narrow stairs, sat down in the broken chair, and demanded absolute silence; how, at the end of fifteen minutes' portentous meditation and fingering of a thin moustache, he sighed heavily as is the custom of Englishmen when they have eaten that which disagrees with them, waved the operator aside, called up the next office, and clicked off a message with a haughty and high-stepping action of the hands. How he lingered long and lovingly over the last click, applied his ear to the instrument as though it could answer, and turning with a large sweet smile said— 'Finis, Babu. Make a note of that,' and swept forth chanting the war-cry of his State:

> 'It is not wealth nor rank nor state,
> But get-up-and-git that makes men great.'

The bullock-cart creaked down the road to Rawut Junction in the first flush of a purple evening, and the low ranges of the Aravallis showed as many-coloured cloud-banks against the turquoise skyline. Behind it the red rock of Rhatore burned angrily on the yellow floors of the desert, speckled with the shadows of the browsing camels. Overhead the crane and the wild duck were flocking back to their beds in the reeds, and grey monkeys, family by family, sat on the roadside, their arms round one another's necks. The evening star came up from behind a jagged peak of rock and brushwood, so that its reflection might swim undisturbed at the bottom of an almost dried reservoir, buttressed with time-yellowed marble and flanked with silver plume-grass. Between the star and the earth wheeled huge fox-headed bats and night-jars hawking for the feather-winged moths. The buffaloes had left their water-holes, and the cattle were lying down for the night. Then villagers in far-away huts began to sing, and the hillsides were studded with home lights. The bullocks grunted as the driver twisted their tails, and the high grass by the roadside brushed with the wash of a wave of the open beach against the slow-turning tyres.

The first breath of a cold-weather night made Kate wrap her rugs about her more closely. Tarvin was sitting at the back of the cart, swinging his legs and staring at Rhatore before the bends of the roads should hide it. The realisation of defeat, remorse, and the torture of an over-well-trained conscience were yet to come to Kate. In that hour, luxuriously disposed upon many cushions, she realised nothing more than a woman's complete contentment with the fact that there was a man in the world to do things for her, though she had not yet learned to lose her interest in how they were done.

The reiterated and passionate farewells of the women in the palace, and the cyclonic sweep of a wedding at which Nick had refused to efface himself as a bridegroom should, but had flung all their world forward on the torrent of his own vitality, had worn her out. The yearning of homesickness—she had seen it in Mrs. Estes' wet eyes at the missionary's house an hour before—lay strong upon her, and she would fain have remembered her plunge into the world's evil as a dream of the night, but—

'Nick,' she said, softly.

'What is it, little woman?'

'Oh, nothing. I was thinking. Nick, what *did* you do about the Maharaj Kunwar?'

'He's fixed, or I'm mistaken. Don't worry your head about that. After I'd explained a thing or two to old man Nolan he seemed to think well of inviting that young man to board with him until he starts for the Mayo College. Tumble?'

'His poor mother! If only I could have——'

'But you couldn't, little woman. Hi! Look quick, Kate! There she goes! The last of Rhatore.'

A string of coloured lights, high up on the hanging gardens of the palace, was being blotted out behind the velvet blackness of a hill shoulder. Tarvin leaped to his feet, caught the side of the cart, and bowed profoundly after the Oriental manner.

The lights disappeared one by one, even as the glories of a necklace had slidden into a Kabuli grape-box, till there remained only the flare from a window on a topmost bastion— a point of light as red and as remote as the blaze of the Black Diamond. That passed too, and the soft darkness rose out of the earth fold upon fold wrapping the man and the woman.

'After all,' said Tarvin, addressing the new-lighted firmament, 'that was distinctly a side issue.'

THE END